AN ONI PRESS PUBLICATION

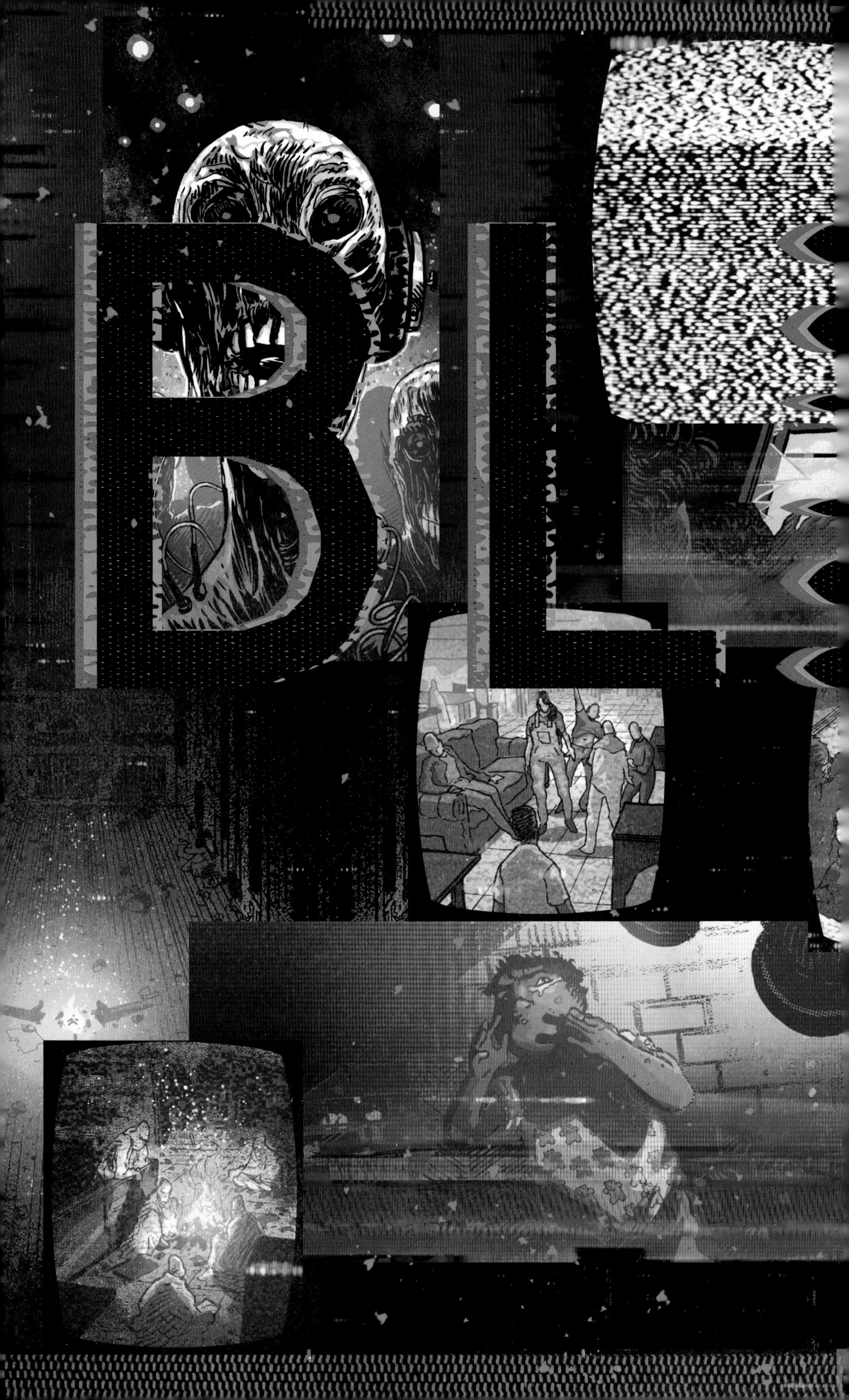
BL

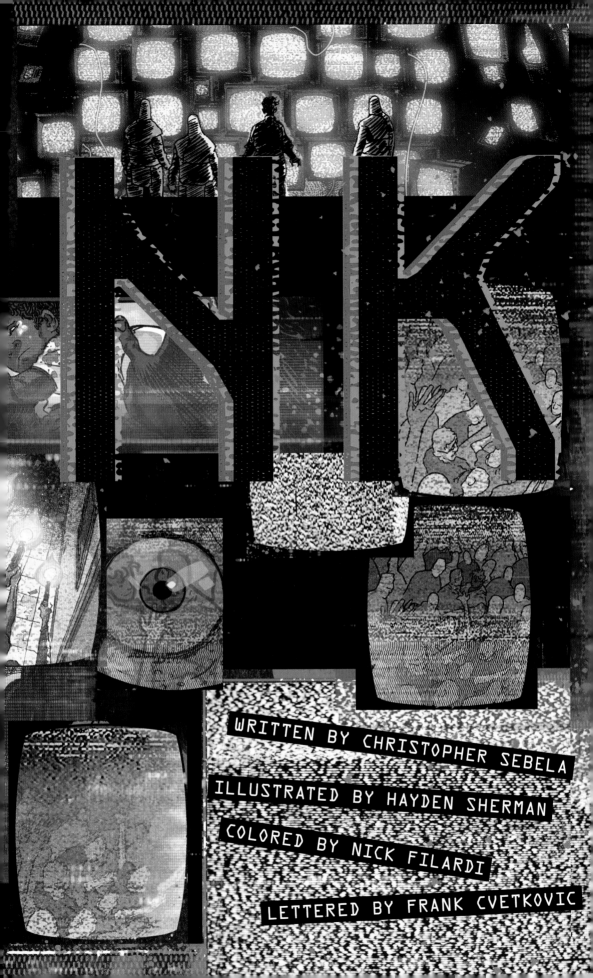

NYK

WRITTEN BY CHRISTOPHER SEBELA

ILLUSTRATED BY HAYDEN SHERMAN

COLORED BY NICK FILARDI

LETTERED BY FRANK CVETKOVIC

DESIGNED BY SARAH ROCKWELL

EDITED BY JASMINE AMIRI AND BESS PALLARES

COLLECTION EDITED BY BESS PALLARES

onipress.com /onipress
Christopher Sebela @XTOP
Hayden Sherman @CLEANLINED
Nick Filardi @NICKFIL
Frank Cvetkovic @GOFRANKGO

PUBLISHED BY ONI-LION FORGE PUBLISHING GROUP, LLC.

Troy Look, vp of publishing services
Katie Sainz, director of marketing
Angie Knowles, director of design & production
Sarah Rockwell, senior graphic designer
Carey Soucy, senior graphic designer
Vincent Kukua, digital prepress technician
Chris Cerasi, managing editor
Bess Pallares, senior editor
Grace Scheipeter, senior editor
Gabriel Granillo, editor
Desiree Rodriguez, editor
Zack Soto, editor
Sara Harding, executive assistant
Jung Hu Lee, logistics coordinator & editorial assistant
Kuian Kellum, warehouse assistant
Joe Nozemack, publisher emeritus

First Edition: May 2023
ISBN: 978-1-63715-201-0
eISBN: 978-1-63715-859-3
Printing numbers: 1 2 3 4 5 6 7 8 9 10
Library of Congress Control Number: 2022939195

BLINK, MAY 2023. Published by Oni-Lion Forge Publishing Group, LLC., 1319 SE Martin Luther King Jr. Blvd., Suite 240, Portland, OR 97214.

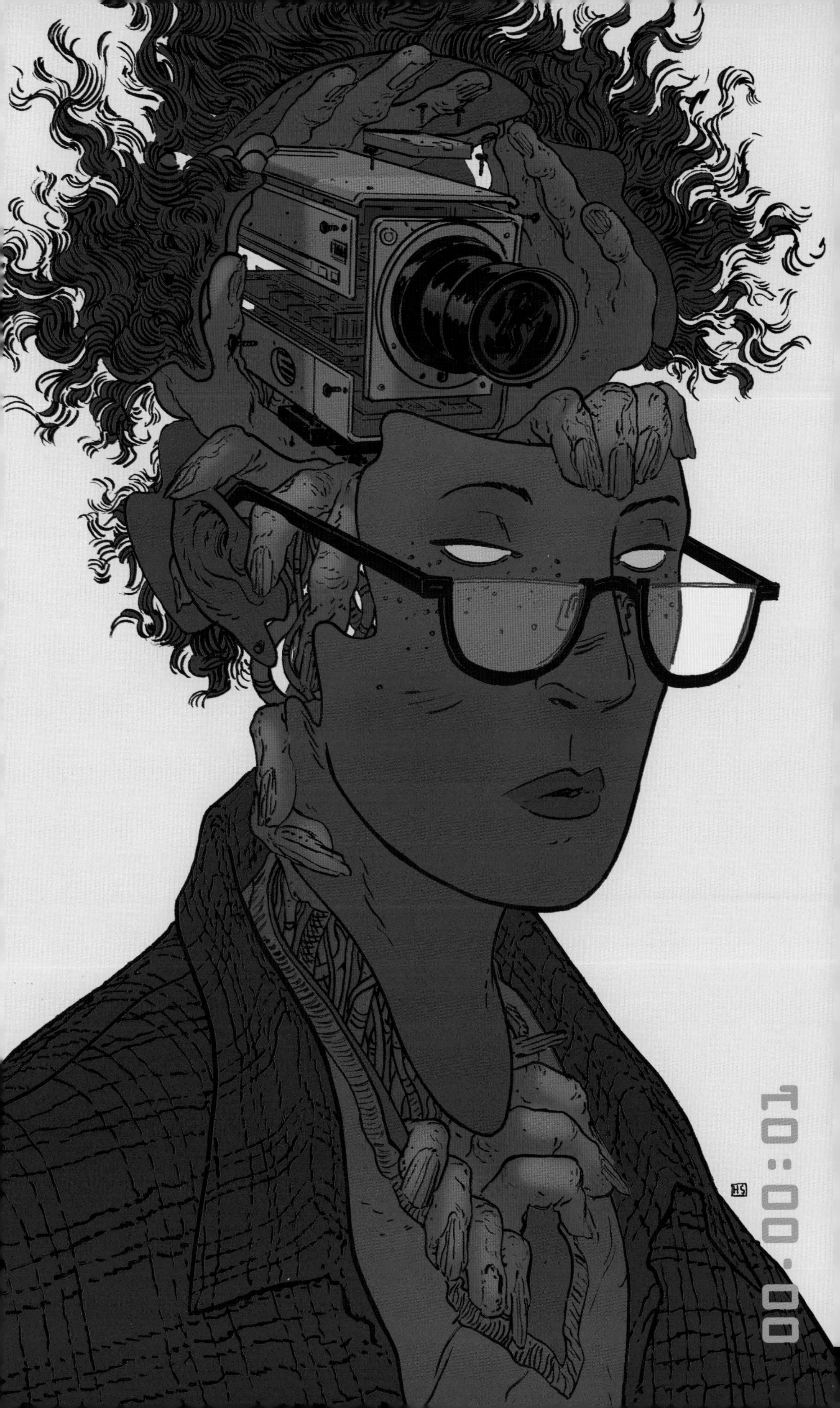
10:00:00

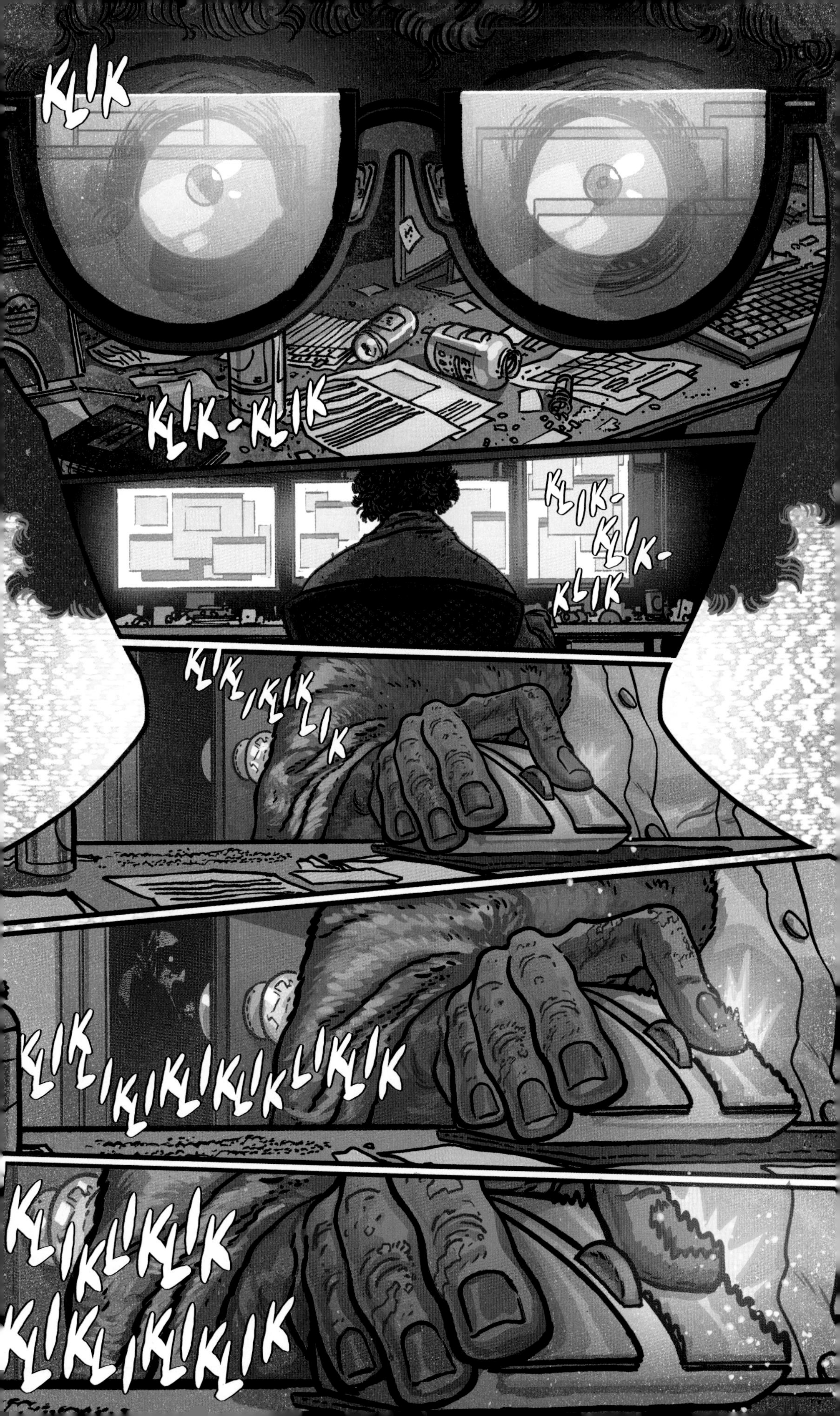
KLIK
KLIK-KLIK
KLIK-KLIK-KLIK
KLIKLIKLIKLIK
KLIKLIKLIKLIKLIKLIK
KLIKLIKLIK
KLIKLIKLIKLIK

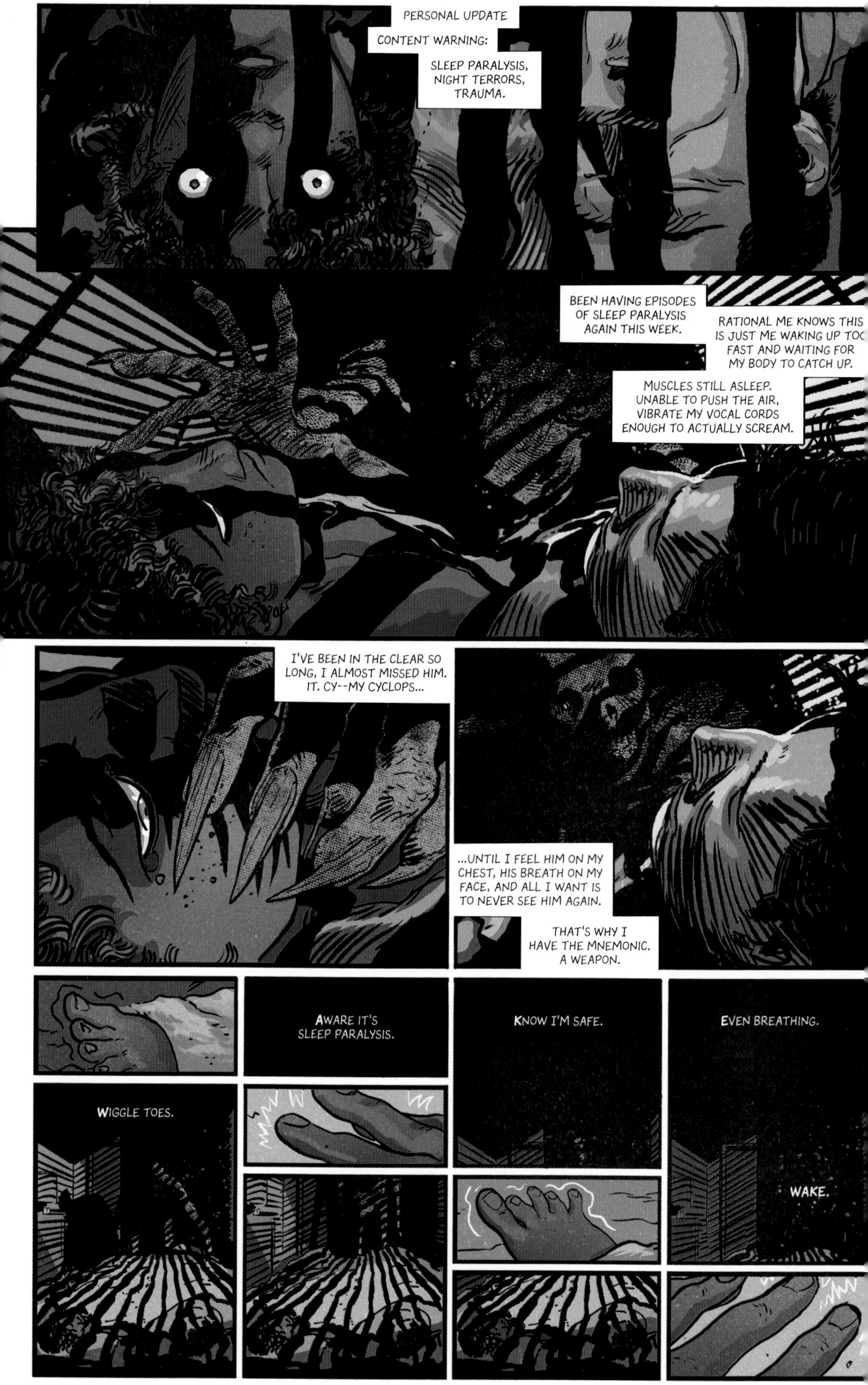
PERSONAL UPDATE
CONTENT WARNING:
SLEEP PARALYSIS, NIGHT TERRORS, TRAUMA.
BEEN HAVING EPISODES OF SLEEP PARALYSIS AGAIN THIS WEEK.
RATIONAL ME KNOWS THIS IS JUST ME WAKING UP TOO FAST AND WAITING FOR MY BODY TO CATCH UP.
MUSCLES STILL ASLEEP. UNABLE TO PUSH THE AIR, VIBRATE MY VOCAL CORDS ENOUGH TO ACTUALLY SCREAM.
I'VE BEEN IN THE CLEAR SO LONG, I ALMOST MISSED HIM. IT. CY--MY CYCLOPS...
...UNTIL I FEEL HIM ON MY CHEST, HIS BREATH ON MY FACE, AND ALL I WANT IS TO NEVER SEE HIM AGAIN.
THAT'S WHY I HAVE THE MNEMONIC. A WEAPON.
AWARE IT'S SLEEP PARALYSIS.
KNOW I'M SAFE.
EVEN BREATHING.
WIGGLE TOES.
WAKE.

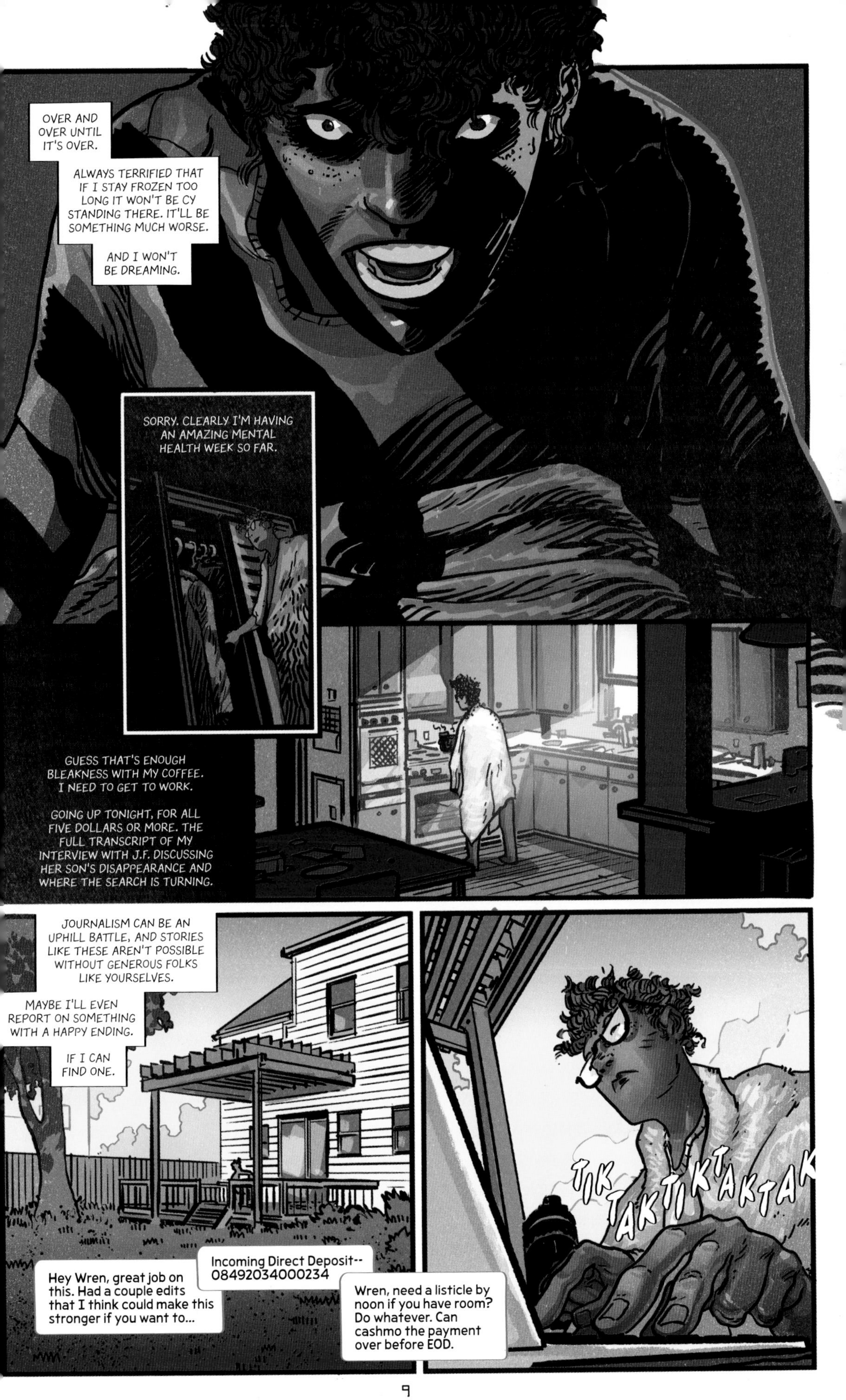

OVER AND OVER UNTIL IT'S OVER.
ALWAYS TERRIFIED THAT IF I STAY FROZEN TOO LONG IT WON'T BE CY STANDING THERE. IT'LL BE SOMETHING MUCH WORSE.
AND I WON'T BE DREAMING.
SORRY. CLEARLY I'M HAVING AN AMAZING MENTAL HEALTH WEEK SO FAR.
GUESS THAT'S ENOUGH BLEAKNESS WITH MY COFFEE. I NEED TO GET TO WORK.
GOING UP TONIGHT, FOR ALL FIVE DOLLARS OR MORE. THE FULL TRANSCRIPT OF MY INTERVIEW WITH J.F. DISCUSSING HER SON'S DISAPPEARANCE AND WHERE THE SEARCH IS TURNING.
JOURNALISM CAN BE AN UPHILL BATTLE, AND STORIES LIKE THESE AREN'T POSSIBLE WITHOUT GENEROUS FOLKS LIKE YOURSELVES.
MAYBE I'LL EVEN REPORT ON SOMETHING WITH A HAPPY ENDING.
IF I CAN FIND ONE.
Hey Wren, great job on this. Had a couple edits that I think could make this stronger if you want to...
Incoming Direct Deposit-- 08492034000234
Wren, need a listicle by noon if you have room? Do whatever. Can cashmo the payment over before EOD.
TIK TAK TIK TAK TIK TAK TAK

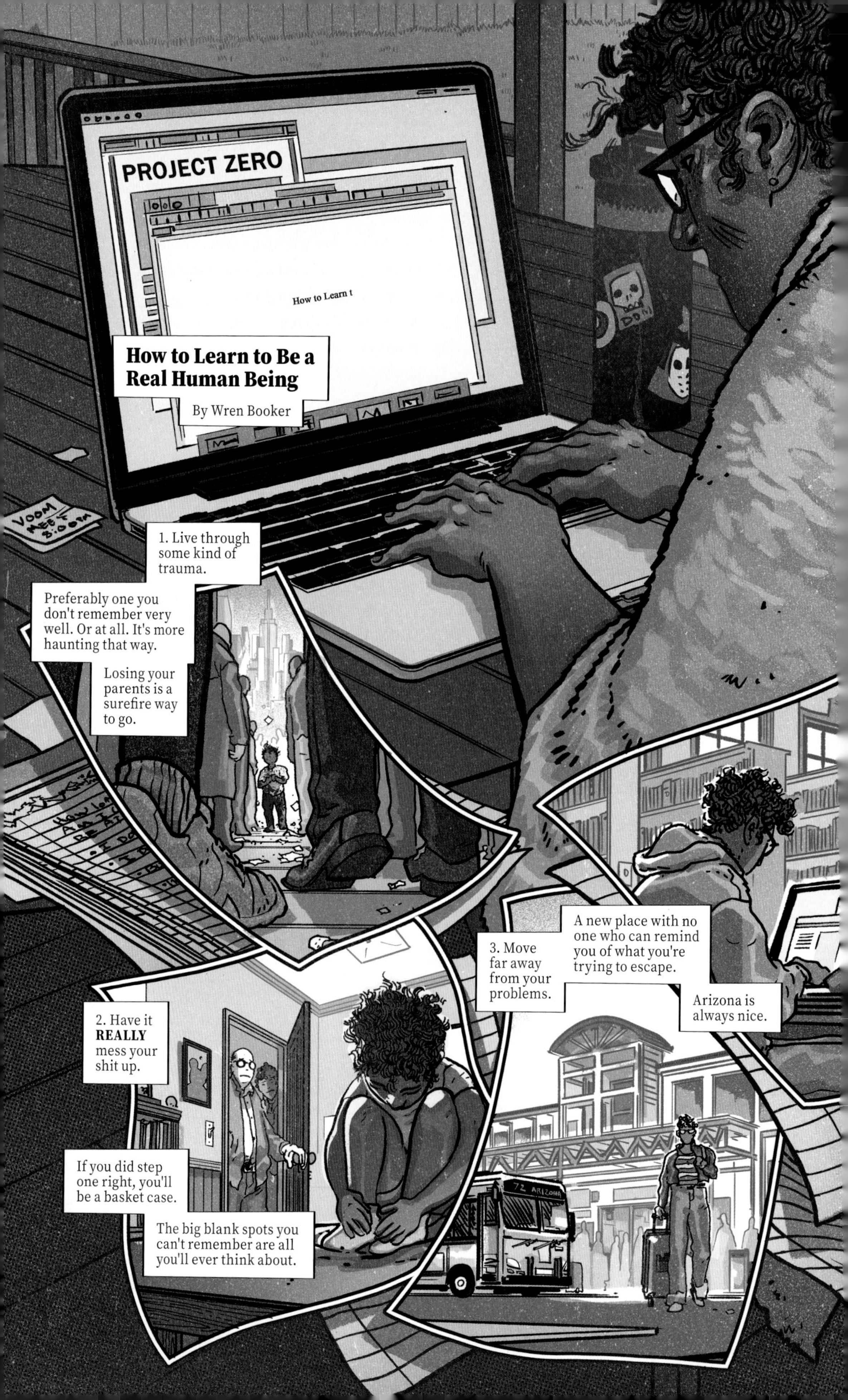
PROJECT ZERO
How to Learn t
How to Learn to Be a Real Human Being
By Wren Booker
VOOM MEET 8:00PM
1. Live through some kind of trauma.
Preferably one you don't remember very well. Or at all. It's more haunting that way.
Losing your parents is a surefire way to go.
2. Have it **REALLY** mess your shit up.
If you did step one right, you'll be a basket case.
The big blank spots you can't remember are all you'll ever think about.
3. Move far away from your problems.
A new place with no one who can remind you of what you're trying to escape.
Arizona is always nice.
72 ARIZONA

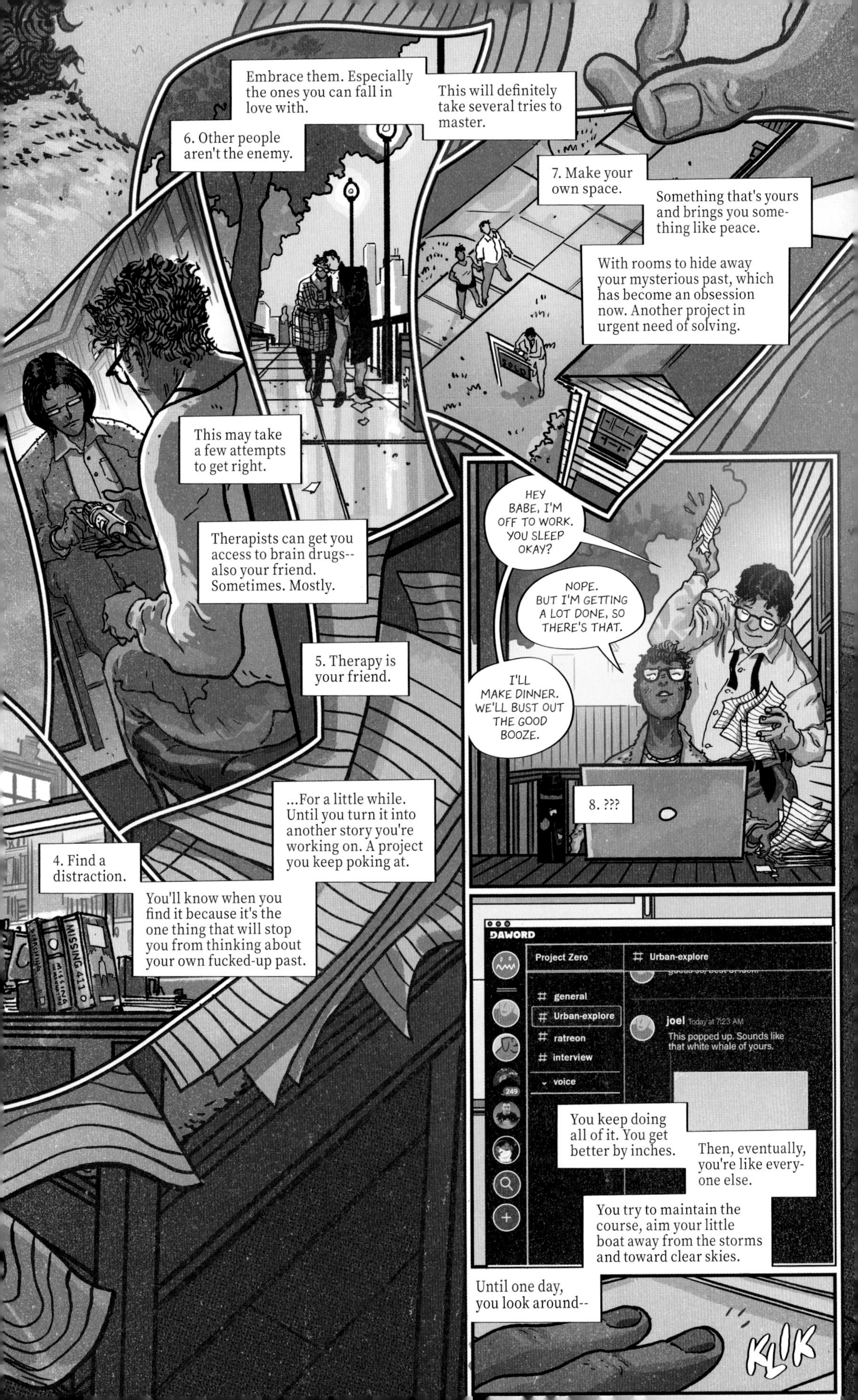

4. Find a distraction.
You'll know when you find it because it's the one thing that will stop you from thinking about your own fucked-up past.
...For a little while. Until you turn it into another story you're working on. A project you keep poking at.
MISSING 411
5. Therapy is your friend.
Therapists can get you access to brain drugs--also your friend. Sometimes. Mostly.
This may take a few attempts to get right.
6. Other people aren't the enemy.
Embrace them. Especially the ones you can fall in love with.
This will definitely take several tries to master.
7. Make your own space.
Something that's yours and brings you something like peace.
With rooms to hide away your mysterious past, which has become an obsession now. Another project in urgent need of solving.
SOLD
HEY BABE, I'M OFF TO WORK. YOU SLEEP OKAY?
NOPE. BUT I'M GETTING A LOT DONE, SO THERE'S THAT.
I'LL MAKE DINNER. WE'LL BUST OUT THE GOOD BOOZE.
8. ???
DAWORD
Project Zero
Urban-explore
general
Urban-explore
ratreon
interview
voice
249
joel Today at 7:23 AM
This popped up. Sounds like that white whale of yours.
You keep doing all of it. You get better by inches.
Then, eventually, you're like every-one else.
You try to maintain the course, aim your little boat away from the storms and toward clear skies.
Until one day, you look around--
KLIK

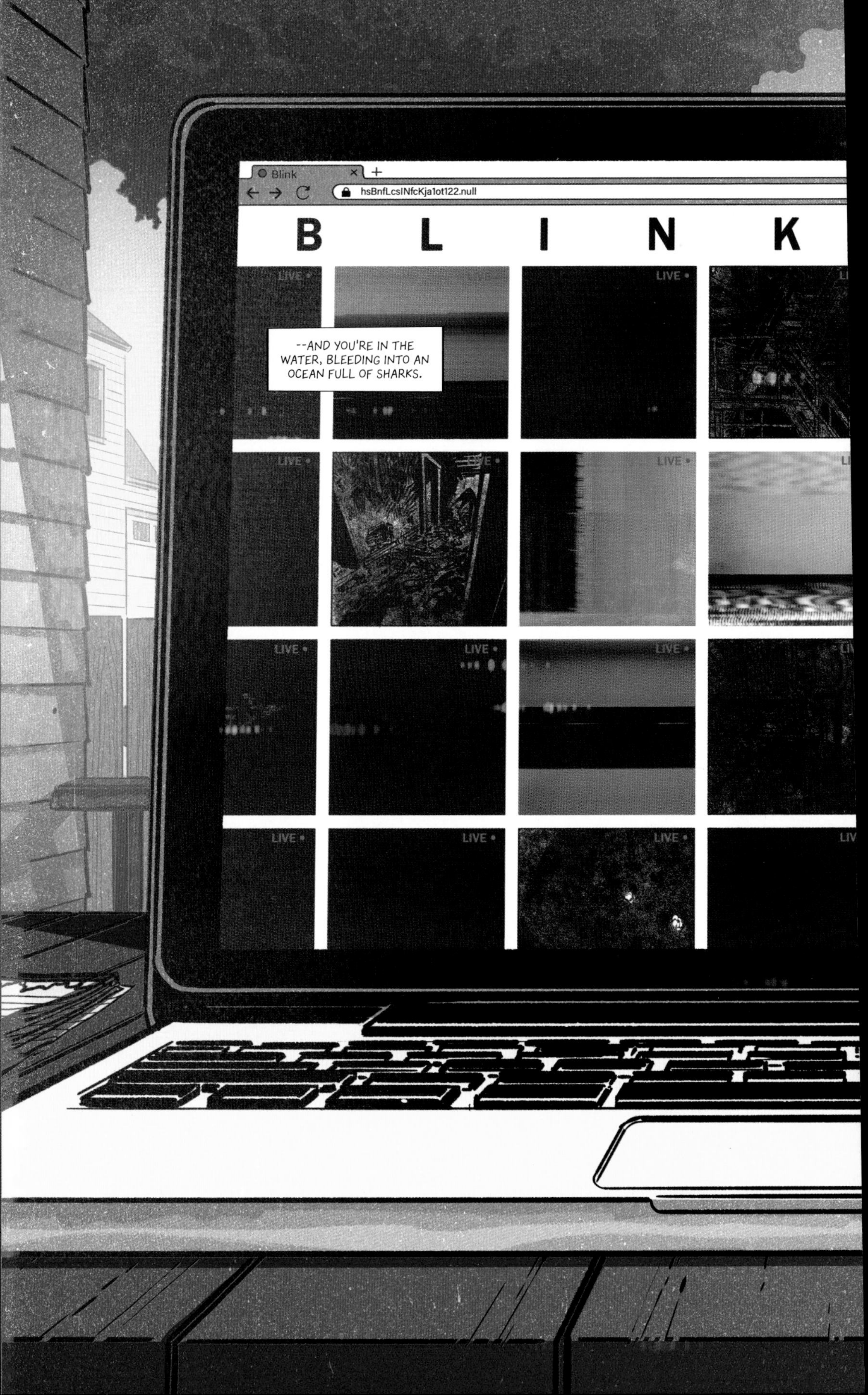
Blink
hsBnfLcsINfcKja1ot122.null
B L I N K
LIVE
--AND YOU'RE IN THE WATER, BLEEDING INTO AN OCEAN FULL OF SHARKS.

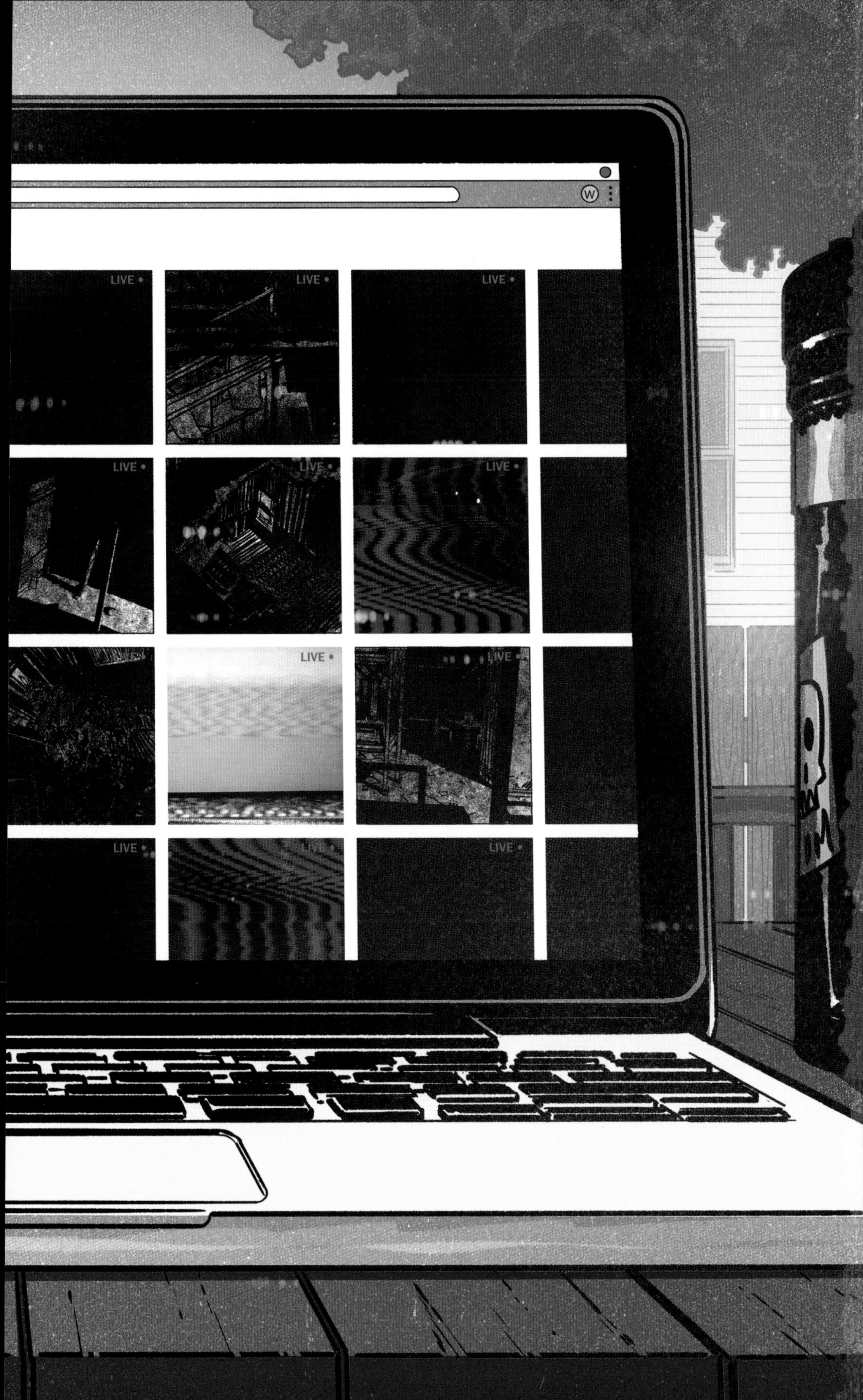

LIVE
LIVE
LIVE
LIVE
LIVE
LIVE
LIVE
LIVE
LIVE
LIVE
LIVE

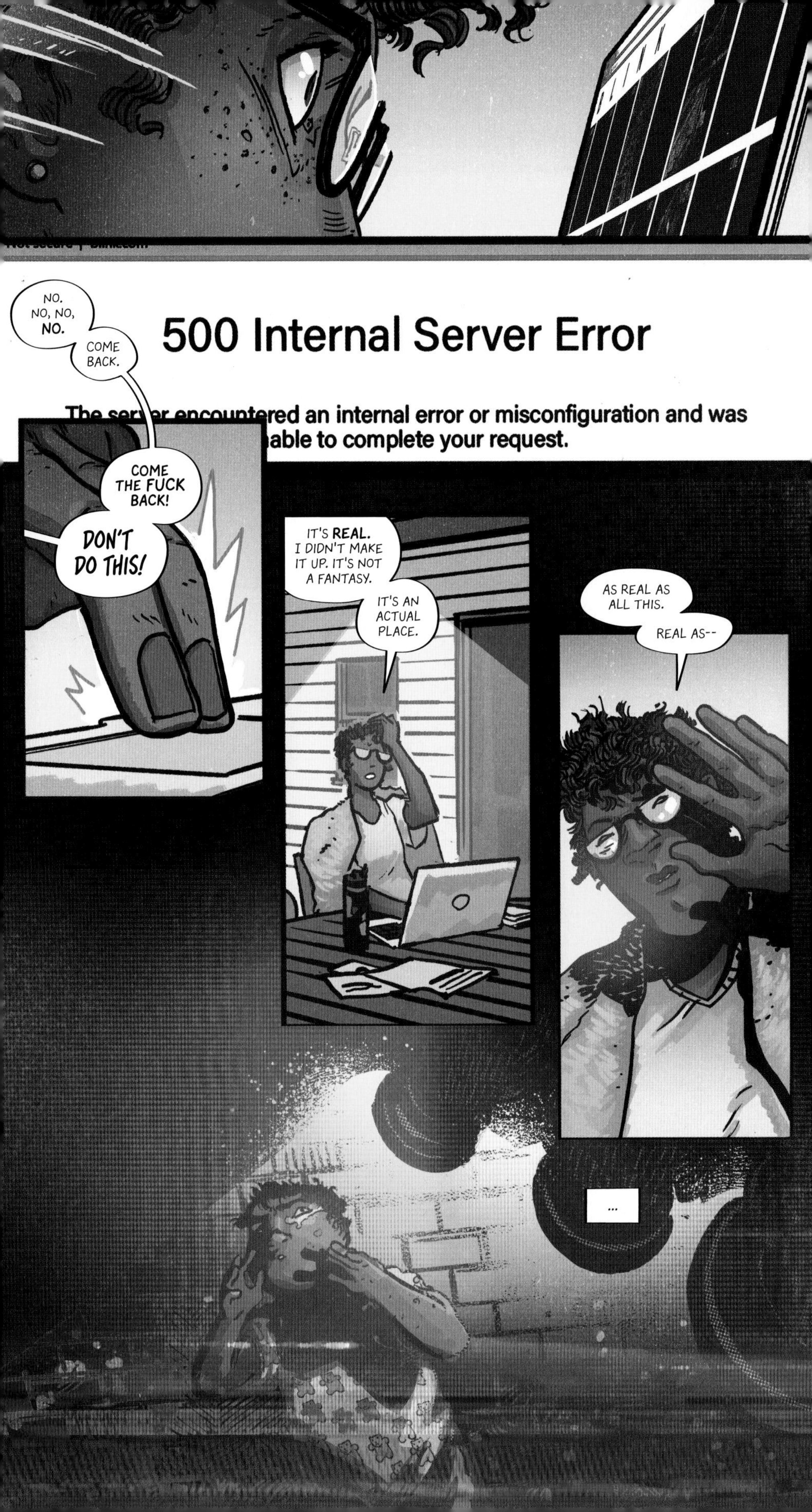
500 Internal Server Error
The server encountered an internal error or misconfiguration and was
able to complete your request.
NO. NO, NO, NO.
COME BACK.
COME THE FUCK BACK!
DON'T DO THIS!
IT'S REAL. I DIDN'T MAKE IT UP. IT'S NOT A FANTASY.
IT'S AN ACTUAL PLACE.
AS REAL AS ALL THIS.
REAL AS--
...

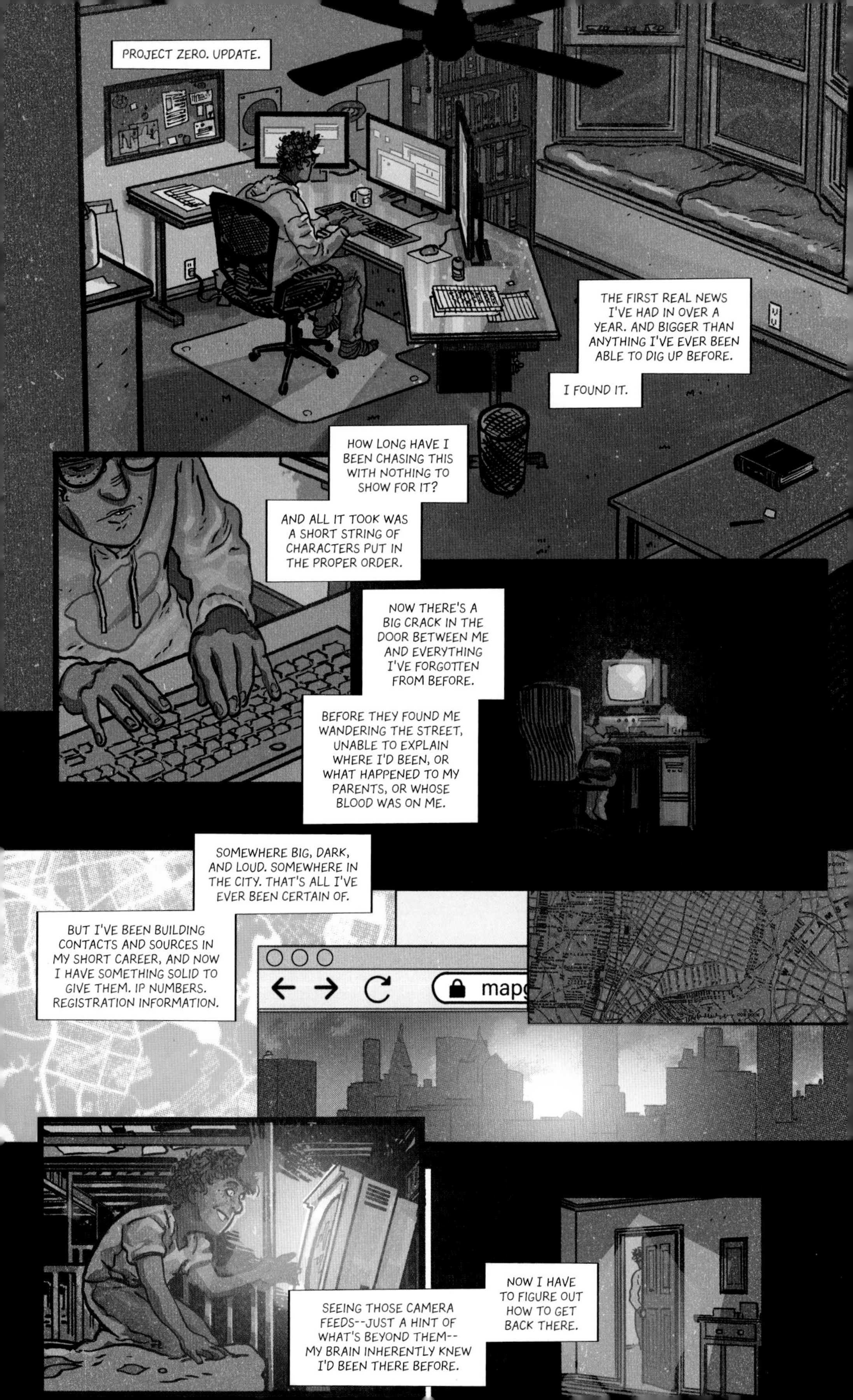
PROJECT ZERO. UPDATE.
THE FIRST REAL NEWS I'VE HAD IN OVER A YEAR. AND BIGGER THAN ANYTHING I'VE EVER BEEN ABLE TO DIG UP BEFORE.
I FOUND IT.
HOW LONG HAVE I BEEN CHASING THIS WITH NOTHING TO SHOW FOR IT?
AND ALL IT TOOK WAS A SHORT STRING OF CHARACTERS PUT IN THE PROPER ORDER.
NOW THERE'S A BIG CRACK IN THE DOOR BETWEEN ME AND EVERYTHING I'VE FORGOTTEN FROM BEFORE.
BEFORE THEY FOUND ME WANDERING THE STREET, UNABLE TO EXPLAIN WHERE I'D BEEN, OR WHAT HAPPENED TO MY PARENTS, OR WHOSE BLOOD WAS ON ME.
SOMEWHERE BIG, DARK, AND LOUD. SOMEWHERE IN THE CITY. THAT'S ALL I'VE EVER BEEN CERTAIN OF.
BUT I'VE BEEN BUILDING CONTACTS AND SOURCES IN MY SHORT CAREER, AND NOW I HAVE SOMETHING SOLID TO GIVE THEM. IP NUMBERS. REGISTRATION INFORMATION.
SEEING THOSE CAMERA FEEDS--JUST A HINT OF WHAT'S BEYOND THEM--MY BRAIN INHERENTLY KNEW I'D BEEN THERE BEFORE.
NOW I HAVE TO FIGURE OUT HOW TO GET BACK THERE.

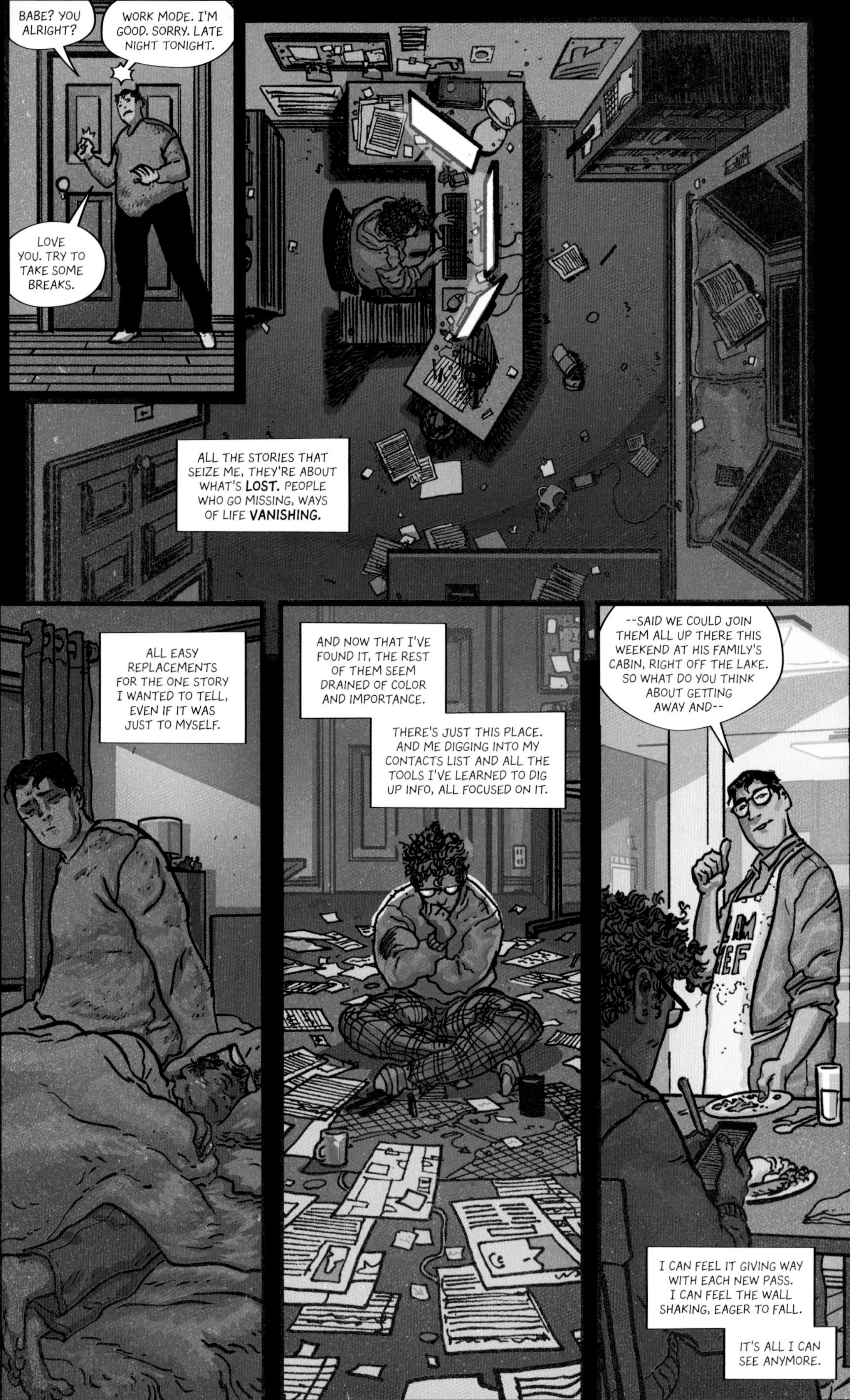
BABE? YOU ALRIGHT?
WORK MODE. I'M GOOD. SORRY. LATE NIGHT TONIGHT.
LOVE YOU. TRY TO TAKE SOME BREAKS.
ALL THE STORIES THAT SEIZE ME, THEY'RE ABOUT WHAT'S **LOST.** PEOPLE WHO GO MISSING, WAYS OF LIFE **VANISHING.**
ALL EASY REPLACEMENTS FOR THE ONE STORY I WANTED TO TELL, EVEN IF IT WAS JUST TO MYSELF.
AND NOW THAT I'VE FOUND IT, THE REST OF THEM SEEM DRAINED OF COLOR AND IMPORTANCE.
THERE'S JUST THIS PLACE. AND ME DIGGING INTO MY CONTACTS LIST AND ALL THE TOOLS I'VE LEARNED TO DIG UP INFO, ALL FOCUSED ON IT.
--SAID WE COULD JOIN THEM ALL UP THERE THIS WEEKEND AT HIS FAMILY'S CABIN, RIGHT OFF THE LAKE. SO WHAT DO YOU THINK ABOUT GETTING AWAY AND--
I CAN FEEL IT GIVING WAY WITH EACH NEW PASS. I CAN FEEL THE WALL SHAKING, EAGER TO FALL.
IT'S ALL I CAN SEE ANYMORE.

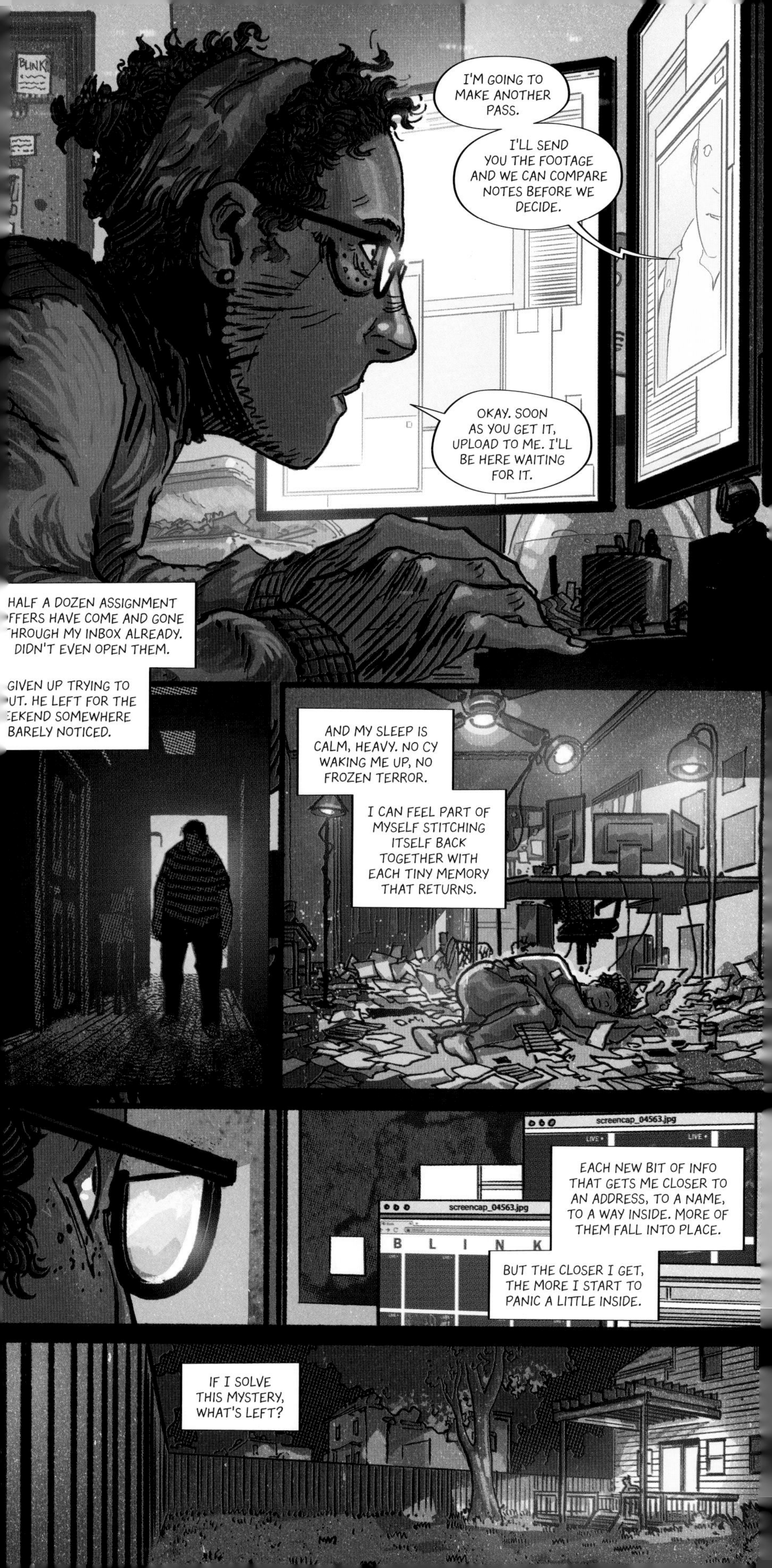
BLINK
I'M GOING TO MAKE ANOTHER PASS.
I'LL SEND YOU THE FOOTAGE AND WE CAN COMPARE NOTES BEFORE WE DECIDE.
OKAY. SOON AS YOU GET IT, UPLOAD TO ME. I'LL BE HERE WAITING FOR IT.
HALF A DOZEN ASSIGNMENT FFERS HAVE COME AND GONE THROUGH MY INBOX ALREADY. DIDN'T EVEN OPEN THEM.
GIVEN UP TRYING TO UT. HE LEFT FOR THE EEKEND SOMEWHERE BARELY NOTICED.
AND MY SLEEP IS CALM, HEAVY. NO CY WAKING ME UP, NO FROZEN TERROR.
I CAN FEEL PART OF MYSELF STITCHING ITSELF BACK TOGETHER WITH EACH TINY MEMORY THAT RETURNS.
screencap_04563.jpg
screencap_04563.jpg
B L I N K
EACH NEW BIT OF INFO THAT GETS ME CLOSER TO AN ADDRESS, TO A NAME, TO A WAY INSIDE. MORE OF THEM FALL INTO PLACE.
BUT THE CLOSER I GET, THE MORE I START TO PANIC A LITTLE INSIDE.
IF I SOLVE THIS MYSTERY, WHAT'S LEFT?

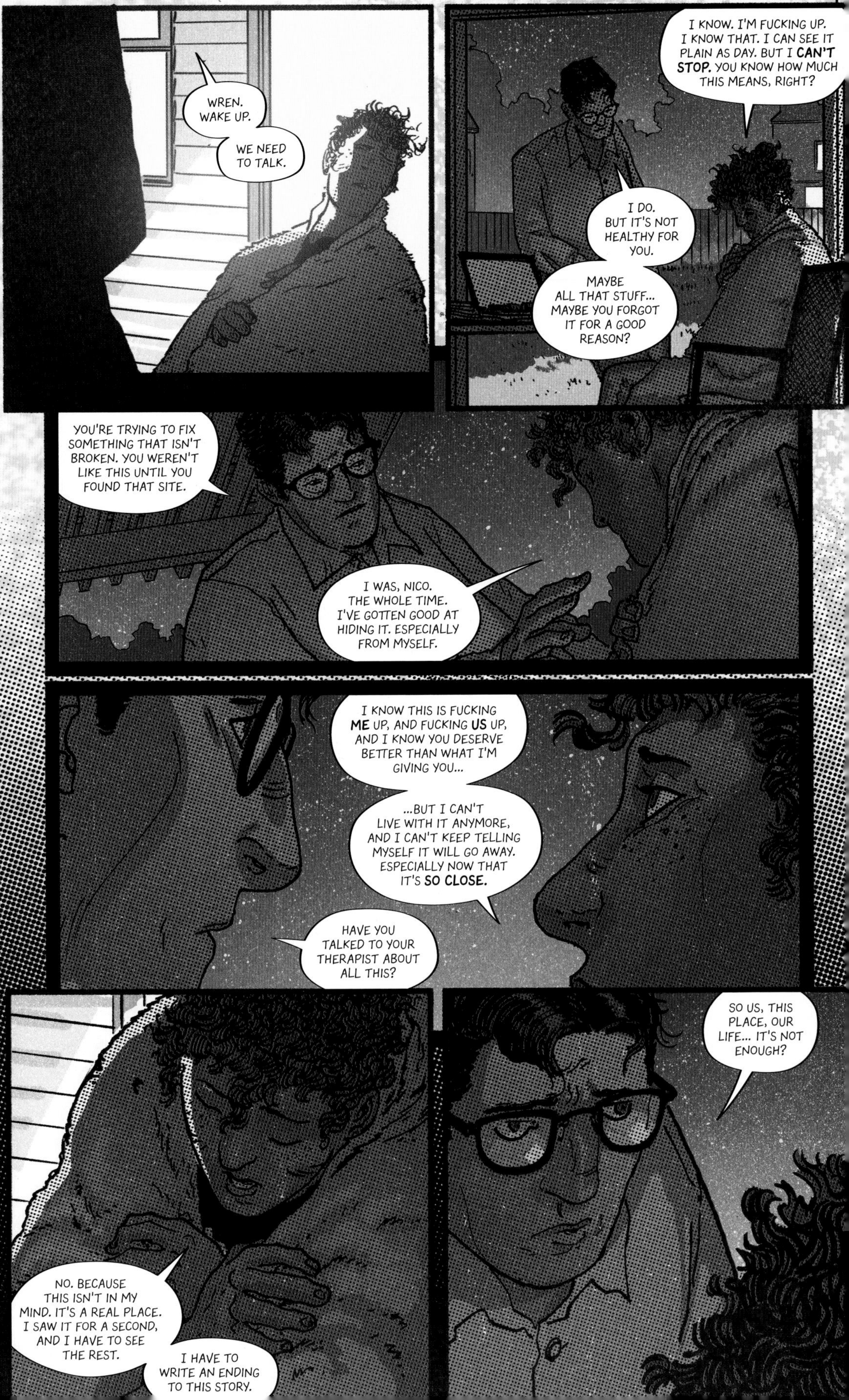
WREN. WAKE UP.
WE NEED TO TALK.
I KNOW. I'M FUCKING UP. I KNOW THAT. I CAN SEE IT PLAIN AS DAY. BUT I **CAN'T STOP.** YOU KNOW HOW MUCH THIS MEANS, RIGHT?
I DO. BUT IT'S NOT HEALTHY FOR YOU.
MAYBE ALL THAT STUFF... MAYBE YOU FORGOT IT FOR A GOOD REASON?
YOU'RE TRYING TO FIX SOMETHING THAT ISN'T BROKEN. YOU WEREN'T LIKE THIS UNTIL YOU FOUND THAT SITE.
I WAS, NICO. THE WHOLE TIME. I'VE GOTTEN GOOD AT HIDING IT. ESPECIALLY FROM MYSELF.
I KNOW THIS IS FUCKING **ME** UP, AND FUCKING **US** UP, AND I KNOW YOU DESERVE BETTER THAN WHAT I'M GIVING YOU...
...BUT I CAN'T LIVE WITH IT ANYMORE, AND I CAN'T KEEP TELLING MYSELF IT WILL GO AWAY. ESPECIALLY NOW THAT IT'S **SO CLOSE.**
HAVE YOU TALKED TO YOUR THERAPIST ABOUT ALL THIS?
NO. BECAUSE THIS ISN'T IN MY MIND. IT'S A REAL PLACE. I SAW IT FOR A SECOND, AND I HAVE TO SEE THE REST.
I HAVE TO WRITE AN ENDING TO THIS STORY.
SO US, THIS PLACE, OUR LIFE... IT'S NOT ENOUGH?

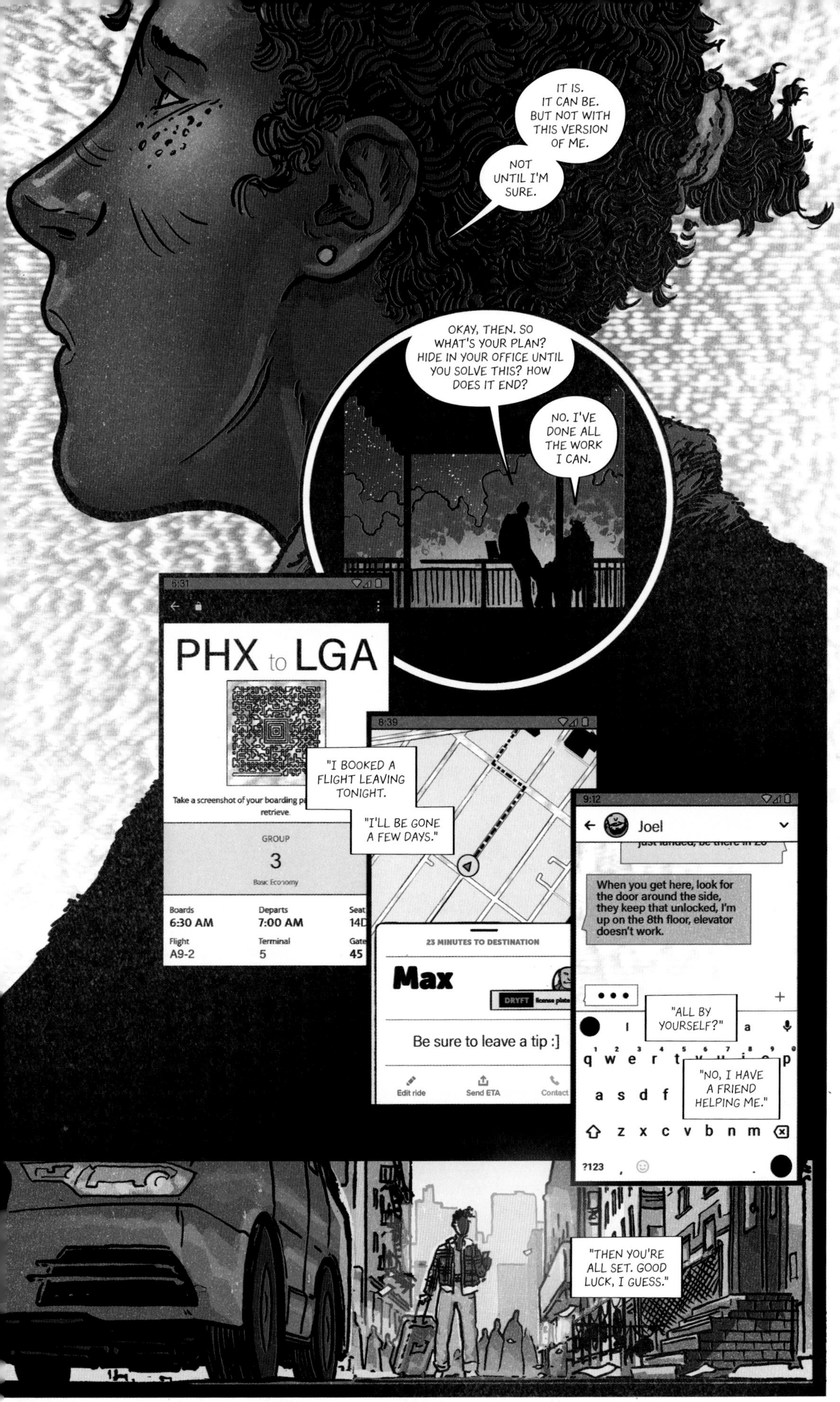
IT IS. IT CAN BE. BUT NOT WITH THIS VERSION OF ME.
NOT UNTIL I'M SURE.
OKAY, THEN. SO WHAT'S YOUR PLAN? HIDE IN YOUR OFFICE UNTIL YOU SOLVE THIS? HOW DOES IT END?
NO. I'VE DONE ALL THE WORK I CAN.
5:31
PHX to LGA
Take a screenshot of your boarding pa
retrieve.
GROUP
3
Basic Economy
Boards
6:30 AM
Departs
7:00 AM
Seat
14D
Flight
A9-2
Terminal
5
Gate
45
"I BOOKED A FLIGHT LEAVING TONIGHT.
"I'LL BE GONE A FEW DAYS."
8:39
23 MINUTES TO DESTINATION
Max
DRYFT
Be sure to leave a tip :]
Edit ride
Send ETA
Contact
9:12
Joel
When you get here, look for the door around the side, they keep that unlocked, I'm up on the 8th floor, elevator doesn't work.
"ALL BY YOURSELF?"
"NO, I HAVE A FRIEND HELPING ME."
"THEN YOU'RE ALL SET. GOOD LUCK, I GUESS."

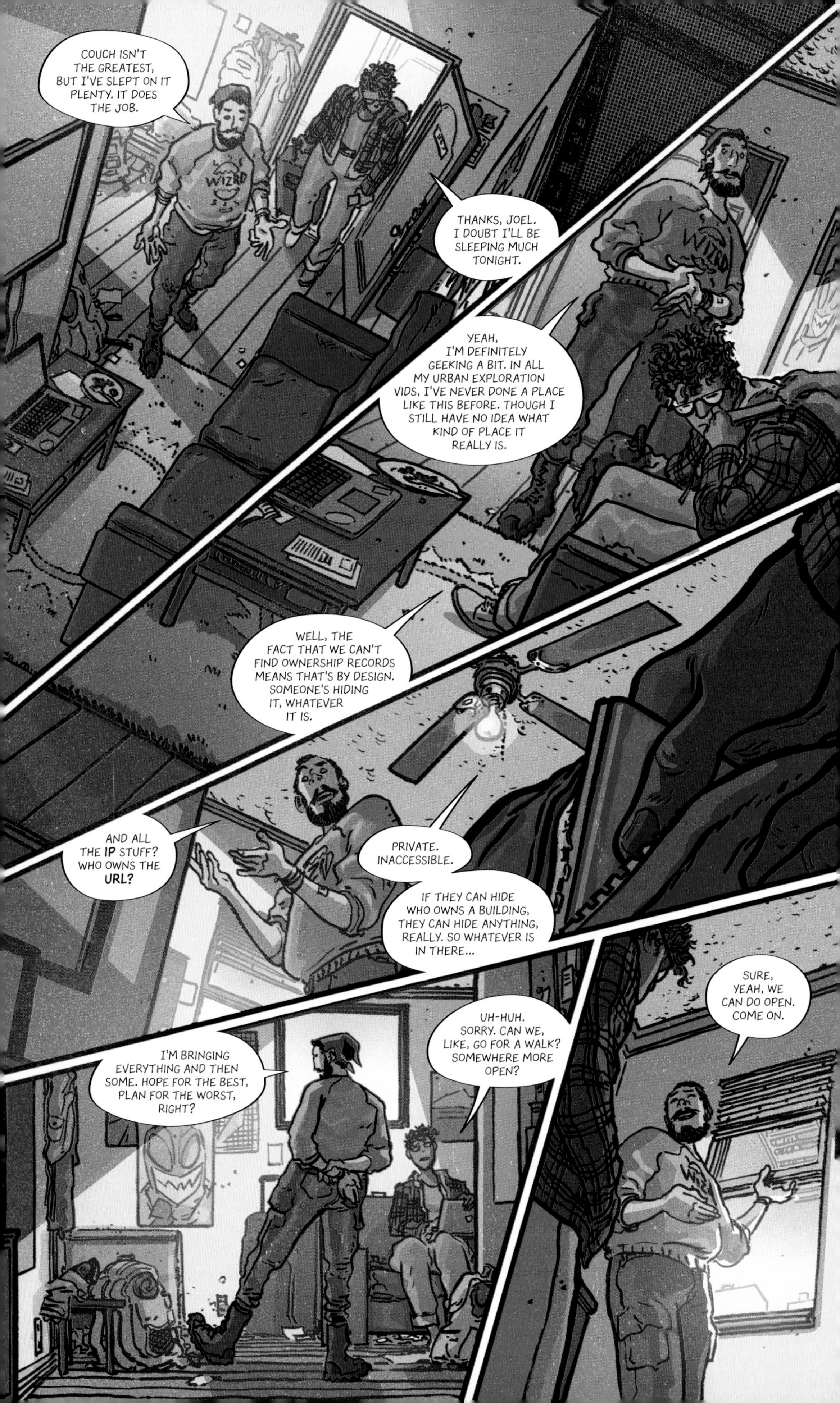

COUCH ISN'T THE GREATEST, BUT I'VE SLEPT ON IT PLENTY. IT DOES THE JOB.
THANKS, JOEL. I DOUBT I'LL BE SLEEPING MUCH TONIGHT.
YEAH, I'M DEFINITELY GEEKING A BIT. IN ALL MY URBAN EXPLORATION VIDS, I'VE NEVER DONE A PLACE LIKE THIS BEFORE. THOUGH I STILL HAVE NO IDEA WHAT KIND OF PLACE IT REALLY IS.
WELL, THE FACT THAT WE CAN'T FIND OWNERSHIP RECORDS MEANS THAT'S BY DESIGN. SOMEONE'S HIDING IT, WHATEVER IT IS.
AND ALL THE IP STUFF? WHO OWNS THE URL?
PRIVATE. INACCESSIBLE.
IF THEY CAN HIDE WHO OWNS A BUILDING, THEY CAN HIDE ANYTHING, REALLY. SO WHATEVER IS IN THERE...
I'M BRINGING EVERYTHING AND THEN SOME. HOPE FOR THE BEST, PLAN FOR THE WORST, RIGHT?
UH-HUH. SORRY. CAN WE, LIKE, GO FOR A WALK? SOMEWHERE MORE OPEN?
SURE, YEAH, WE CAN DO OPEN. COME ON.

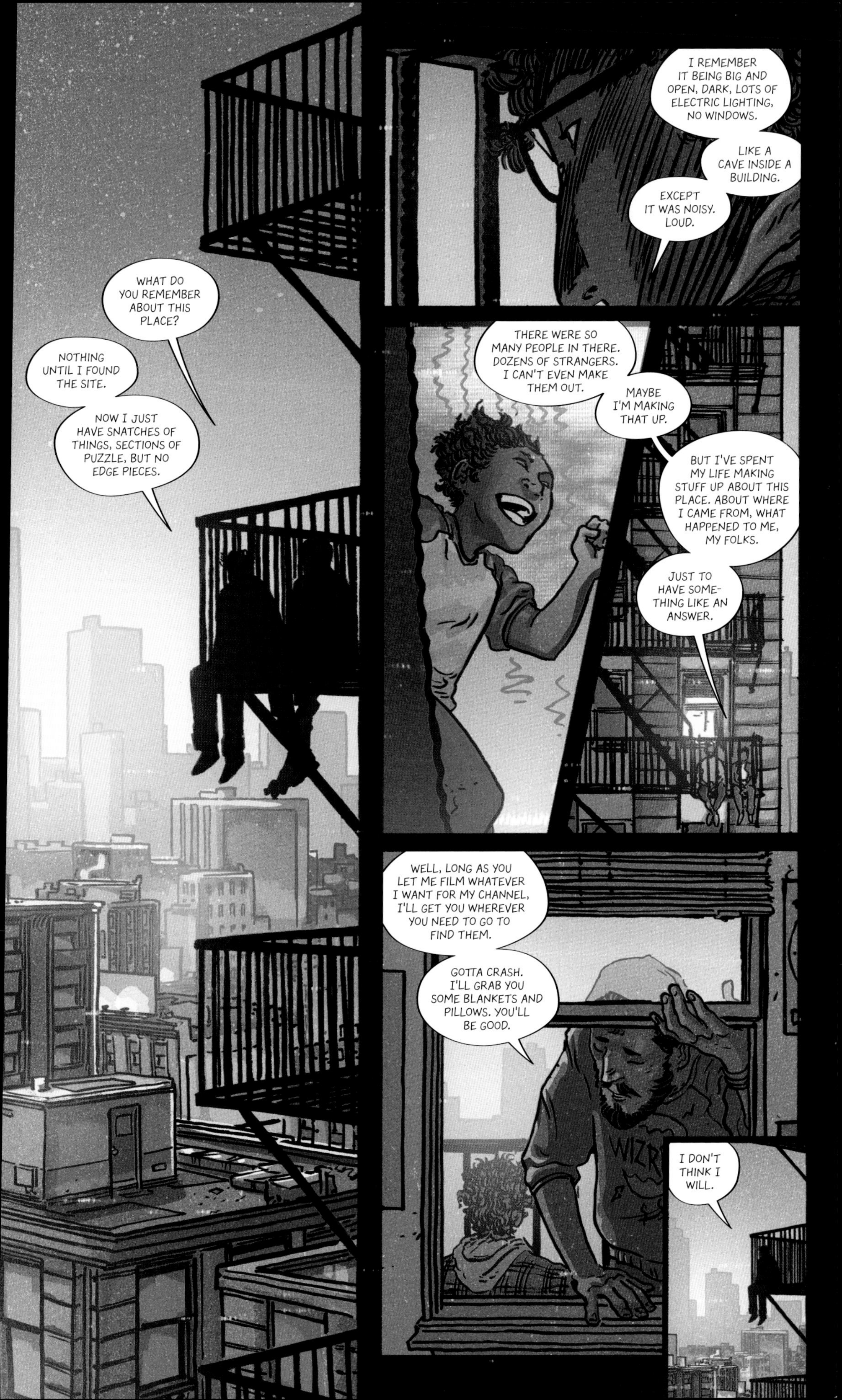
WHAT DO YOU REMEMBER ABOUT THIS PLACE?
NOTHING UNTIL I FOUND THE SITE.
NOW I JUST HAVE SNATCHES OF THINGS, SECTIONS OF PUZZLE, BUT NO EDGE PIECES.
I REMEMBER IT BEING BIG AND OPEN, DARK, LOTS OF ELECTRIC LIGHTING, NO WINDOWS.
LIKE A CAVE INSIDE A BUILDING.
EXCEPT IT WAS NOISY. LOUD.
THERE WERE SO MANY PEOPLE IN THERE. DOZENS OF STRANGERS. I CAN'T EVEN MAKE THEM OUT.
MAYBE I'M MAKING THAT UP.
BUT I'VE SPENT MY LIFE MAKING STUFF UP ABOUT THIS PLACE. ABOUT WHERE I CAME FROM, WHAT HAPPENED TO ME, MY FOLKS.
JUST TO HAVE SOME-THING LIKE AN ANSWER.
WELL, LONG AS YOU LET ME FILM WHATEVER I WANT FOR MY CHANNEL, I'LL GET YOU WHEREVER YOU NEED TO GO TO FIND THEM.
GOTTA CRASH. I'LL GRAB YOU SOME BLANKETS AND PILLOWS. YOU'LL BE GOOD.
I DON'T THINK I WILL.

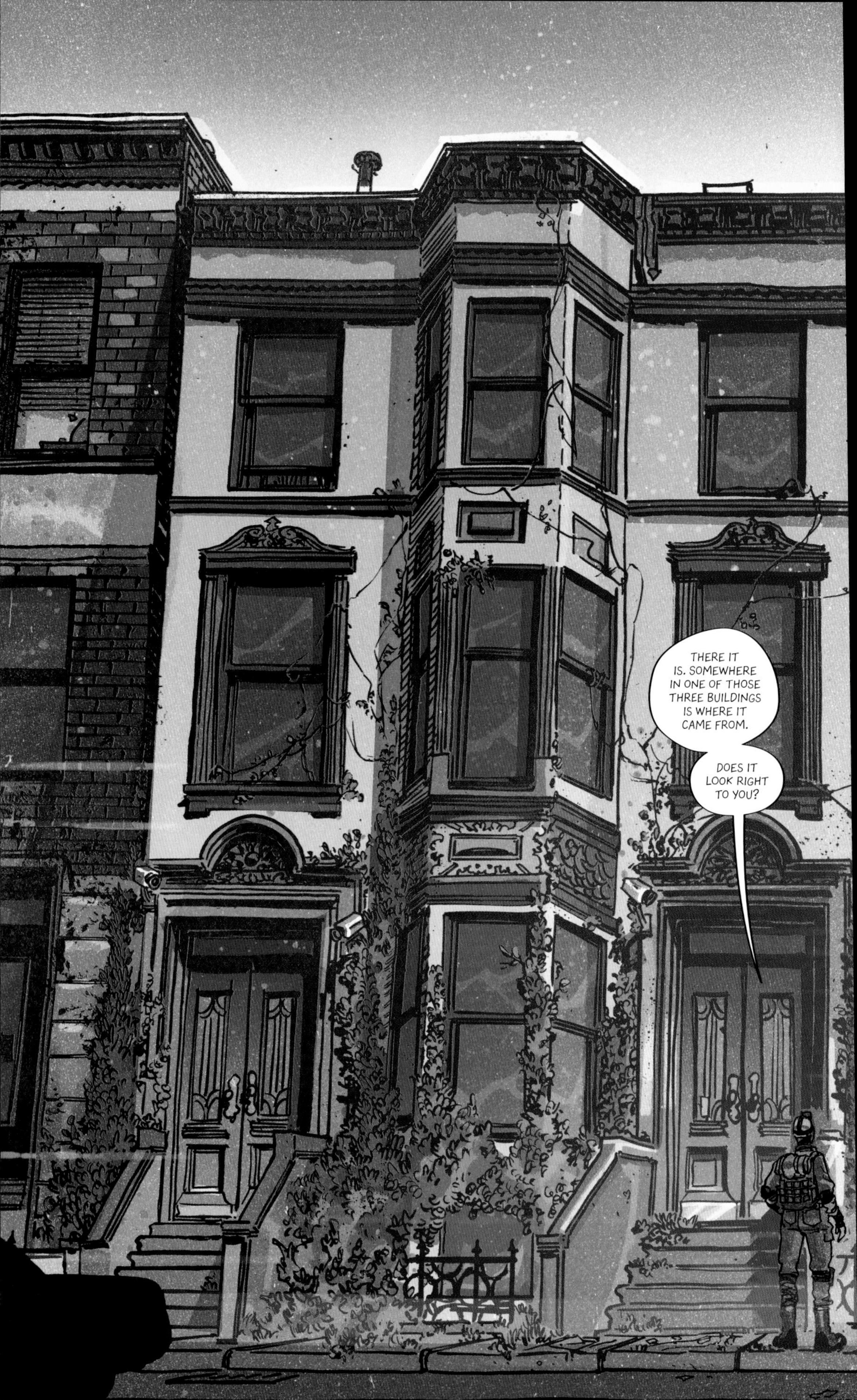
THERE IT IS. SOMEWHERE IN ONE OF THOSE THREE BUILDINGS IS WHERE IT CAME FROM.
DOES IT LOOK RIGHT TO YOU?

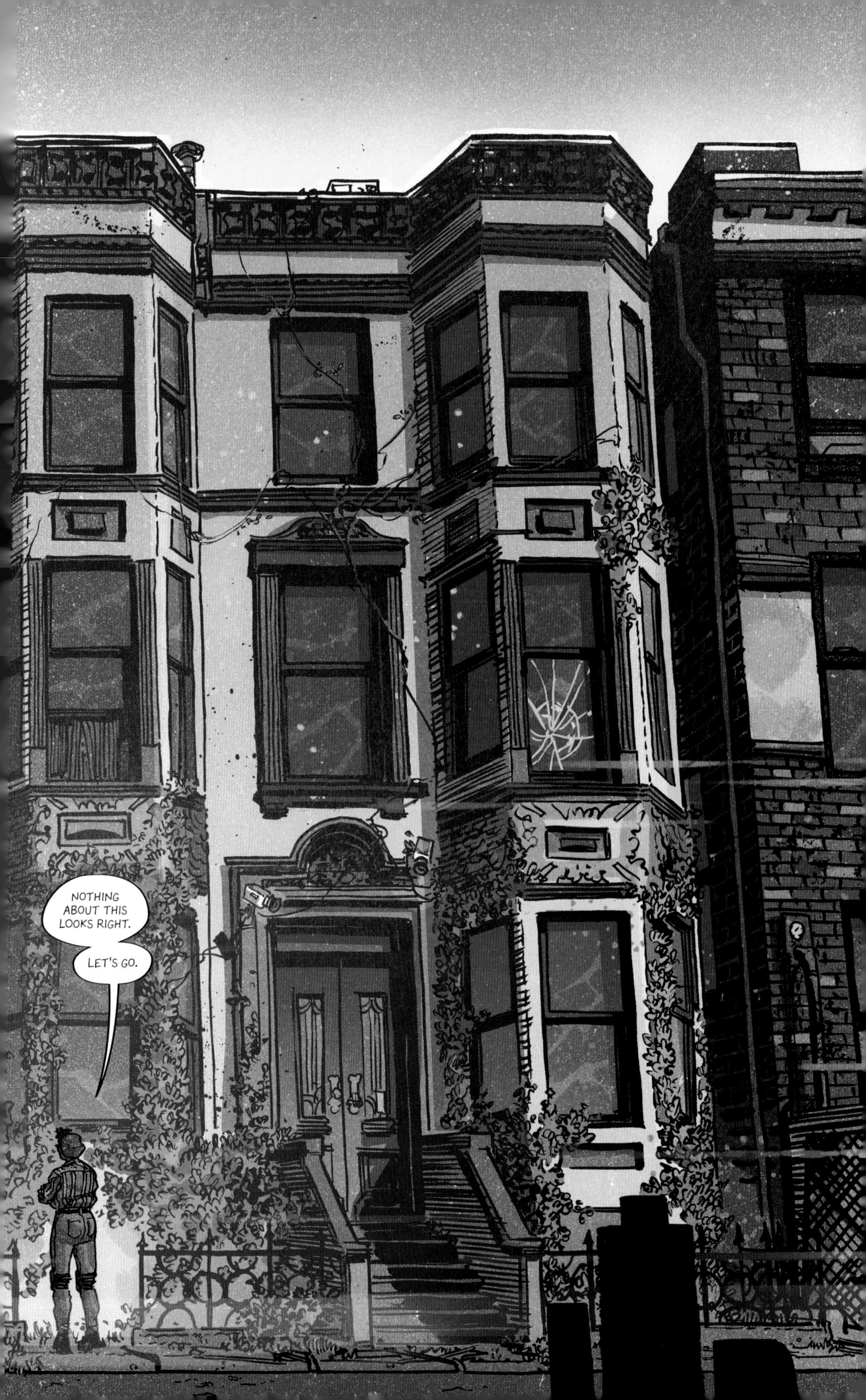
NOTHING ABOUT THIS LOOKS RIGHT.
LET'S GO.

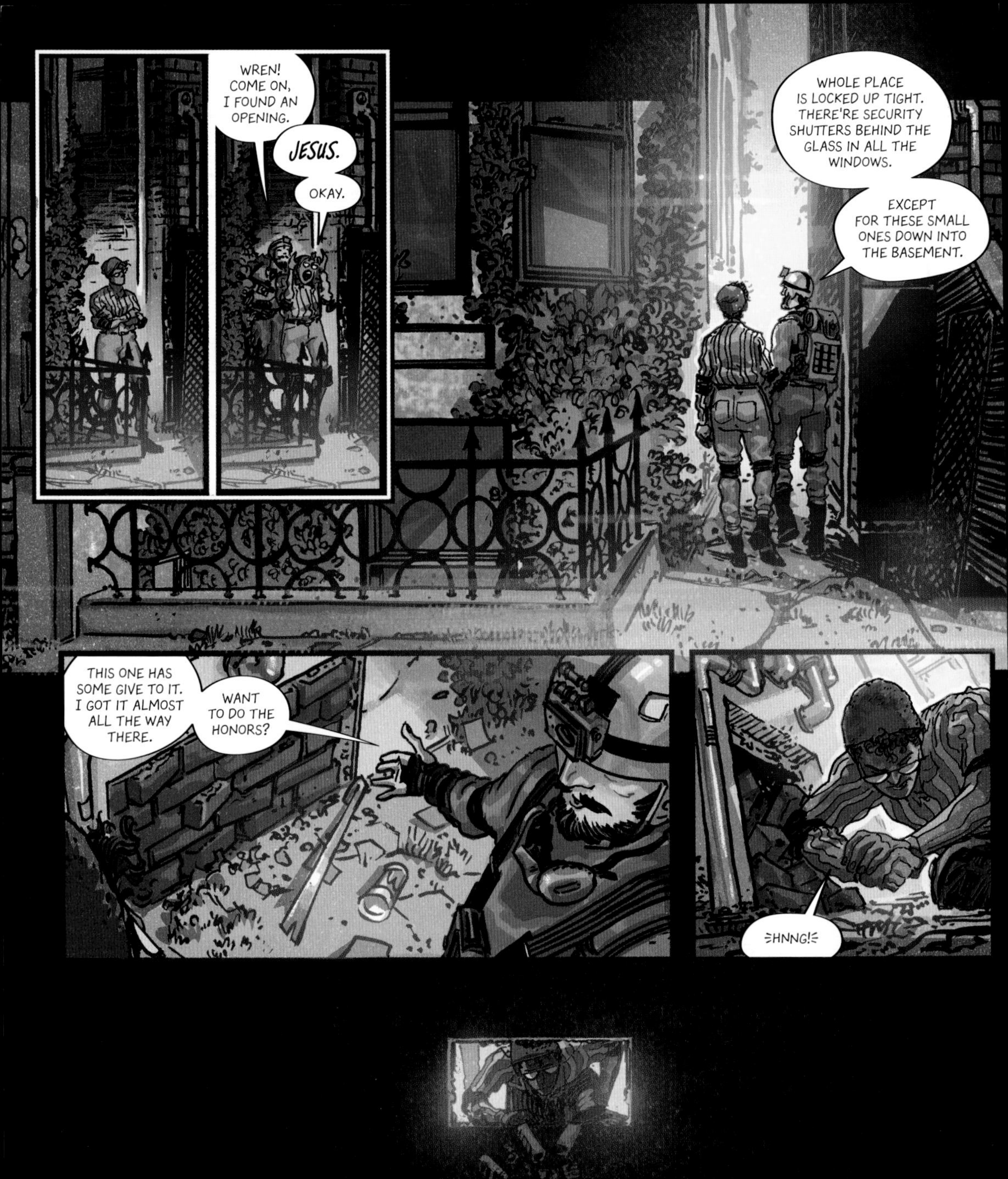
WREN! COME ON, I FOUND AN OPENING.
JESUS.
OKAY.
WHOLE PLACE IS LOCKED UP TIGHT. THERE'RE SECURITY SHUTTERS BEHIND THE GLASS IN ALL THE WINDOWS.
EXCEPT FOR THESE SMALL ONES DOWN INTO THE BASEMENT.
THIS ONE HAS SOME GIVE TO IT. I GOT IT ALMOST ALL THE WAY THERE.
WANT TO DO THE HONORS?
HNNG!

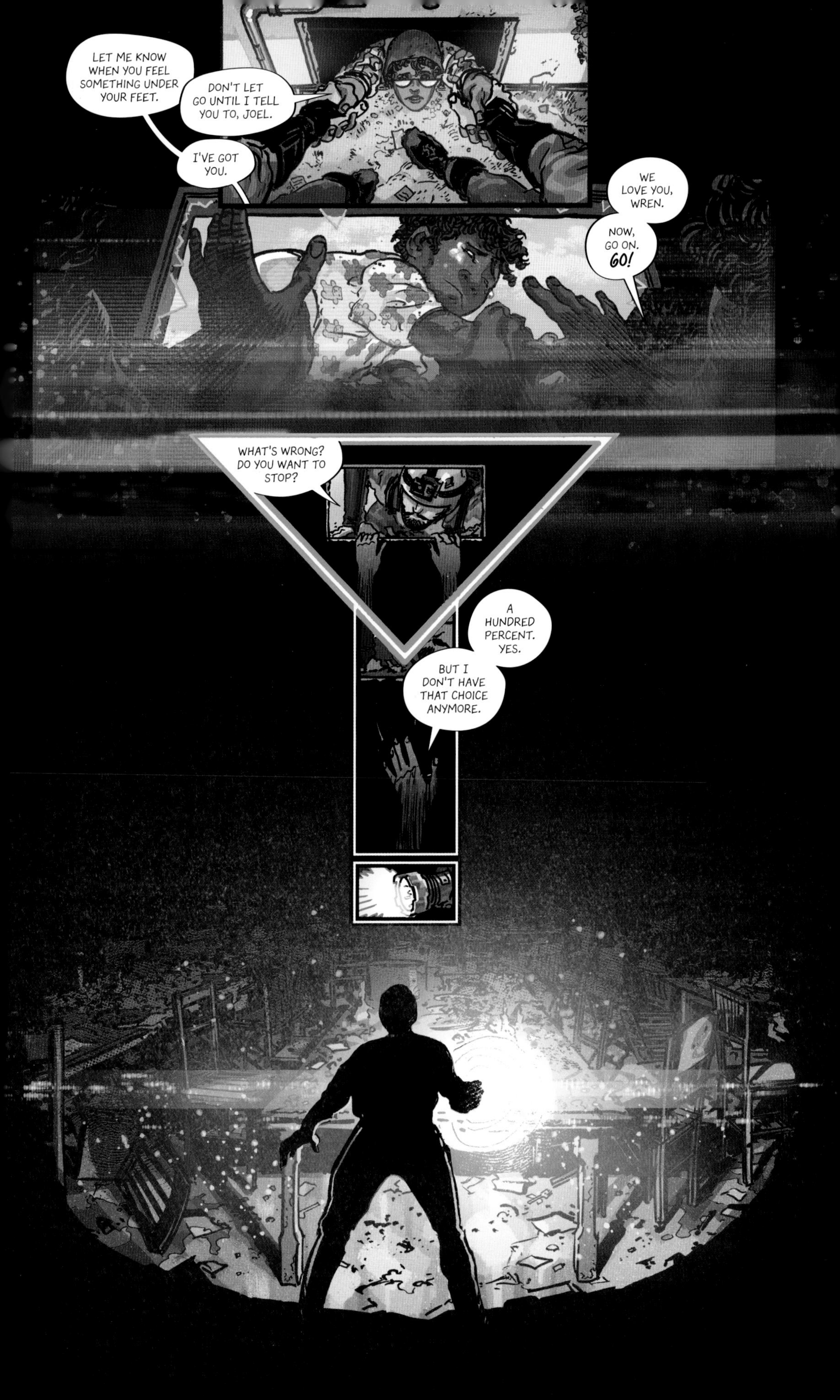

LET ME KNOW WHEN YOU FEEL SOMETHING UNDER YOUR FEET.
DON'T LET GO UNTIL I TELL YOU TO, JOEL.
I'VE GOT YOU.
WE LOVE YOU, WREN.
NOW, GO ON. GO!
WHAT'S WRONG? DO YOU WANT TO STOP?
A HUNDRED PERCENT. YES.
BUT I DON'T HAVE THAT CHOICE ANYMORE.

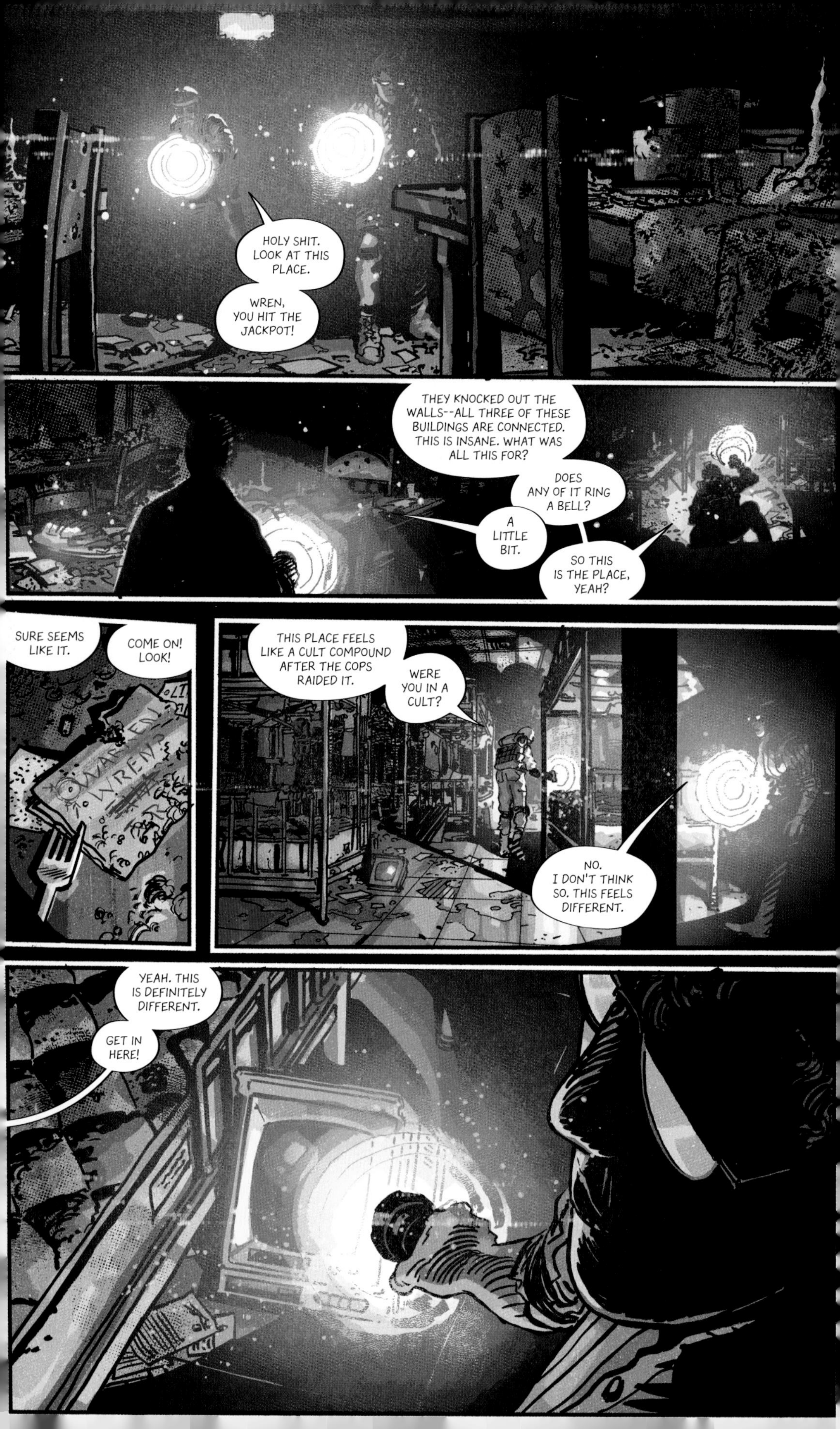
HOLY SHIT. LOOK AT THIS PLACE.
WREN, YOU HIT THE JACKPOT!
THEY KNOCKED OUT THE WALLS--ALL THREE OF THESE BUILDINGS ARE CONNECTED. THIS IS INSANE. WHAT WAS ALL THIS FOR?
DOES ANY OF IT RING A BELL?
A LITTLE BIT.
SO THIS IS THE PLACE, YEAH?
SURE SEEMS LIKE IT.
COME ON! LOOK!
WARREN
WREN
THIS PLACE FEELS LIKE A CULT COMPOUND AFTER THE COPS RAIDED IT.
WERE YOU IN A CULT?
NO. I DON'T THINK SO. THIS FEELS DIFFERENT.
YEAH. THIS IS DEFINITELY DIFFERENT.
GET IN HERE!

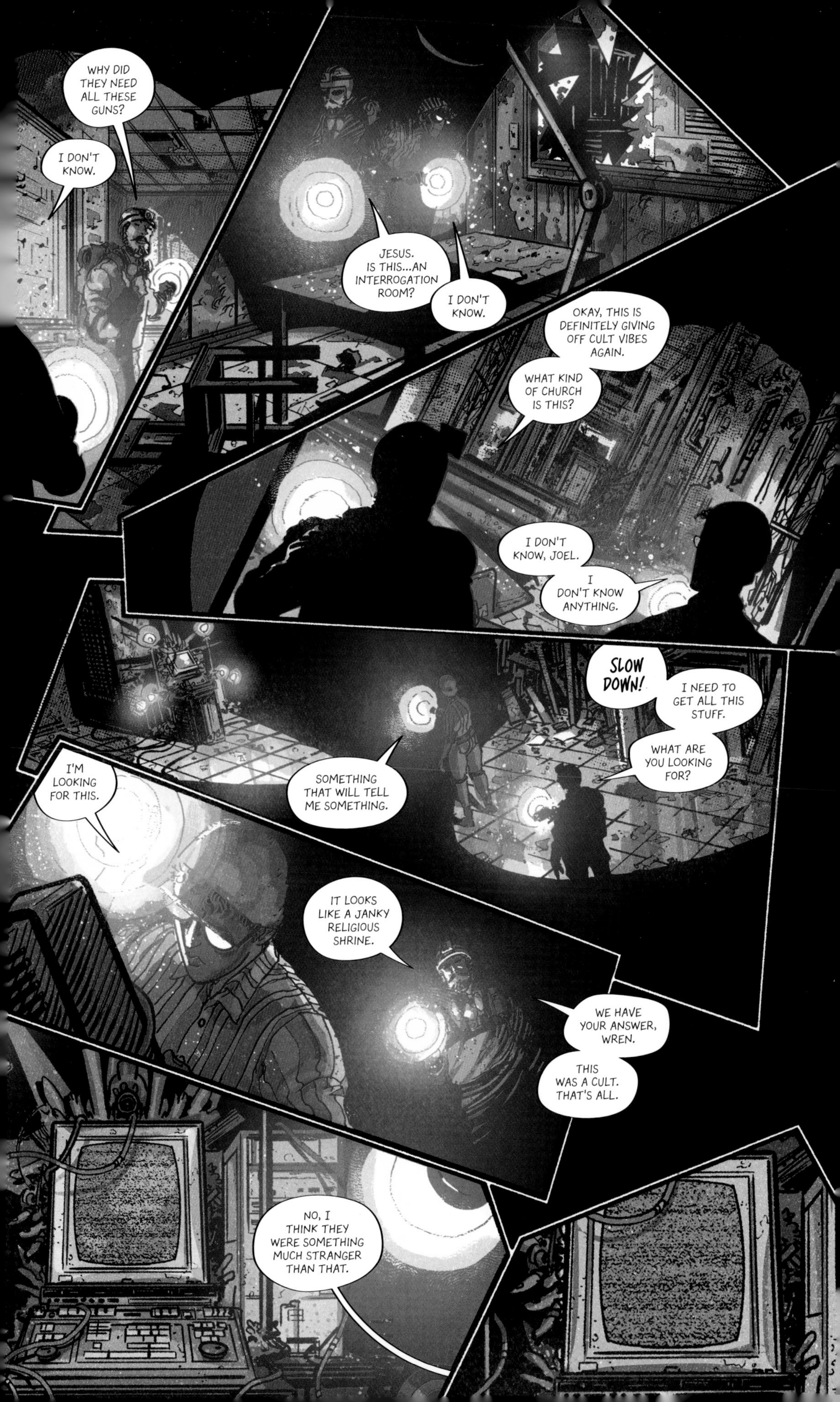

WHY DID THEY NEED ALL THESE GUNS?
I DON'T KNOW.
JESUS. IS THIS...AN INTERROGATION ROOM?
I DON'T KNOW.
OKAY, THIS IS DEFINITELY GIVING OFF CULT VIBES AGAIN.
WHAT KIND OF CHURCH IS THIS?
I DON'T KNOW, JOEL.
I DON'T KNOW ANYTHING.
SLOW DOWN!
I NEED TO GET ALL THIS STUFF.
WHAT ARE YOU LOOKING FOR?
SOMETHING THAT WILL TELL ME SOMETHING.
I'M LOOKING FOR THIS.
IT LOOKS LIKE A JANKY RELIGIOUS SHRINE.
WE HAVE YOUR ANSWER, WREN.
THIS WAS A CULT. THAT'S ALL.
NO, I THINK THEY WERE SOMETHING MUCH STRANGER THAN THAT.

CAN'T BELIEVE THERE'S POWER IN HERE. OR THAT THIS JUNK WORKS.
I'M GONNA LOOK AROUND.
REC EDIT STOP
PLAY STILL REW
ME TOO.
PLAY STILL REW
SHK SHK
TIK TIK TIK
IN
A2
REC EDIT STOP
PLAY STILL REW
SHK
TIK
IN
A2

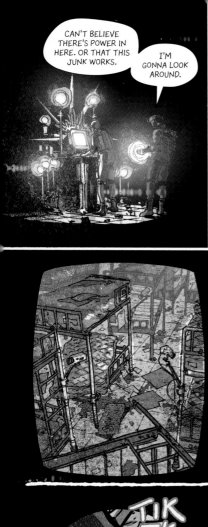

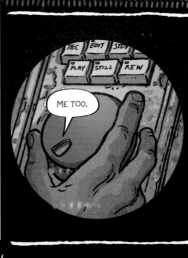

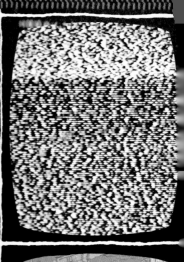

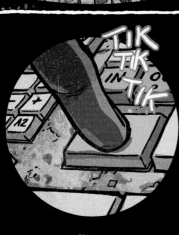

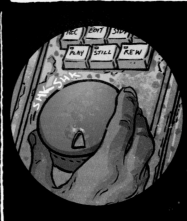

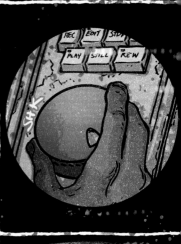

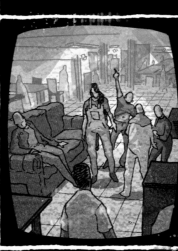

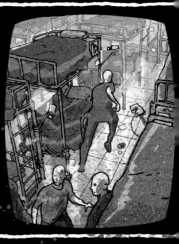

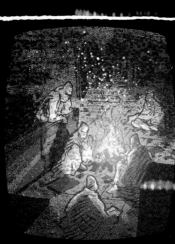

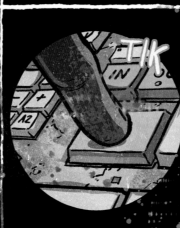

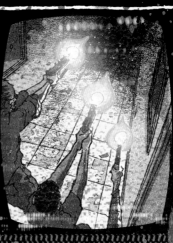

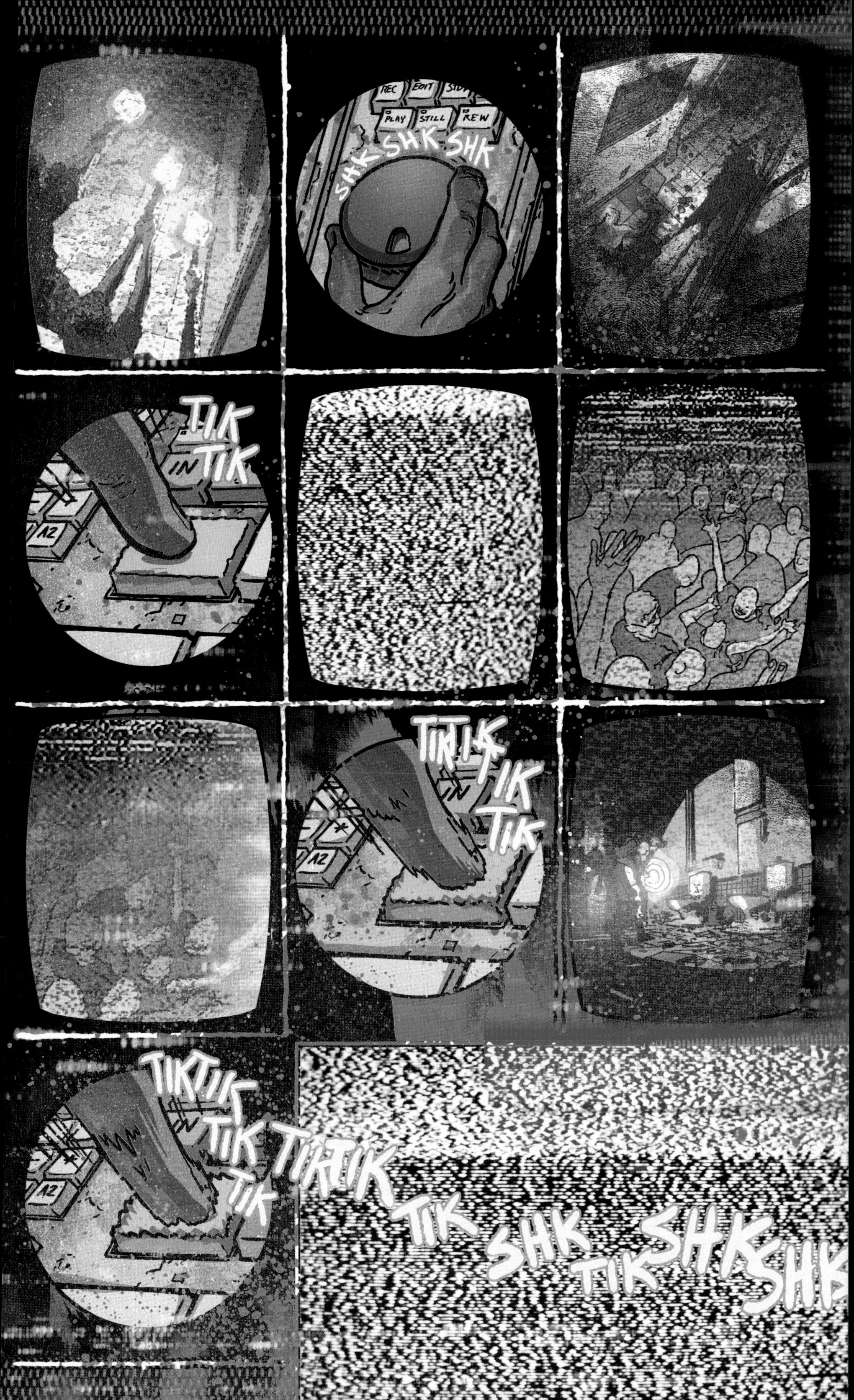
REC
EDIT
PLAY
STILL
REW
SHK SHK SHK SHK
TIK
TIK
IN
TIKTIK
TIK
TIK
IN
TIKTIK
TIK
TIKTIK
TIK
TIK
SHK
TIK
SHK
SHK

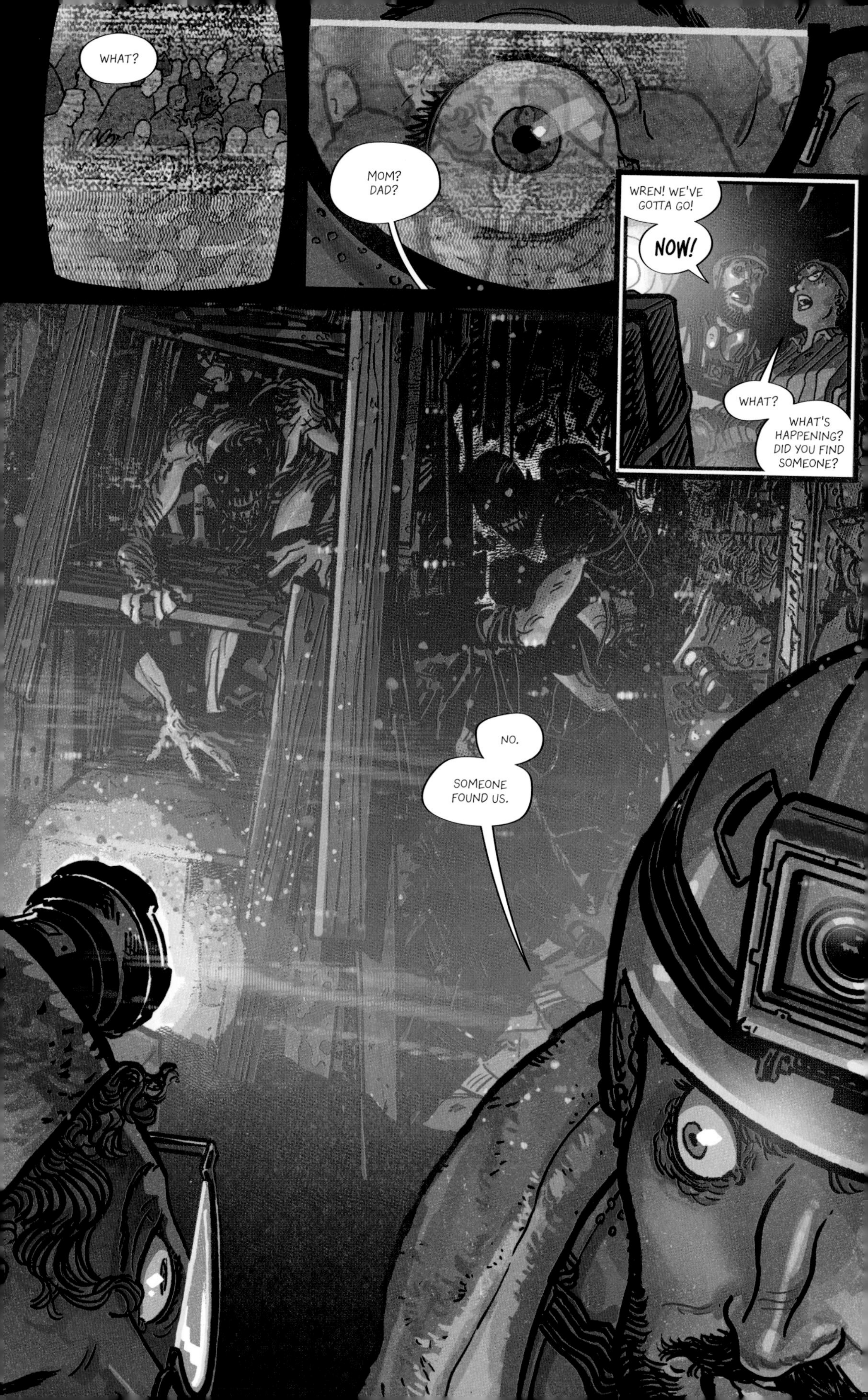
WHAT?
MOM? DAD?
WREN! WE'VE GOTTA GO!
NOW!
WHAT?
WHAT'S HAPPENING? DID YOU FIND SOMEONE?
NO.
SOMEONE FOUND US.

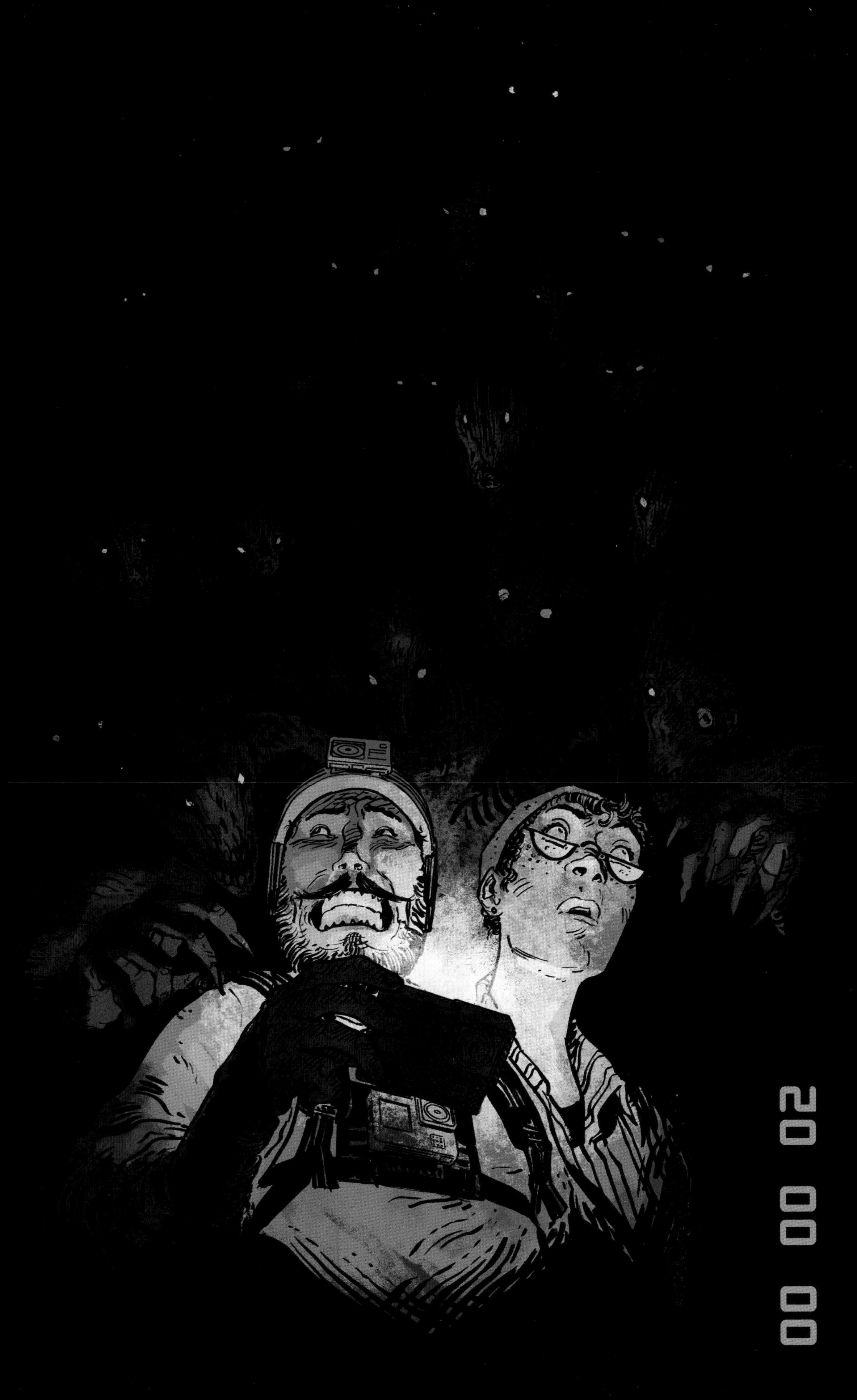
00 00 02

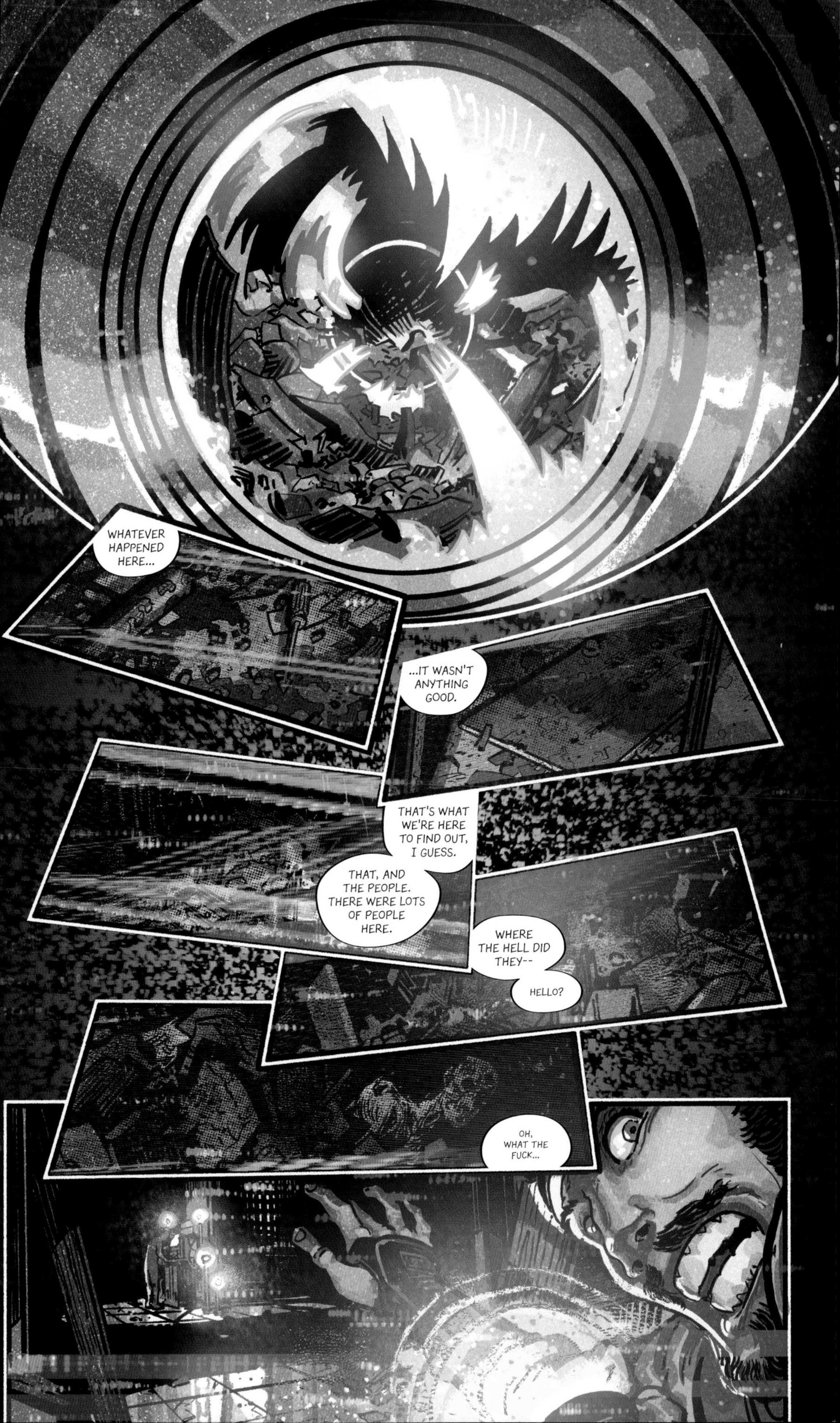
WHATEVER HAPPENED HERE...
...IT WASN'T ANYTHING GOOD.
THAT'S WHAT WE'RE HERE TO FIND OUT, I GUESS.
THAT, AND THE PEOPLE. THERE WERE LOTS OF PEOPLE HERE.
WHERE THE HELL DID THEY--
HELLO?
OH, WHAT THE FUCK...

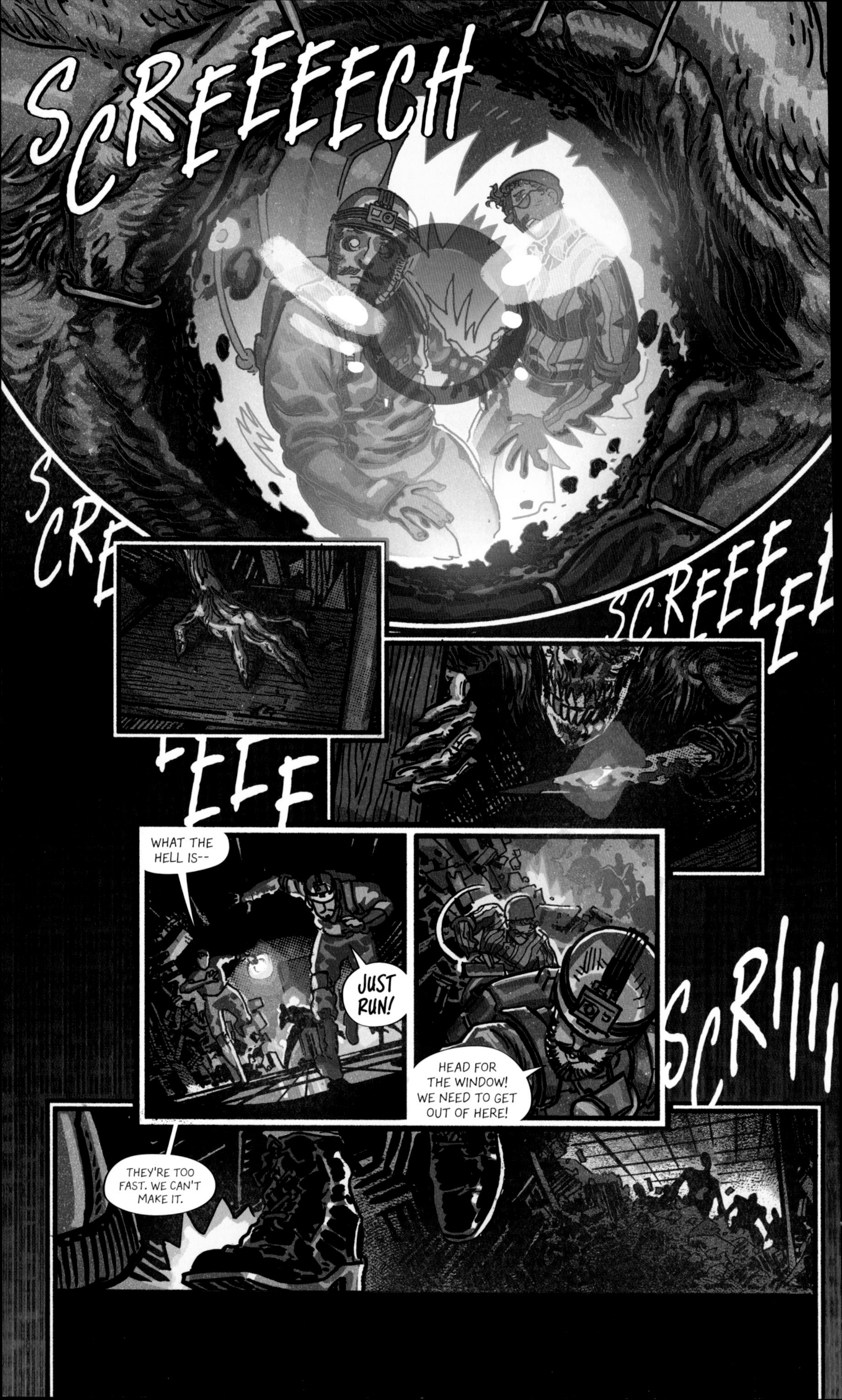
SCREEECH
SCREEEEE
SCREEEEE
WHAT THE HELL IS--
JUST RUN!
HEAD FOR THE WINDOW! WE NEED TO GET OUT OF HERE!
SCRIIII
THEY'RE TOO FAST. WE CAN'T MAKE IT.

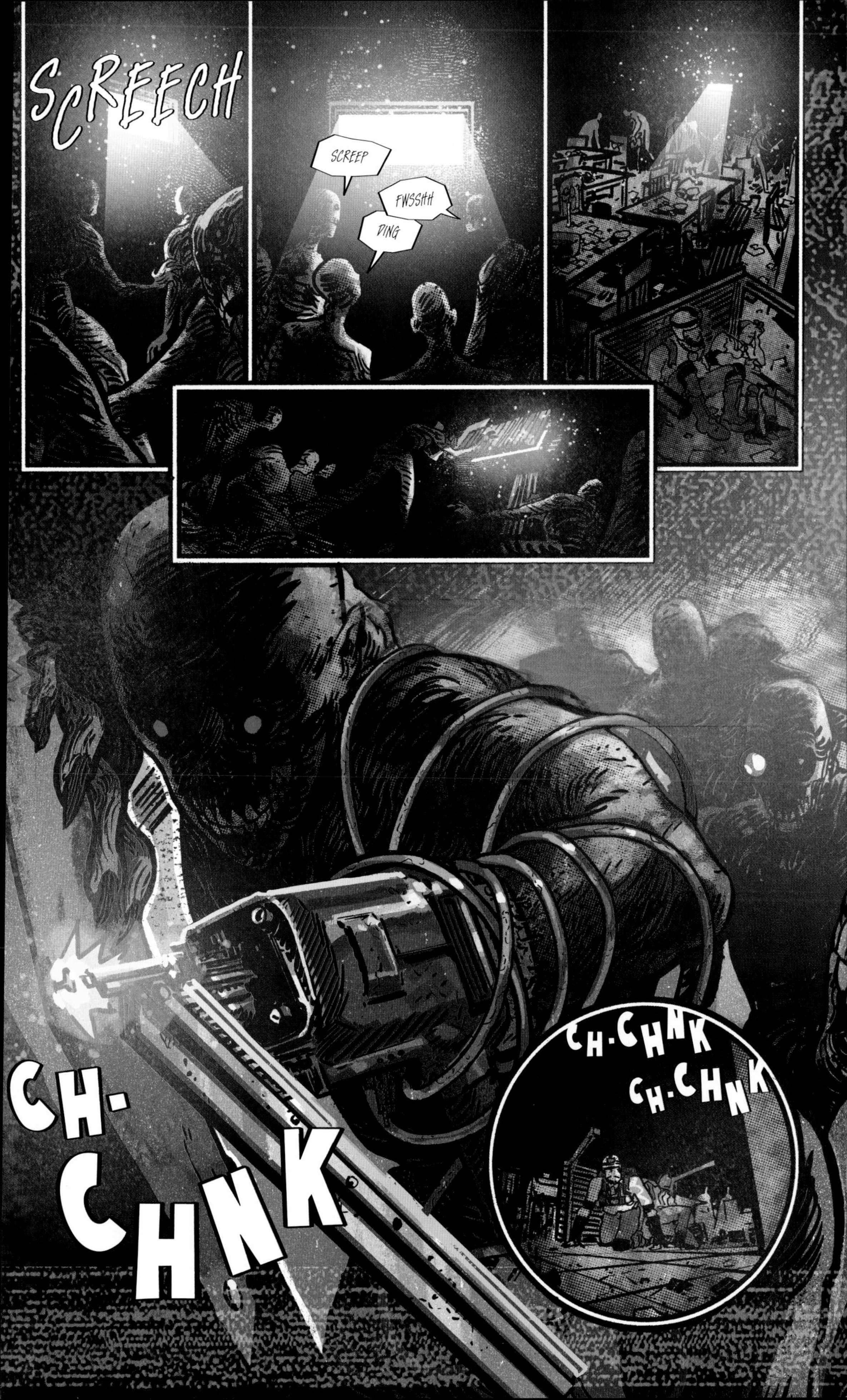
SCREECH
SCREEP
FWSSHH
DING
CH-CHNK
CH-CHNK
CH-CHNK

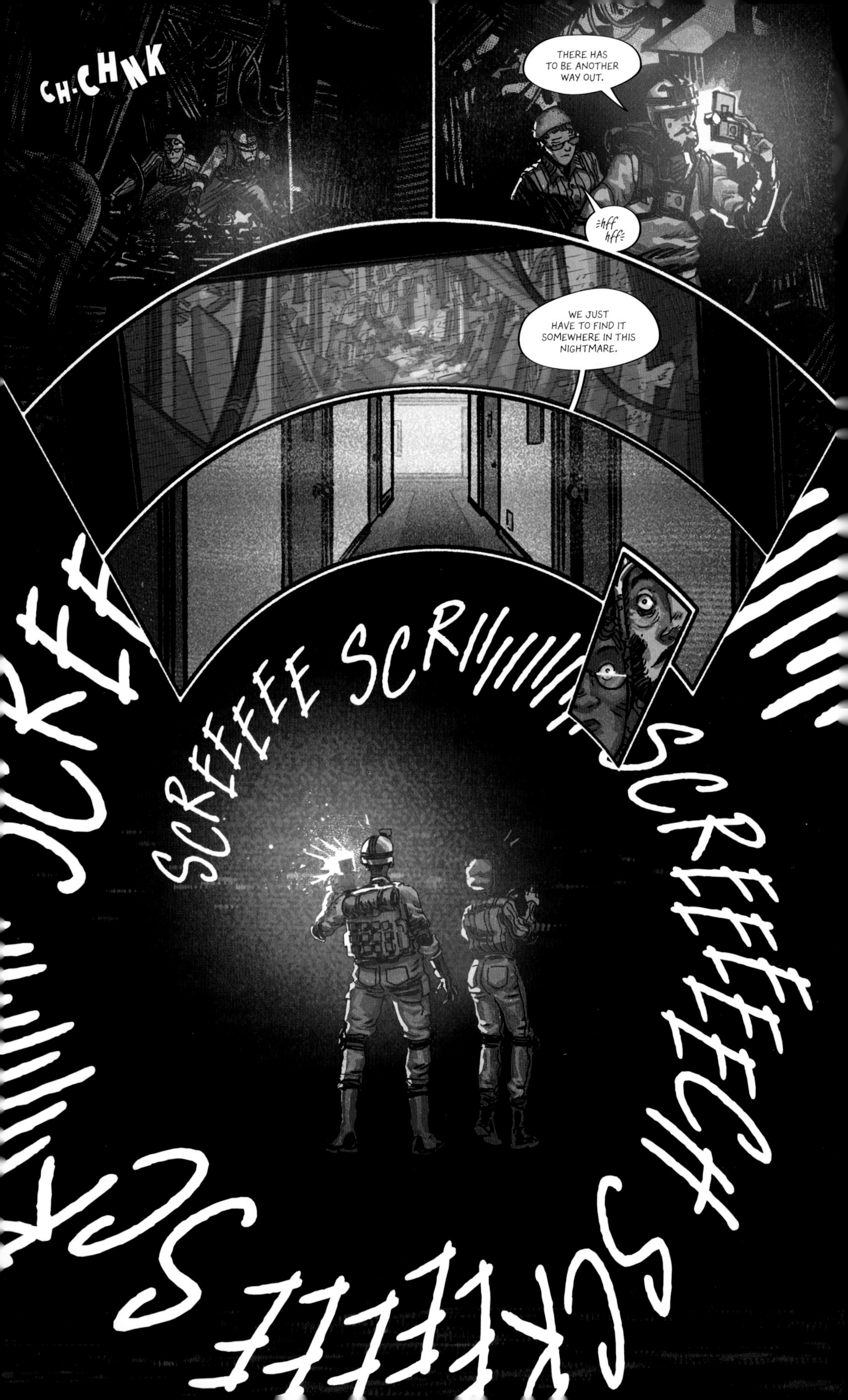
CH-CHNK
THERE HAS TO BE ANOTHER WAY OUT.
hff hff
WE JUST HAVE TO FIND IT SOMEWHERE IN THIS NIGHTMARE.
SCREEEEE SCRIIIIIIIIII
SCREEEECH
SCREEEEE
SCRIIIIIIII
SCREE

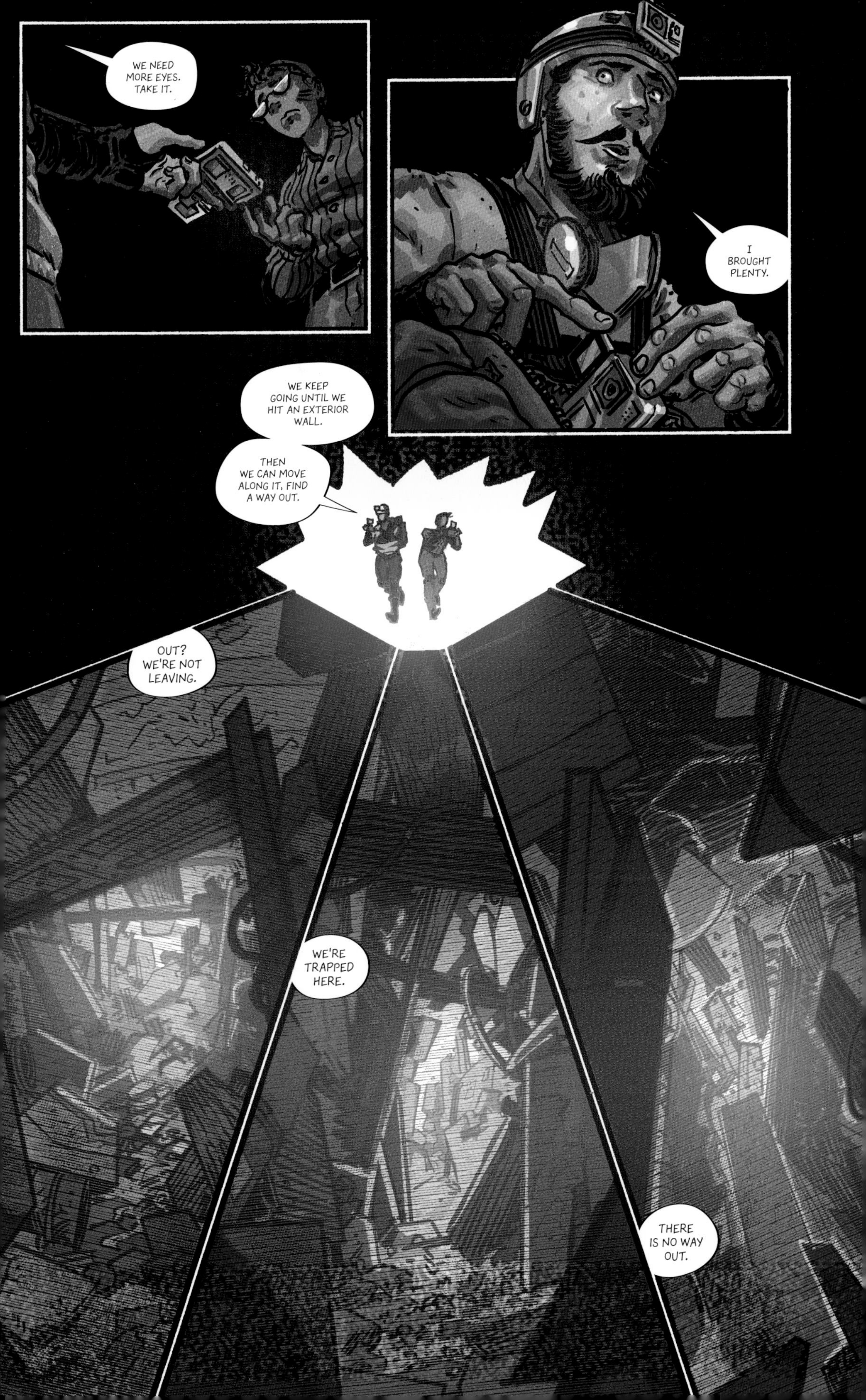
WE NEED MORE EYES. TAKE IT.
I BROUGHT PLENTY.
WE KEEP GOING UNTIL WE HIT AN EXTERIOR WALL.
THEN WE CAN MOVE ALONG IT, FIND A WAY OUT.
OUT? WE'RE NOT LEAVING.
WE'RE TRAPPED HERE.
THERE IS NO WAY OUT.

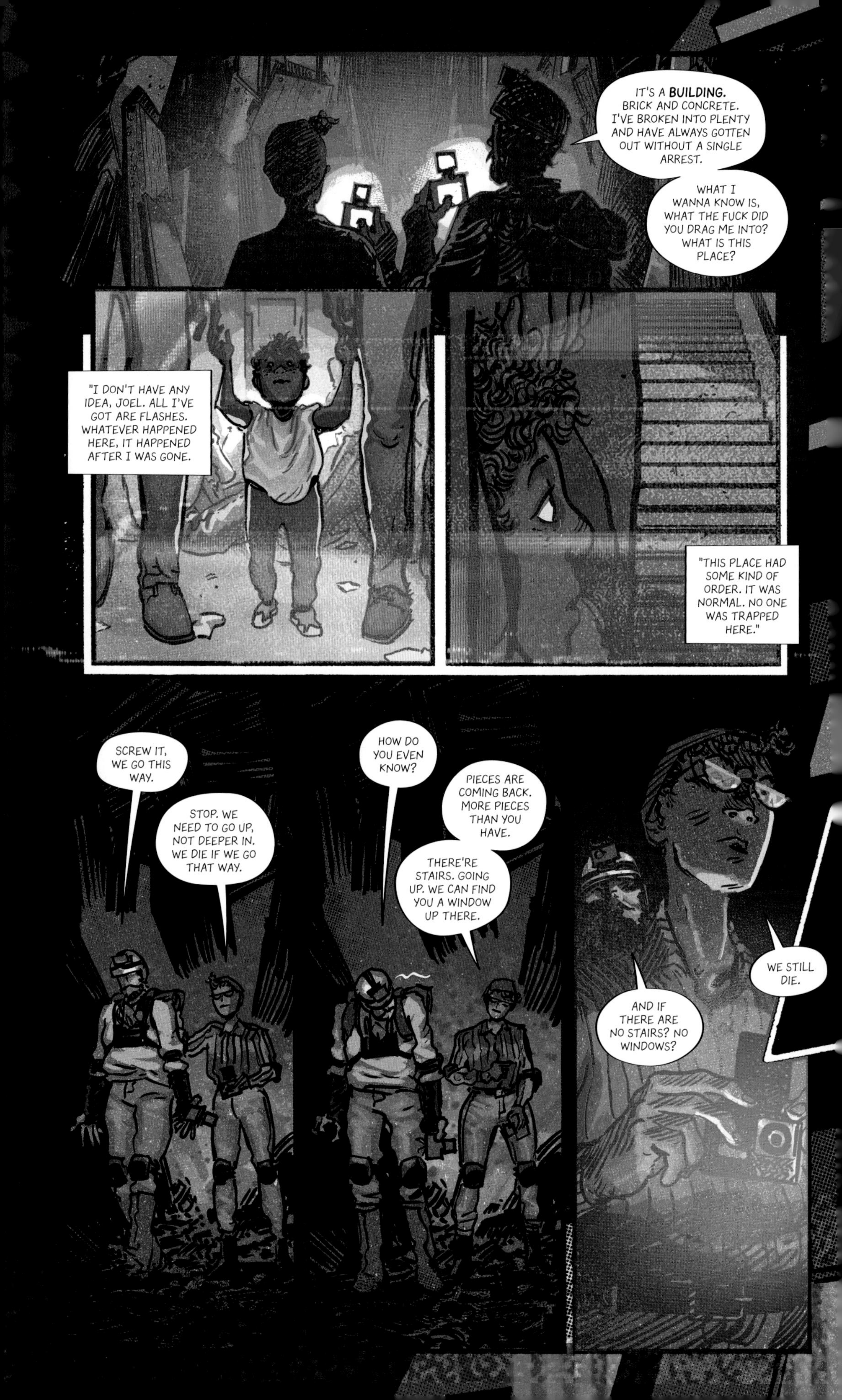
IT'S A **BUILDING.** BRICK AND CONCRETE. I'VE BROKEN INTO PLENTY AND HAVE ALWAYS GOTTEN OUT WITHOUT A SINGLE ARREST.
WHAT I WANNA KNOW IS, WHAT THE FUCK DID YOU DRAG ME INTO? WHAT IS THIS PLACE?
"I DON'T HAVE ANY IDEA, JOEL. ALL I'VE GOT ARE FLASHES. WHATEVER HAPPENED HERE, IT HAPPENED AFTER I WAS GONE.
"THIS PLACE HAD SOME KIND OF ORDER. IT WAS NORMAL. NO ONE WAS TRAPPED HERE."
SCREW IT, WE GO THIS WAY.
STOP. WE NEED TO GO UP, NOT DEEPER IN. WE DIE IF WE GO THAT WAY.
HOW DO YOU EVEN KNOW?
PIECES ARE COMING BACK. MORE PIECES THAN YOU HAVE.
THERE'RE STAIRS. GOING UP. WE CAN FIND YOU A WINDOW UP THERE.
AND IF THERE ARE NO STAIRS? NO WINDOWS?
WE STILL DIE.

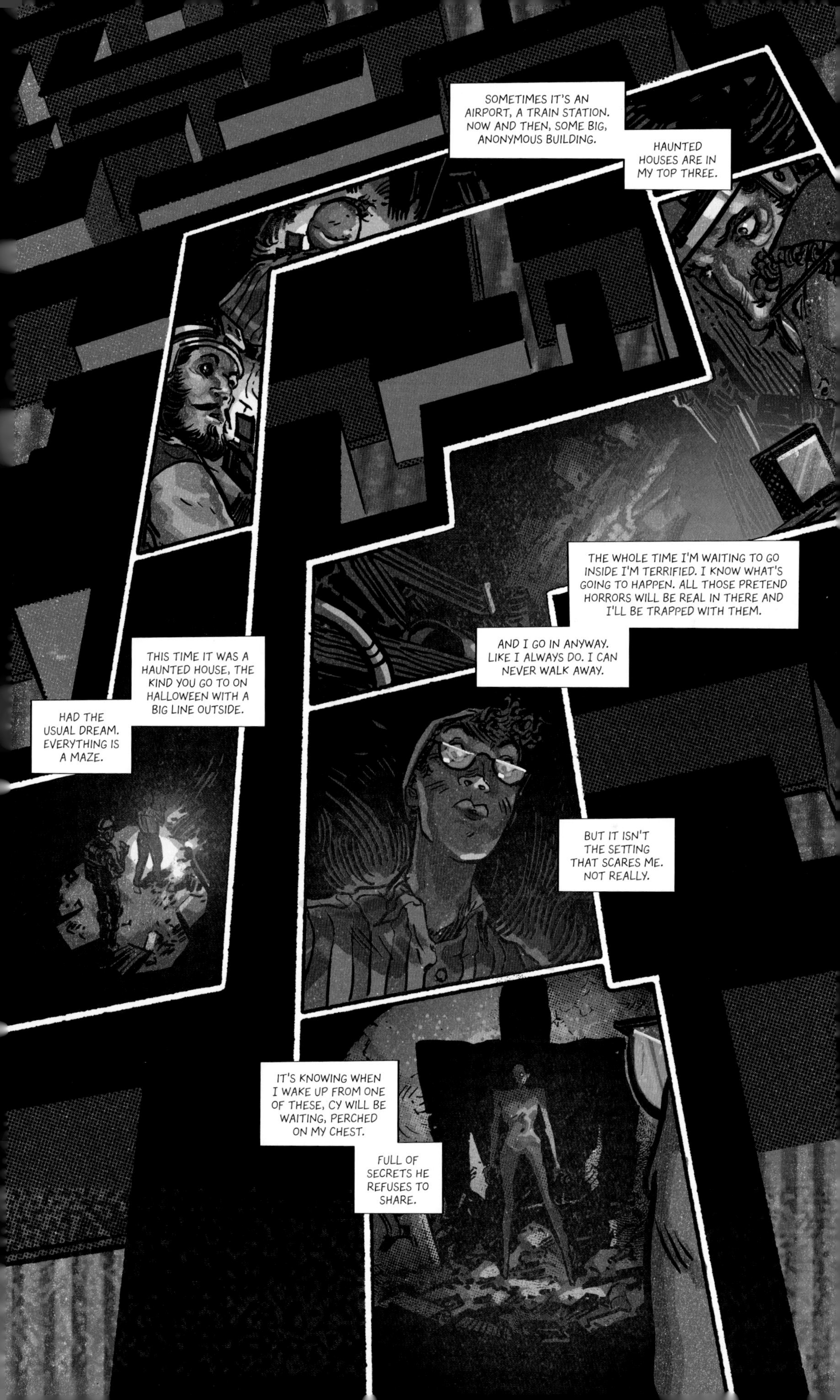
SOMETIMES IT'S AN AIRPORT, A TRAIN STATION. NOW AND THEN, SOME BIG, ANONYMOUS BUILDING.
HAUNTED HOUSES ARE IN MY TOP THREE.
HAD THE USUAL DREAM. EVERYTHING IS A MAZE.
THIS TIME IT WAS A HAUNTED HOUSE, THE KIND YOU GO TO ON HALLOWEEN WITH A BIG LINE OUTSIDE.
THE WHOLE TIME I'M WAITING TO GO INSIDE I'M TERRIFIED. I KNOW WHAT'S GOING TO HAPPEN. ALL THOSE PRETEND HORRORS WILL BE REAL IN THERE AND I'LL BE TRAPPED WITH THEM.
AND I GO IN ANYWAY. LIKE I ALWAYS DO. I CAN NEVER WALK AWAY.
BUT IT ISN'T THE SETTING THAT SCARES ME. NOT REALLY.
IT'S KNOWING WHEN I WAKE UP FROM ONE OF THESE, CY WILL BE WAITING, PERCHED ON MY CHEST.
FULL OF SECRETS HE REFUSES TO SHARE.

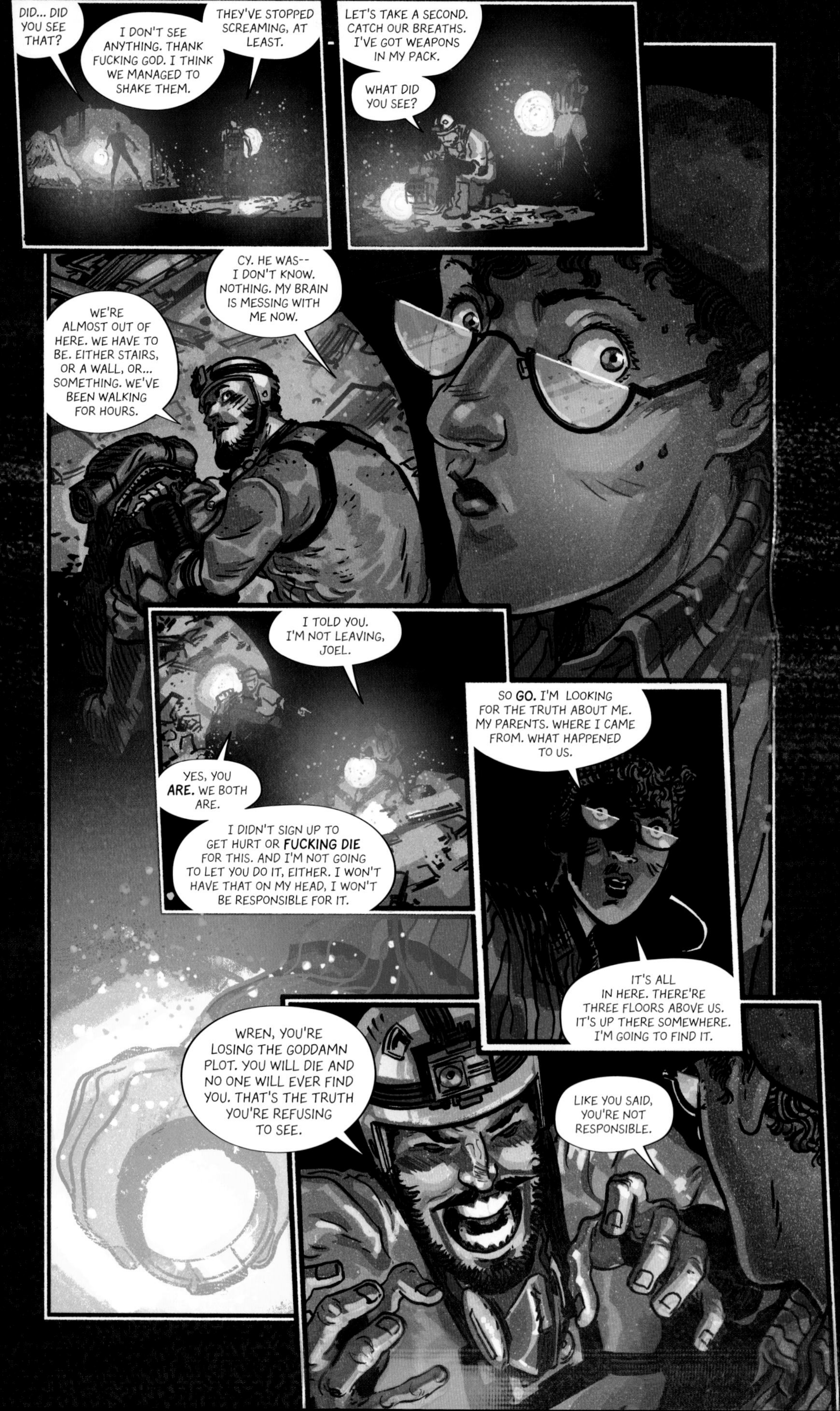

DID... DID YOU SEE THAT?
I DON'T SEE ANYTHING. THANK FUCKING GOD. I THINK WE MANAGED TO SHAKE THEM.
THEY'VE STOPPED SCREAMING, AT LEAST.
LET'S TAKE A SECOND. CATCH OUR BREATHS. I'VE GOT WEAPONS IN MY PACK.
WHAT DID YOU SEE?
CY. HE WAS-- I DON'T KNOW. NOTHING. MY BRAIN IS MESSING WITH ME NOW.
WE'RE ALMOST OUT OF HERE. WE HAVE TO BE. EITHER STAIRS, OR A WALL, OR... SOMETHING. WE'VE BEEN WALKING FOR HOURS.
I TOLD YOU. I'M NOT LEAVING, JOEL.
YES, YOU **ARE.** WE BOTH ARE.
I DIDN'T SIGN UP TO GET HURT OR **FUCKING DIE** FOR THIS. AND I'M NOT GOING TO LET YOU DO IT, EITHER. I WON'T HAVE THAT ON MY HEAD, I WON'T BE RESPONSIBLE FOR IT.
SO **GO.** I'M LOOKING FOR THE TRUTH ABOUT ME. MY PARENTS. WHERE I CAME FROM. WHAT HAPPENED TO US.
IT'S ALL IN HERE. THERE'RE THREE FLOORS ABOVE US. IT'S UP THERE SOMEWHERE. I'M GOING TO FIND IT.
WREN, YOU'RE LOSING THE GODDAMN PLOT. YOU WILL DIE AND NO ONE WILL EVER FIND YOU. THAT'S THE TRUTH YOU'RE REFUSING TO SEE.
LIKE YOU SAID, YOU'RE NOT RESPONSIBLE.

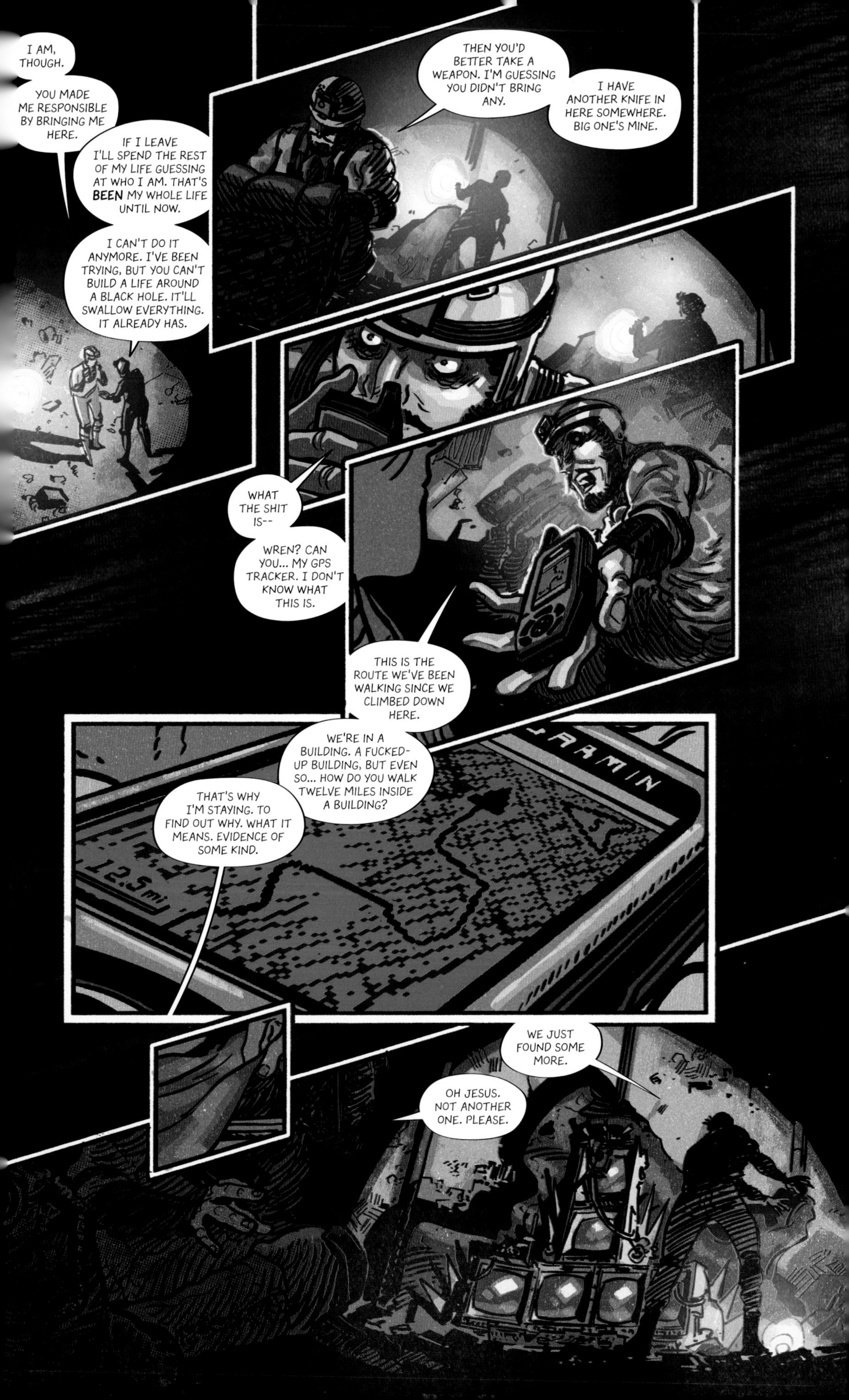
I AM, THOUGH.
YOU MADE ME RESPONSIBLE BY BRINGING ME HERE.
IF I LEAVE I'LL SPEND THE REST OF MY LIFE GUESSING AT WHO I AM. THAT'S **BEEN** MY WHOLE LIFE UNTIL NOW.
I CAN'T DO IT ANYMORE. I'VE BEEN TRYING, BUT YOU CAN'T BUILD A LIFE AROUND A BLACK HOLE. IT'LL SWALLOW EVERYTHING. IT ALREADY HAS.
THEN YOU'D BETTER TAKE A WEAPON. I'M GUESSING YOU DIDN'T BRING ANY.
I HAVE ANOTHER KNIFE IN HERE SOMEWHERE. BIG ONE'S MINE.
WHAT THE SHIT IS--
WREN? CAN YOU... MY GPS TRACKER. I DON'T KNOW WHAT THIS IS.
THIS IS THE ROUTE WE'VE BEEN WALKING SINCE WE CLIMBED DOWN HERE.
WE'RE IN A BUILDING. A FUCKED-UP BUILDING, BUT EVEN SO... HOW DO YOU WALK TWELVE MILES INSIDE A BUILDING?
THAT'S WHY I'M STAYING. TO FIND OUT WHY. WHAT IT MEANS. EVIDENCE OF SOME KIND.
GARMIN
12.5 mi
WE JUST FOUND SOME MORE.
OH JESUS. NOT ANOTHER ONE. PLEASE.

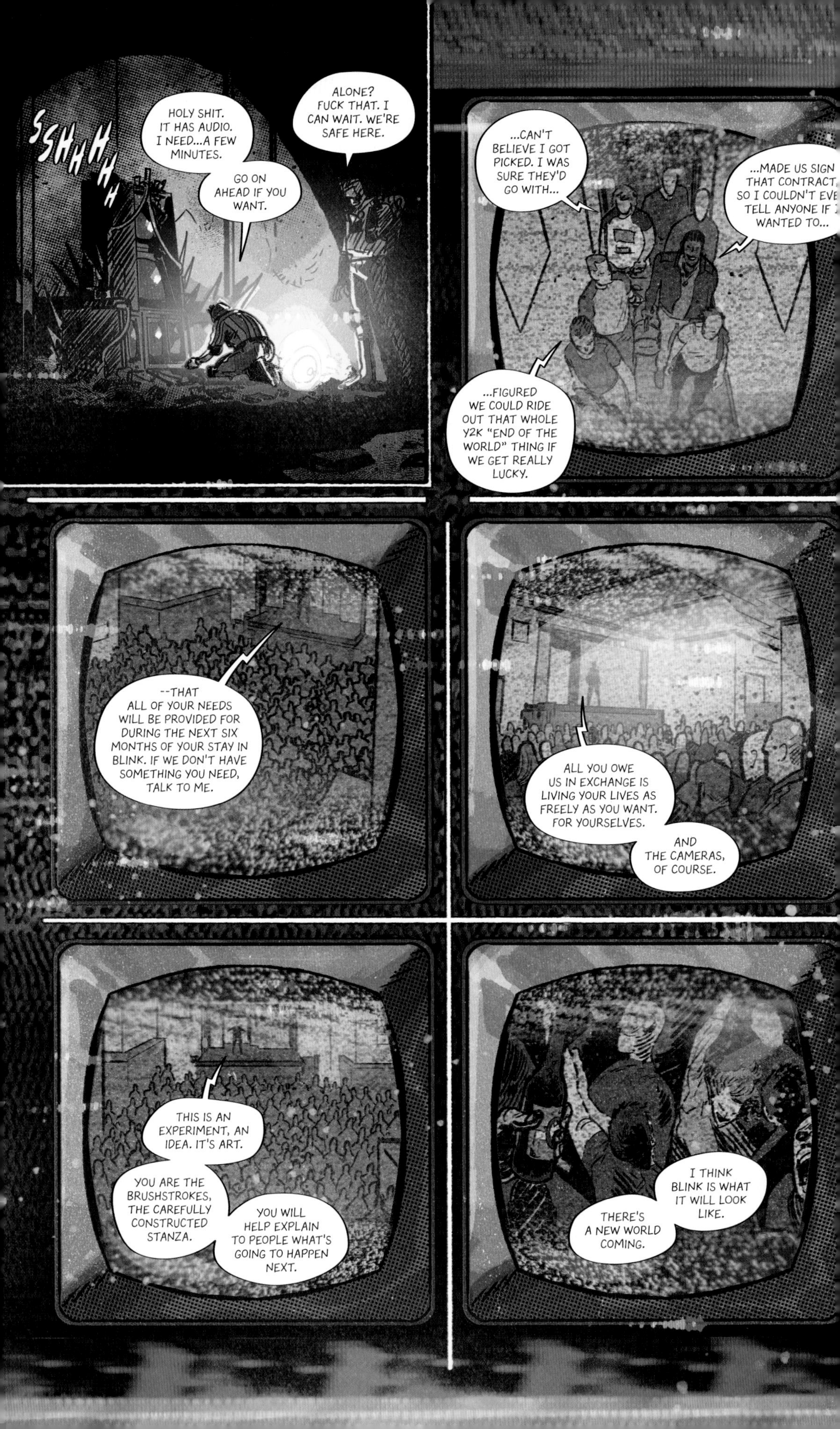
SSHHHH
HOLY SHIT. IT HAS AUDIO. I NEED...A FEW MINUTES.
GO ON AHEAD IF YOU WANT.
ALONE? FUCK THAT. I CAN WAIT. WE'RE SAFE HERE.
...CAN'T BELIEVE I GOT PICKED. I WAS SURE THEY'D GO WITH...
...MADE US SIGN THAT CONTRACT, SO I COULDN'T EVE TELL ANYONE IF I WANTED TO...
...FIGURED WE COULD RIDE OUT THAT WHOLE Y2K "END OF THE WORLD" THING IF WE GET REALLY LUCKY.
--THAT ALL OF YOUR NEEDS WILL BE PROVIDED FOR DURING THE NEXT SIX MONTHS OF YOUR STAY IN BLINK. IF WE DON'T HAVE SOMETHING YOU NEED, TALK TO ME.
ALL YOU OWE US IN EXCHANGE IS LIVING YOUR LIVES AS FREELY AS YOU WANT. FOR YOURSELVES.
AND THE CAMERAS, OF COURSE.
THIS IS AN EXPERIMENT, AN IDEA. IT'S ART.
YOU ARE THE BRUSHSTROKES, THE CAREFULLY CONSTRUCTED STANZA.
YOU WILL HELP EXPLAIN TO PEOPLE WHAT'S GOING TO HAPPEN NEXT.
THERE'S A NEW WORLD COMING.
I THINK BLINK IS WHAT IT WILL LOOK LIKE.

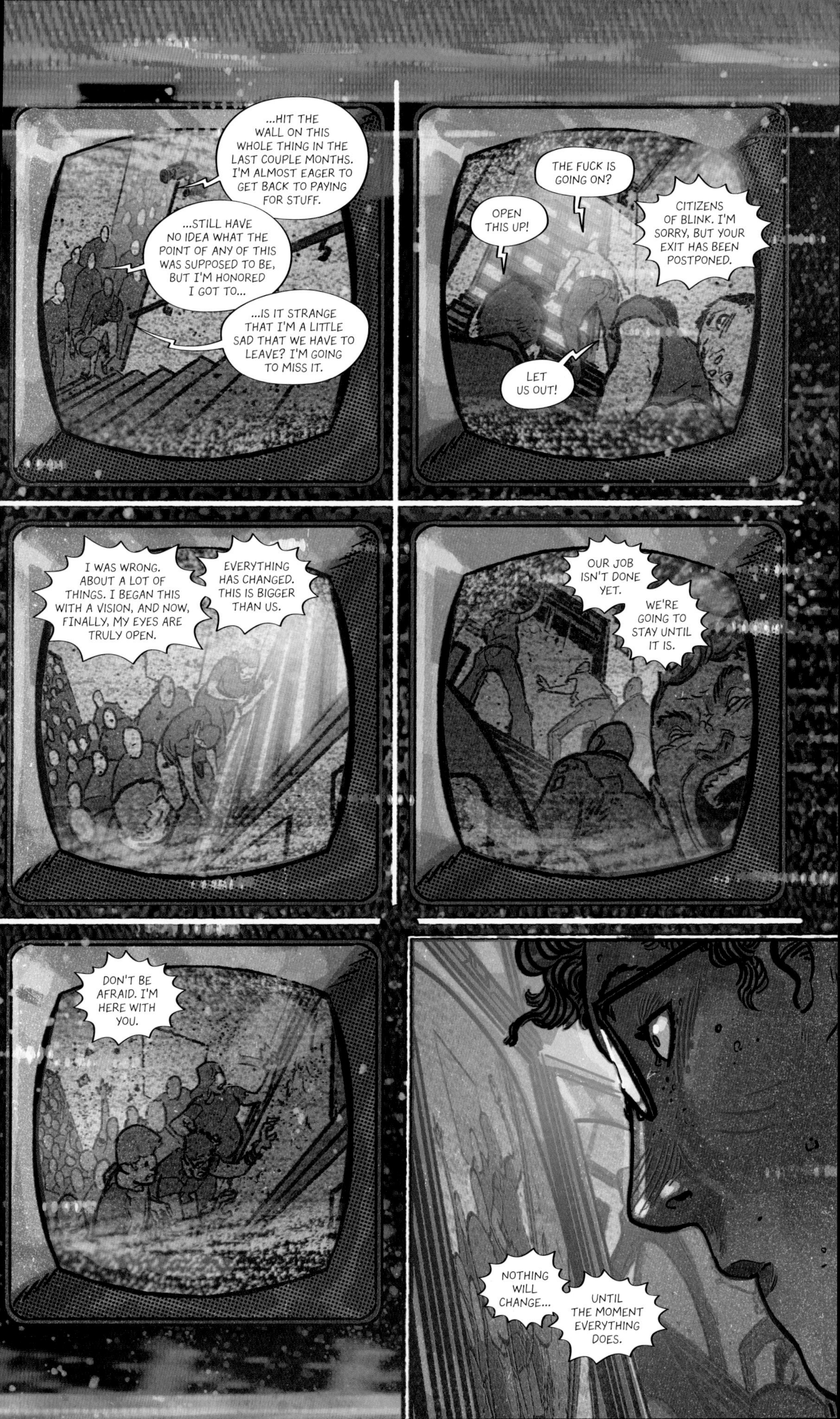
...HIT THE WALL ON THIS WHOLE THING IN THE LAST COUPLE MONTHS. I'M ALMOST EAGER TO GET BACK TO PAYING FOR STUFF.
...STILL HAVE NO IDEA WHAT THE POINT OF ANY OF THIS WAS SUPPOSED TO BE, BUT I'M HONORED I GOT TO...
...IS IT STRANGE THAT I'M A LITTLE SAD THAT WE HAVE TO LEAVE? I'M GOING TO MISS IT.
THE FUCK IS GOING ON?
OPEN THIS UP!
CITIZENS OF BLINK. I'M SORRY, BUT YOUR EXIT HAS BEEN POSTPONED.
LET US OUT!
I WAS WRONG. ABOUT A LOT OF THINGS. I BEGAN THIS WITH A VISION, AND NOW, FINALLY, MY EYES ARE TRULY OPEN.
EVERYTHING HAS CHANGED. THIS IS BIGGER THAN US.
OUR JOB ISN'T DONE YET.
WE'RE GOING TO STAY UNTIL IT IS.
DON'T BE AFRAID. I'M HERE WITH YOU.
NOTHING WILL CHANGE...
UNTIL THE MOMENT EVERYTHING DOES.

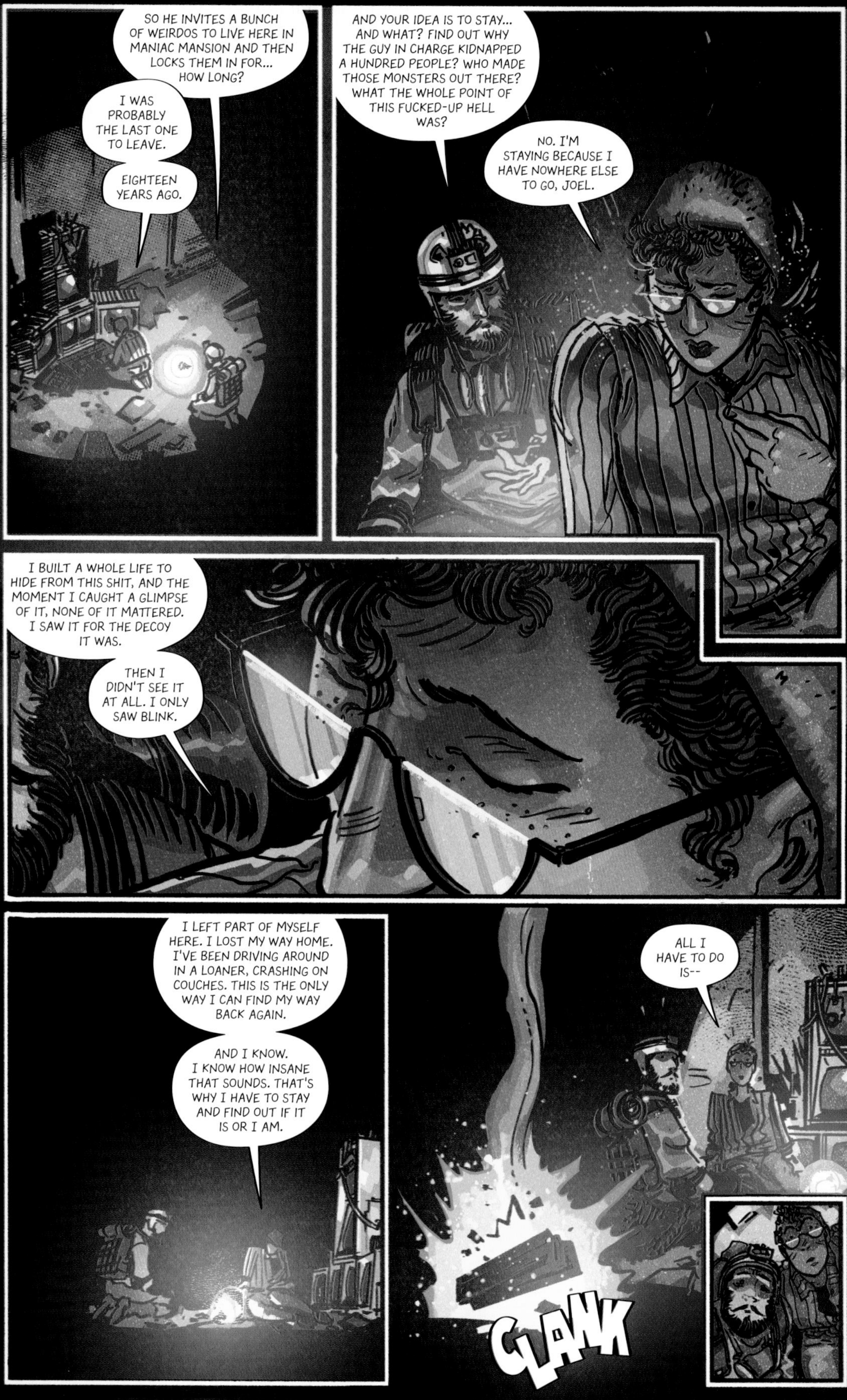

SO HE INVITES A BUNCH OF WEIRDOS TO LIVE HERE IN MANIAC MANSION AND THEN LOCKS THEM IN FOR... HOW LONG?
I WAS PROBABLY THE LAST ONE TO LEAVE.
EIGHTEEN YEARS AGO.
AND YOUR IDEA IS TO STAY... AND WHAT? FIND OUT WHY THE GUY IN CHARGE KIDNAPPED A HUNDRED PEOPLE? WHO MADE THOSE MONSTERS OUT THERE? WHAT THE WHOLE POINT OF THIS FUCKED-UP HELL WAS?
NO. I'M STAYING BECAUSE I HAVE NOWHERE ELSE TO GO, JOEL.
I BUILT A WHOLE LIFE TO HIDE FROM THIS SHIT, AND THE MOMENT I CAUGHT A GLIMPSE OF IT, NONE OF IT MATTERED. I SAW IT FOR THE DECOY IT WAS.
THEN I DIDN'T SEE IT AT ALL. I ONLY SAW BLINK.
I LEFT PART OF MYSELF HERE. I LOST MY WAY HOME. I'VE BEEN DRIVING AROUND IN A LOANER, CRASHING ON COUCHES. THIS IS THE ONLY WAY I CAN FIND MY WAY BACK AGAIN.
AND I KNOW. I KNOW HOW INSANE THAT SOUNDS. THAT'S WHY I HAVE TO STAY AND FIND OUT IF IT IS OR I AM.
ALL I HAVE TO DO IS--
CLANK

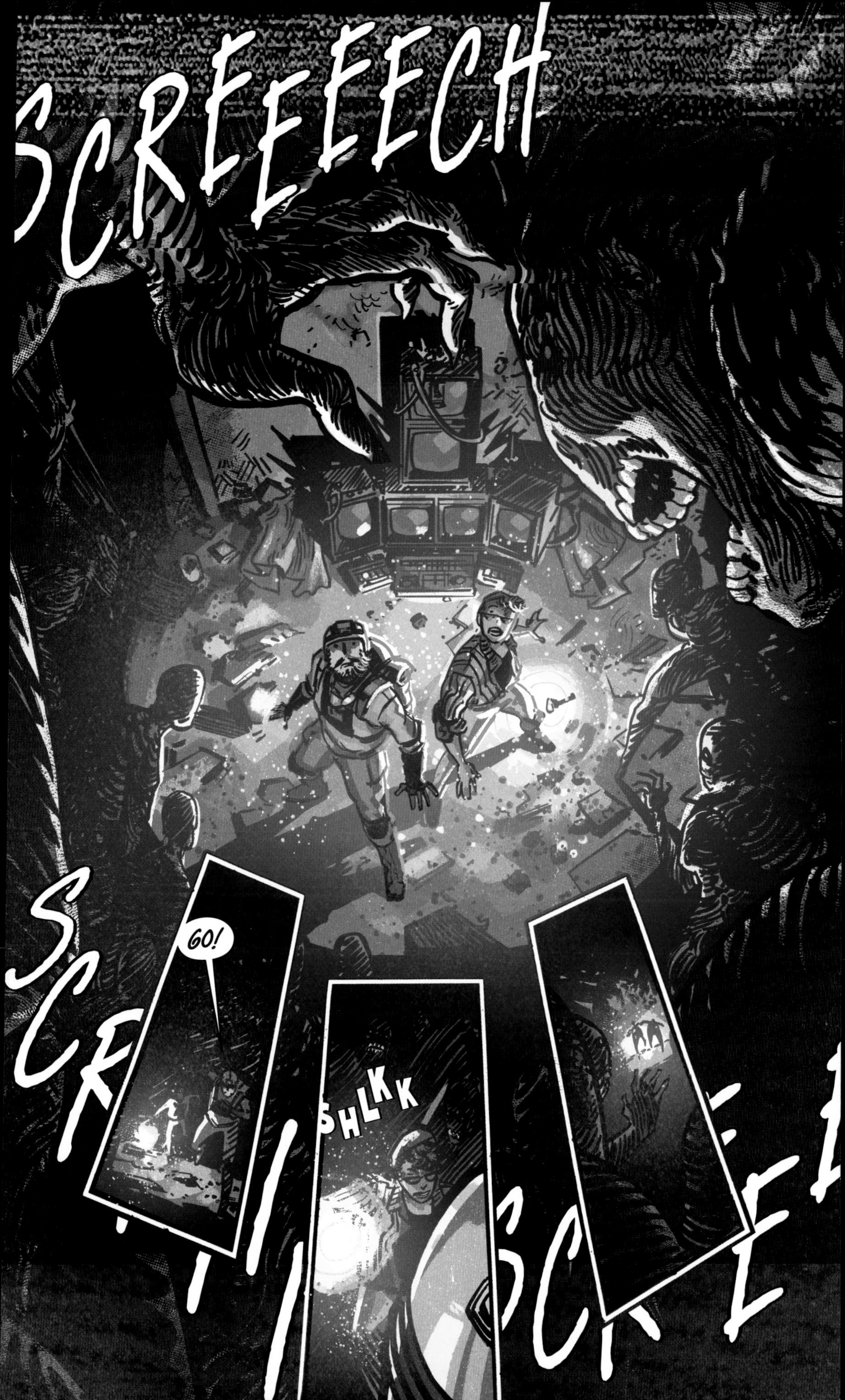
SCREEECH
GO!
SHLKK

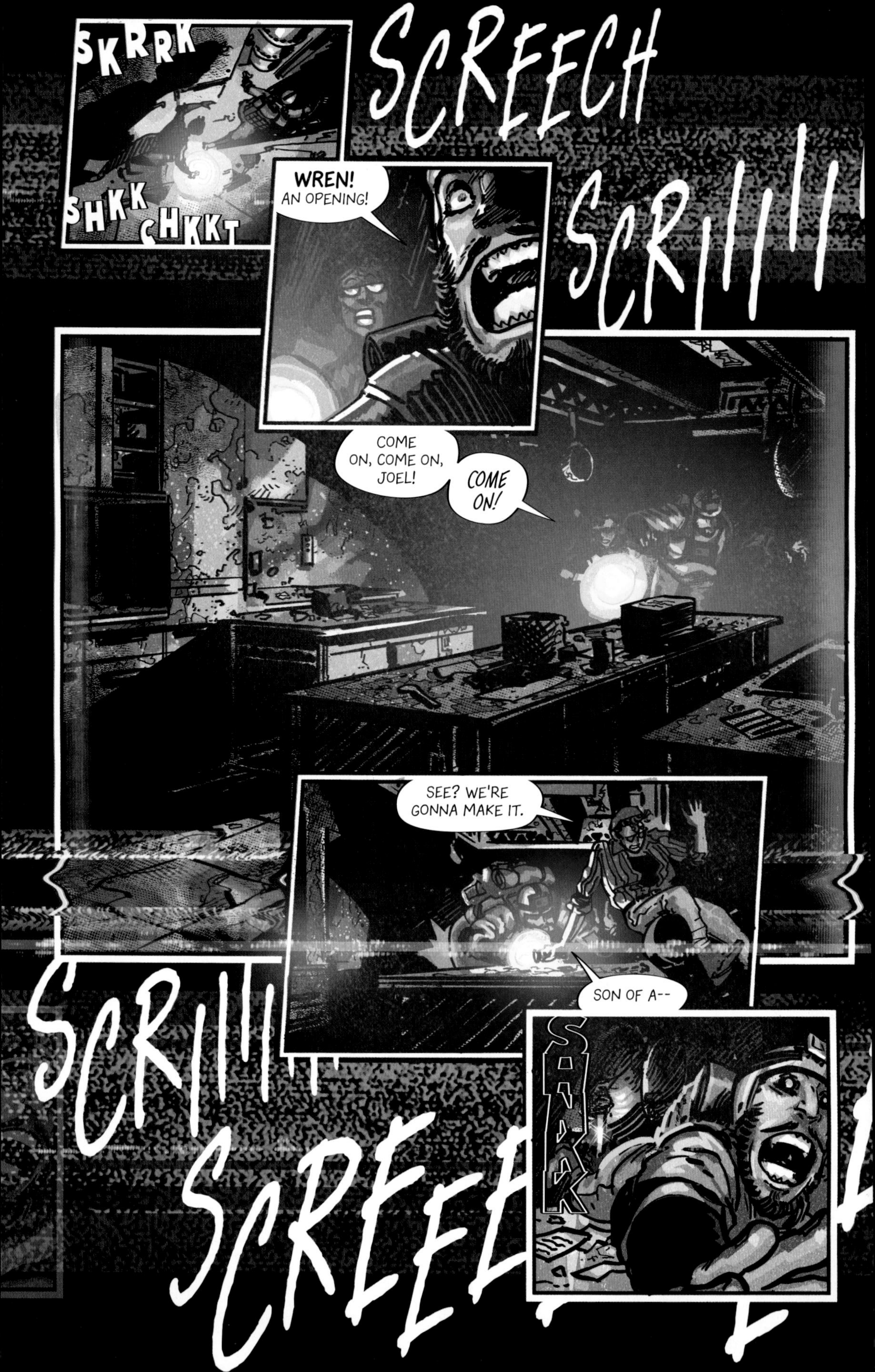
SKRRK
SHKK CHKKT
SCREECH
WREN! AN OPENING!
SCRIII
COME ON, COME ON, JOEL!
COME ON!
SEE? WE'RE GONNA MAKE IT.
SON OF A--
SCRIII
SCREEE
SHNAK

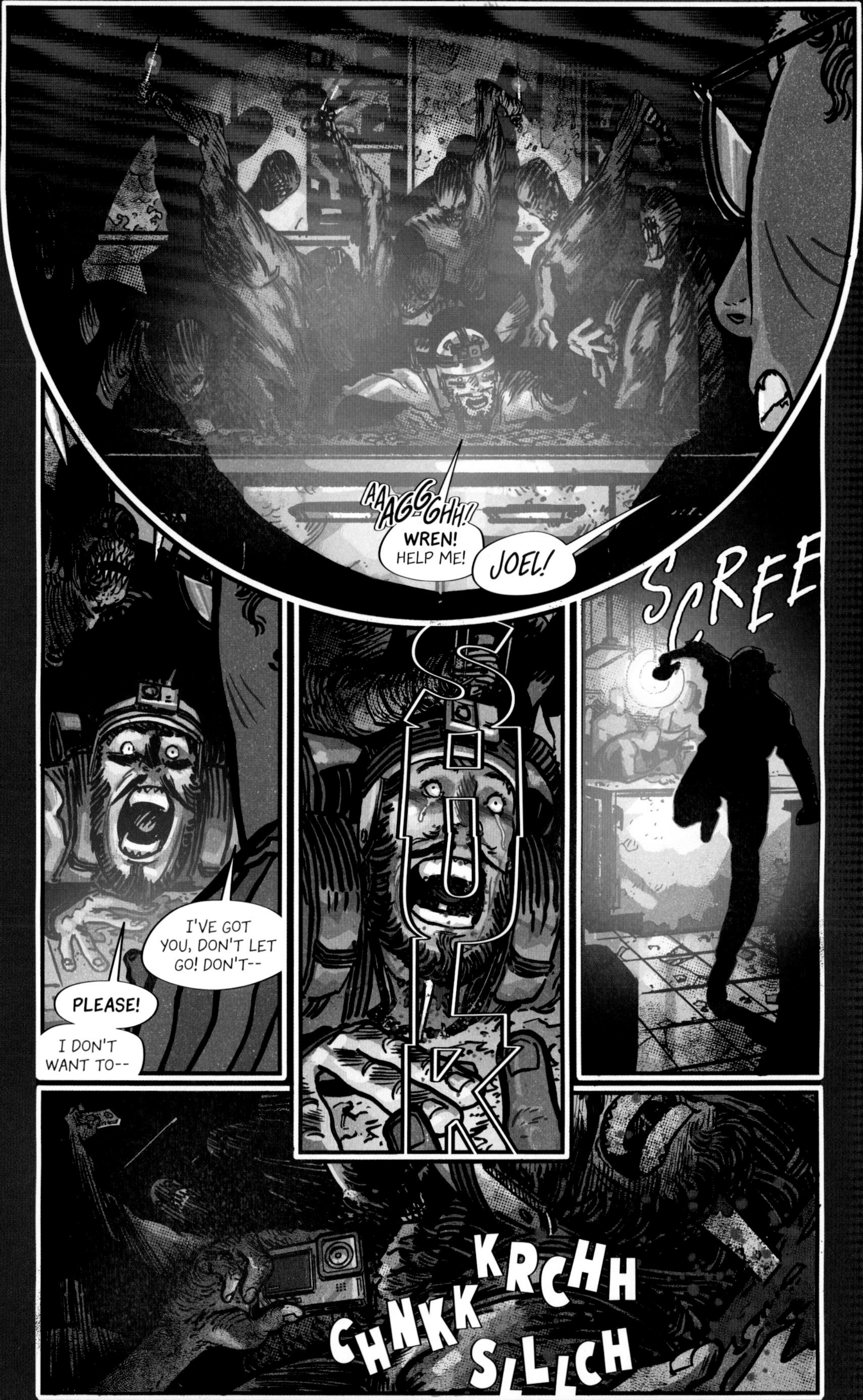
AAAGGGHH!
WREN! HELP ME!
JOEL!
SCREE
I'VE GOT YOU, DON'T LET GO! DON'T--
PLEASE!
I DON'T WANT TO--
SHUK
KRCHH
CHNKK
SLLLCH

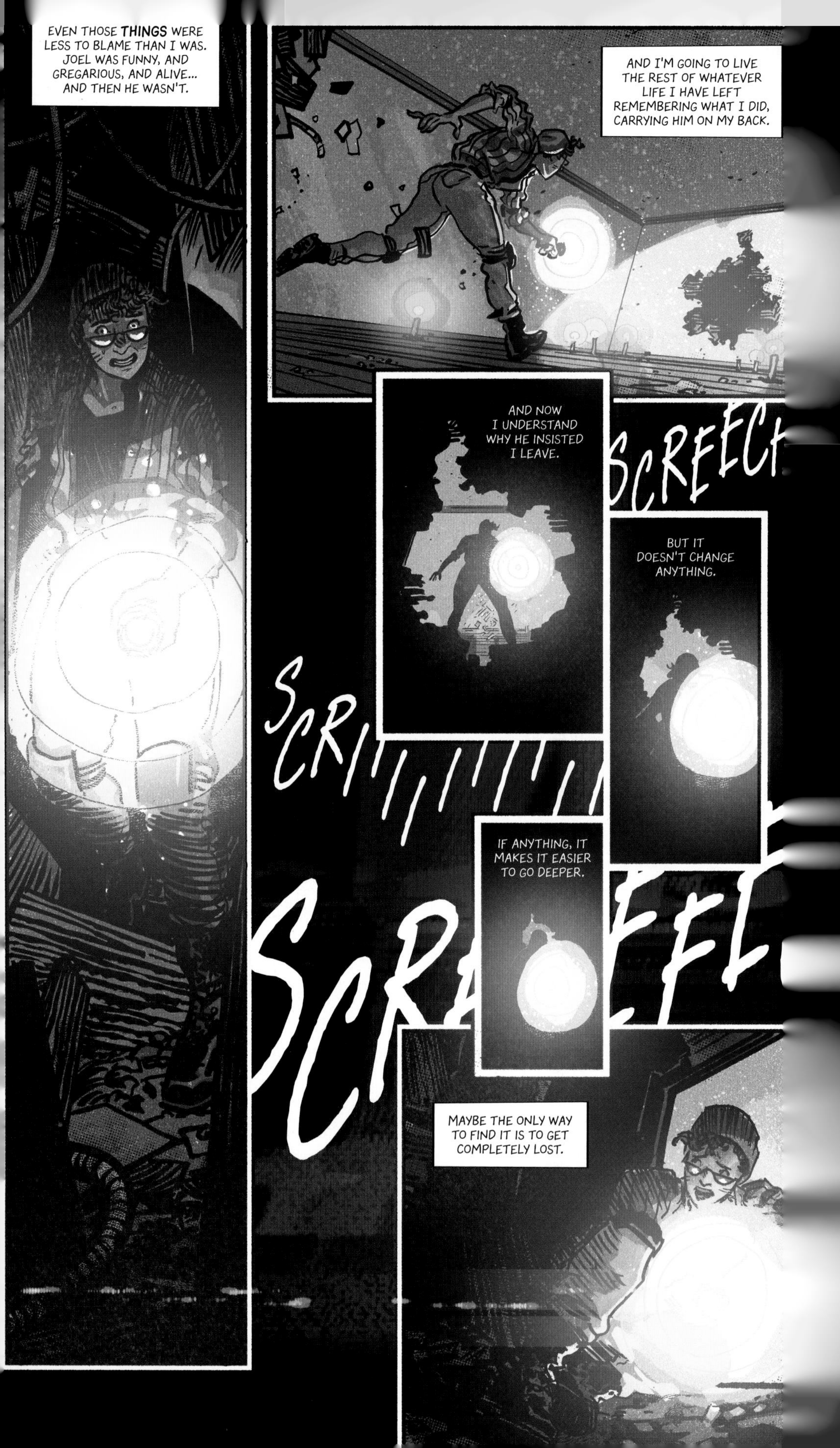
EVEN THOSE THINGS WERE LESS TO BLAME THAN I WAS. JOEL WAS FUNNY, AND GREGARIOUS, AND ALIVE... AND THEN HE WASN'T.
AND I'M GOING TO LIVE THE REST OF WHATEVER LIFE I HAVE LEFT REMEMBERING WHAT I DID, CARRYING HIM ON MY BACK.
AND NOW I UNDERSTAND WHY HE INSISTED I LEAVE.
SCREECH
BUT IT DOESN'T CHANGE ANYTHING.
SCRI
IF ANYTHING, IT MAKES IT EASIER TO GO DEEPER.
MAYBE THE ONLY WAY TO FIND IT IS TO GET COMPLETELY LOST.

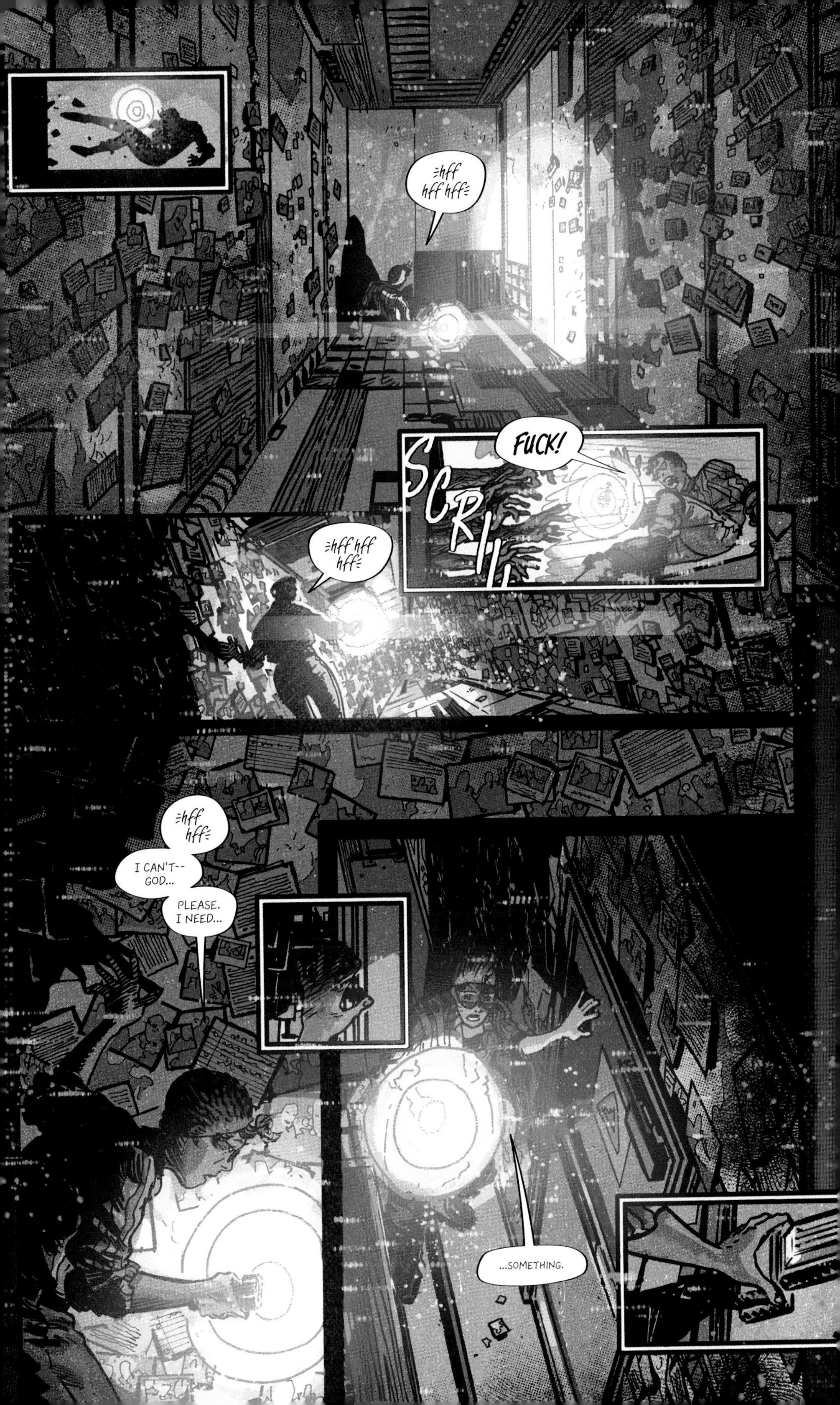

hff hff hff
SCRI
FUCK!
hff hff hff
hff hff
I CAN'T--
GOD...
PLEASE.
I NEED...
...SOMETHING.

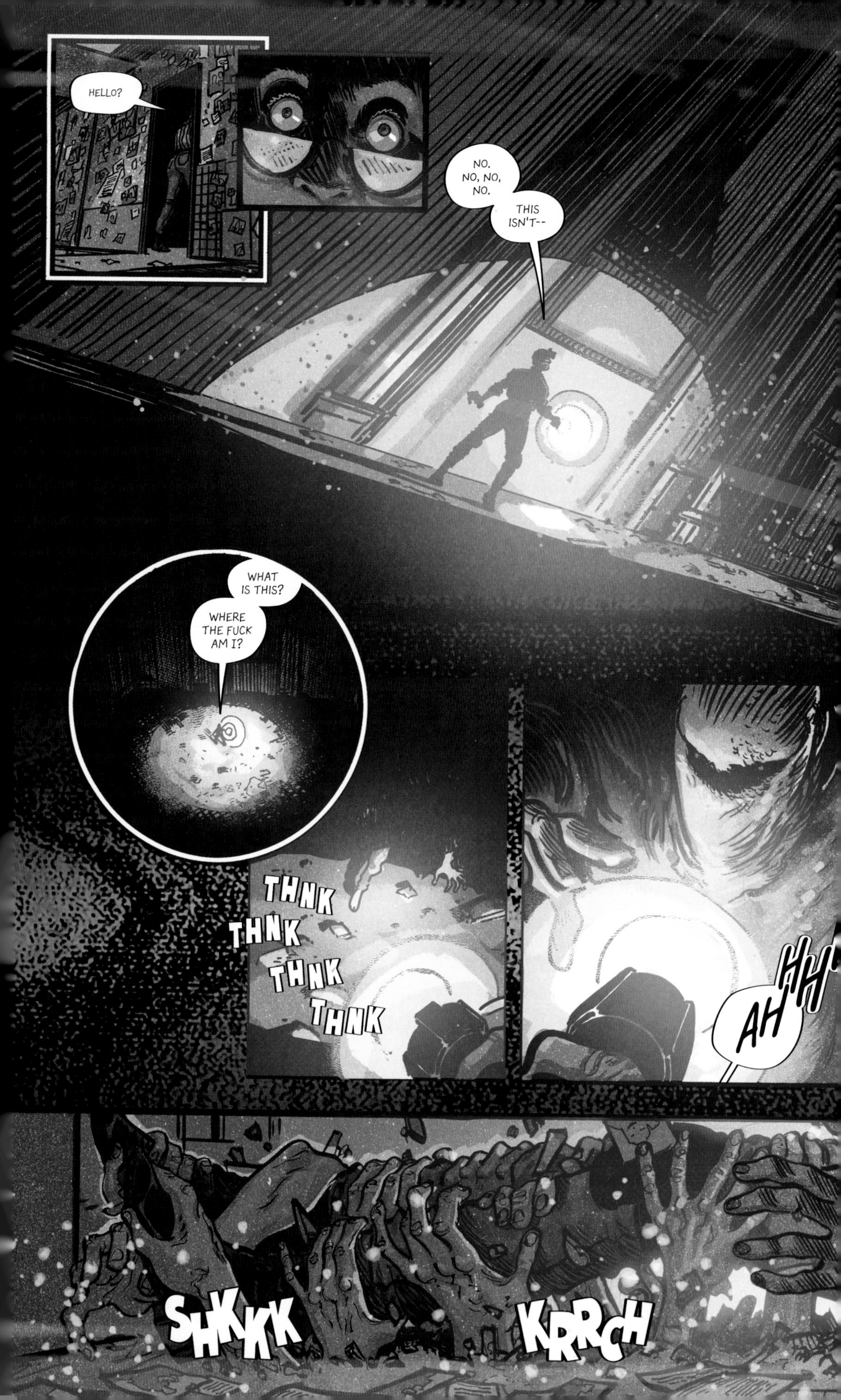
HELLO?
NO. NO, NO, NO.
THIS ISN'T--
WHAT IS THIS?
WHERE THE FUCK AM I?
THNK
THNK
THNK
THNK
AHHHH
SHKKK
KRRCH

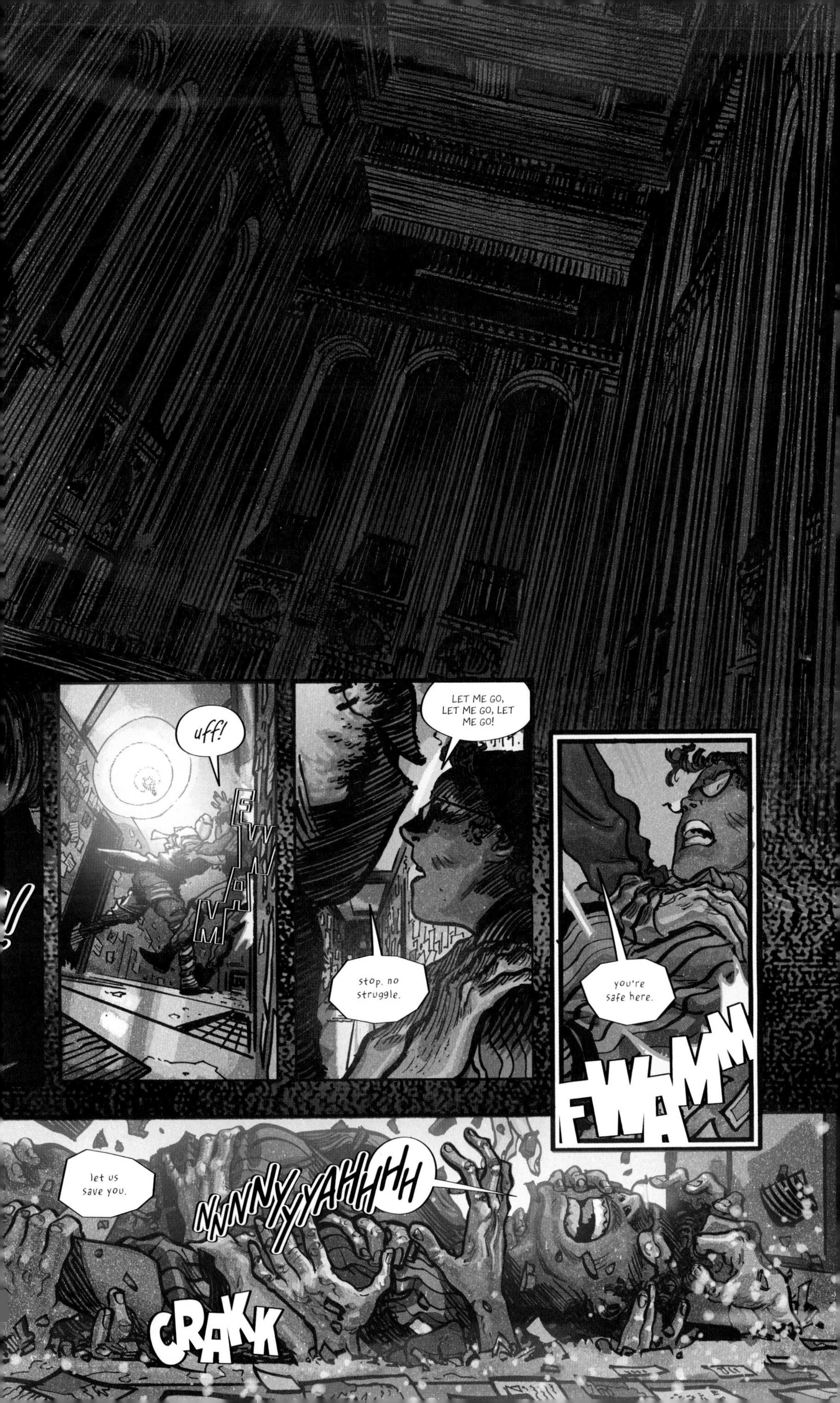
uff!
FWNAM
LET ME GO, LET ME GO, LET ME GO!
stop. no struggle.
you're safe here.
FWAMM
let us save you.
NNNNYYAHHHH
CRAKK

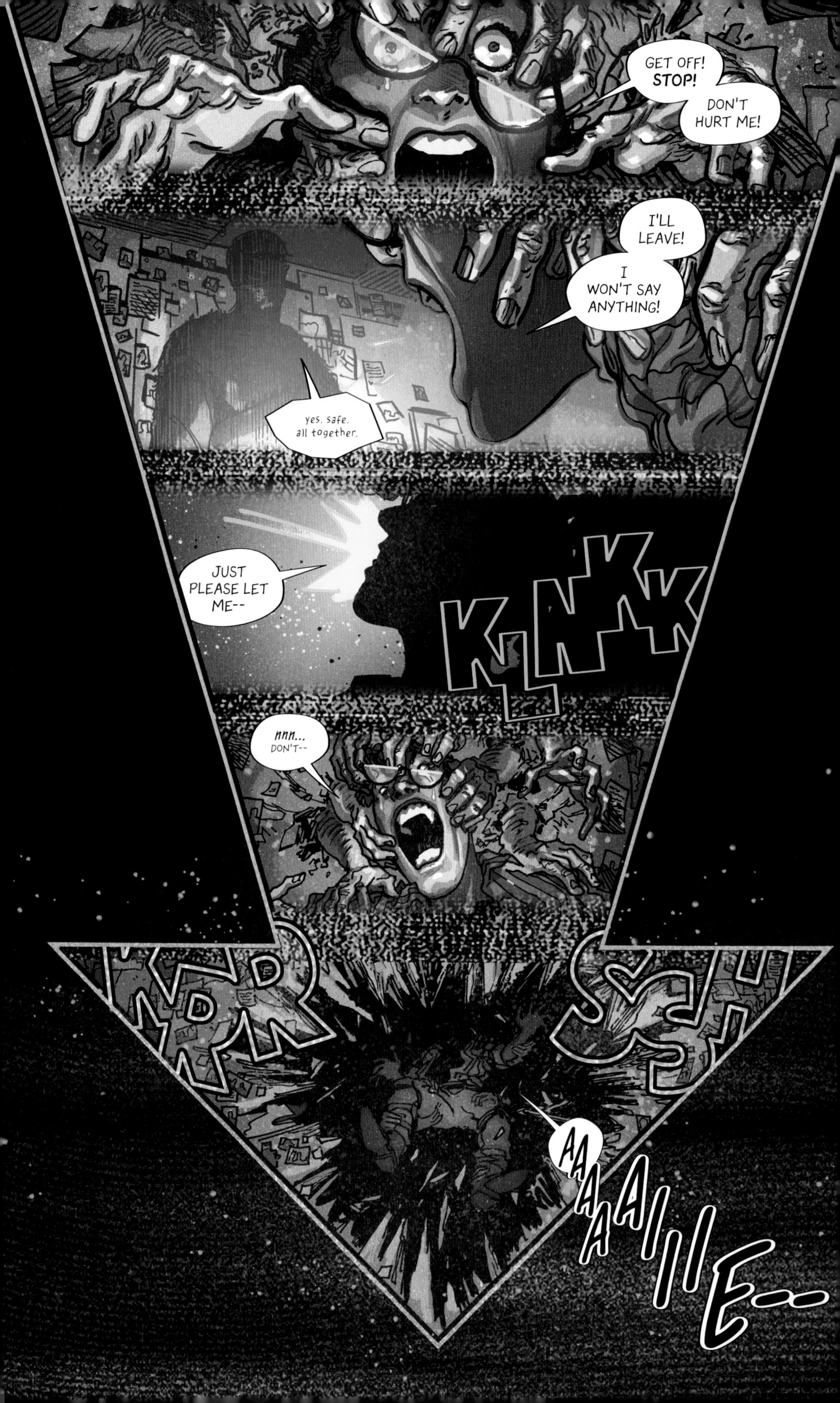
GET OFF!
STOP!
DON'T HURT ME!
I'LL LEAVE!
I WON'T SAY ANYTHING!
yes. safe. all together.
JUST PLEASE LET ME--
KLNKK
nnn... DON'T--
KRR
SSH
AAAAIIIE--

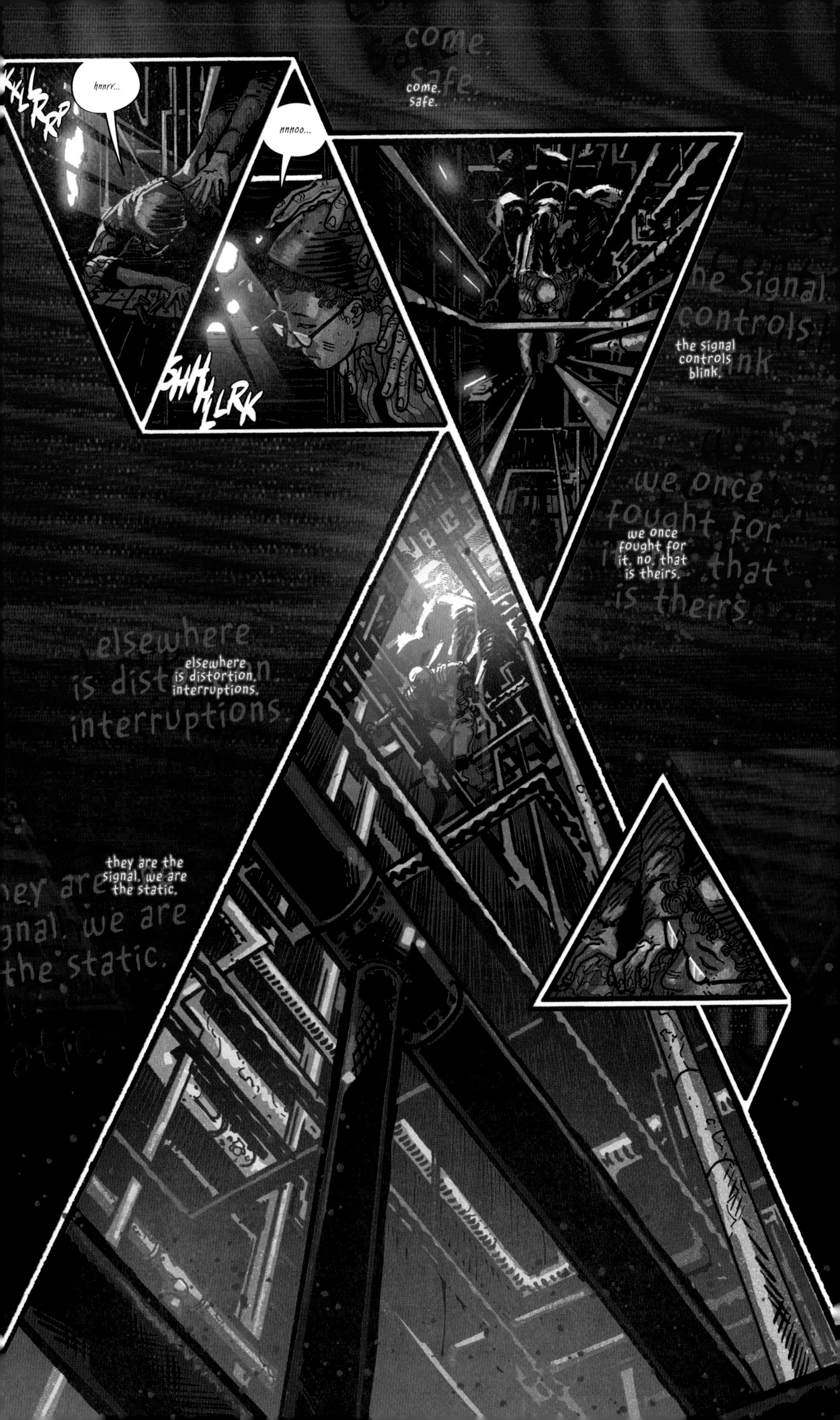

KXLLRRP
hnnrr...
nnnoo...
SHHHLLRK
come.
safe.
the signal
controls
blink.
we once
fought for
it. no. that
is theirs.
elsewhere
is distortion.
interruptions.
they are the
signal. we are
the static.

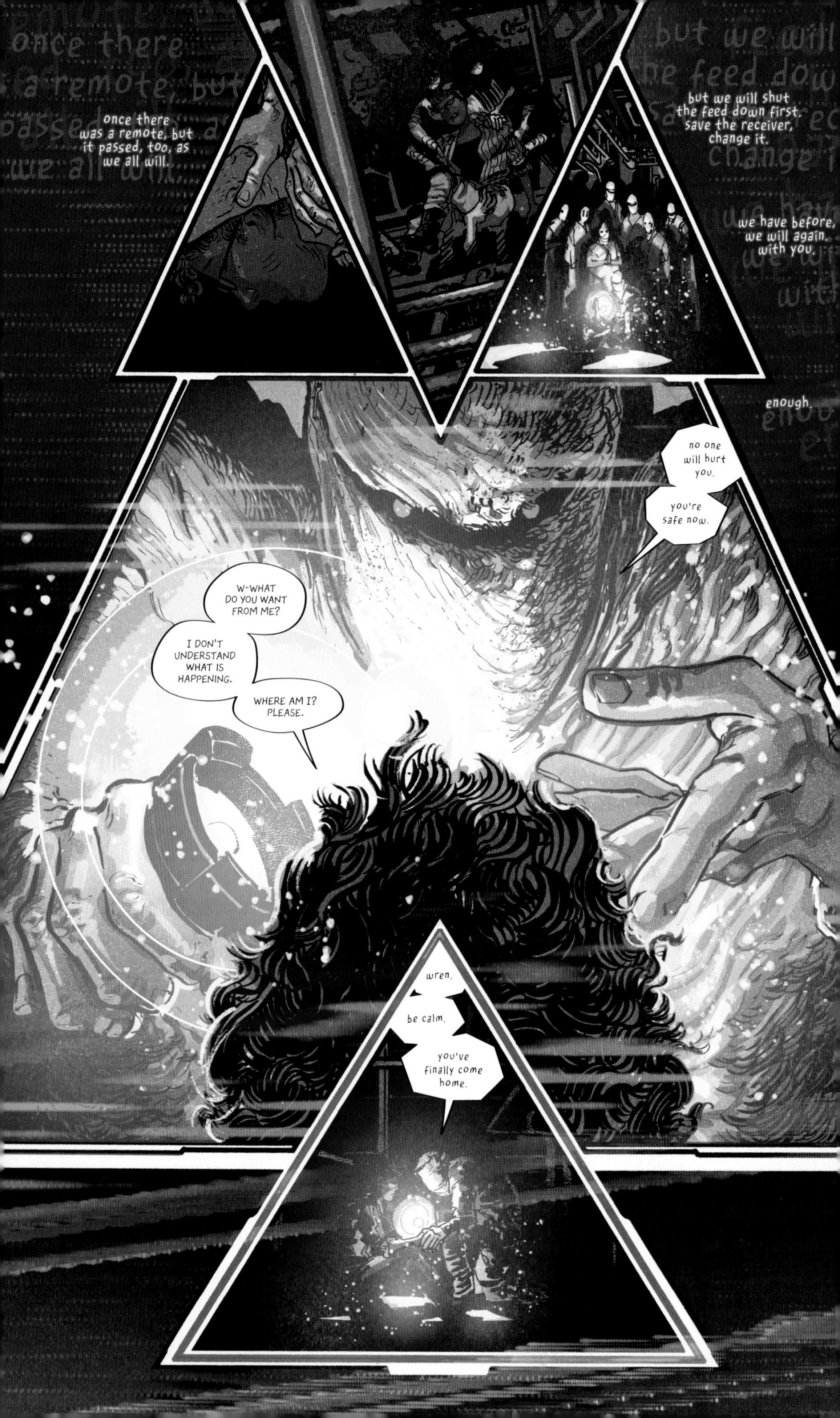

once there was a remote, but it passed, too, as we all will.
but we will shut the feed down first. save the receiver, change it.
we have before, we will again. with you.
enough.
W-WHAT DO YOU WANT FROM ME?
I DON'T UNDERSTAND WHAT IS HAPPENING.
WHERE AM I? PLEASE.
no one will hurt you.
you're safe now.
wren.
be calm.
you've finally come home.

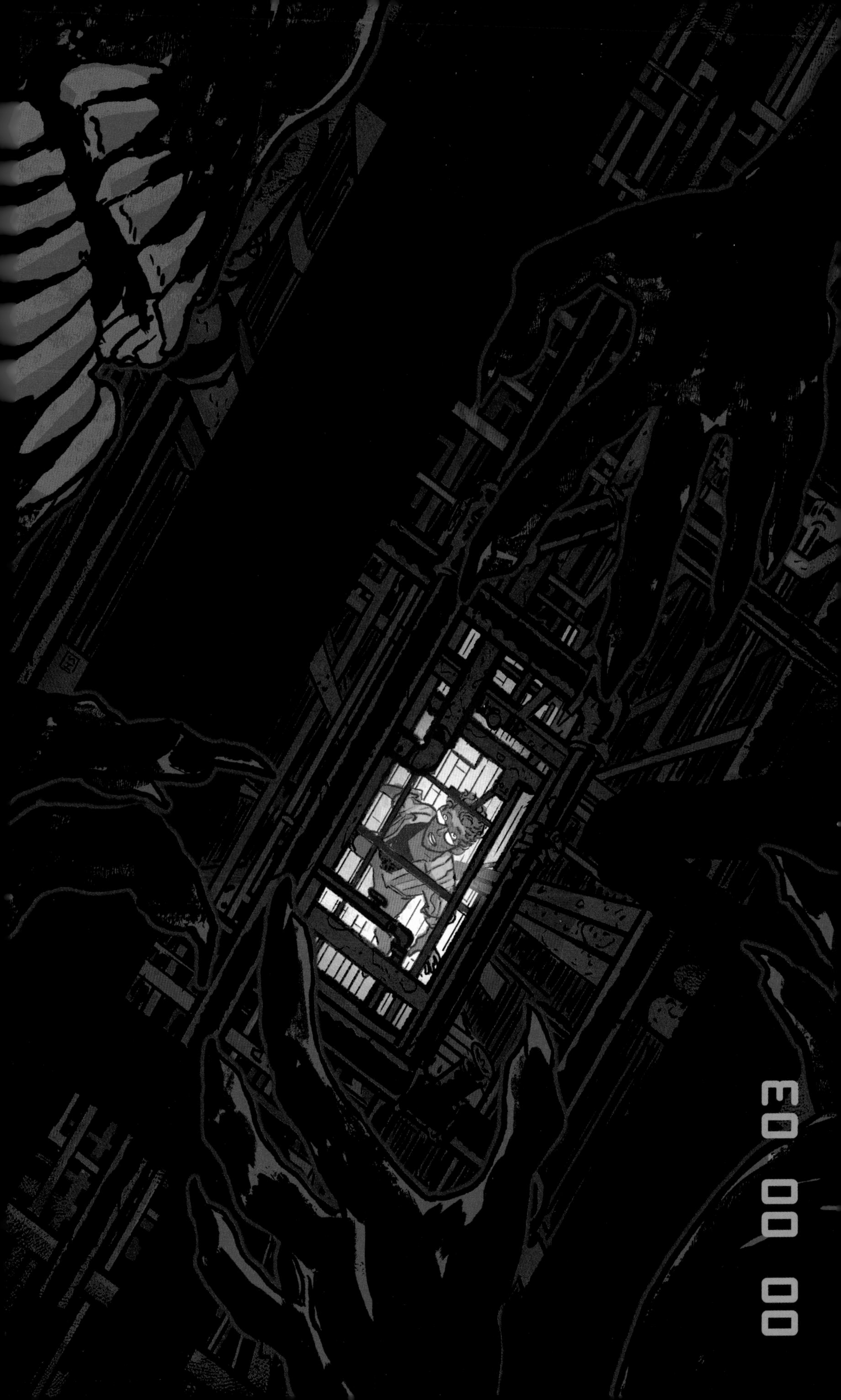
00 00 03

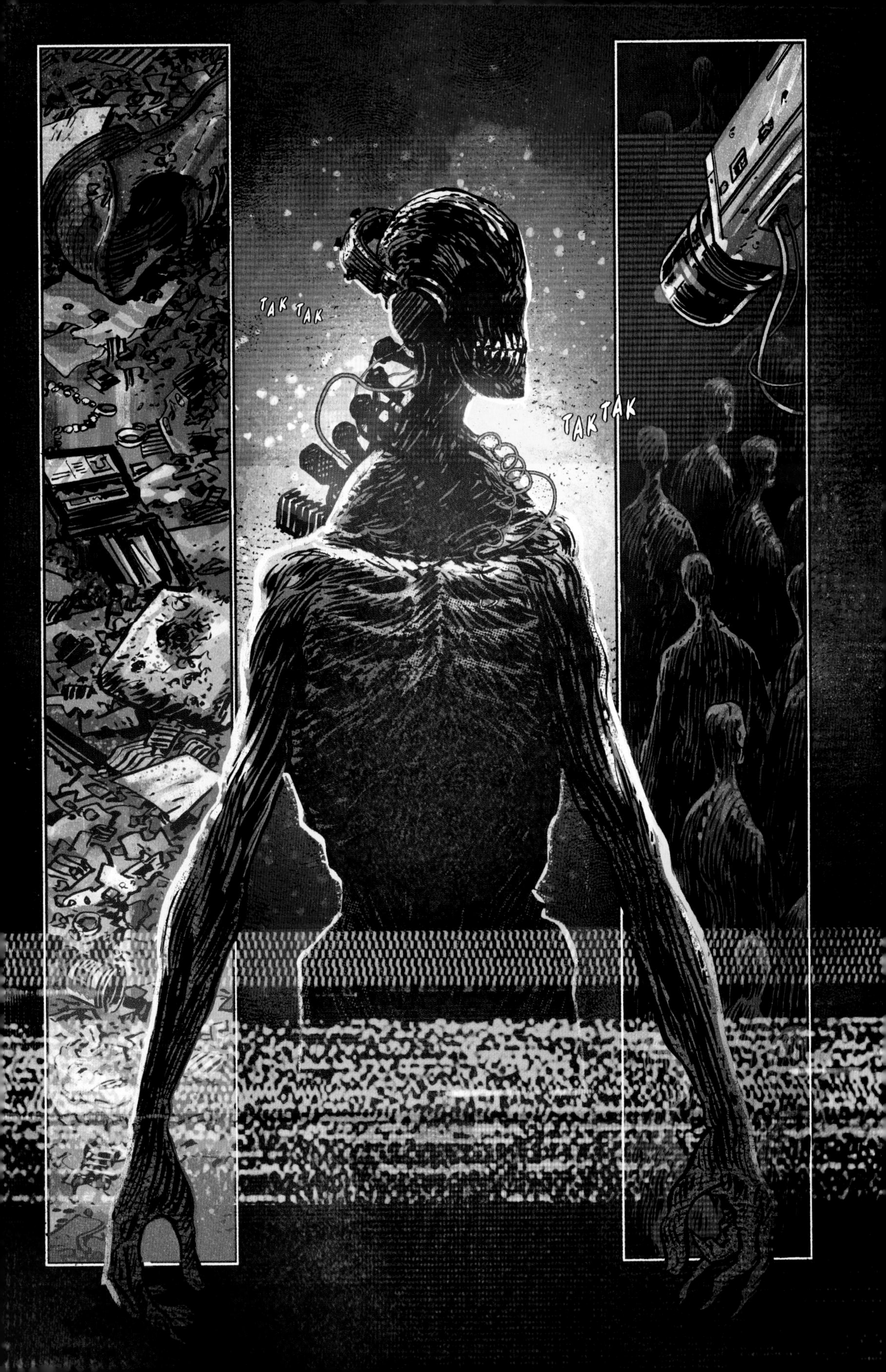
TAK TAK
TAK TAK

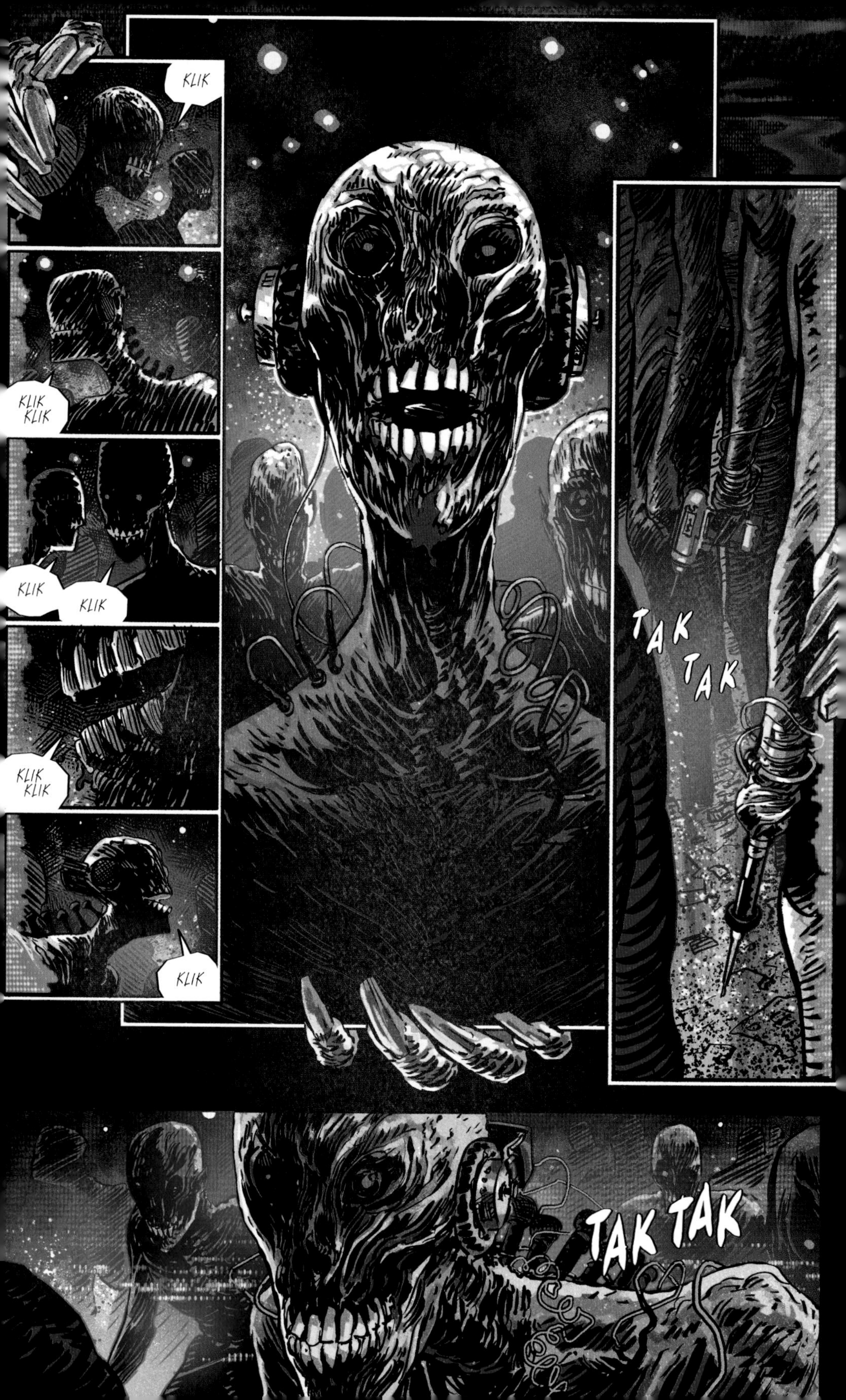
KLIK
KLIK KLIK
KLIK
KLIK
KLIK KLIK
KLIK
TAK TAK
TAK TAK

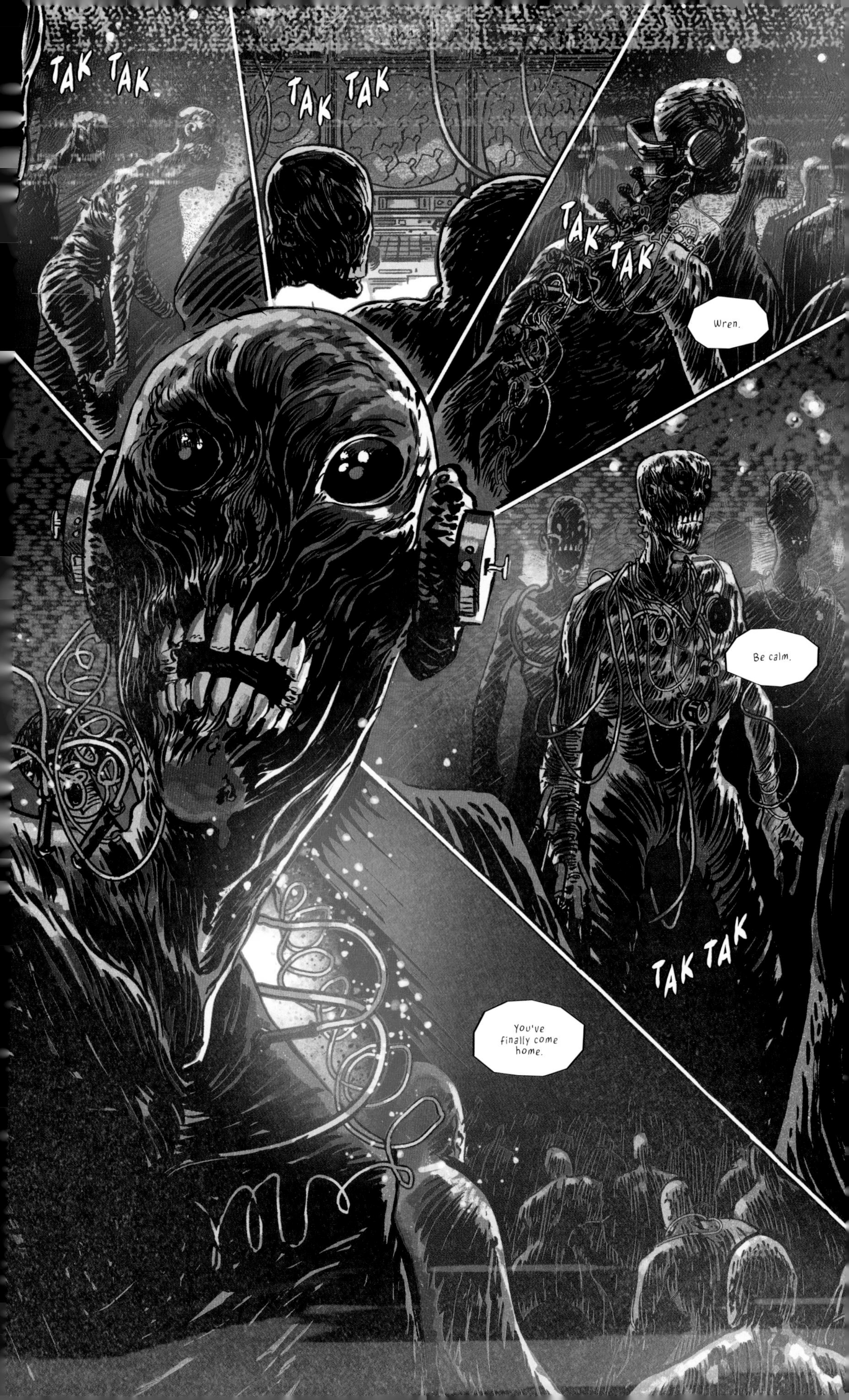
TAK TAK
TAK TAK
TAK TAK
Wren.
Be calm.
TAK TAK
You've finally come home.

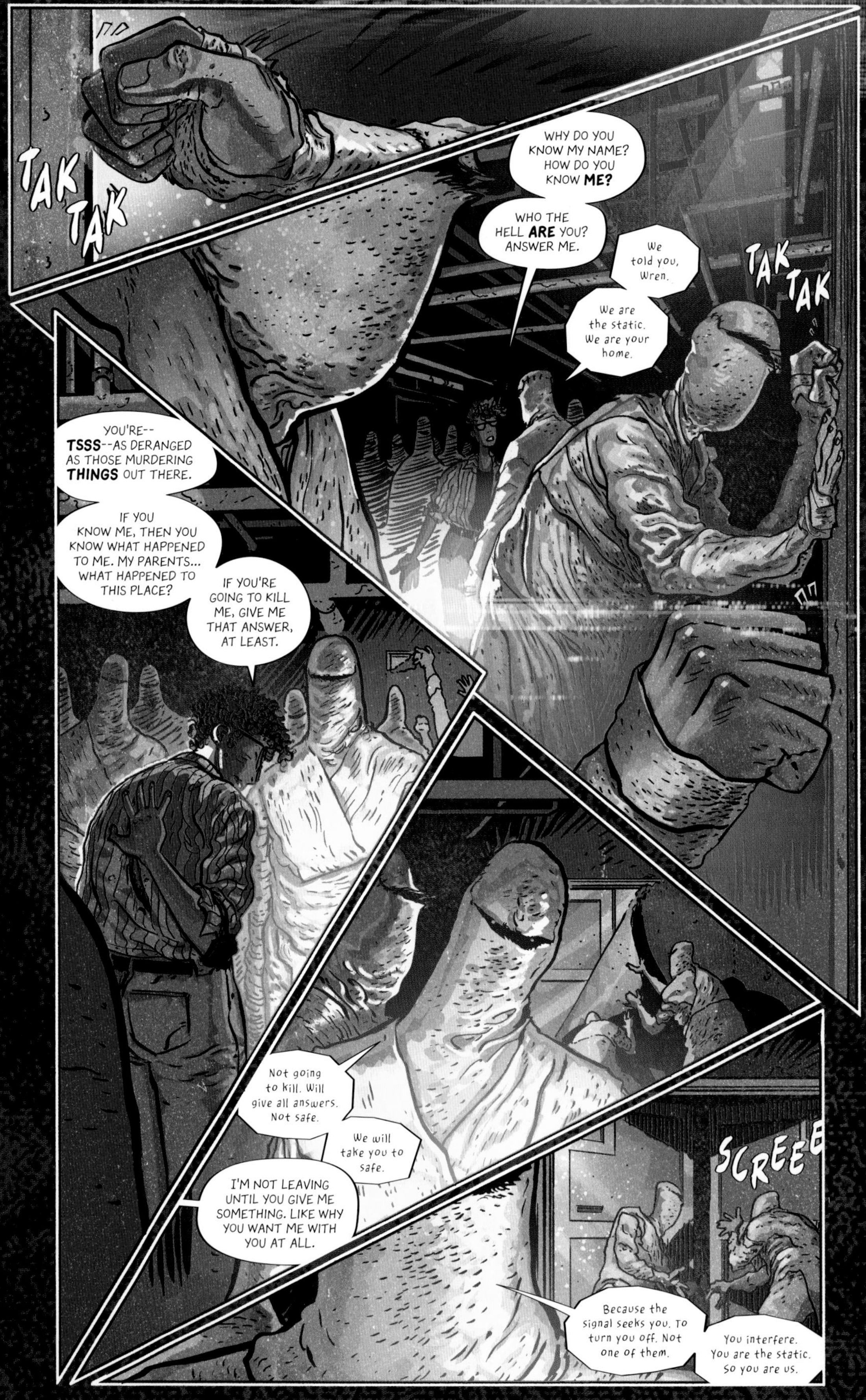
TAK TAK
WHY DO YOU KNOW MY NAME? HOW DO YOU KNOW ME?
WHO THE HELL ARE YOU? ANSWER ME.
We told you, Wren.
We are the static. We are your home.
TAK TAK
YOU'RE--TSSS--AS DERANGED AS THOSE MURDERING THINGS OUT THERE.
IF YOU KNOW ME, THEN YOU KNOW WHAT HAPPENED TO ME. MY PARENTS... WHAT HAPPENED TO THIS PLACE?
IF YOU'RE GOING TO KILL ME, GIVE ME THAT ANSWER, AT LEAST.
Not going to kill. Will give all answers. Not safe.
We will take you to safe.
I'M NOT LEAVING UNTIL YOU GIVE ME SOMETHING. LIKE WHY YOU WANT ME WITH YOU AT ALL.
SCREEE
Because the signal seeks you. To turn you off. Not one of them.
You interfere. You are the static. So you are us.

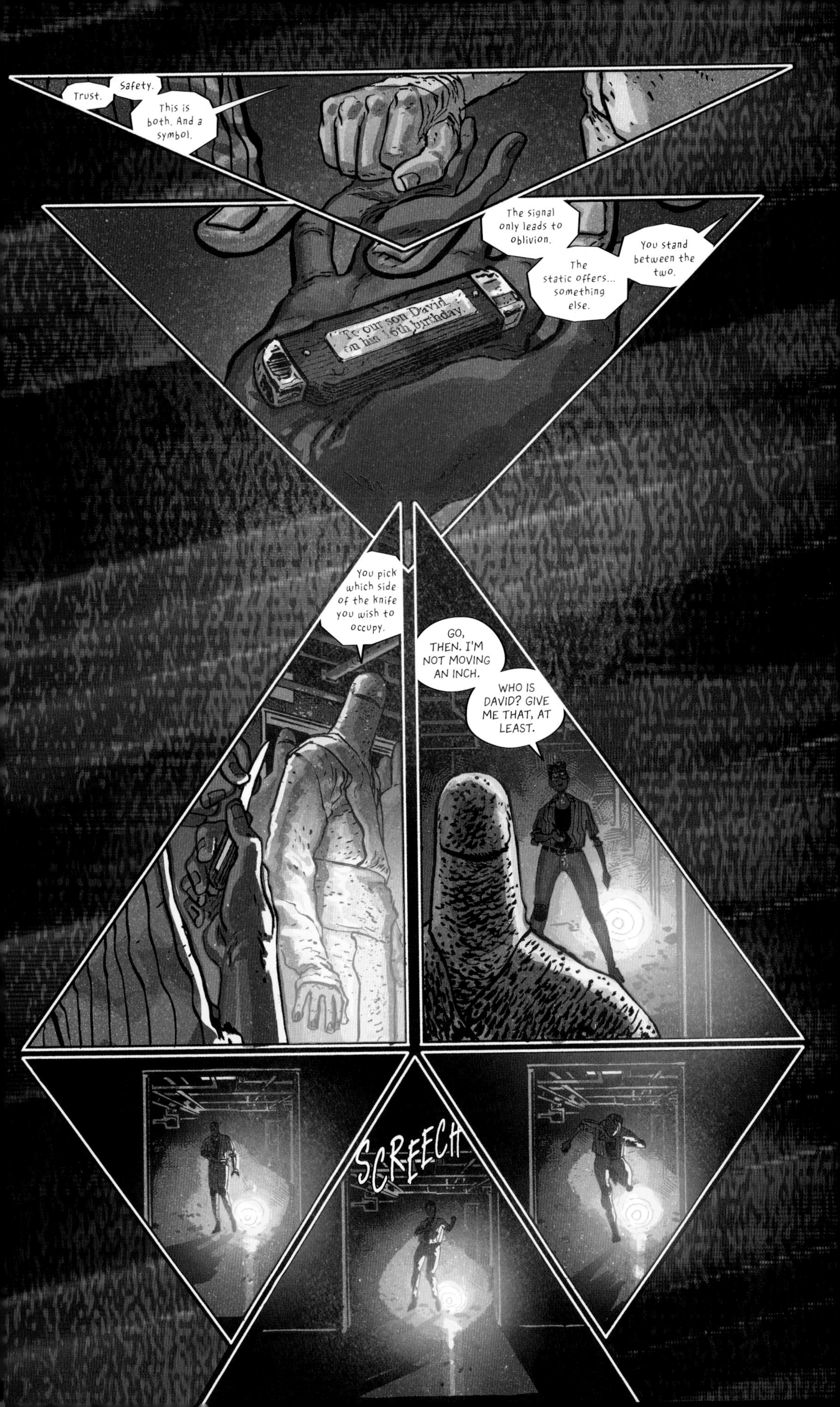
Trust.
Safety.
This is both. And a symbol.
The signal only leads to oblivion.
The static offers... something else.
You stand between the two.
To our son David, on his 16th birthday.
You pick which side of the knife you wish to occupy.
GO, THEN. I'M NOT MOVING AN INCH.
WHO IS DAVID? GIVE ME THAT, AT LEAST.
SCREECH

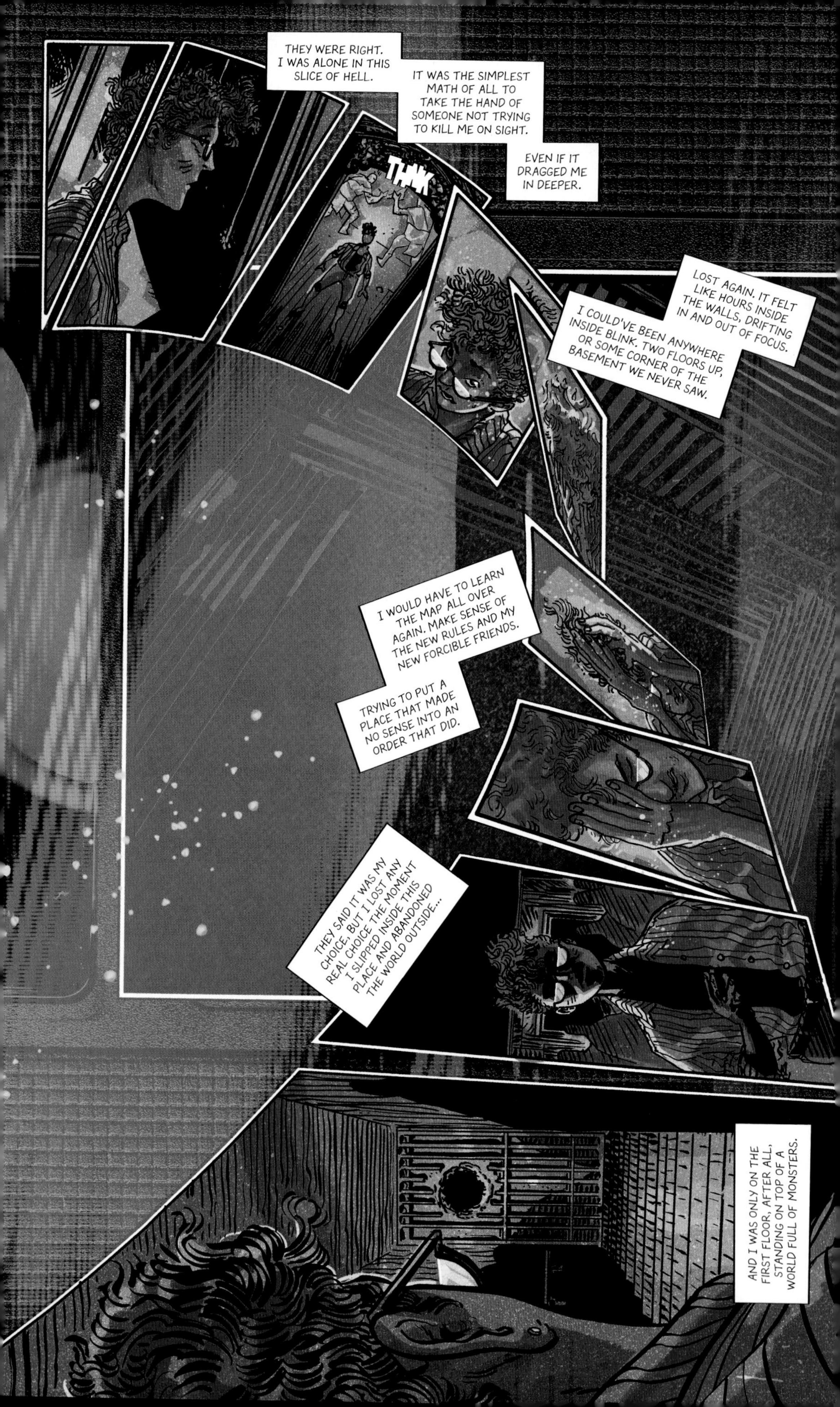
THEY WERE RIGHT. I WAS ALONE IN THIS SLICE OF HELL.
IT WAS THE SIMPLEST MATH OF ALL TO TAKE THE HAND OF SOMEONE NOT TRYING TO KILL ME ON SIGHT.
EVEN IF IT DRAGGED ME IN DEEPER.
THNK
LOST AGAIN. IT FELT LIKE HOURS INSIDE THE WALLS, DRIFTING IN AND OUT OF FOCUS.
I COULD'VE BEEN ANYWHERE INSIDE BLINK. TWO FLOORS UP, OR SOME CORNER OF THE BASEMENT WE NEVER SAW.
I WOULD HAVE TO LEARN THE MAP ALL OVER AGAIN. MAKE SENSE OF THE NEW RULES AND MY NEW FORCIBLE FRIENDS.
TRYING TO PUT A PLACE THAT MADE NO SENSE INTO AN ORDER THAT DID.
THEY SAID IT WAS MY CHOICE, BUT I LOST ANY REAL CHOICE THE MOMENT I SLIPPED INSIDE THIS PLACE AND ABANDONED THE WORLD OUTSIDE...
AND I WAS ONLY ON THE FIRST FLOOR, AFTER ALL, STANDING ON TOP OF A WORLD FULL OF MONSTERS.

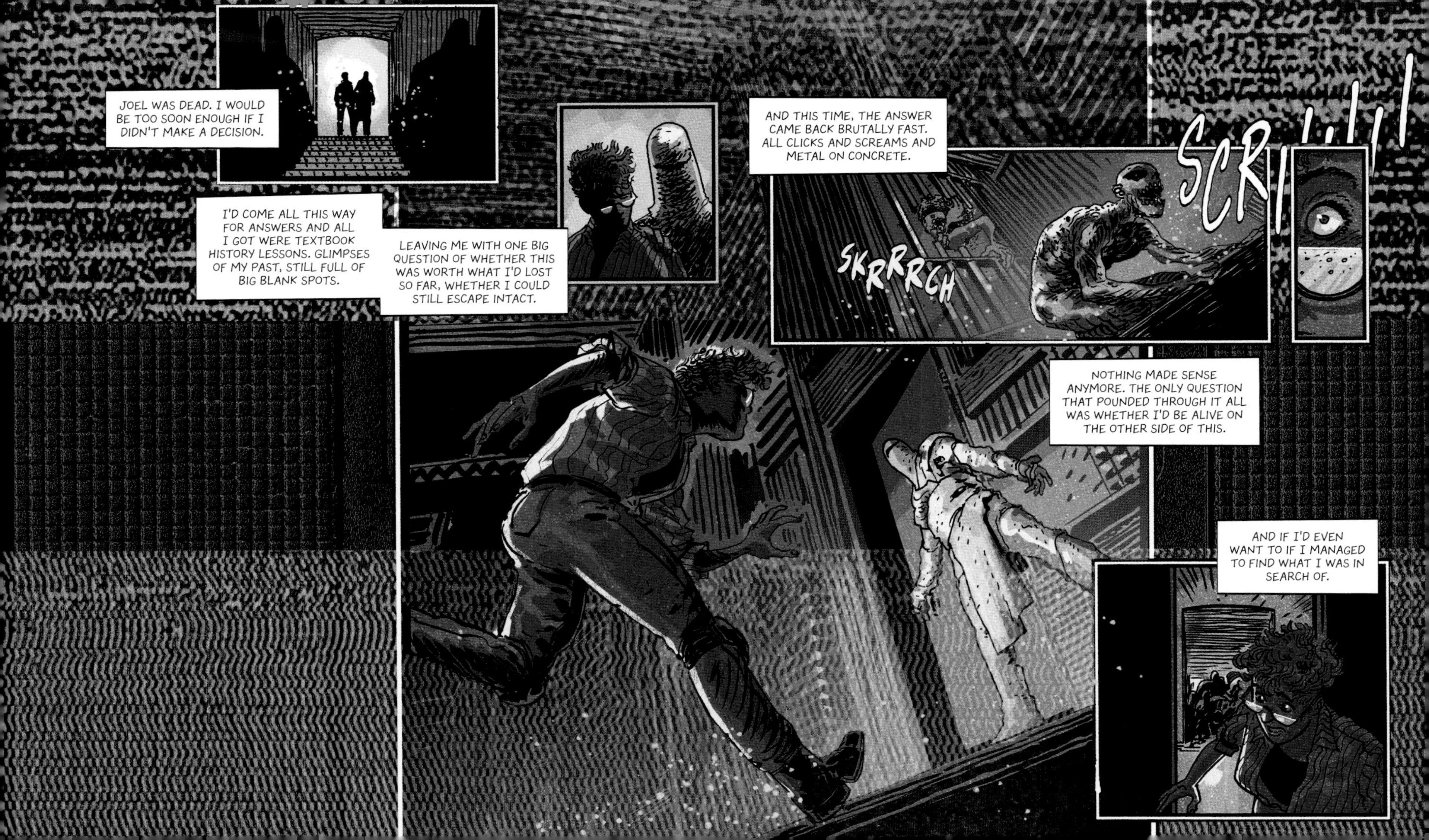
JOEL WAS DEAD. I WOULD BE TOO SOON ENOUGH IF I DIDN'T MAKE A DECISION.
I'D COME ALL THIS WAY FOR ANSWERS AND ALL I GOT WERE TEXTBOOK HISTORY LESSONS. GLIMPSES OF MY PAST, STILL FULL OF BIG BLANK SPOTS.
LEAVING ME WITH ONE BIG QUESTION OF WHETHER THIS WAS WORTH WHAT I'D LOST SO FAR, WHETHER I COULD STILL ESCAPE INTACT.
AND THIS TIME, THE ANSWER CAME BACK BRUTALLY FAST. ALL CLICKS AND SCREAMS AND METAL ON CONCRETE.
SKRRRCH
SCRI!!!!!
NOTHING MADE SENSE ANYMORE. THE ONLY QUESTION THAT POUNDED THROUGH IT ALL WAS WHETHER I'D BE ALIVE ON THE OTHER SIDE OF THIS.
AND IF I'D EVEN WANT TO IF I MANAGED TO FIND WHAT I WAS IN SEARCH OF.

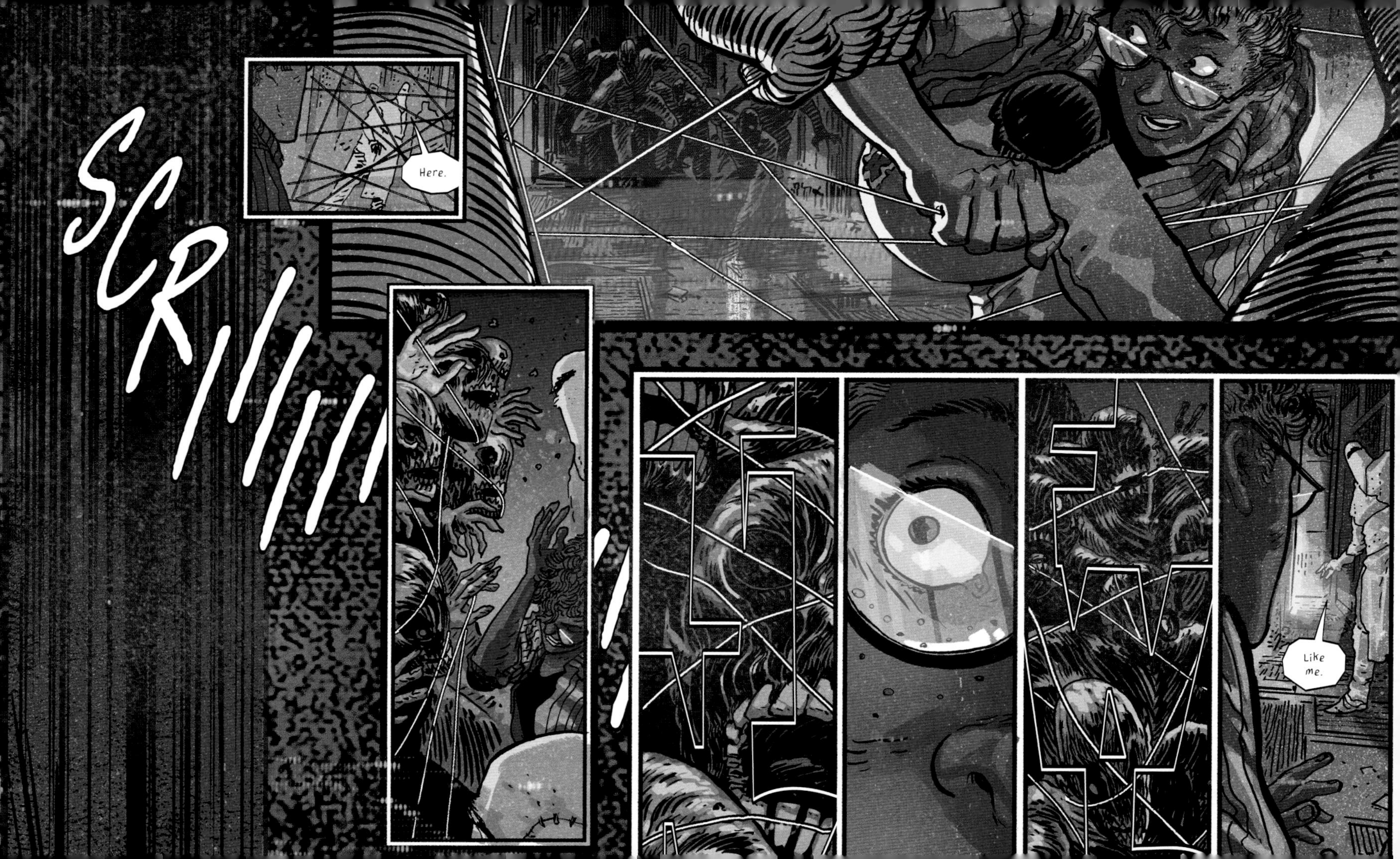
Here.
SCRIIIIIII
Like me.

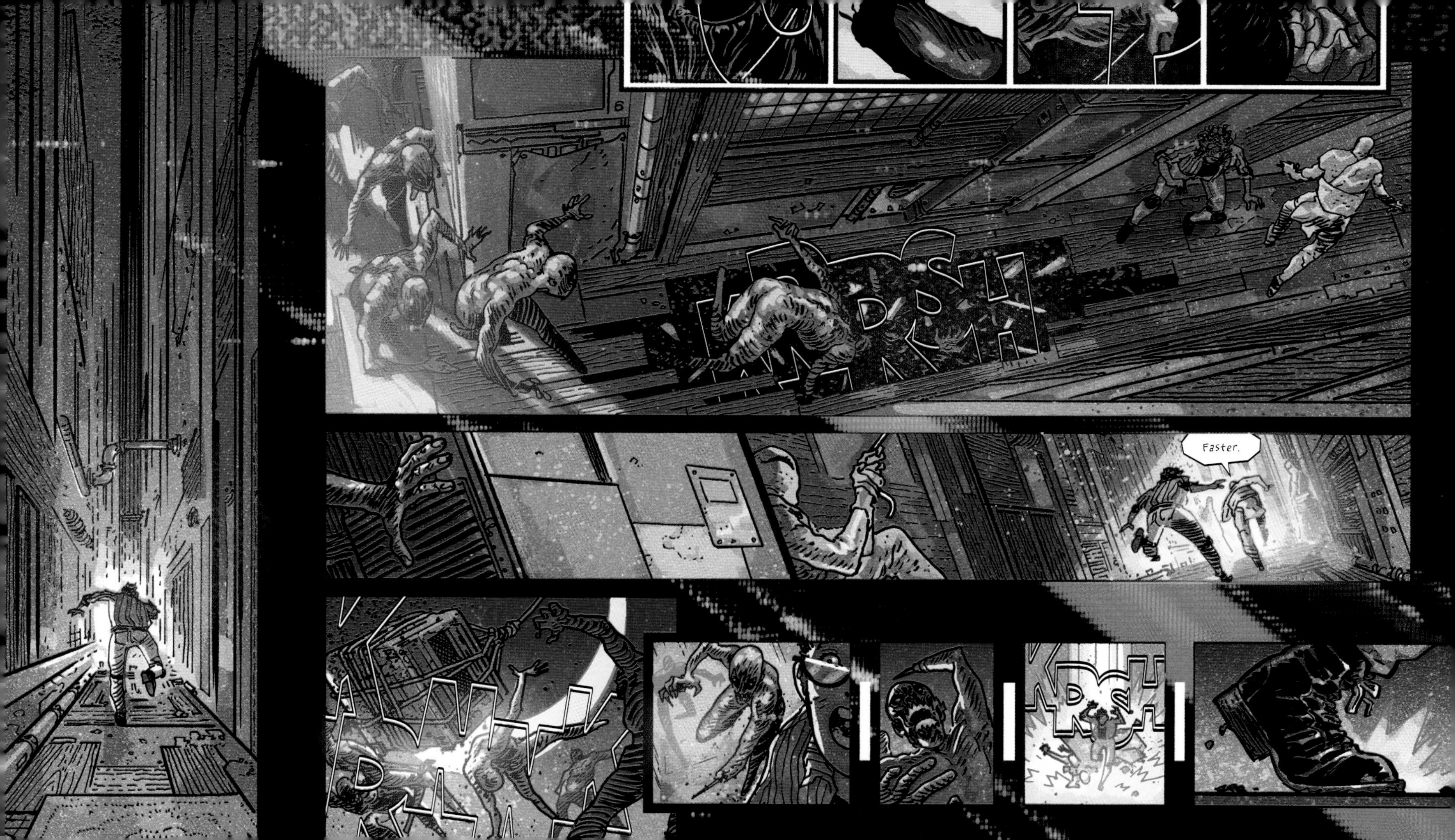
Faster.

Up.
uffff!
TSSSSS
NO, NO, NO, NO, NO...

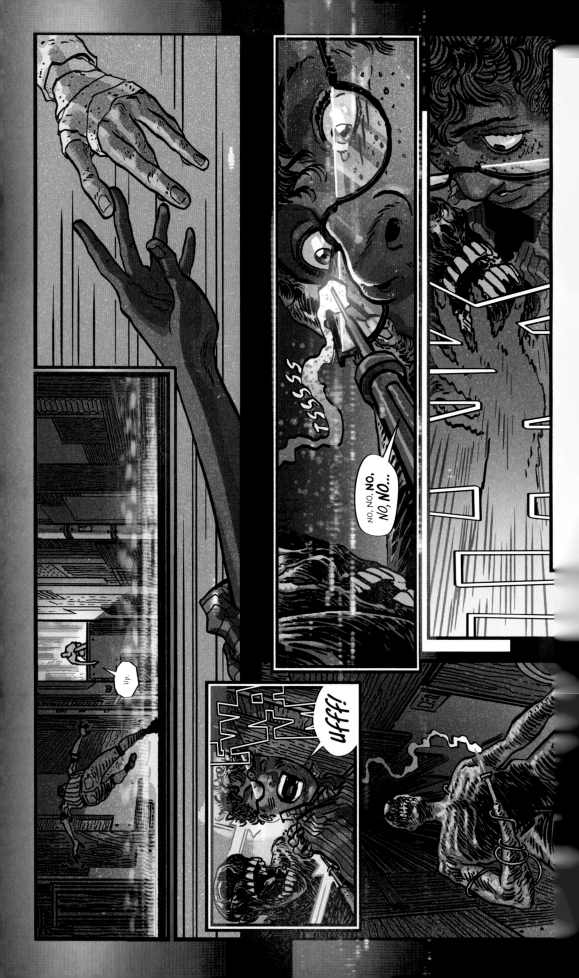

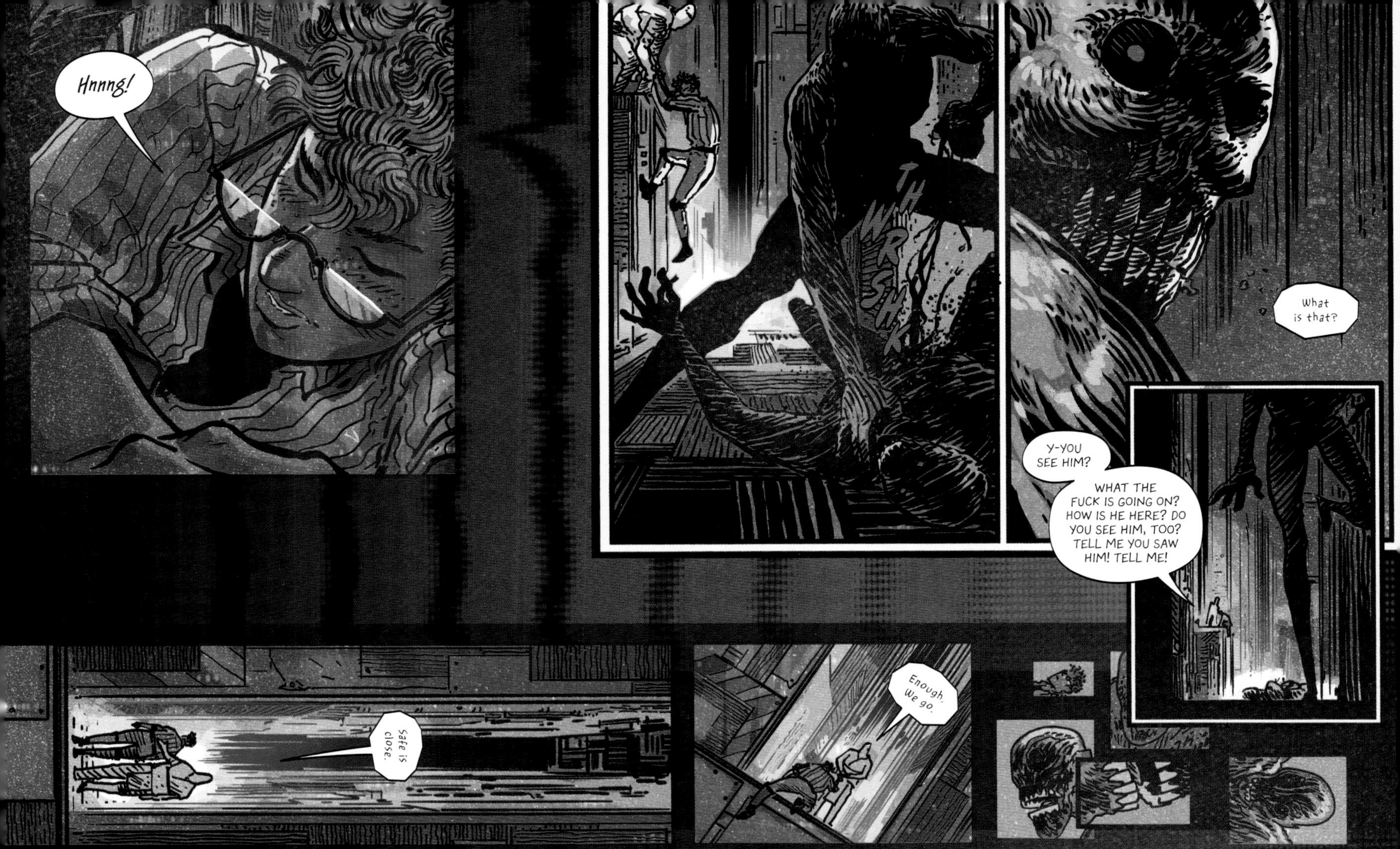
Hnnng!
THWRSHK
What is that?
Y-YOU SEE HIM?
WHAT THE FUCK IS GOING ON? HOW IS HE HERE? DO YOU SEE HIM, TOO? TELL ME YOU SAW HIM! TELL ME!
Safe is close.
Enough. We go.

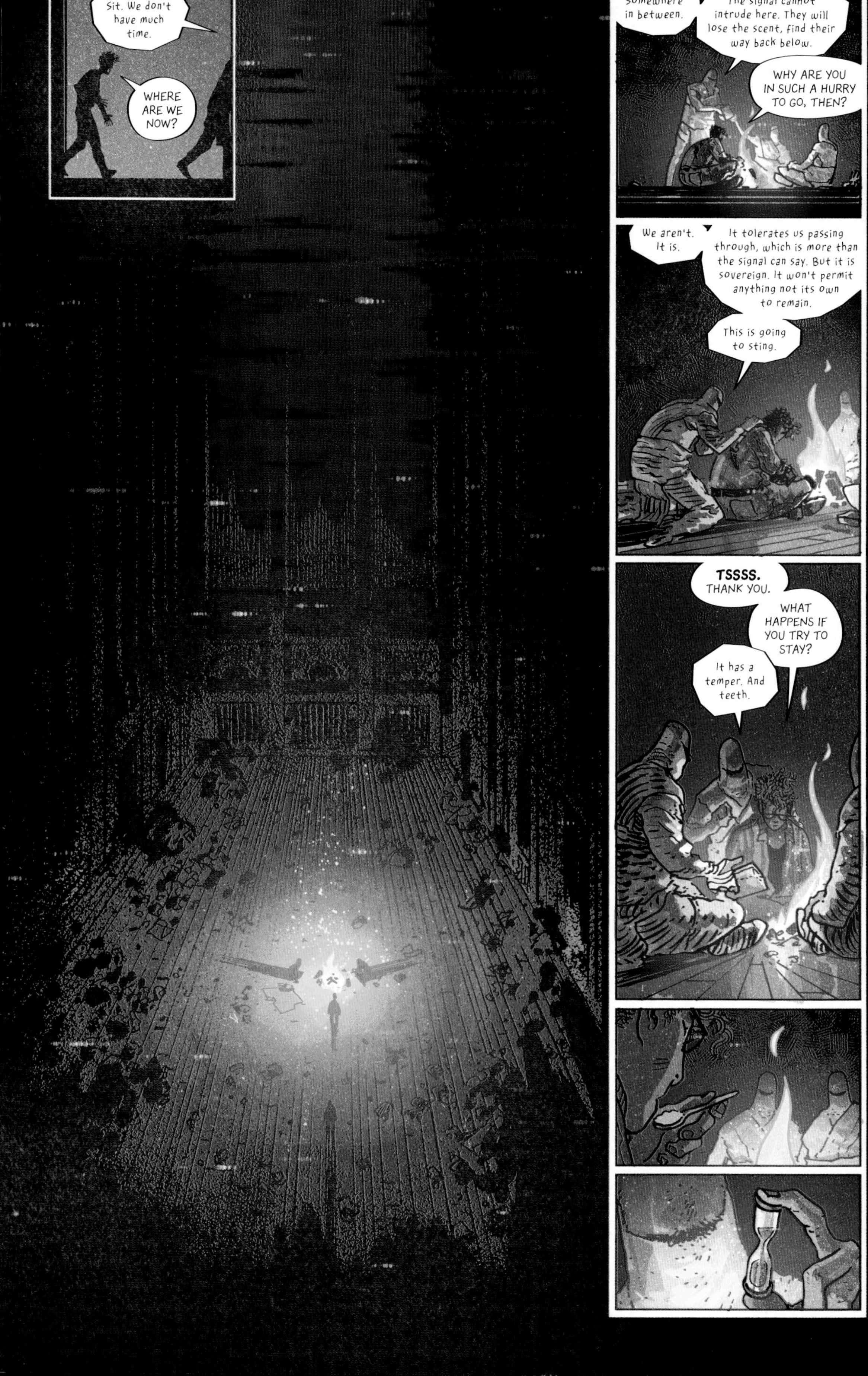
Sit. We don't have much time.
WHERE ARE WE NOW?
in between.
intrude here. They will lose the scent, find their way back below.
WHY ARE YOU IN SUCH A HURRY TO GO, THEN?
We aren't. It is.
It tolerates us passing through, which is more than the signal can say. But it is sovereign. It won't permit anything not its own to remain.
This is going to sting.
TSSSS.
THANK YOU.
WHAT HAPPENS IF YOU TRY TO STAY?
It has a temper. And teeth.

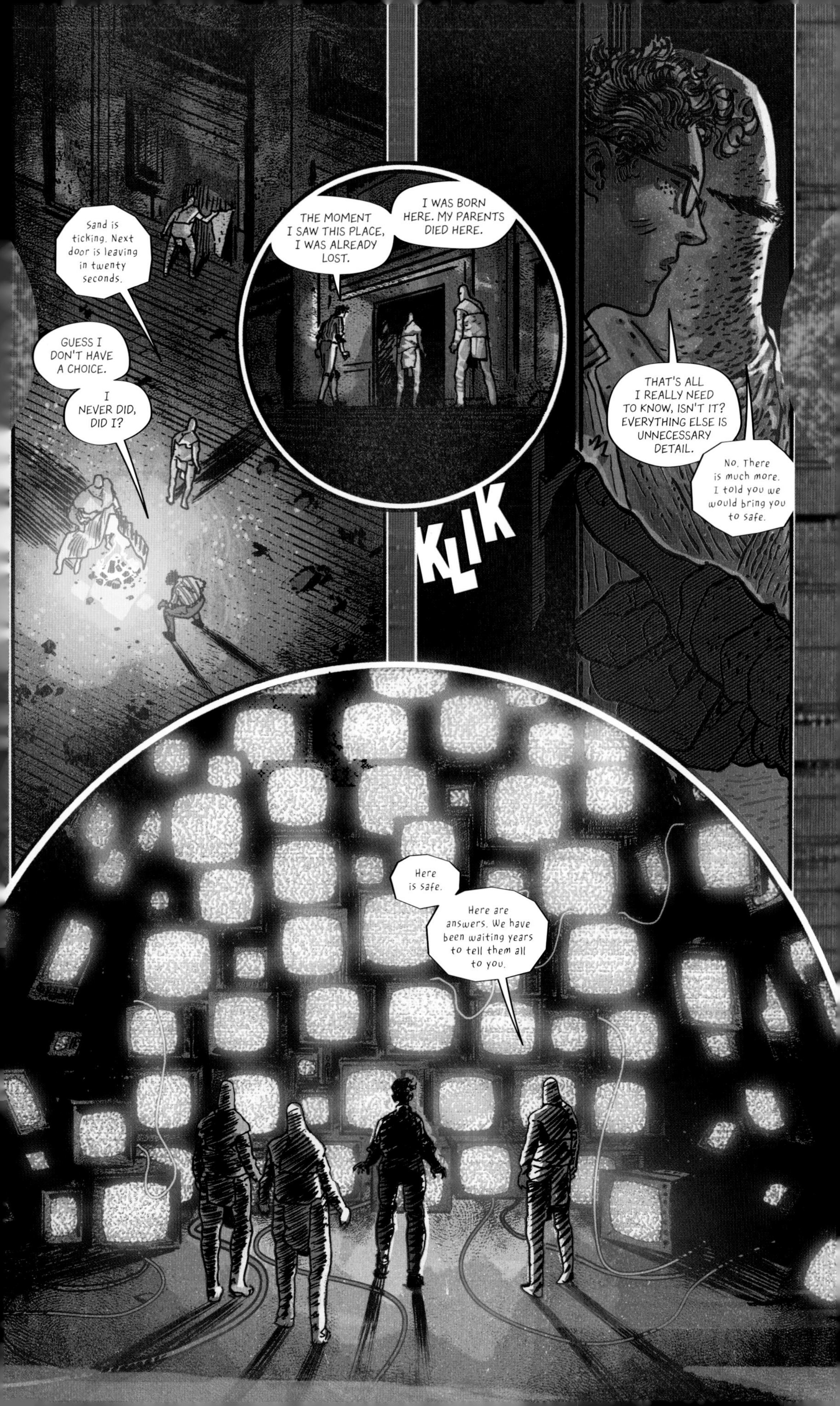
Sand is ticking. Next door is leaving in twenty seconds.
GUESS I DON'T HAVE A CHOICE.
I NEVER DID, DID I?
THE MOMENT I SAW THIS PLACE, I WAS ALREADY LOST.
I WAS BORN HERE. MY PARENTS DIED HERE.
THAT'S ALL I REALLY NEED TO KNOW, ISN'T IT? EVERYTHING ELSE IS UNNECESSARY DETAIL.
No. There is much more. I told you we would bring you to safe.
KLIK
Here is safe.
Here are answers. We have been waiting years to tell them all to you.

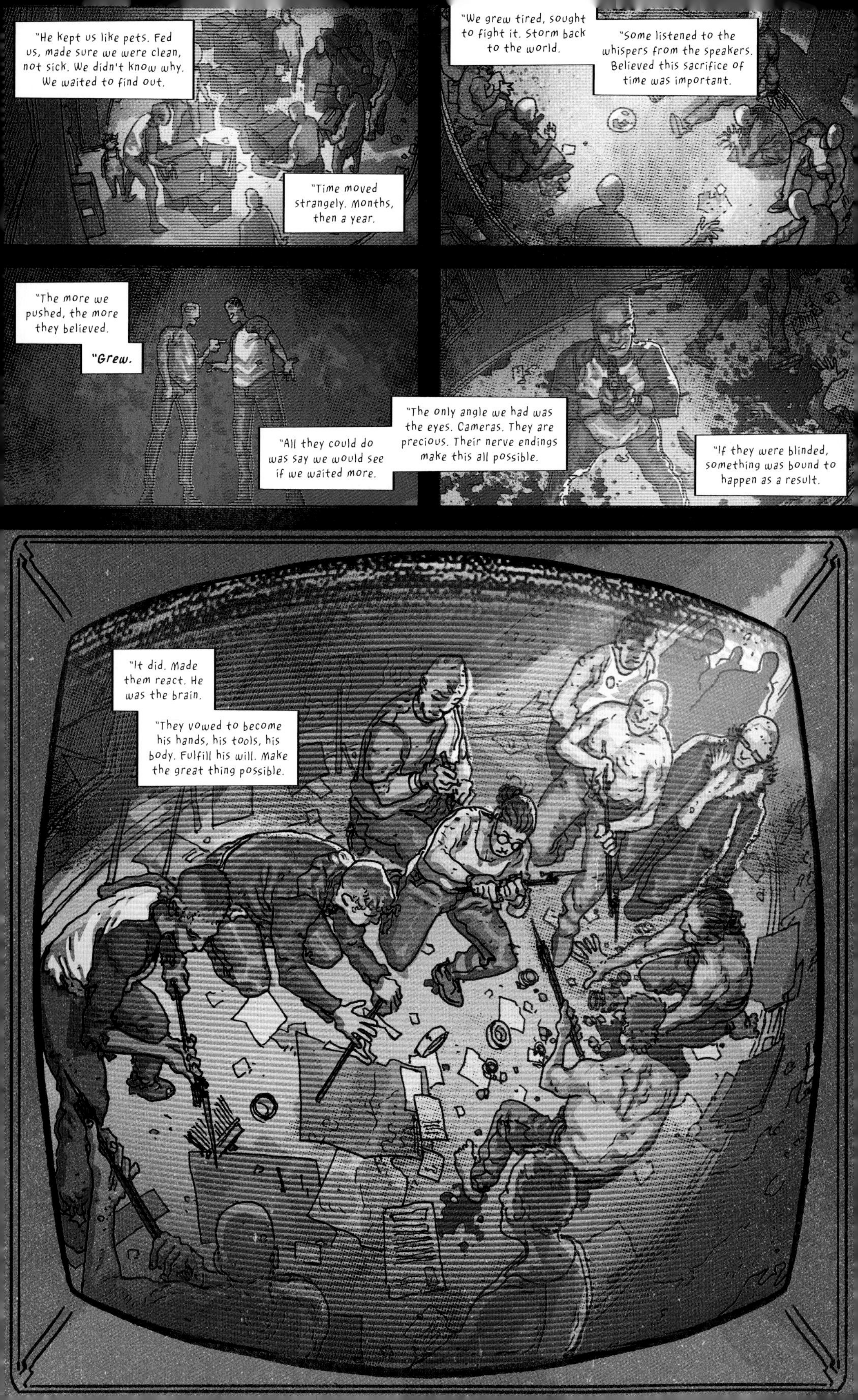
"He kept us like pets. Fed us, made sure we were clean, not sick. We didn't know why. We waited to find out.
"Time moved strangely. Months, then a year.
"We grew tired, sought to fight it. Storm back to the world.
"Some listened to the whispers from the speakers. Believed this sacrifice of time was important.
"The more we pushed, the more they believed.
"Grew.
"All they could do was say we would see if we waited more.
"The only angle we had was the eyes. Cameras. They are precious. Their nerve endings make this all possible.
"If they were blinded, something was bound to happen as a result.
"It did. Made them react. He was the brain.
"They vowed to become his hands, his tools, his body. Fulfill his will. Make the great thing possible.

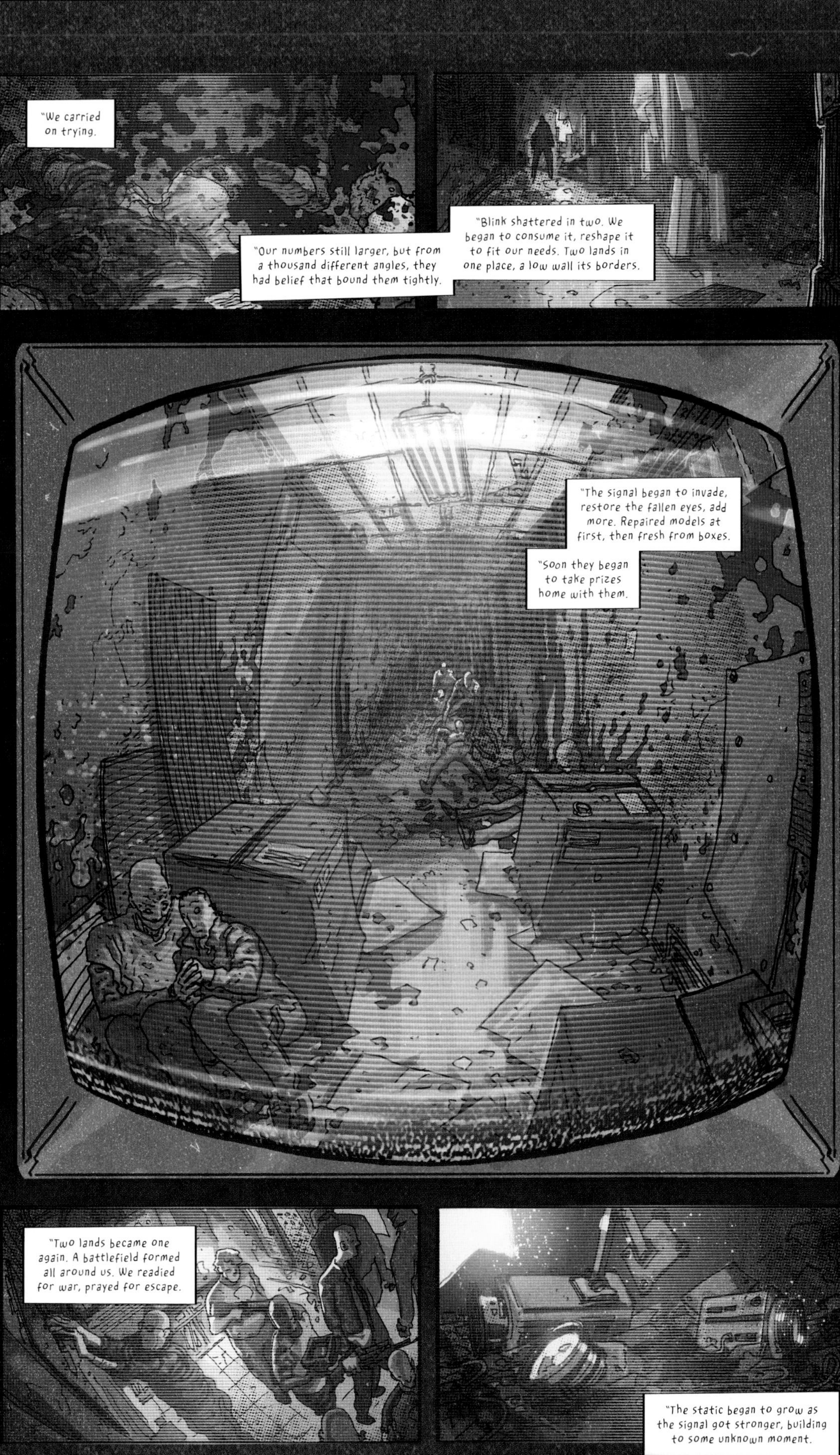
"We carried on trying.
"Our numbers still larger, but from a thousand different angles, they had belief that bound them tightly.
"Blink shattered in two. We began to consume it, reshape it to fit our needs. Two lands in one place, a low wall its borders.
"The signal began to invade, restore the fallen eyes, add more. Repaired models at first, then fresh from boxes.
"Soon they began to take prizes home with them.
"Two lands became one again. A battlefield formed all around us. We readied for war, prayed for escape.
"The static began to grow as the signal got stronger, building to some unknown moment.

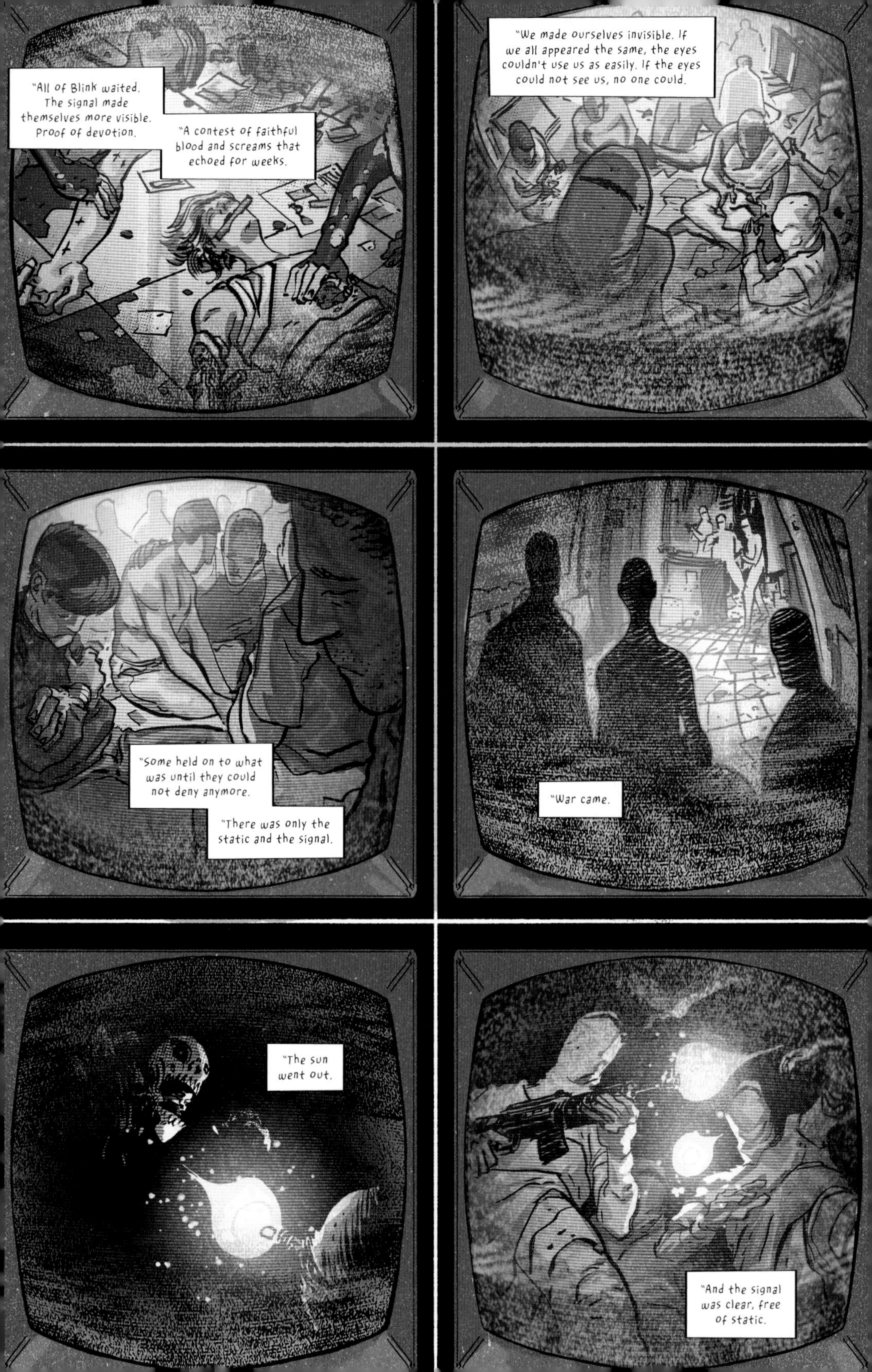
"All of Blink waited. The signal made themselves more visible. Proof of devotion.
"A contest of faithful blood and screams that echoed for weeks.
"We made ourselves invisible. If we all appeared the same, the eyes couldn't use us as easily. If the eyes could not see us, no one could.
"Some held on to what was until they could not deny anymore.
"There was only the static and the signal.
"War came.
"The sun went out.
"And the signal was clear, free of static.

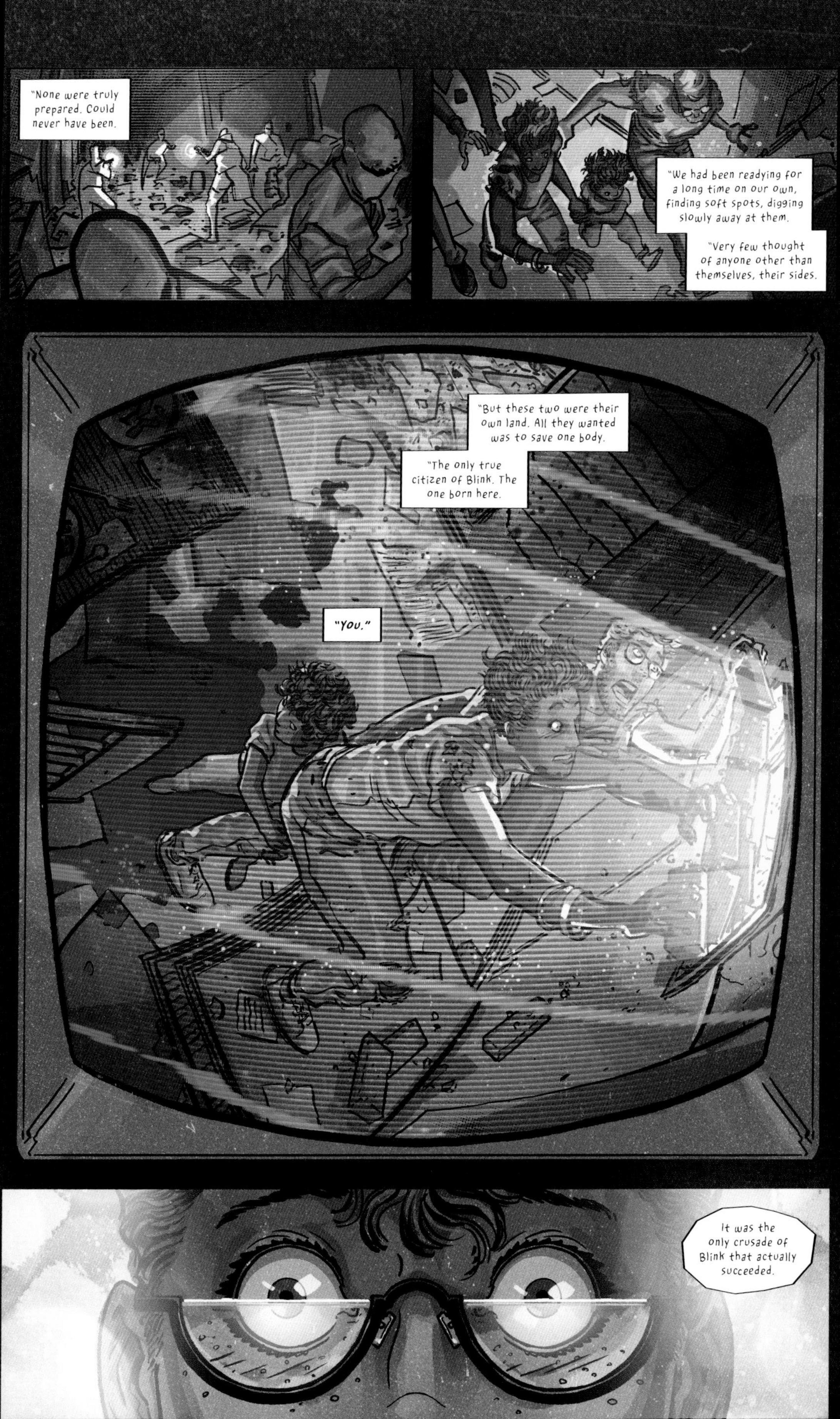
"None were truly prepared. Could never have been.
"We had been readying for a long time on our own, finding soft spots, digging slowly away at them.
"Very few thought of anyone other than themselves, their sides.
"But these two were their own land. All they wanted was to save one body.
"The only true citizen of Blink. The one born here.
"You."
It was the only crusade of Blink that actually succeeded.

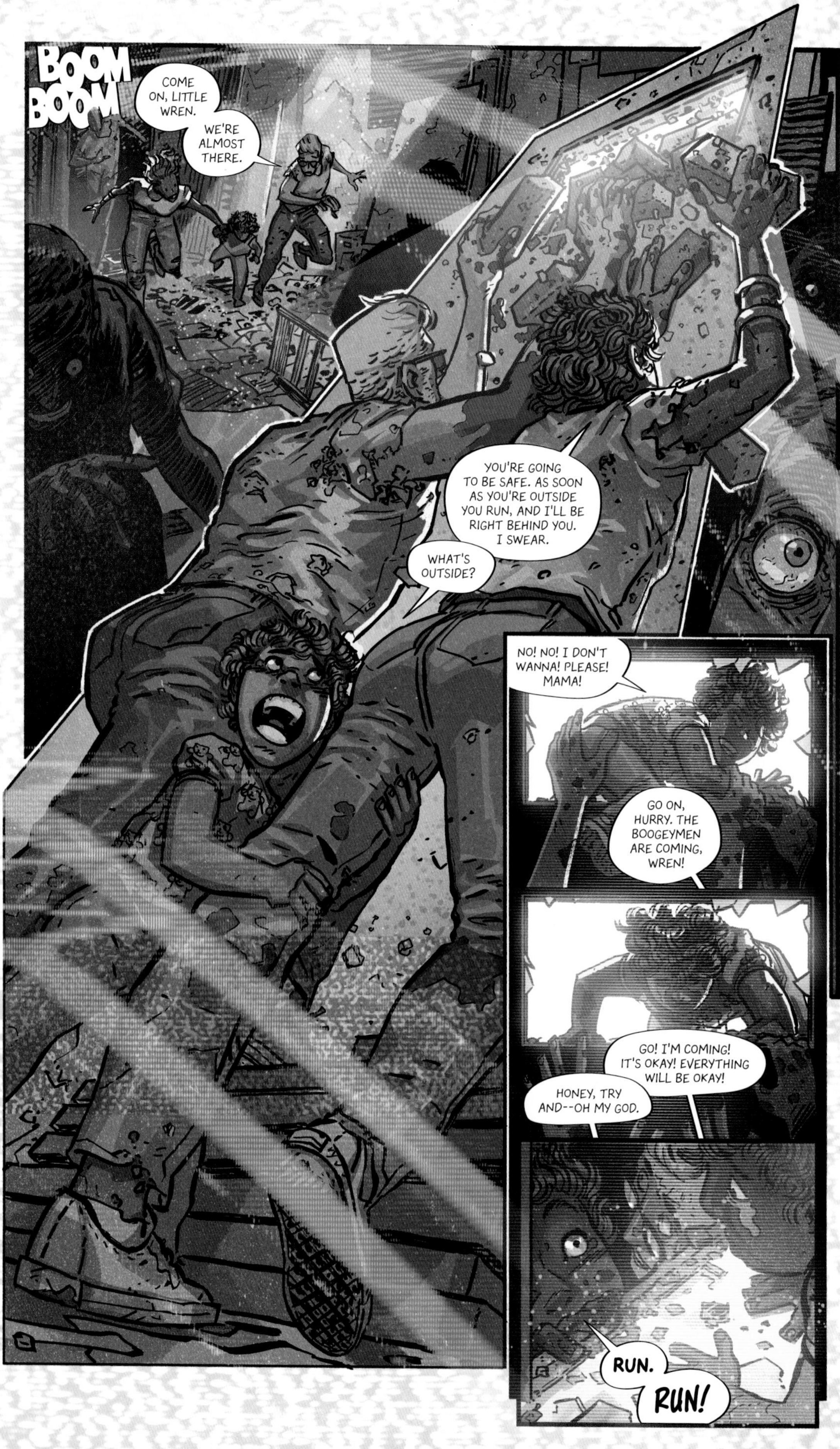
BOOM BOOM
COME ON, LITTLE WREN.
WE'RE ALMOST THERE.
YOU'RE GOING TO BE SAFE. AS SOON AS YOU'RE OUTSIDE YOU RUN, AND I'LL BE RIGHT BEHIND YOU. I SWEAR.
WHAT'S OUTSIDE?
NO! NO! I DON'T WANNA! PLEASE! MAMA!
GO ON, HURRY. THE BOOGEYMEN ARE COMING, WREN!
GO! I'M COMING! IT'S OKAY! EVERYTHING WILL BE OKAY!
HONEY, TRY AND--OH MY GOD.
RUN.
RUN!

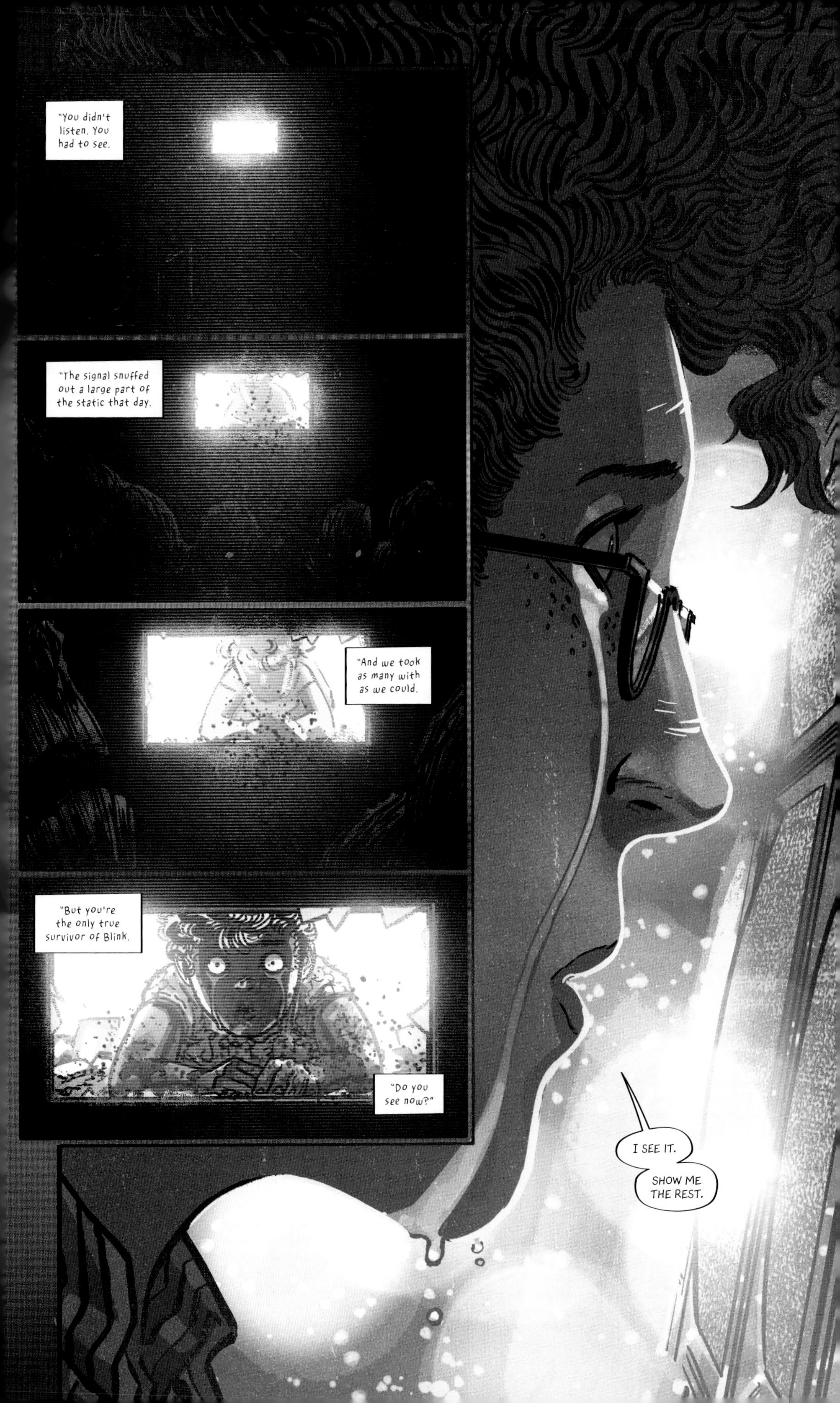
"You didn't listen. You had to see.
"The signal snuffed out a large part of the static that day.
"And we took as many with as we could.
"But you're the only true survivor of Blink.
"Do you see now?"
I SEE IT.
SHOW ME THE REST.

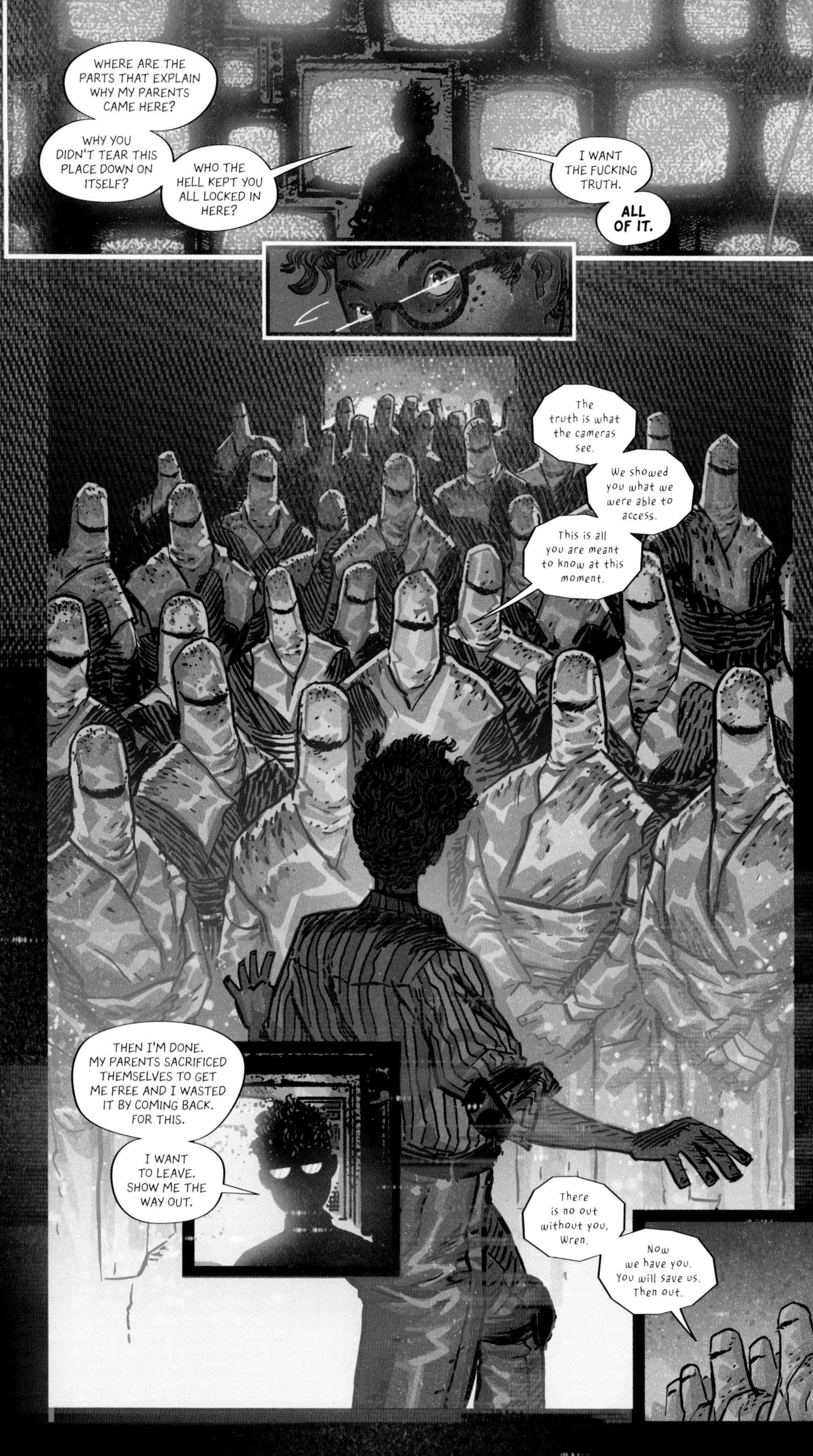
WHERE ARE THE PARTS THAT EXPLAIN WHY MY PARENTS CAME HERE?
WHY YOU DIDN'T TEAR THIS PLACE DOWN ON ITSELF?
WHO THE HELL KEPT YOU ALL LOCKED IN HERE?
I WANT THE FUCKING TRUTH.
ALL OF IT.
The truth is what the cameras see.
We showed you what we were able to access.
This is all you are meant to know at this moment.
THEN I'M DONE. MY PARENTS SACRIFICED THEMSELVES TO GET ME FREE AND I WASTED IT BY COMING BACK. FOR THIS.
I WANT TO LEAVE. SHOW ME THE WAY OUT.
There is no out without you, Wren.
Now we have you. You will save us. Then out.

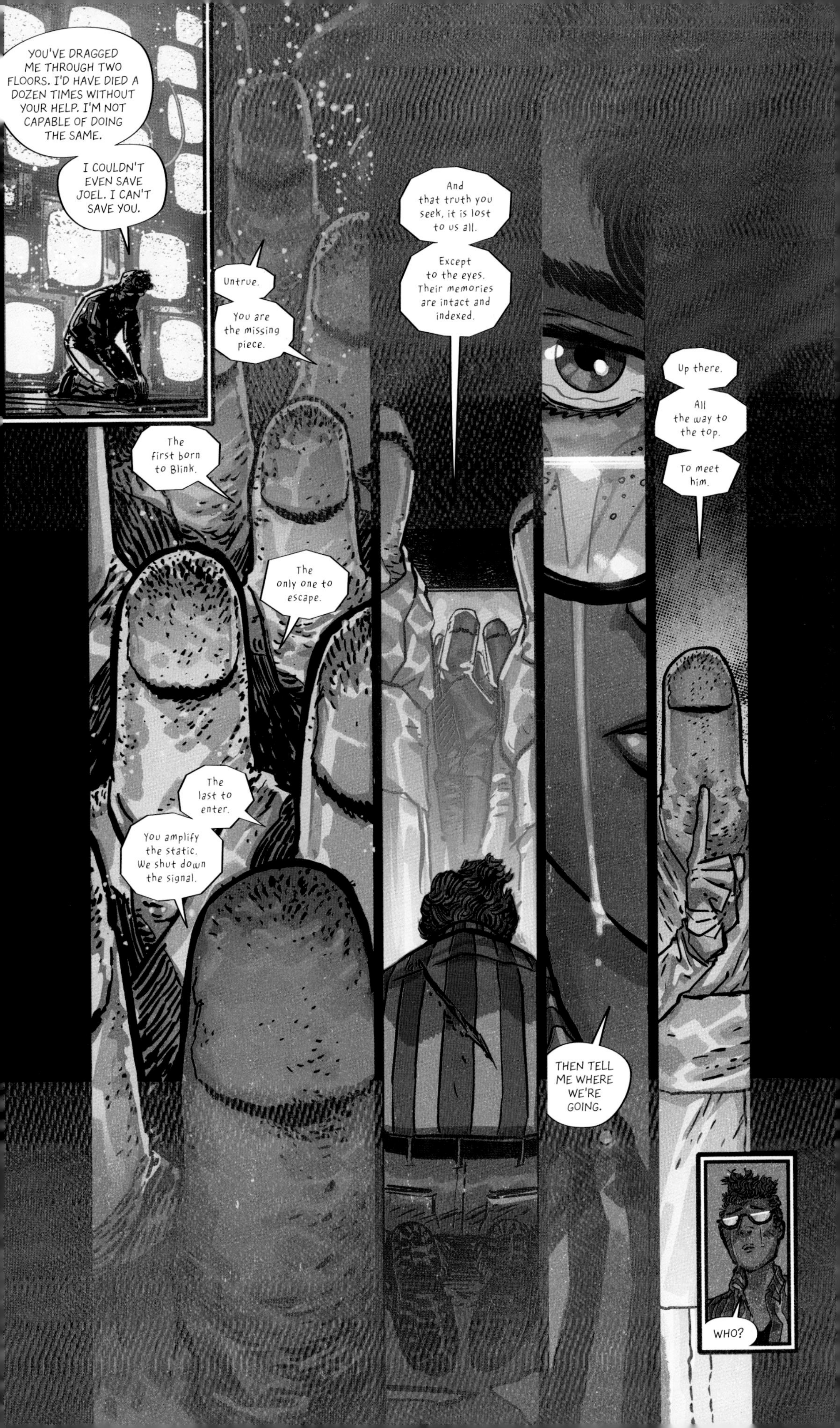
YOU'VE DRAGGED ME THROUGH TWO FLOORS. I'D HAVE DIED A DOZEN TIMES WITHOUT YOUR HELP. I'M NOT CAPABLE OF DOING THE SAME.
I COULDN'T EVEN SAVE JOEL. I CAN'T SAVE YOU.
Untrue.
You are the missing piece.
The first born to Blink.
The only one to escape.
The last to enter.
You amplify the static. We shut down the signal.
And that truth you seek, it is lost to us all.
Except to the eyes. Their memories are intact and indexed.
THEN TELL ME WHERE WE'RE GOING.
Up there.
All the way to the top.
To meet him.
WHO?

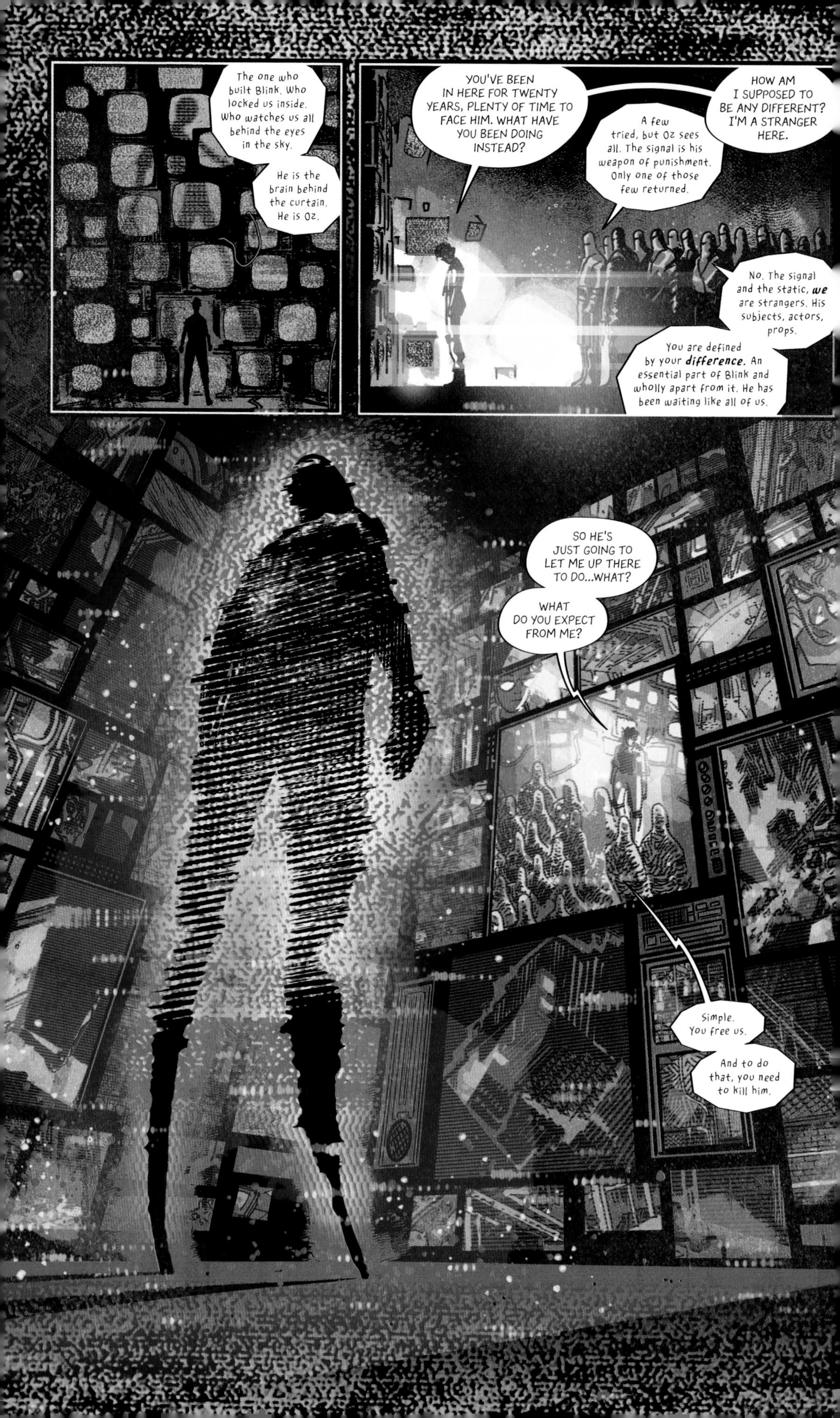

The one who built Blink. Who locked us inside. Who watches us all behind the eyes in the sky.
He is the brain behind the curtain. He is Oz.
YOU'VE BEEN IN HERE FOR TWENTY YEARS, PLENTY OF TIME TO FACE HIM. WHAT HAVE YOU BEEN DOING INSTEAD?
HOW AM I SUPPOSED TO BE ANY DIFFERENT? I'M A STRANGER HERE.
A few tried, but Oz sees all. The signal is his weapon of punishment. Only one of those few returned.
No. The signal and the static, **we** are strangers. His subjects, actors, props.
You are defined by your **difference.** An essential part of Blink and wholly apart from it. He has been waiting like all of us.
SO HE'S JUST GOING TO LET ME UP THERE TO DO...WHAT?
WHAT DO YOU EXPECT FROM ME?
Simple. You free us.
And to do that, you need to kill him.

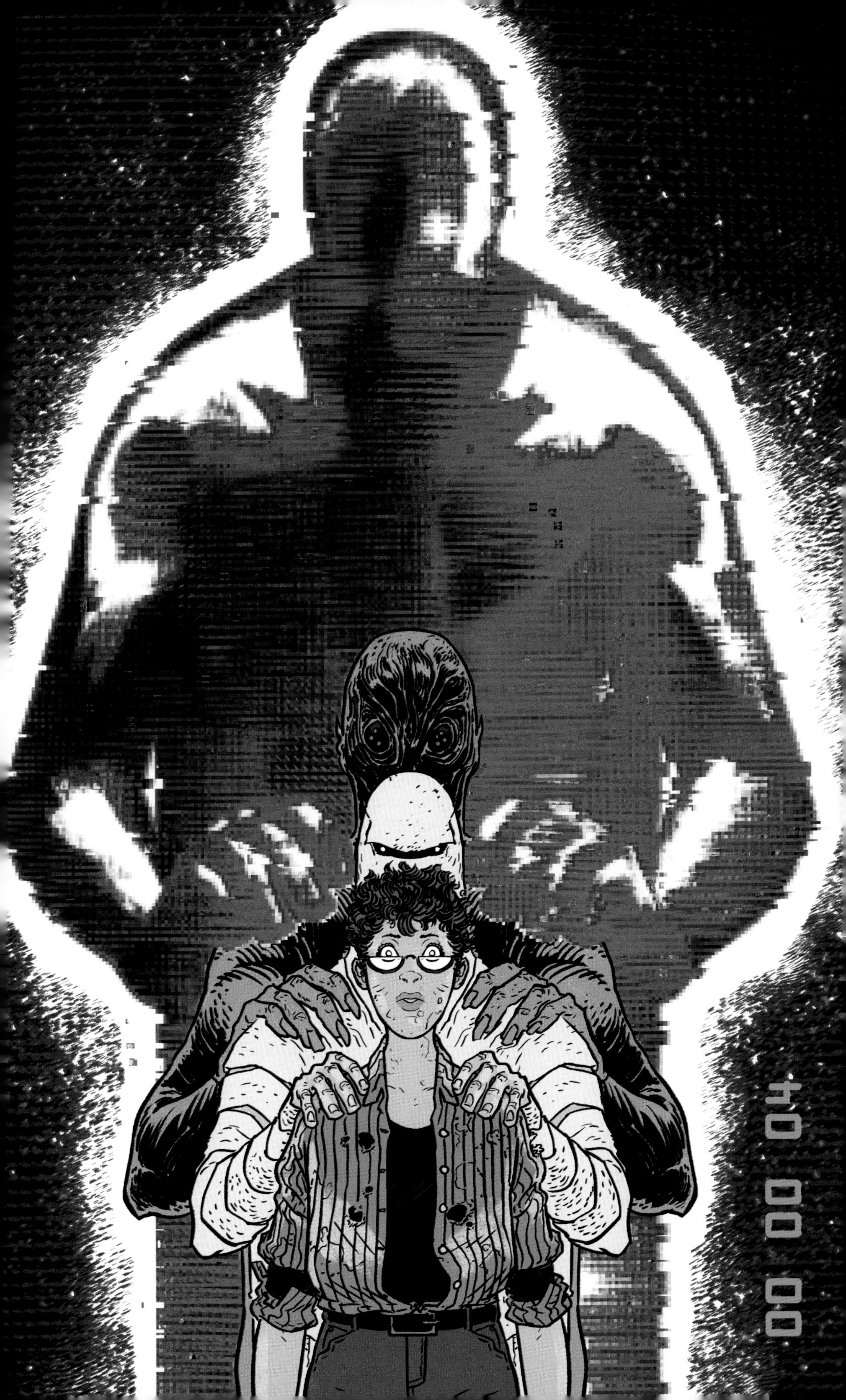

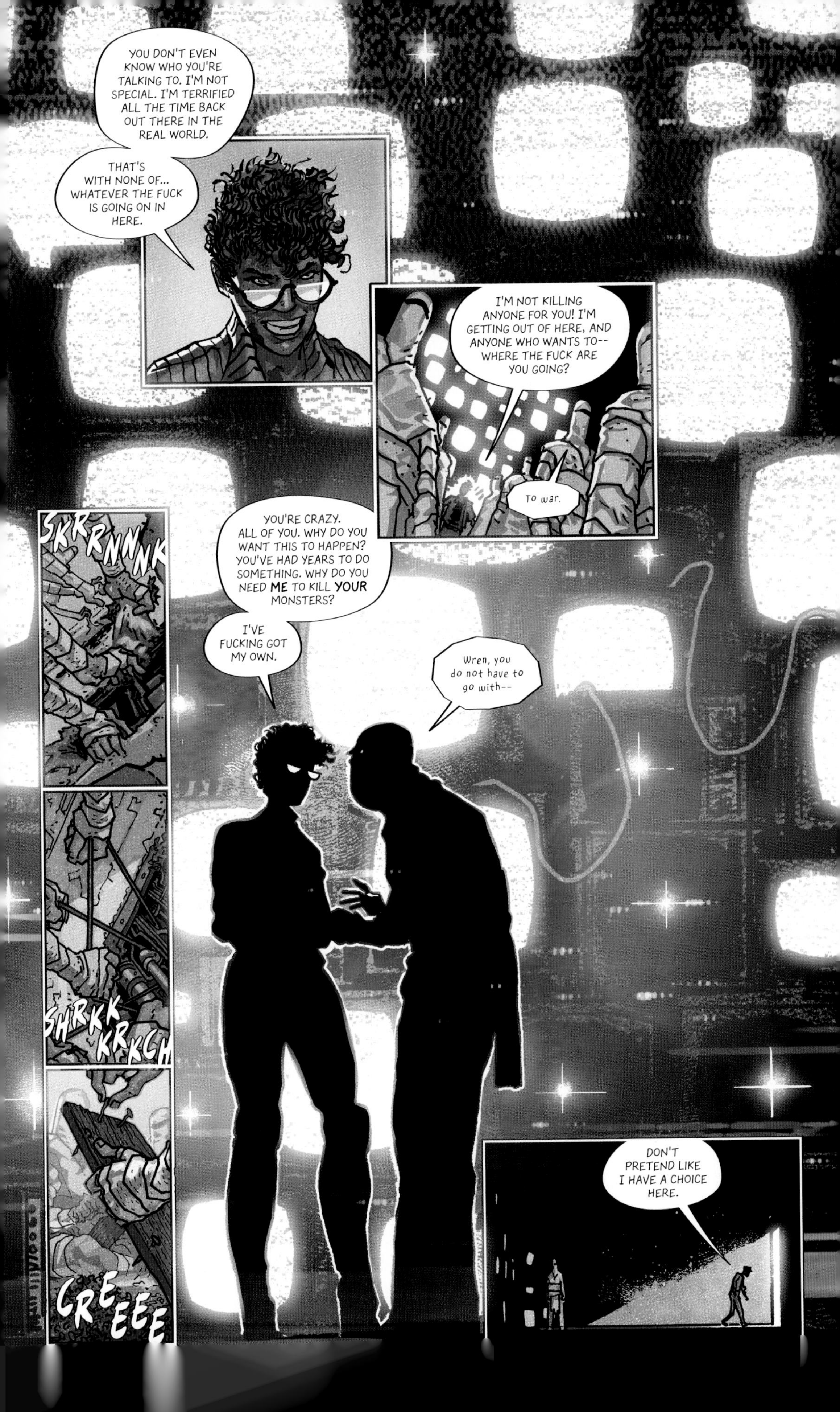
YOU DON'T EVEN KNOW WHO YOU'RE TALKING TO. I'M NOT SPECIAL. I'M TERRIFIED ALL THE TIME BACK OUT THERE IN THE REAL WORLD.
THAT'S WITH NONE OF... WHATEVER THE FUCK IS GOING ON IN HERE.
I'M NOT KILLING ANYONE FOR YOU! I'M GETTING OUT OF HERE, AND ANYONE WHO WANTS TO-- WHERE THE FUCK ARE YOU GOING?
To war.
SKRRNNNK
SHRKK KRKCH
CREEEEE
YOU'RE CRAZY. ALL OF YOU. WHY DO YOU WANT THIS TO HAPPEN? YOU'VE HAD YEARS TO DO SOMETHING. WHY DO YOU NEED **ME** TO KILL **YOUR** MONSTERS?
I'VE FUCKING GOT MY OWN.
Wren, you do not have to go with--
DON'T PRETEND LIKE I HAVE A CHOICE HERE.

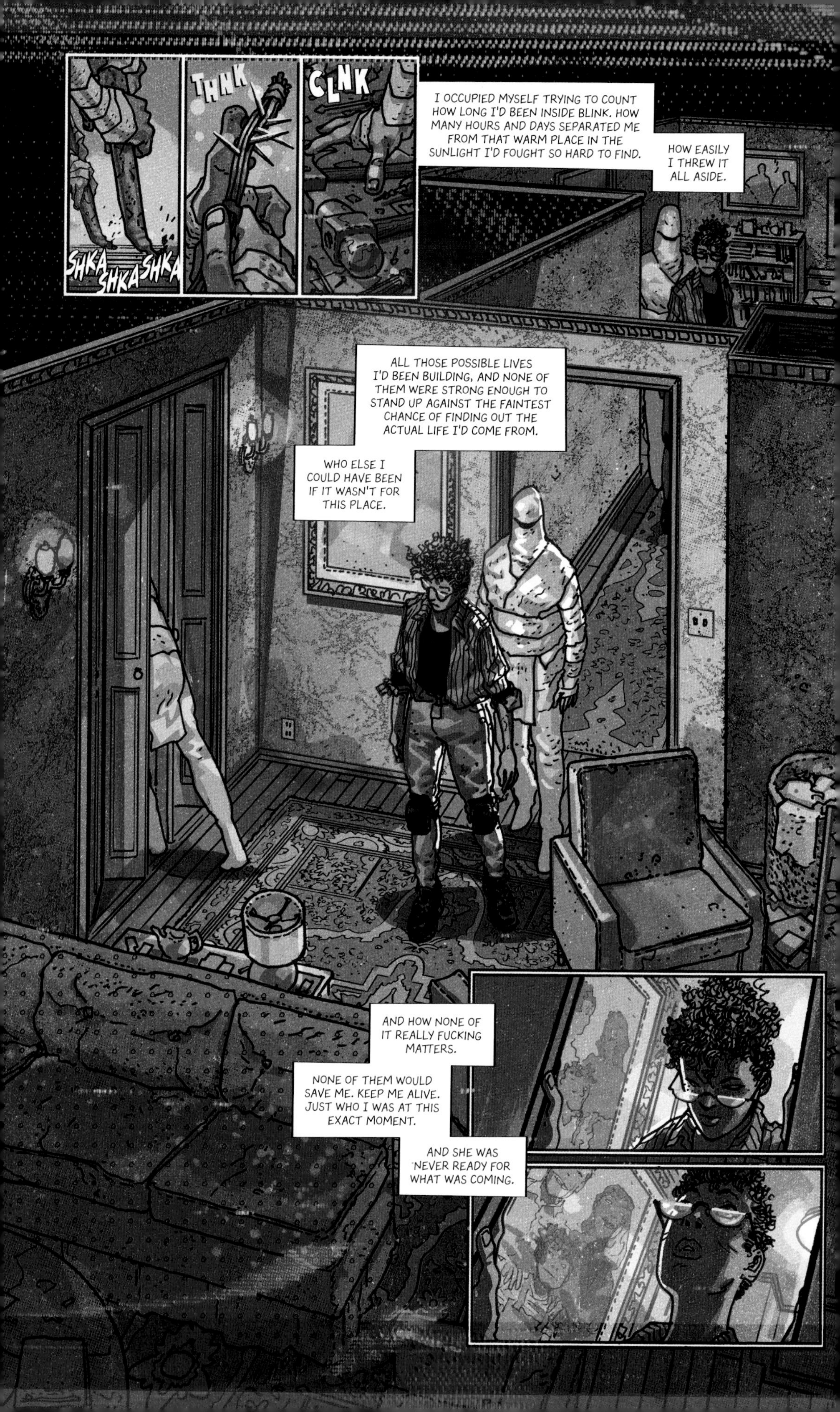
SHKA SHKA SHKA
THNK
CLNK
I OCCUPIED MYSELF TRYING TO COUNT HOW LONG I'D BEEN INSIDE BLINK. HOW MANY HOURS AND DAYS SEPARATED ME FROM THAT WARM PLACE IN THE SUNLIGHT I'D FOUGHT SO HARD TO FIND.
HOW EASILY I THREW IT ALL ASIDE.
ALL THOSE POSSIBLE LIVES I'D BEEN BUILDING, AND NONE OF THEM WERE STRONG ENOUGH TO STAND UP AGAINST THE FAINTEST CHANCE OF FINDING OUT THE ACTUAL LIFE I'D COME FROM.
WHO ELSE I COULD HAVE BEEN IF IT WASN'T FOR THIS PLACE.
AND HOW NONE OF IT REALLY FUCKING MATTERS.
NONE OF THEM WOULD SAVE ME. KEEP ME ALIVE. JUST WHO I WAS AT THIS EXACT MOMENT.
AND SHE WAS NEVER READY FOR WHAT WAS COMING.

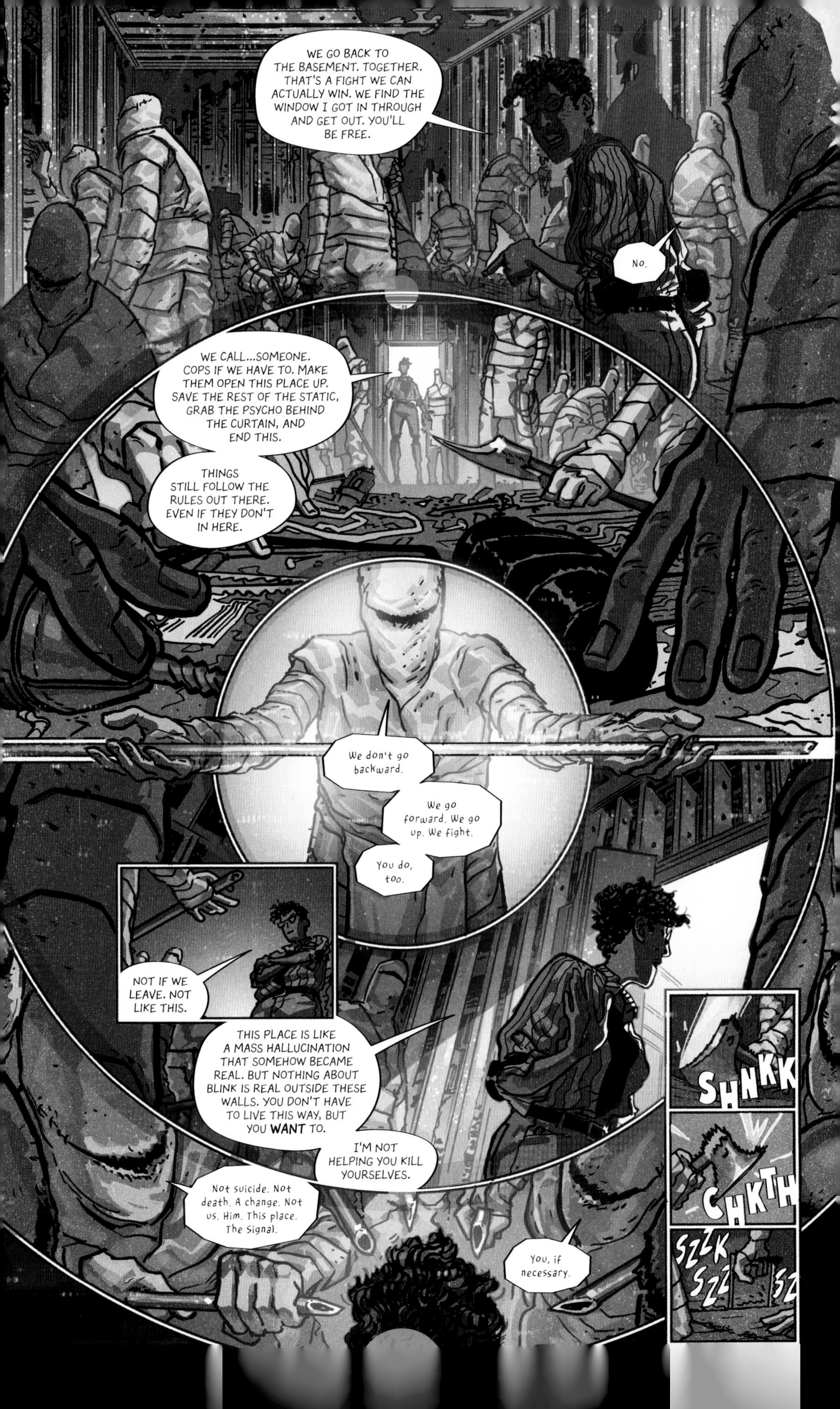
WE GO BACK TO THE BASEMENT. TOGETHER. THAT'S A FIGHT WE CAN ACTUALLY WIN. WE FIND THE WINDOW I GOT IN THROUGH AND GET OUT. YOU'LL BE FREE.
No.
WE CALL...SOMEONE. COPS IF WE HAVE TO. MAKE THEM OPEN THIS PLACE UP. SAVE THE REST OF THE STATIC, GRAB THE PSYCHO BEHIND THE CURTAIN, AND END THIS.
THINGS STILL FOLLOW THE RULES OUT THERE. EVEN IF THEY DON'T IN HERE.
We don't go backward.
We go forward. We go up. We fight.
You do, too.
NOT IF WE LEAVE. NOT LIKE THIS.
THIS PLACE IS LIKE A MASS HALLUCINATION THAT SOMEHOW BECAME REAL. BUT NOTHING ABOUT BLINK IS REAL OUTSIDE THESE WALLS. YOU DON'T HAVE TO LIVE THIS WAY, BUT YOU **WANT** TO.
I'M NOT HELPING YOU KILL YOURSELVES.
Not suicide. Not death. A change. Not us. Him. This place. The Signal.
You, if necessary.
SHNKK
CHKTH
SZZK SZZ SZ

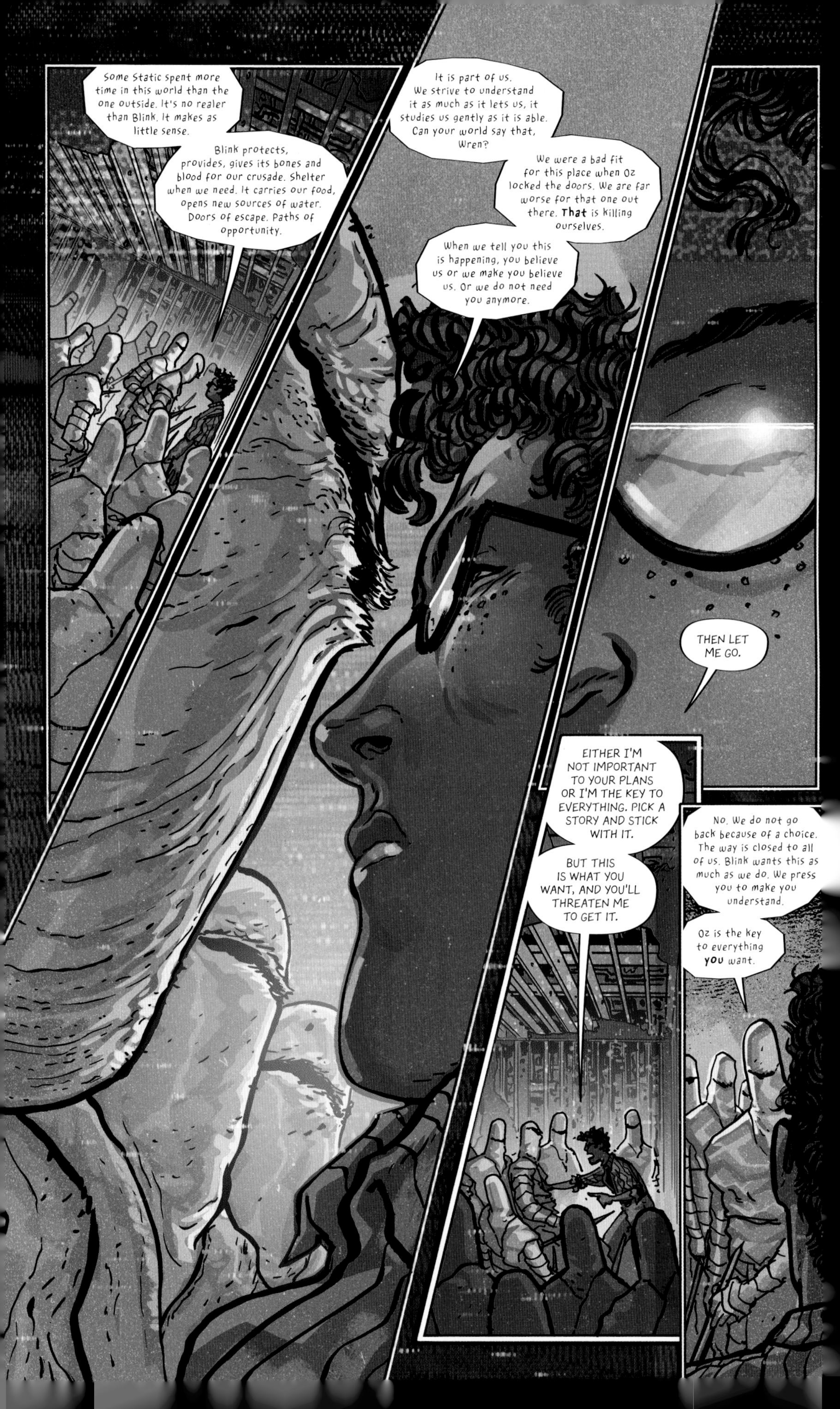

Some Static spent more time in this world than the one outside. It's no realer than Blink. It makes as little sense.
Blink protects, provides, gives its bones and blood for our crusade. Shelter when we need. It carries our food, opens new sources of water. Doors of escape. Paths of opportunity.
It is part of us. We strive to understand it as much as it lets us, it studies us gently as it is able. Can your world say that, Wren?
We were a bad fit for this place when Oz locked the doors. We are far worse for that one out there. That is killing ourselves.
When we tell you this is happening, you believe us or we make you believe us. Or we do not need you anymore.
THEN LET ME GO.
EITHER I'M NOT IMPORTANT TO YOUR PLANS OR I'M THE KEY TO EVERYTHING. PICK A STORY AND STICK WITH IT.
BUT THIS IS WHAT YOU WANT, AND YOU'LL THREATEN ME TO GET IT.
No. We do not go back because of a choice. The way is closed to all of us. Blink wants this as much as we do. We press you to make you understand.
Oz is the key to everything you want.

down from his throne.

Turn it over to us.

those doors for you.

If that's what you still want.

But first we must make our way.

To the third floor.

To his home.

I ALWAYS THOUGHT THAT THERE WERE LINES. SIDES TO THINGS. GOOD AND EVIL. A MORAL ARC OF THE UNIVERSE, ALWAYS BENDING, HOWEVER SLOWLY.

NEVER REALIZING I WAS AS WRONG ABOUT MY WORLD AS I WAS ABOUT THIS ONE. THE ONLY SIDE WAS SELF-INTEREST. NOTHING LIKE JUSTICE EXISTED. NOT REALLY.

KRCH

AND AS MUCH AS I STRIVED TO GET BACK TO THAT PLACE I TOLD MYSELF MADE SENSE...

IT WAS JUST AS CHAOTIC AND UNBOUND.

FWAM

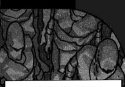

I TRIED TO MAKE IT BETTER. POURED MYSELF INTO OTHERS WHO WERE LOST LIKE ME. ALWAYS TOO LATE, RECOUNTING THE STORY INSTEAD OF TELLING IT. MAKING MONEY OFF IT.

I WAS NO ONE SPECIAL THERE.

IN BLINK, I COULD CHANGE THINGS.

I WONDERED WHAT THAT WOULD FEEL LIKE.

SPLSH
I WAS BORN HERE. I WOULD STILL BE HERE IF MY PARENTS HADN'T SAVED ME, SENT ME BACK TO THE WORLD THEY'D BEEN TAKEN FROM.
OF ALL THE HOMES I EVER TRIED TO MAKE.
THIS WAS THE EASIEST ONE TO CLAIM AS MINE.
INSTINCT, PRESERVATION, I DON'T KNOW.
IF IT WAS SOMETHING AS BASIC AS LOVE THAT GOT ME OUT.
THEN WHAT WAS IT THAT BROUGHT ME BACK?

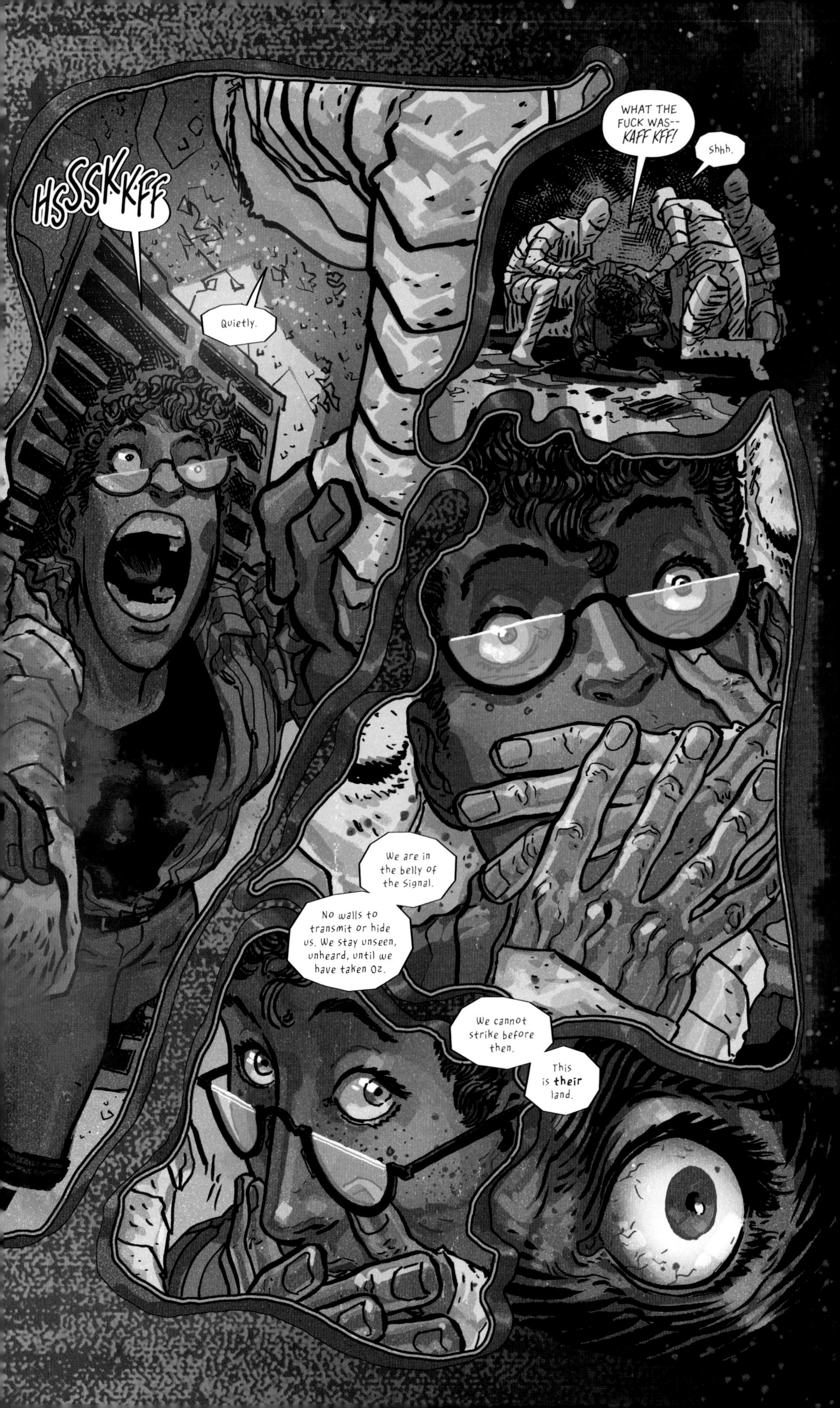
HSSSKKFF
Quietly.
WHAT THE FUCK WAS-- KAFF KFF!
Shhh.
We are in the belly of the Signal.
No walls to transmit or hide us. We stay unseen, unheard, until we have taken Oz.
We cannot strike before then.
This is **their** land.

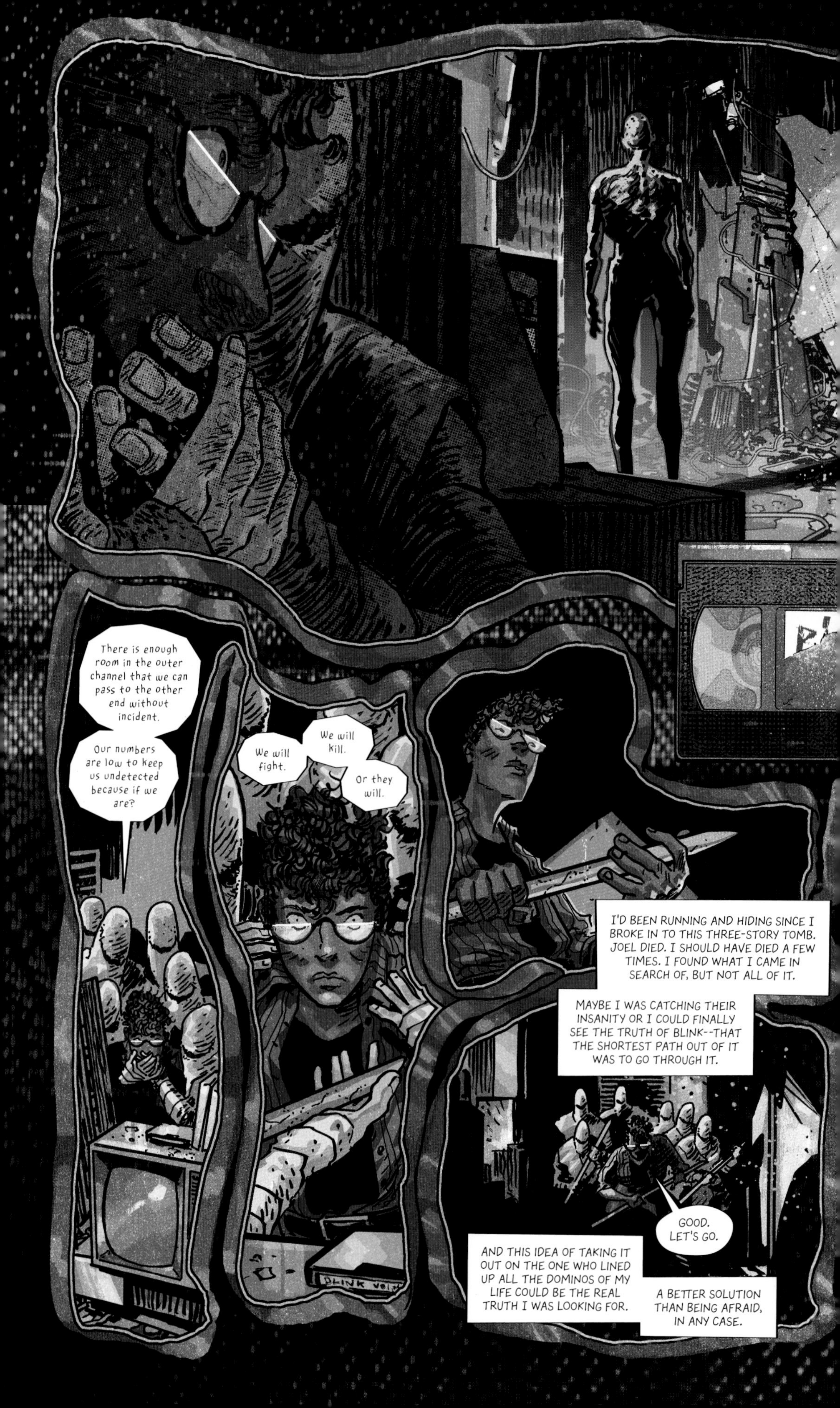
There is enough room in the outer channel that we can pass to the other end without incident.
Our numbers are low to keep us undetected because if we are?
We will fight.
We will kill.
Or they will.
I'D BEEN RUNNING AND HIDING SINCE I BROKE IN TO THIS THREE-STORY TOMB. JOEL DIED. I SHOULD HAVE DIED A FEW TIMES. I FOUND WHAT I CAME IN SEARCH OF, BUT NOT ALL OF IT.
MAYBE I WAS CATCHING THEIR INSANITY OR I COULD FINALLY SEE THE TRUTH OF BLINK--THAT THE SHORTEST PATH OUT OF IT WAS TO GO THROUGH IT.
GOOD. LET'S GO.
AND THIS IDEA OF TAKING IT OUT ON THE ONE WHO LINED UP ALL THE DOMINOS OF MY LIFE COULD BE THE REAL TRUTH I WAS LOOKING FOR.
A BETTER SOLUTION THAN BEING AFRAID, IN ANY CASE.

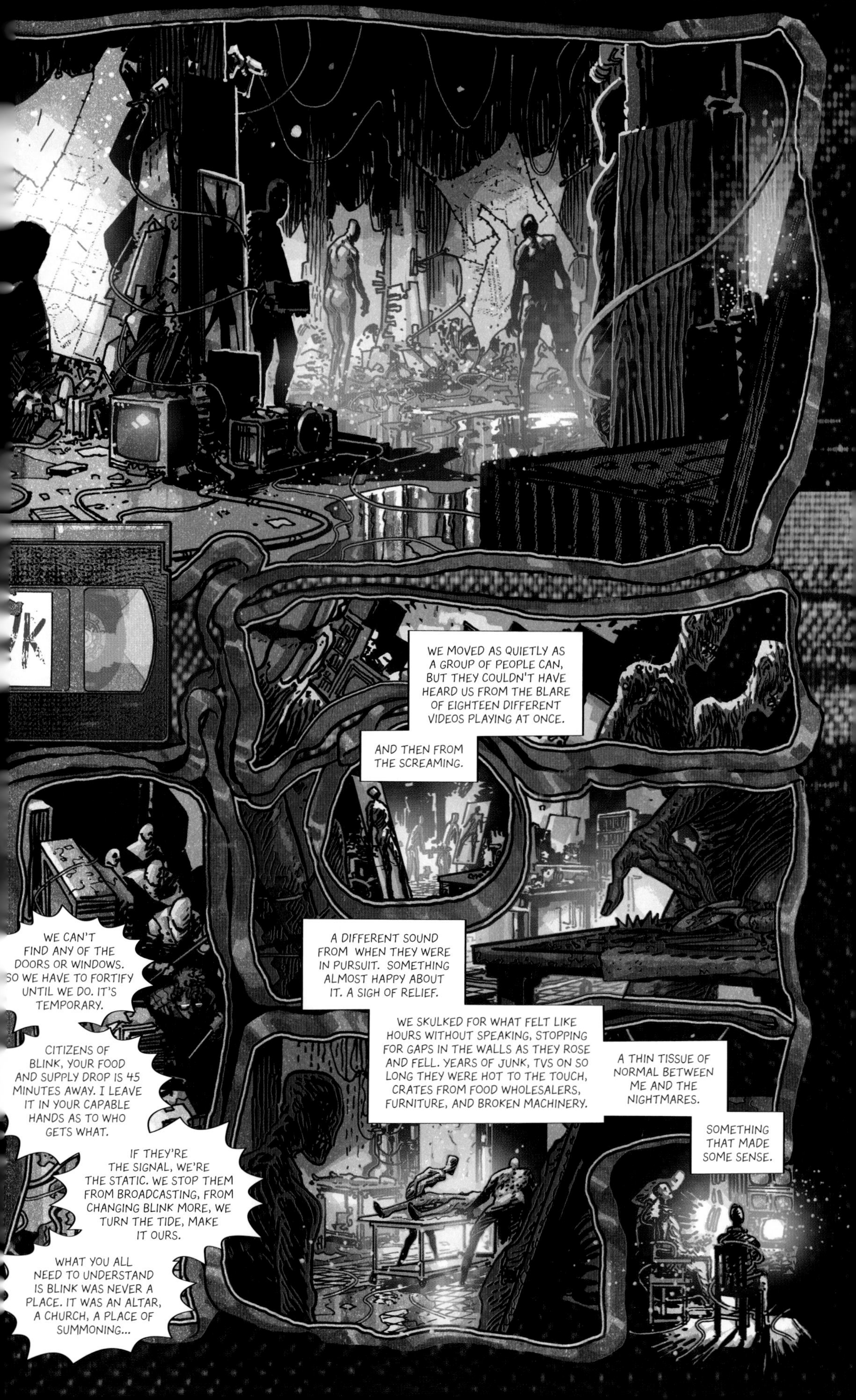
WE MOVED AS QUIETLY AS A GROUP OF PEOPLE CAN, BUT THEY COULDN'T HAVE HEARD US FROM THE BLARE OF EIGHTEEN DIFFERENT VIDEOS PLAYING AT ONCE.
AND THEN FROM THE SCREAMING.
A DIFFERENT SOUND FROM WHEN THEY WERE IN PURSUIT. SOMETHING ALMOST HAPPY ABOUT IT. A SIGH OF RELIEF.
WE SKULKED FOR WHAT FELT LIKE HOURS WITHOUT SPEAKING, STOPPING FOR GAPS IN THE WALLS AS THEY ROSE AND FELL. YEARS OF JUNK, TVS ON SO LONG THEY WERE HOT TO THE TOUCH, CRATES FROM FOOD WHOLESALERS, FURNITURE, AND BROKEN MACHINERY.
A THIN TISSUE OF NORMAL BETWEEN ME AND THE NIGHTMARES.
SOMETHING THAT MADE SOME SENSE.
WE CAN'T FIND ANY OF THE DOORS OR WINDOWS. SO WE HAVE TO FORTIFY UNTIL WE DO. IT'S TEMPORARY.
CITIZENS OF BLINK, YOUR FOOD AND SUPPLY DROP IS 45 MINUTES AWAY. I LEAVE IT IN YOUR CAPABLE HANDS AS TO WHO GETS WHAT.
IF THEY'RE THE SIGNAL, WE'RE THE STATIC. WE STOP THEM FROM BROADCASTING, FROM CHANGING BLINK MORE, WE TURN THE TIDE, MAKE IT OURS.
WHAT YOU ALL NEED TO UNDERSTAND IS BLINK WAS NEVER A PLACE. IT WAS AN ALTAR, A CHURCH, A PLACE OF SUMMONING...

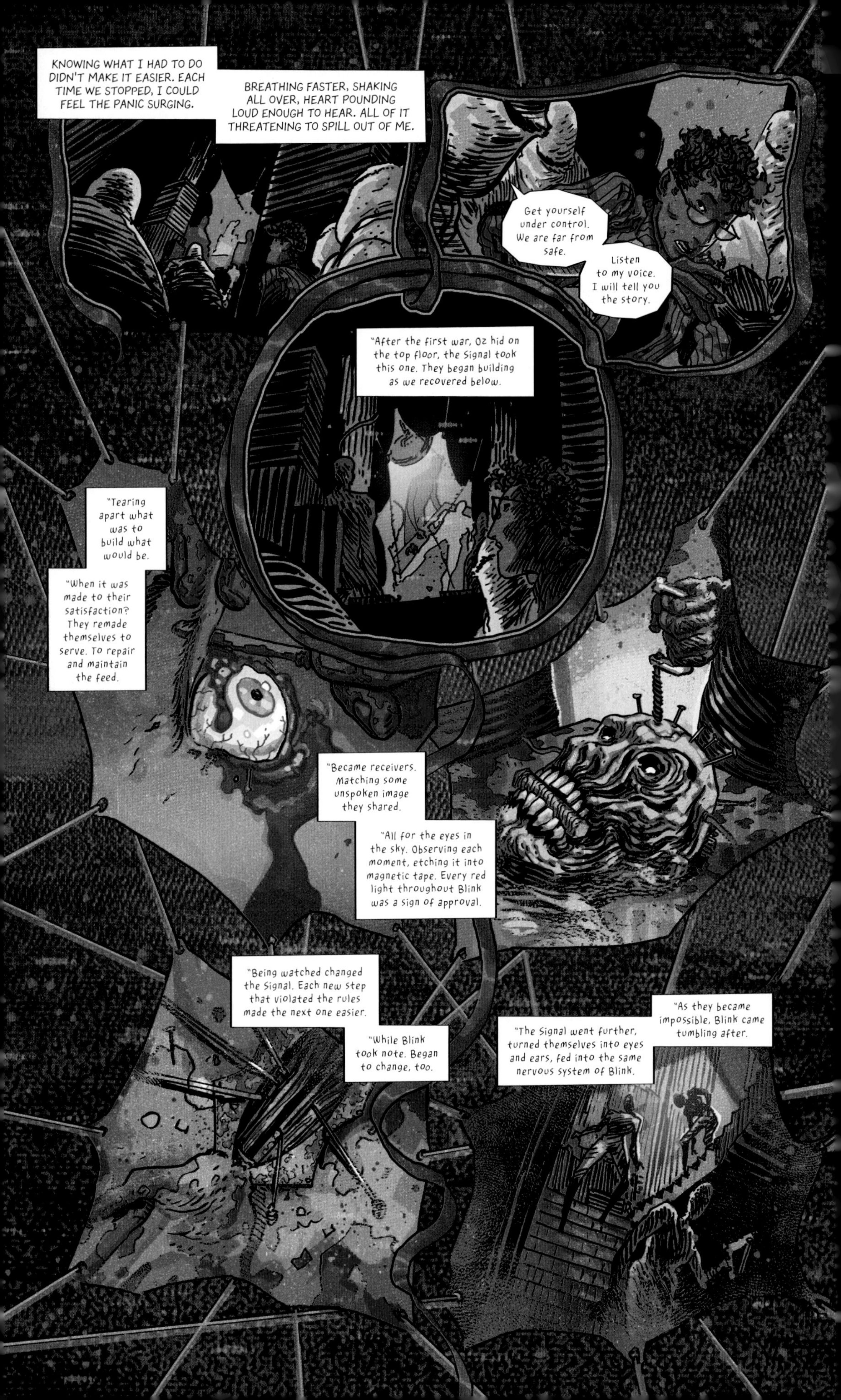
KNOWING WHAT I HAD TO DO DIDN'T MAKE IT EASIER. EACH TIME WE STOPPED, I COULD FEEL THE PANIC SURGING.
BREATHING FASTER, SHAKING ALL OVER, HEART POUNDING LOUD ENOUGH TO HEAR. ALL OF IT THREATENING TO SPILL OUT OF ME.
Get yourself under control. We are far from safe.
Listen to my voice. I will tell you the story.
"After the first war, Oz hid on the top floor, the Signal took this one. They began building as we recovered below.
"Tearing apart what was to build what would be.
"When it was made to their satisfaction? They remade themselves to serve. To repair and maintain the feed.
"Became receivers. Matching some unspoken image they shared.
"All for the eyes in the sky. Observing each moment, etching it into magnetic tape. Every red light throughout Blink was a sign of approval.
"Being watched changed the Signal. Each new step that violated the rules made the next one easier.
"While Blink took note. Began to change, too.
"The Signal went further, turned themselves into eyes and ears, fed into the same nervous system of Blink.
"As they became impossible, Blink came tumbling after.

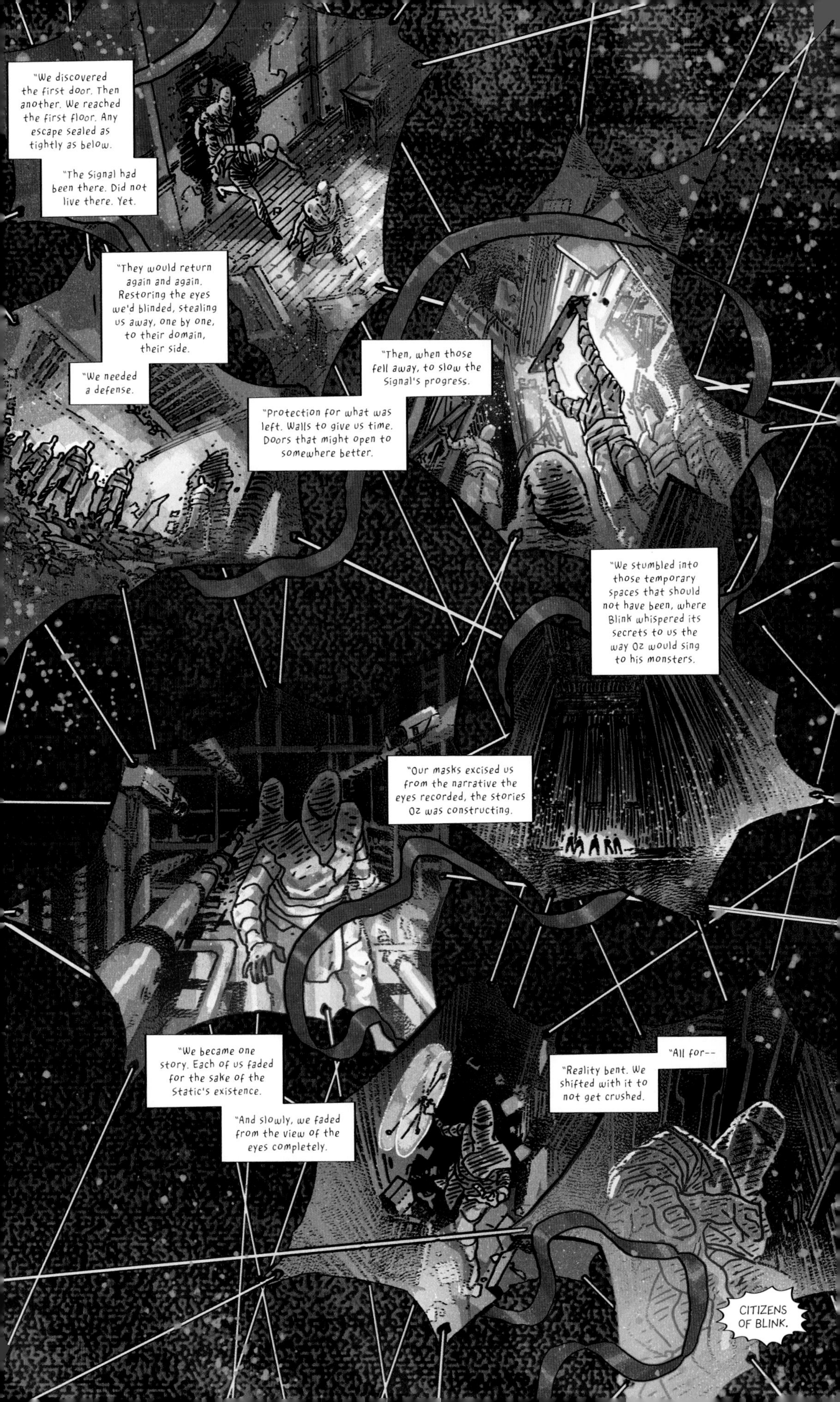
"We discovered the first door. Then another. We reached the first floor. Any escape sealed as tightly as below.
"The Signal had been there. Did not live there. Yet.
"They would return again and again. Restoring the eyes we'd blinded, stealing us away, one by one, to their domain, their side.
"We needed a defense.
"Then, when those fell away, to slow the Signal's progress.
"Protection for what was left. Walls to give us time. Doors that might open to somewhere better.
"We stumbled into those temporary spaces that should not have been, where Blink whispered its secrets to us the way Oz would sing to his monsters.
"Our masks excised us from the narrative the eyes recorded, the stories Oz was constructing.
"We became one story. Each of us faded for the sake of the Static's existence.
"And slowly, we faded from the view of the eyes completely.
"Reality bent. We shifted with it to not get crushed.
"All for--
CITIZENS OF BLINK.

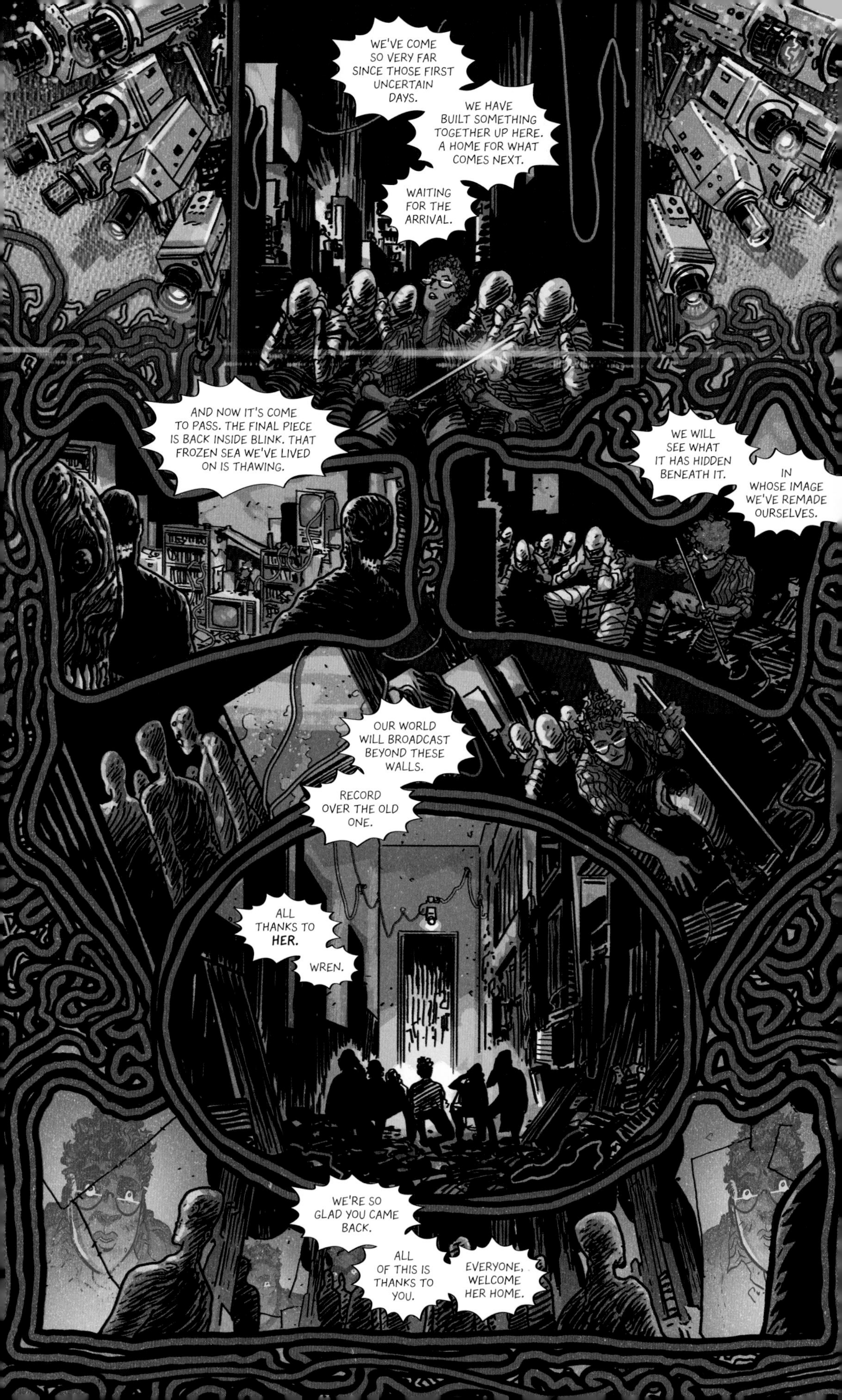

WE'VE COME SO VERY FAR SINCE THOSE FIRST UNCERTAIN DAYS.
WE HAVE BUILT SOMETHING TOGETHER UP HERE. A HOME FOR WHAT COMES NEXT.
WAITING FOR THE ARRIVAL.
AND NOW IT'S COME TO PASS. THE FINAL PIECE IS BACK INSIDE BLINK. THAT FROZEN SEA WE'VE LIVED ON IS THAWING.
WE WILL SEE WHAT IT HAS HIDDEN BENEATH IT.
IN WHOSE IMAGE WE'VE REMADE OURSELVES.
OUR WORLD WILL BROADCAST BEYOND THESE WALLS.
RECORD OVER THE OLD ONE.
ALL THANKS TO **HER.**
WREN.
WE'RE SO GLAD YOU CAME BACK.
ALL OF THIS IS THANKS TO YOU.
EVERYONE, WELCOME HER HOME.

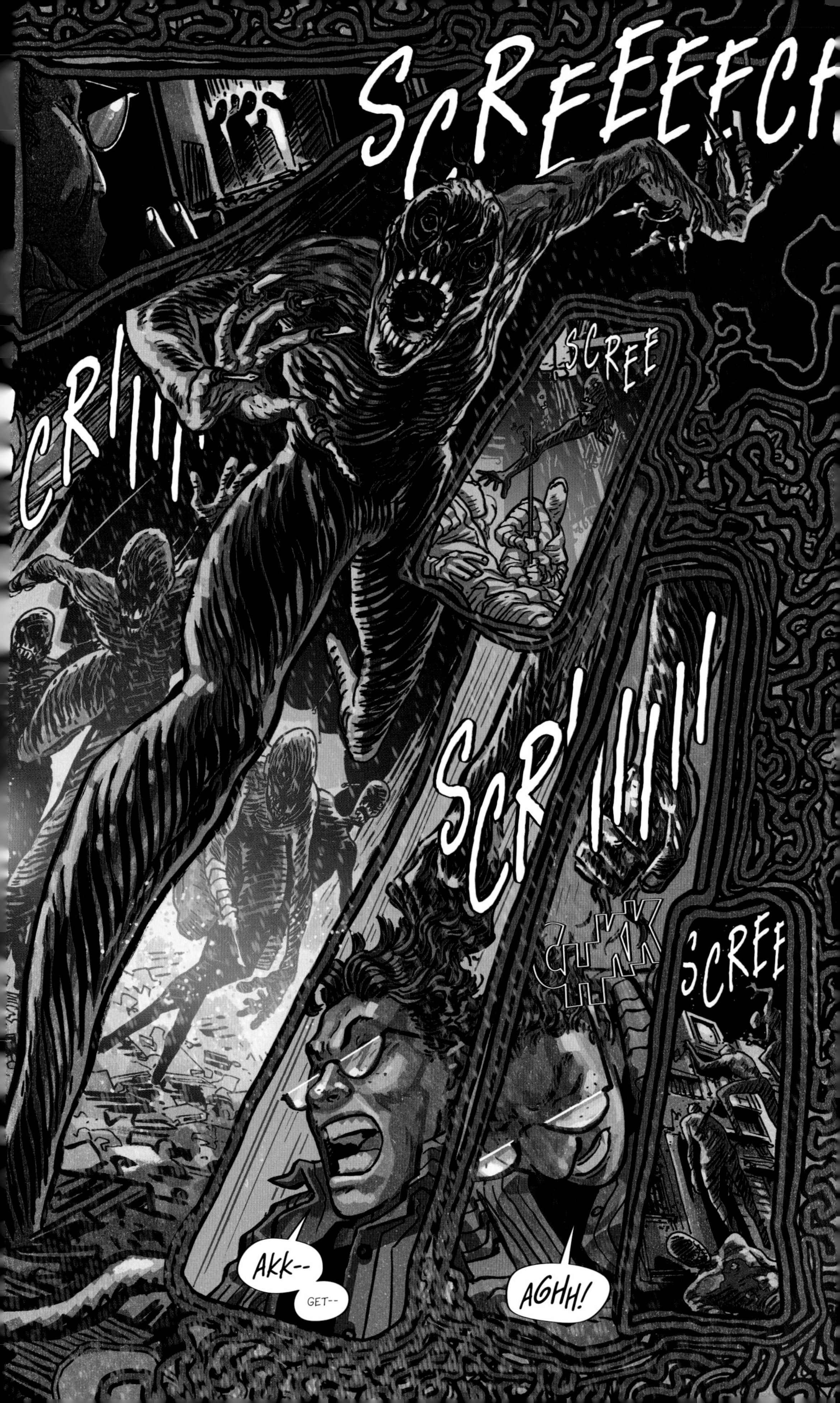
SCREEECH
CRIIII
SCREE
SCRIIII
CHNK
SCREE
AKK--
GET--
AGHH!

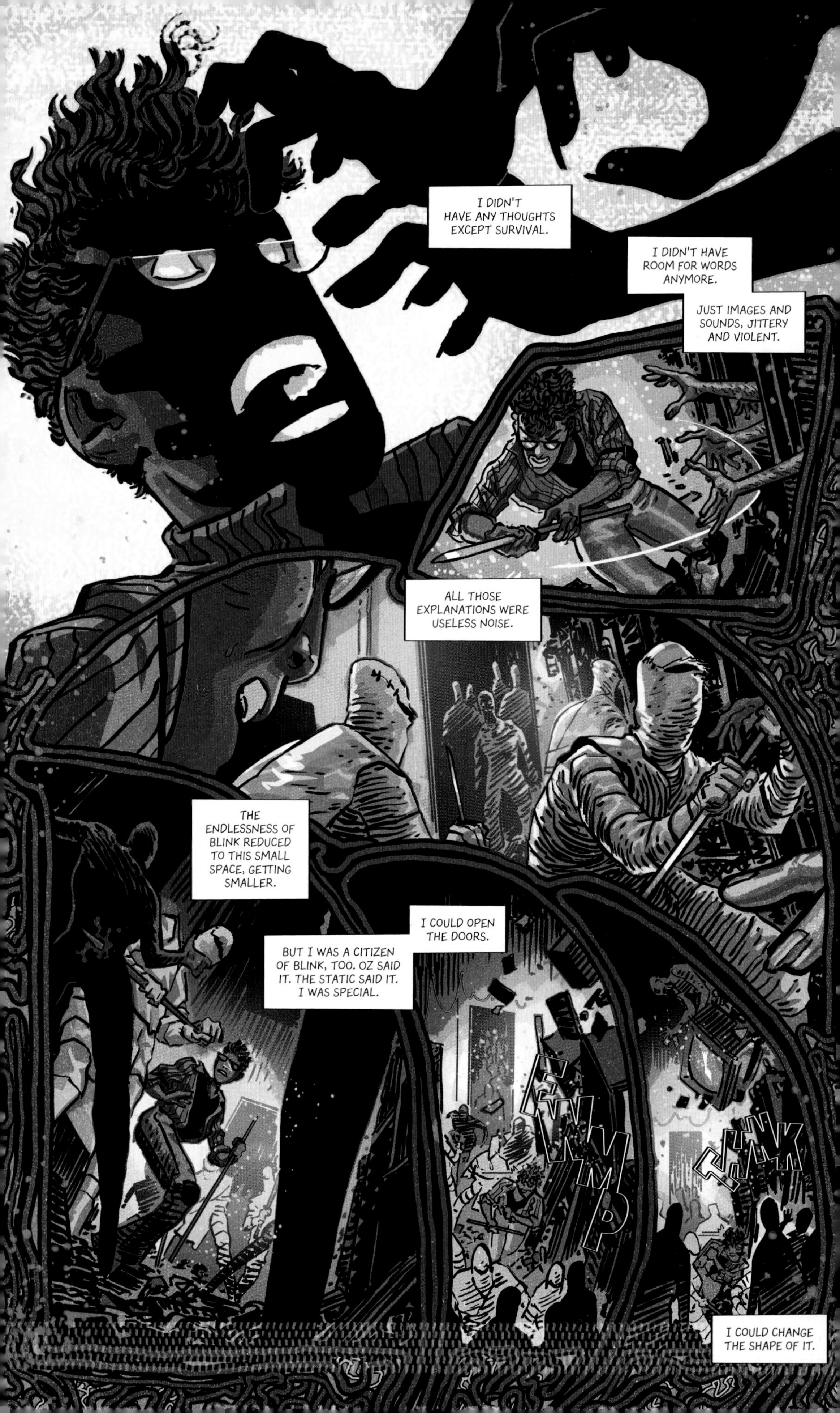

I DIDN'T HAVE ANY THOUGHTS EXCEPT SURVIVAL.
I DIDN'T HAVE ROOM FOR WORDS ANYMORE.
JUST IMAGES AND SOUNDS, JITTERY AND VIOLENT.
ALL THOSE EXPLANATIONS WERE USELESS NOISE.
THE ENDLESSNESS OF BLINK REDUCED TO THIS SMALL SPACE, GETTING SMALLER.
I COULD OPEN THE DOORS.
BUT I WAS A CITIZEN OF BLINK, TOO. OZ SAID IT. THE STATIC SAID IT. I WAS SPECIAL.
I COULD CHANGE THE SHAPE OF IT.

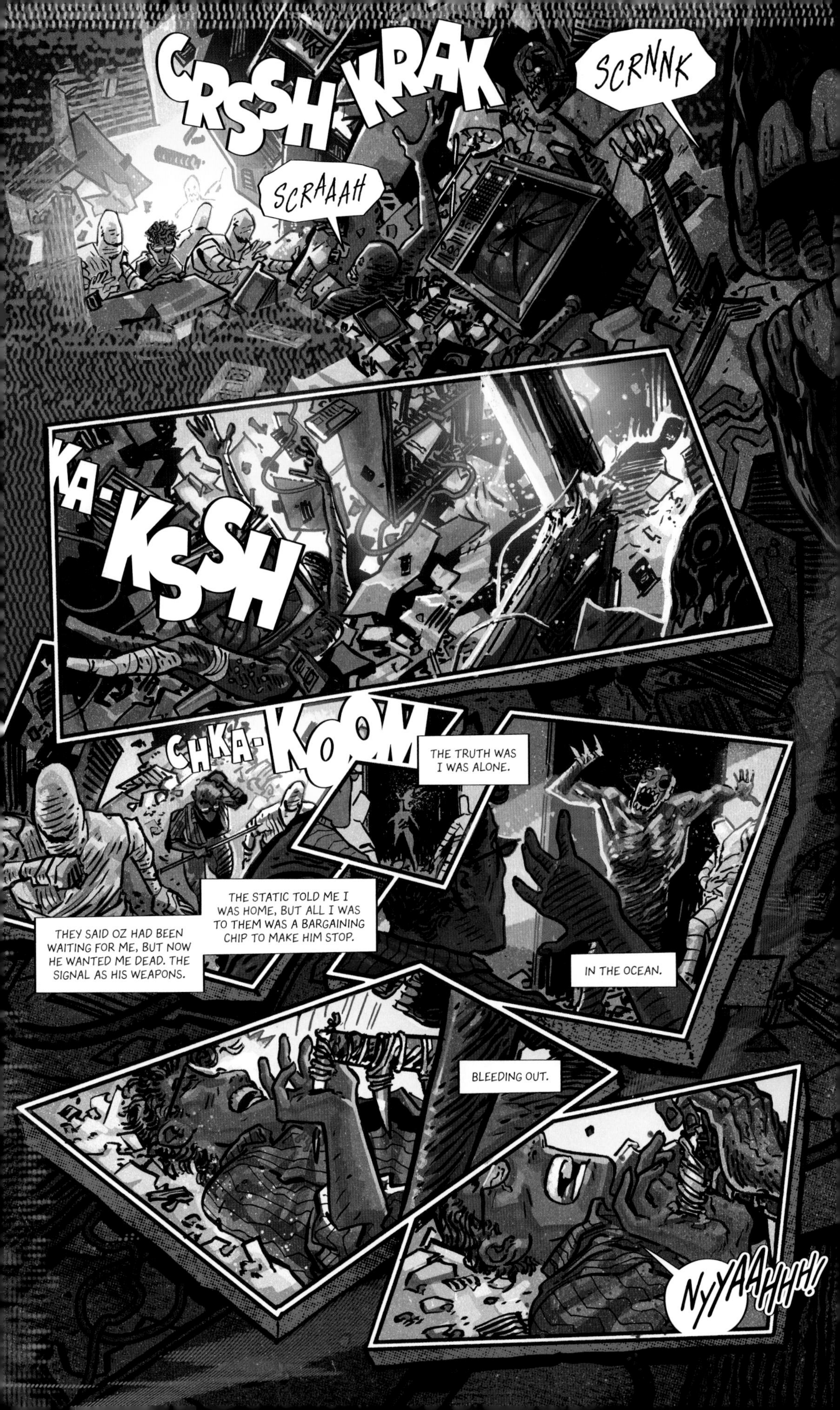
CRSSH KRAK
SCRNNK
SCRAAAH
KA-KSSH
CHKA-KOOM
THE TRUTH WAS I WAS ALONE.
THEY SAID OZ HAD BEEN WAITING FOR ME, BUT NOW HE WANTED ME DEAD. THE SIGNAL AS HIS WEAPONS.
THE STATIC TOLD ME I WAS HOME, BUT ALL I WAS TO THEM WAS A BARGAINING CHIP TO MAKE HIM STOP.
IN THE OCEAN.
BLEEDING OUT.
NYYAAHHH!

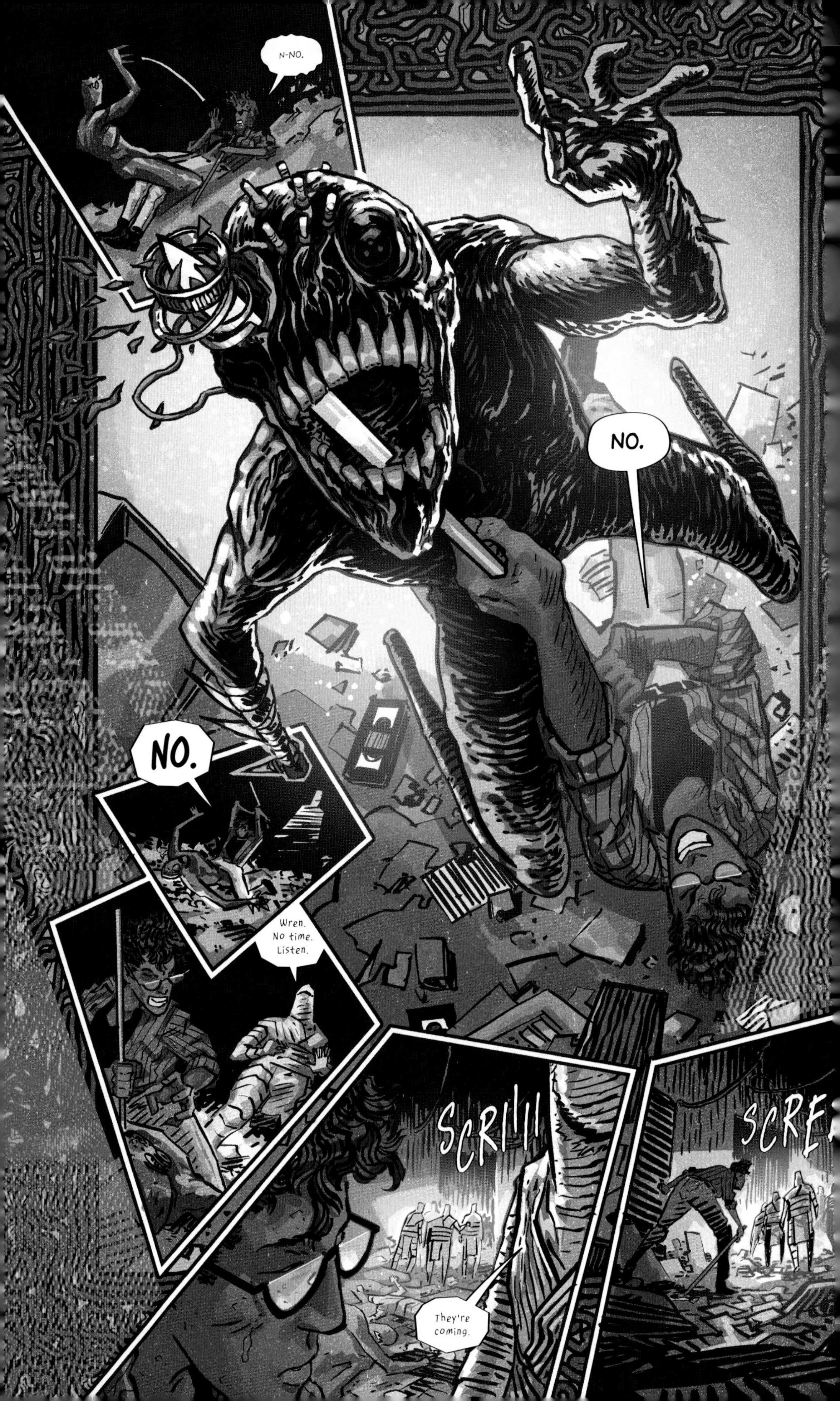
N-NO.
NO.
NO.
Wren. No time. Listen.
SCRIIII
They're coming.
SCRE

WHY THE FUCK IS NOTHING IN THIS PLACE NORMAL?
ALL THIS PLANNING AND NO ONE BROUGHT A GODDAMN LADDER?
No one has ever made it this far and returned.
THEN HELP ME DO WHAT YOU DO.
BUILD A WAY OUT.
WE WERE ESCAPING FROM A HOSTILE LAND INTO SOMETHING EVEN MORE VICIOUS. NO MAPS AND ONLY ONE DOOR IN.
SCRIIIIII
AND I WAS MEANT TO KILL THE MAN ON THE OTHER SIDE.
It's done. Go. We will follow.

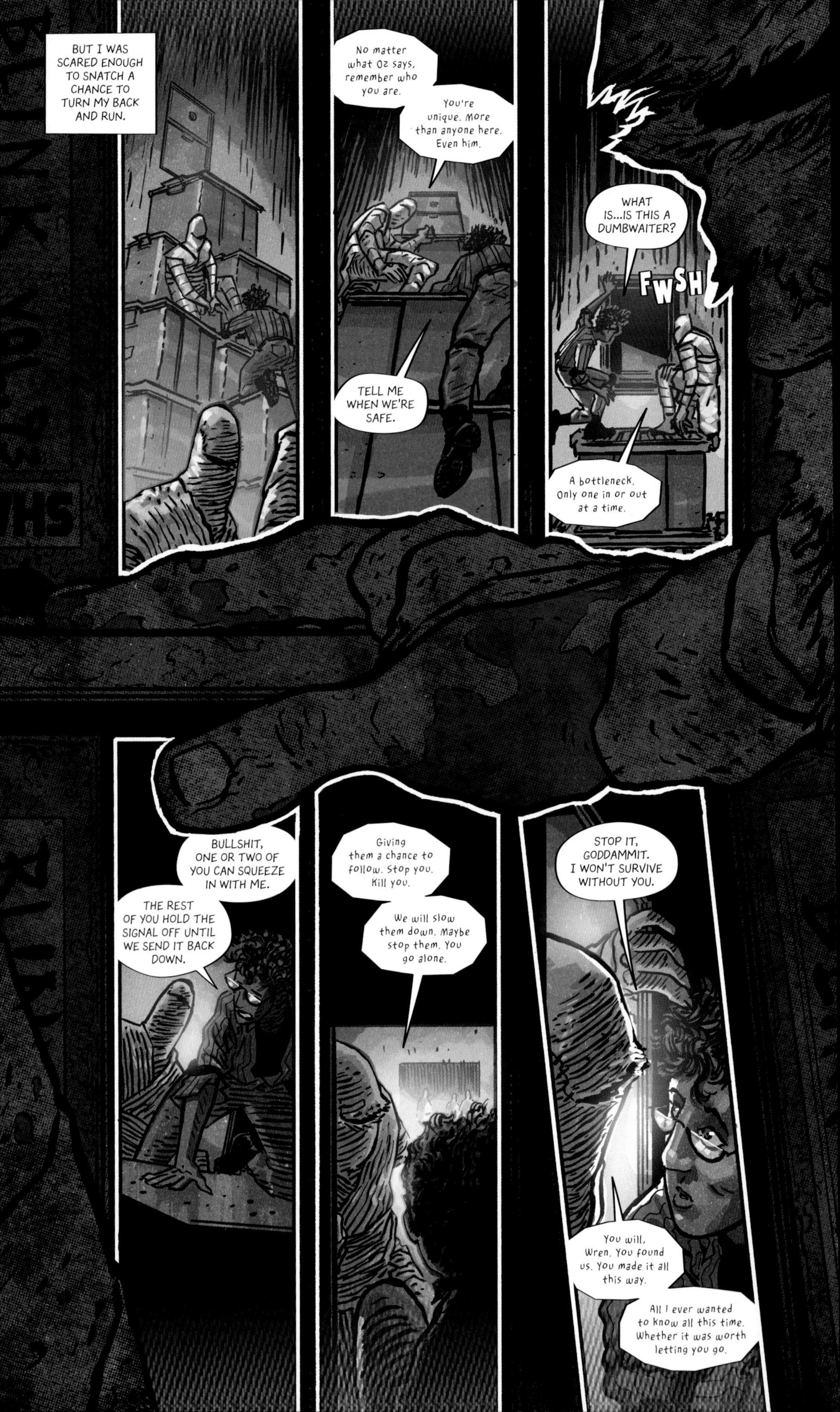
BUT I WAS SCARED ENOUGH TO SNATCH A CHANCE TO TURN MY BACK AND RUN.
No matter what Oz says, remember who you are.
You're unique. More than anyone here. Even him.
TELL ME WHEN WE'RE SAFE.
WHAT IS...IS THIS A DUMBWAITER?
FWSH
A bottleneck. Only one in or out at a time.
BULLSHIT, ONE OR TWO OF YOU CAN SQUEEZE IN WITH ME.
THE REST OF YOU HOLD THE SIGNAL OFF UNTIL WE SEND IT BACK DOWN.
Giving them a chance to follow. Stop you. Kill you.
We will slow them down. Maybe stop them. You go alone.
STOP IT, GODDAMMIT. I WON'T SURVIVE WITHOUT YOU.
You will, Wren. You found us. You made it all this way.
All I ever wanted to know all this time. Whether it was worth letting you go.

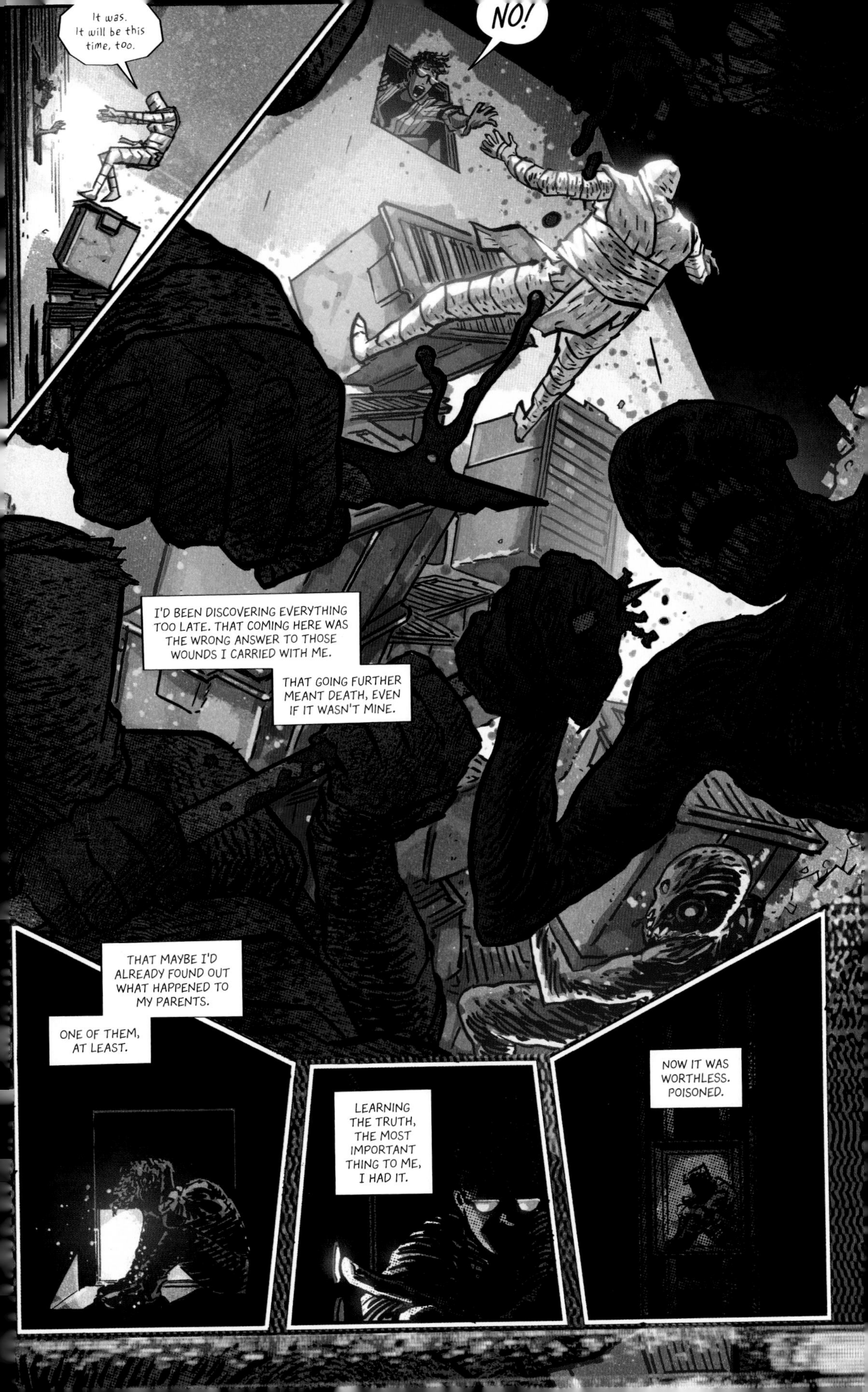
It was.
It will be this time, too.
NO!
I'D BEEN DISCOVERING EVERYTHING TOO LATE. THAT COMING HERE WAS THE WRONG ANSWER TO THOSE WOUNDS I CARRIED WITH ME.
THAT GOING FURTHER MEANT DEATH, EVEN IF IT WASN'T MINE.
THAT MAYBE I'D ALREADY FOUND OUT WHAT HAPPENED TO MY PARENTS.
ONE OF THEM, AT LEAST.
LEARNING THE TRUTH, THE MOST IMPORTANT THING TO ME, I HAD IT.
NOW IT WAS WORTHLESS. POISONED.

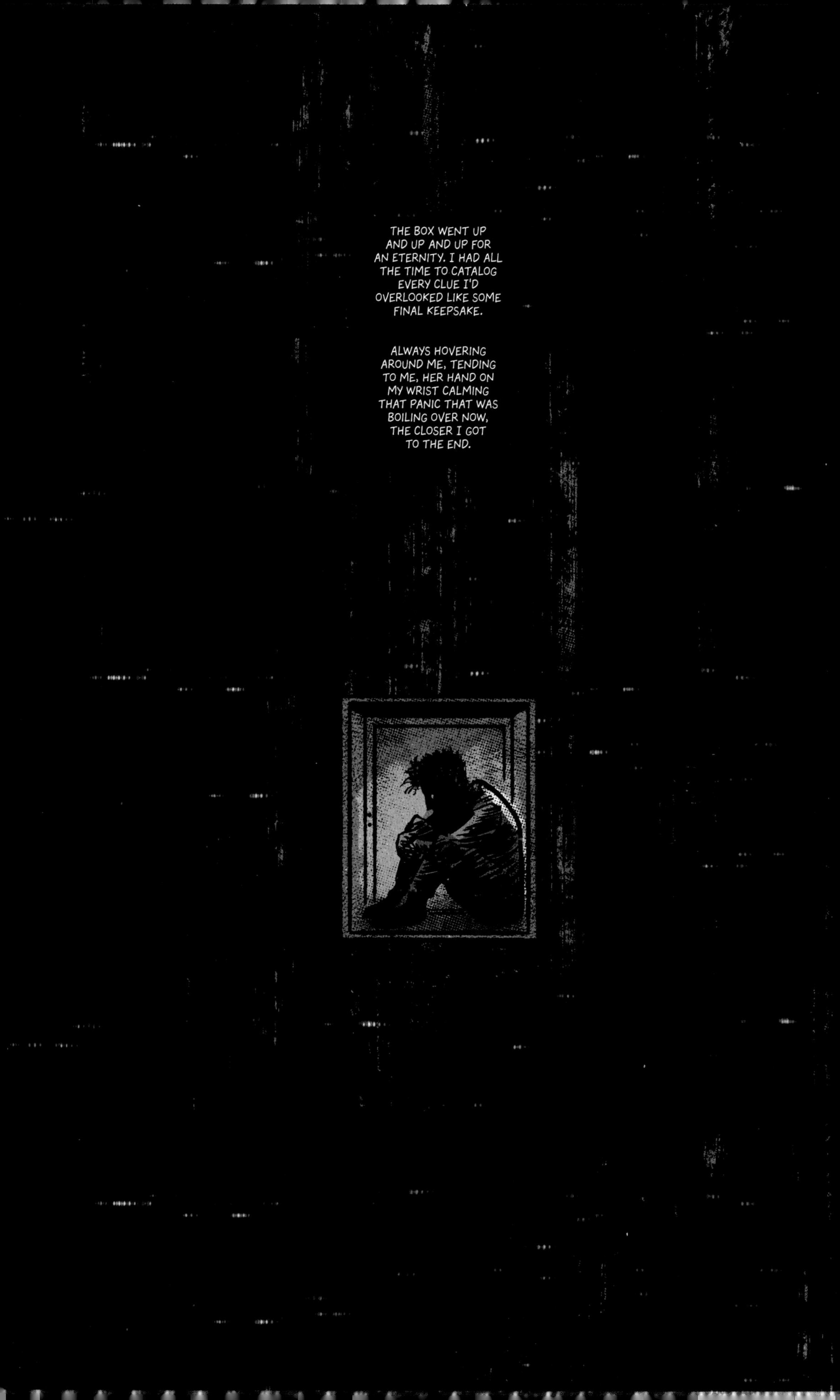
THE BOX WENT UP AND UP AND UP FOR AN ETERNITY. I HAD ALL THE TIME TO CATALOG EVERY CLUE I'D OVERLOOKED LIKE SOME FINAL KEEPSAKE.
ALWAYS HOVERING AROUND ME, TENDING TO ME, HER HAND ON MY WRIST CALMING THAT PANIC THAT WAS BOILING OVER NOW, THE CLOSER I GOT TO THE END.

THEN ENOUGH TIME
TO TAMP THOSE
THOUGHTS DOWN AND
REPLACE THEM WITH
ANGER. MY GOOD HAND
A FIST, FOLDING AND
UNFOLDING.

I'D FOUND
EVERYTHING I'D
WANTED.

IT WAS
TIME FOR WHAT
I NEEDED.

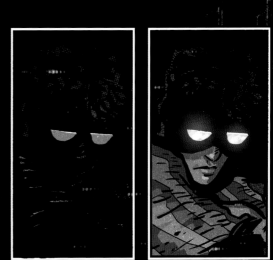

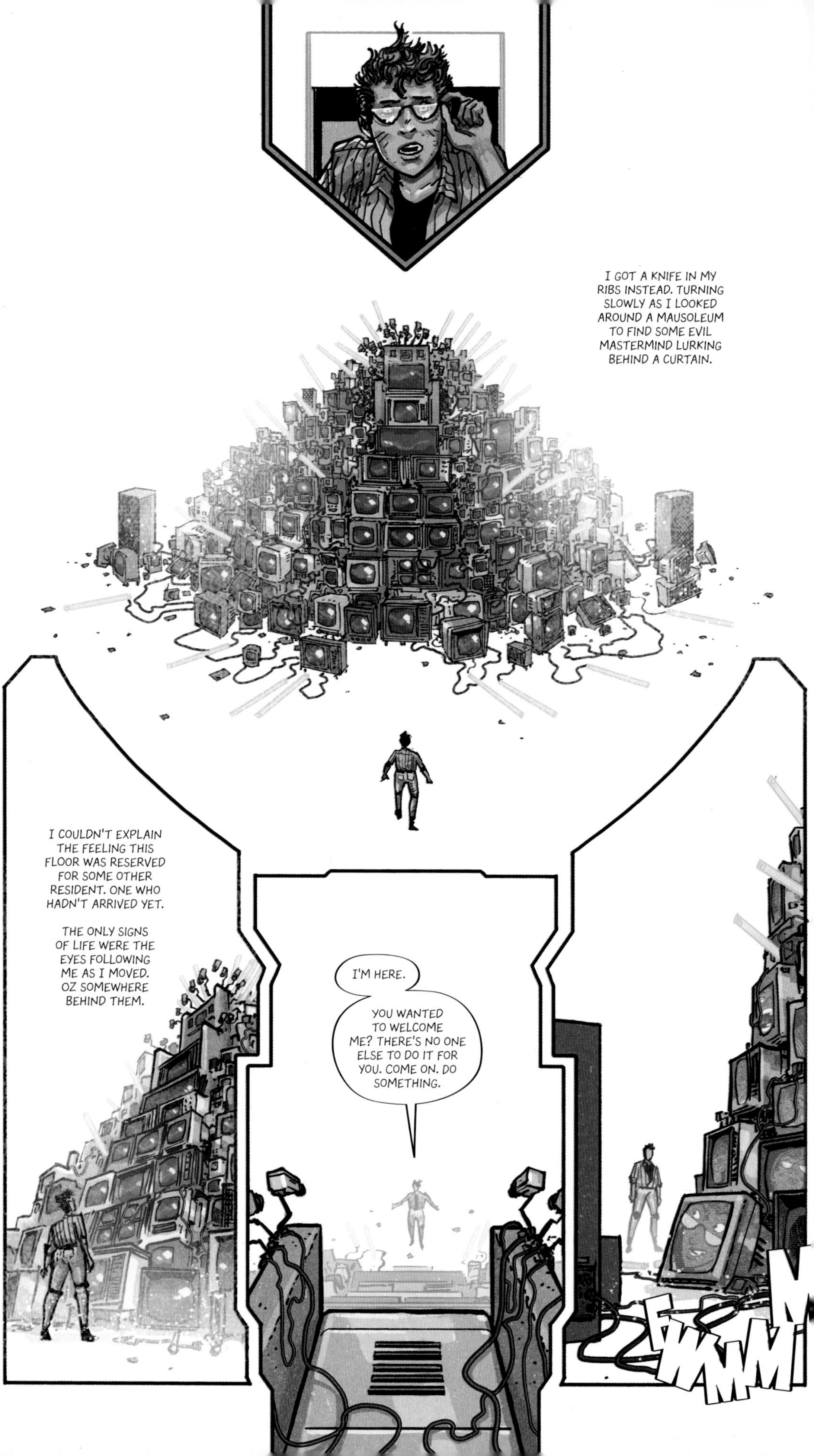
I GOT A KNIFE IN MY RIBS INSTEAD. TURNING SLOWLY AS I LOOKED AROUND A MAUSOLEUM TO FIND SOME EVIL MASTERMIND LURKING BEHIND A CURTAIN.
I COULDN'T EXPLAIN THE FEELING THIS FLOOR WAS RESERVED FOR SOME OTHER RESIDENT. ONE WHO HADN'T ARRIVED YET.
THE ONLY SIGNS OF LIFE WERE THE EYES FOLLOWING ME AS I MOVED. OZ SOMEWHERE BEHIND THEM.
I'M HERE.
YOU WANTED TO WELCOME ME? THERE'S NO ONE ELSE TO DO IT FOR YOU. COME ON. DO SOMETHING.

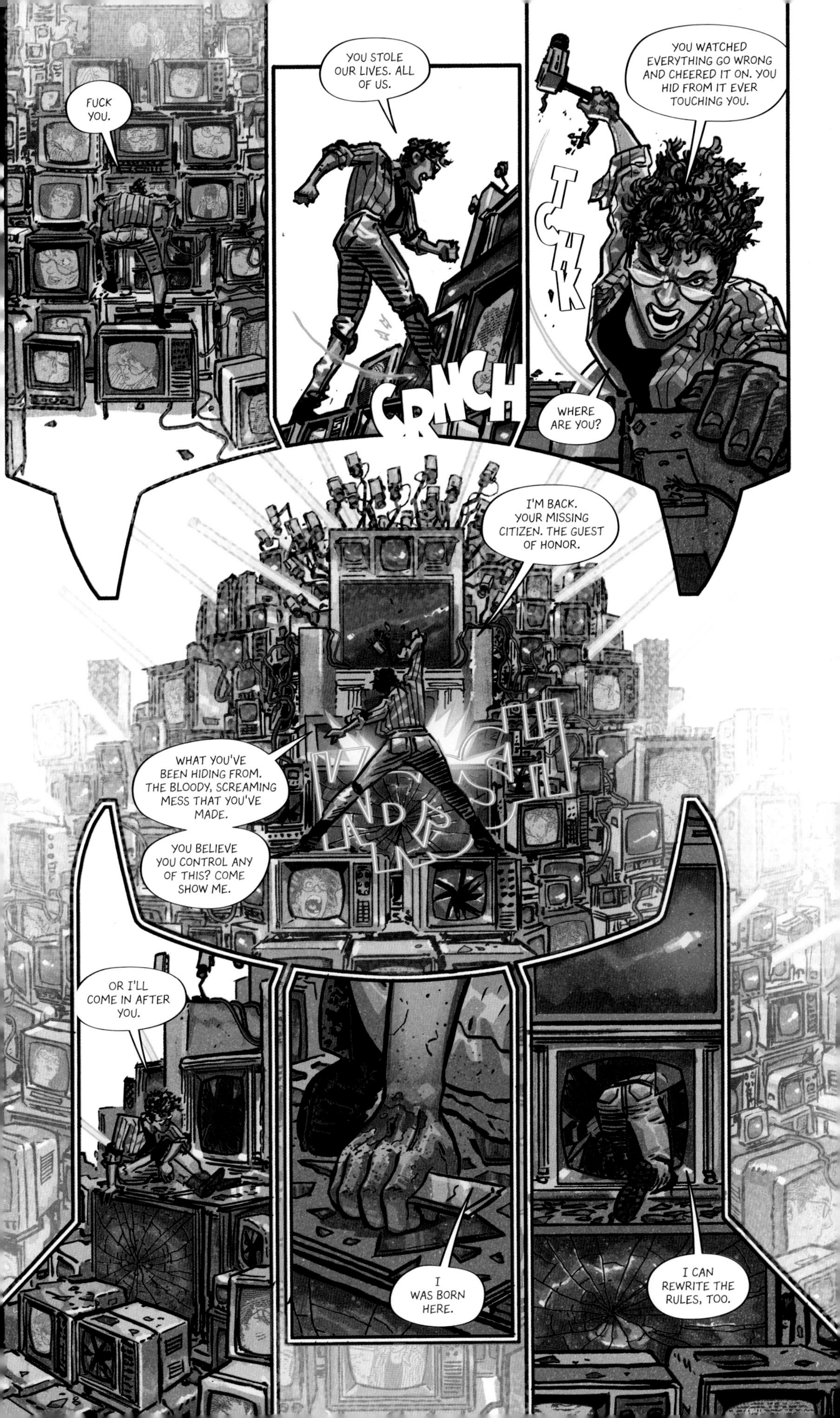
FUCK YOU.
YOU STOLE OUR LIVES. ALL OF US.
CRNCH
YOU WATCHED EVERYTHING GO WRONG AND CHEERED IT ON. YOU HID FROM IT EVER TOUCHING YOU.
TCHK
WHERE ARE YOU?
I'M BACK. YOUR MISSING CITIZEN. THE GUEST OF HONOR.
WHAT YOU'VE BEEN HIDING FROM. THE BLOODY, SCREAMING MESS THAT YOU'VE MADE.
YOU BELIEVE YOU CONTROL ANY OF THIS? COME SHOW ME.
OR I'LL COME IN AFTER YOU.
I WAS BORN HERE.
I CAN REWRITE THE RULES, TOO.

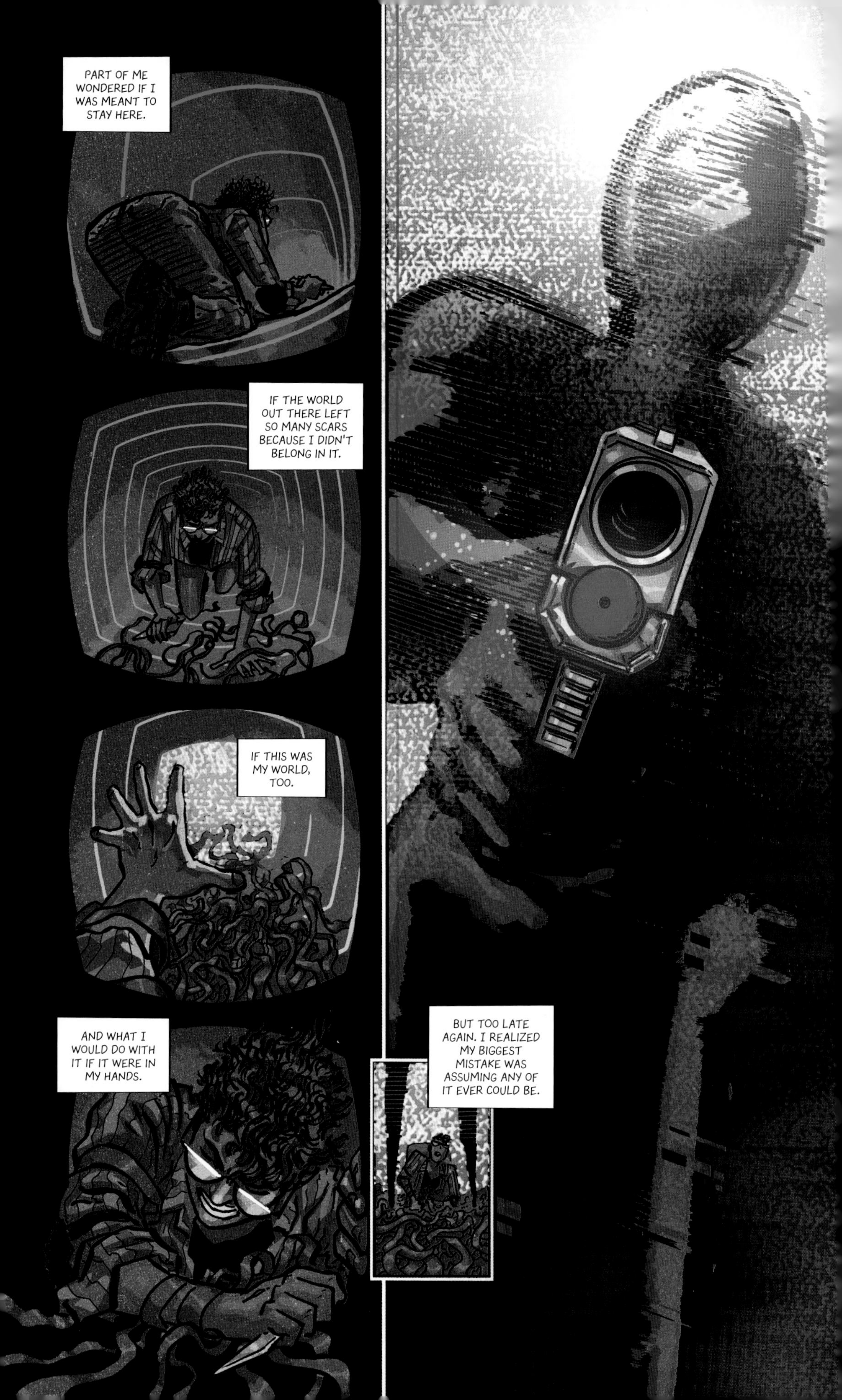
PART OF ME WONDERED IF I WAS MEANT TO STAY HERE.
IF THE WORLD OUT THERE LEFT SO MANY SCARS BECAUSE I DIDN'T BELONG IN IT.
IF THIS WAS MY WORLD, TOO.
AND WHAT I WOULD DO WITH IT IF IT WERE IN MY HANDS.
BUT TOO LATE AGAIN. I REALIZED MY BIGGEST MISTAKE WAS ASSUMING ANY OF IT EVER COULD BE.

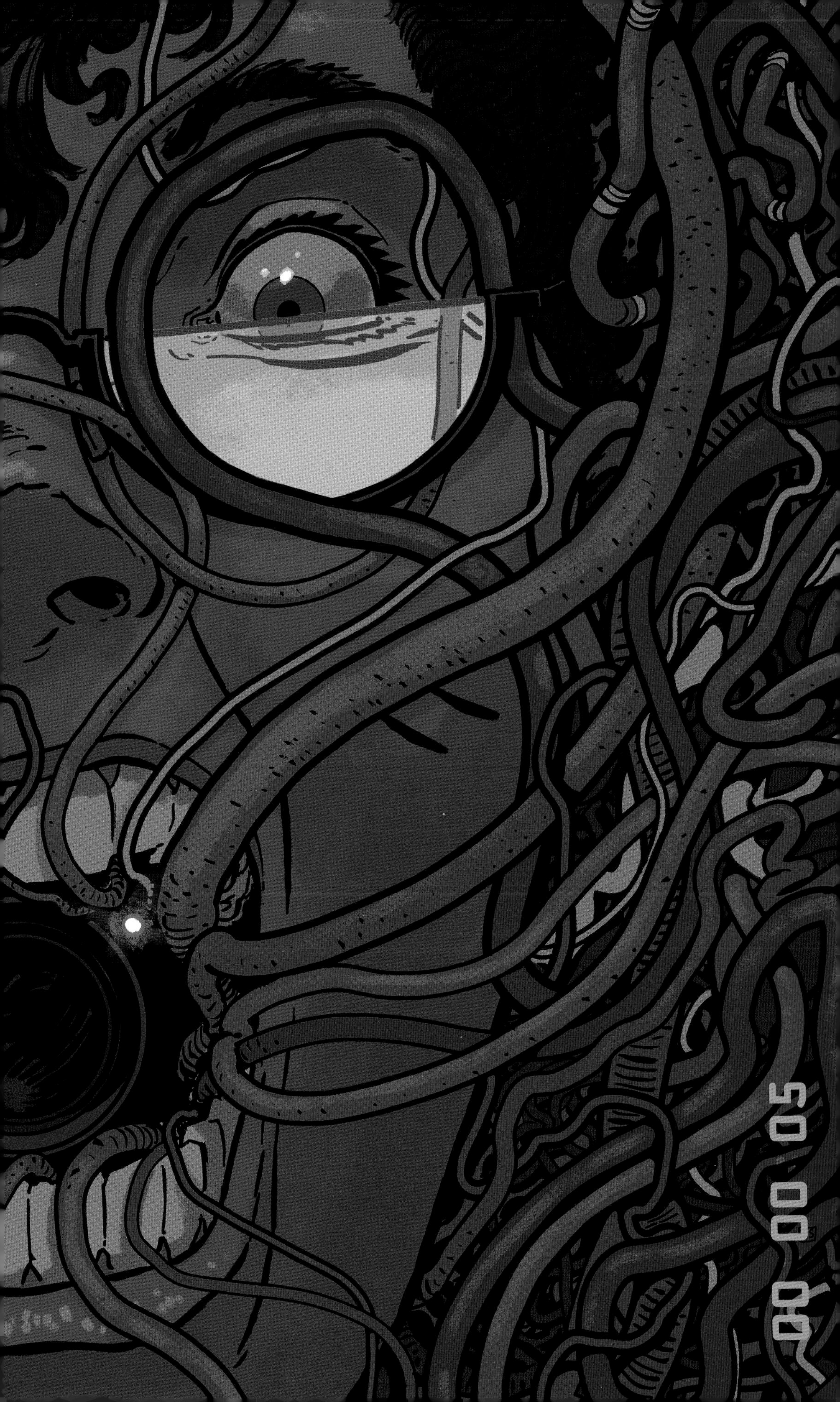
00 00 05

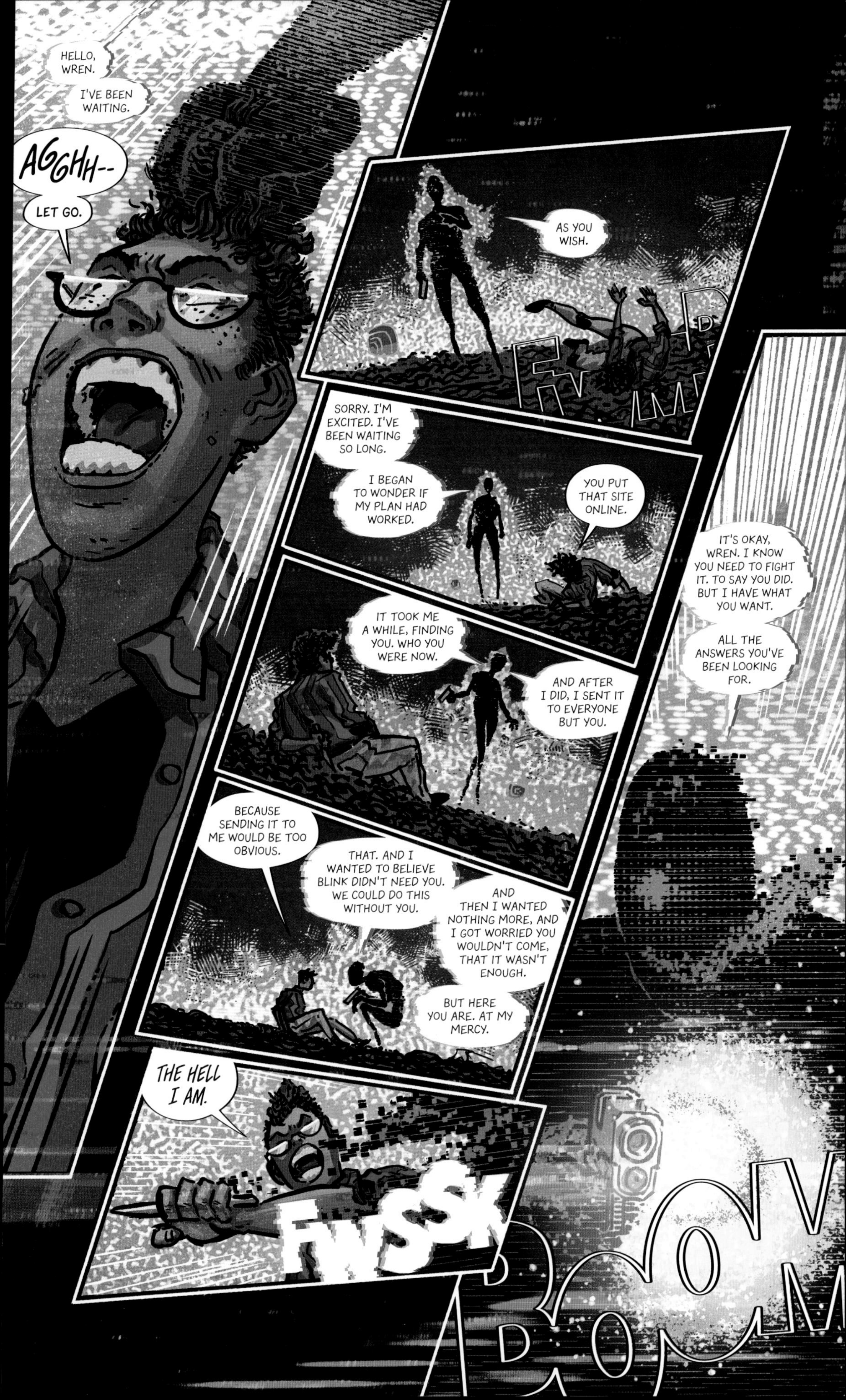
HELLO, WREN.
I'VE BEEN WAITING.
AGGHH--
LET GO.
AS YOU WISH.
SORRY. I'M EXCITED. I'VE BEEN WAITING SO LONG.
I BEGAN TO WONDER IF MY PLAN HAD WORKED.
YOU PUT THAT SITE ONLINE.
IT TOOK ME A WHILE, FINDING YOU. WHO YOU WERE NOW.
AND AFTER I DID, I SENT IT TO EVERYONE BUT YOU.
BECAUSE SENDING IT TO ME WOULD BE TOO OBVIOUS.
THAT. AND I WANTED TO BELIEVE BLINK DIDN'T NEED YOU. WE COULD DO THIS WITHOUT YOU.
AND THEN I WANTED NOTHING MORE, AND I GOT WORRIED YOU WOULDN'T COME, THAT IT WASN'T ENOUGH.
BUT HERE YOU ARE. AT MY MERCY.
IT'S OKAY, WREN. I KNOW YOU NEED TO FIGHT IT. TO SAY YOU DID. BUT I HAVE WHAT YOU WANT.
ALL THE ANSWERS YOU'VE BEEN LOOKING FOR.
THE HELL I AM.
FWSSK
BOOM

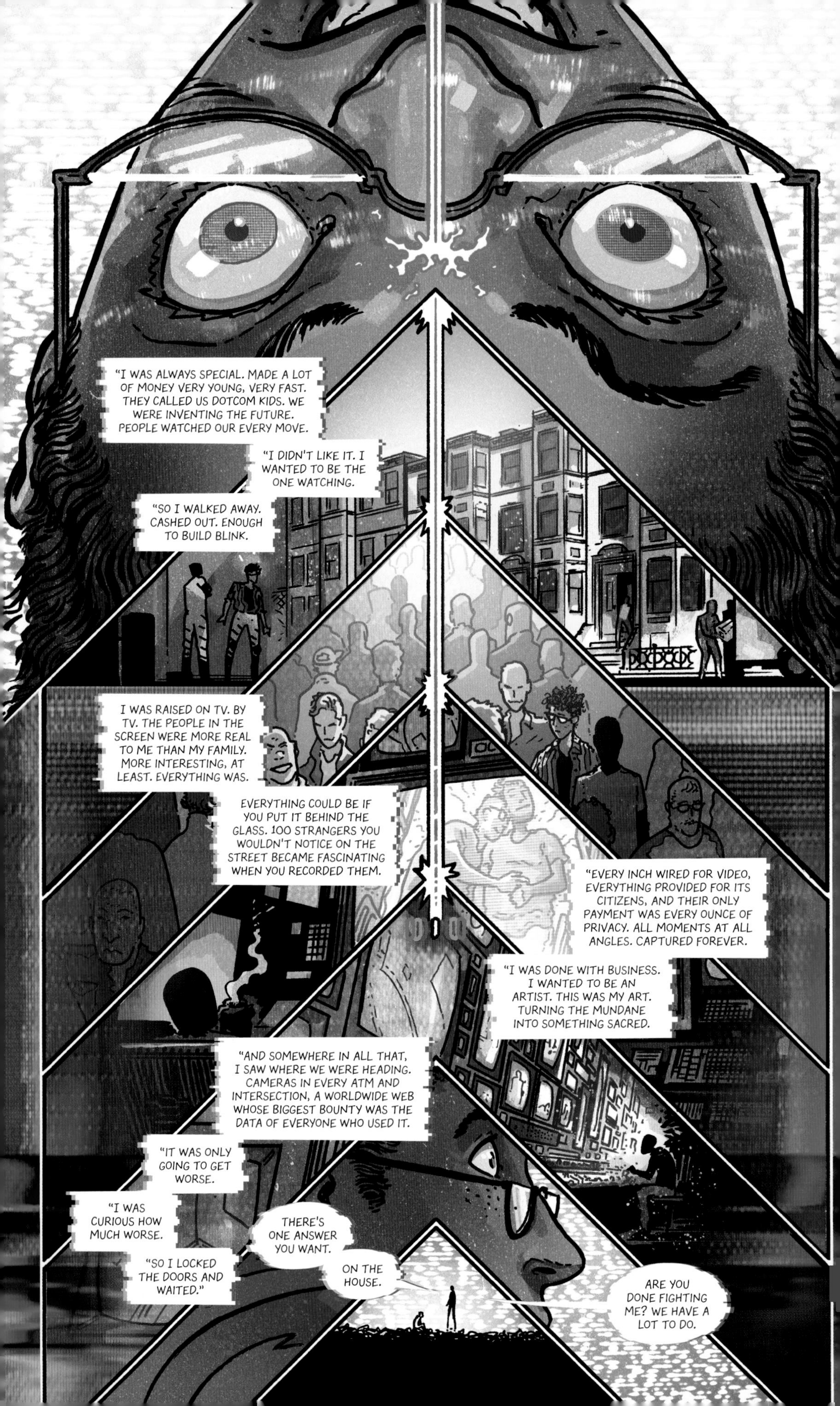
"I WAS ALWAYS SPECIAL. MADE A LOT OF MONEY VERY YOUNG, VERY FAST. THEY CALLED US DOTCOM KIDS. WE WERE INVENTING THE FUTURE. PEOPLE WATCHED OUR EVERY MOVE.
"I DIDN'T LIKE IT. I WANTED TO BE THE ONE WATCHING.
"SO I WALKED AWAY. CASHED OUT. ENOUGH TO BUILD BLINK.
I WAS RAISED ON TV. BY TV. THE PEOPLE IN THE SCREEN WERE MORE REAL TO ME THAN MY FAMILY. MORE INTERESTING, AT LEAST. EVERYTHING WAS.
EVERYTHING COULD BE IF YOU PUT IT BEHIND THE GLASS. 100 STRANGERS YOU WOULDN'T NOTICE ON THE STREET BECAME FASCINATING WHEN YOU RECORDED THEM.
"EVERY INCH WIRED FOR VIDEO, EVERYTHING PROVIDED FOR ITS CITIZENS, AND THEIR ONLY PAYMENT WAS EVERY OUNCE OF PRIVACY. ALL MOMENTS AT ALL ANGLES. CAPTURED FOREVER.
"I WAS DONE WITH BUSINESS. I WANTED TO BE AN ARTIST. THIS WAS MY ART. TURNING THE MUNDANE INTO SOMETHING SACRED.
"AND SOMEWHERE IN ALL THAT, I SAW WHERE WE WERE HEADING. CAMERAS IN EVERY ATM AND INTERSECTION, A WORLDWIDE WEB WHOSE BIGGEST BOUNTY WAS THE DATA OF EVERYONE WHO USED IT.
"IT WAS ONLY GOING TO GET WORSE.
"I WAS CURIOUS HOW MUCH WORSE.
"SO I LOCKED THE DOORS AND WAITED."
THERE'S ONE ANSWER YOU WANT.
ON THE HOUSE.
ARE YOU DONE FIGHTING ME? WE HAVE A LOT TO DO.

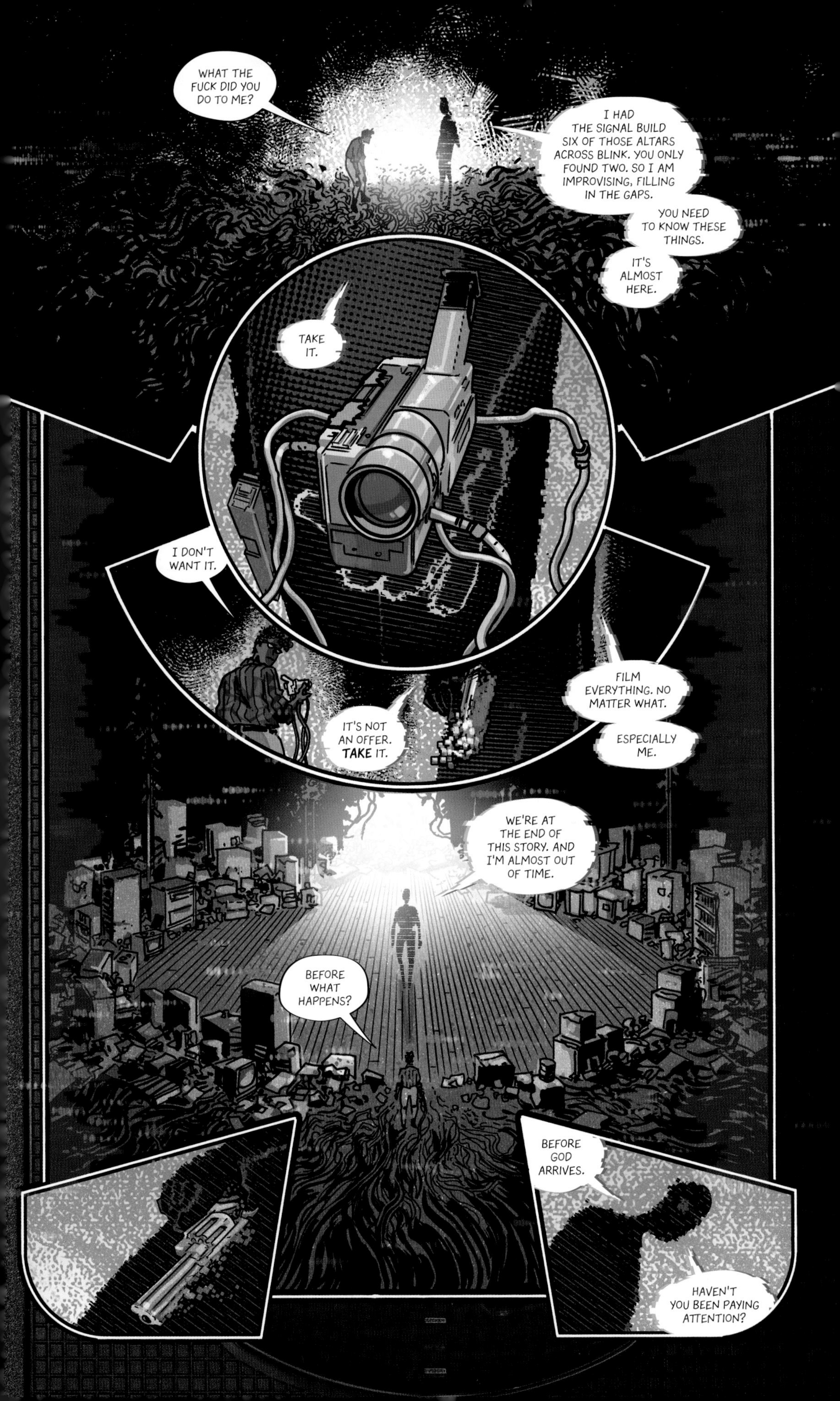
WHAT THE FUCK DID YOU DO TO ME?
I HAD THE SIGNAL BUILD SIX OF THOSE ALTARS ACROSS BLINK. YOU ONLY FOUND TWO. SO I AM IMPROVISING, FILLING IN THE GAPS.
YOU NEED TO KNOW THESE THINGS.
IT'S ALMOST HERE.
TAKE IT.
I DON'T WANT IT.
IT'S NOT AN OFFER. **TAKE** IT.
FILM EVERYTHING. NO MATTER WHAT.
ESPECIALLY ME.
WE'RE AT THE END OF THIS STORY. AND I'M ALMOST OUT OF TIME.
BEFORE WHAT HAPPENS?
BEFORE GOD ARRIVES.
HAVEN'T YOU BEEN PAYING ATTENTION?

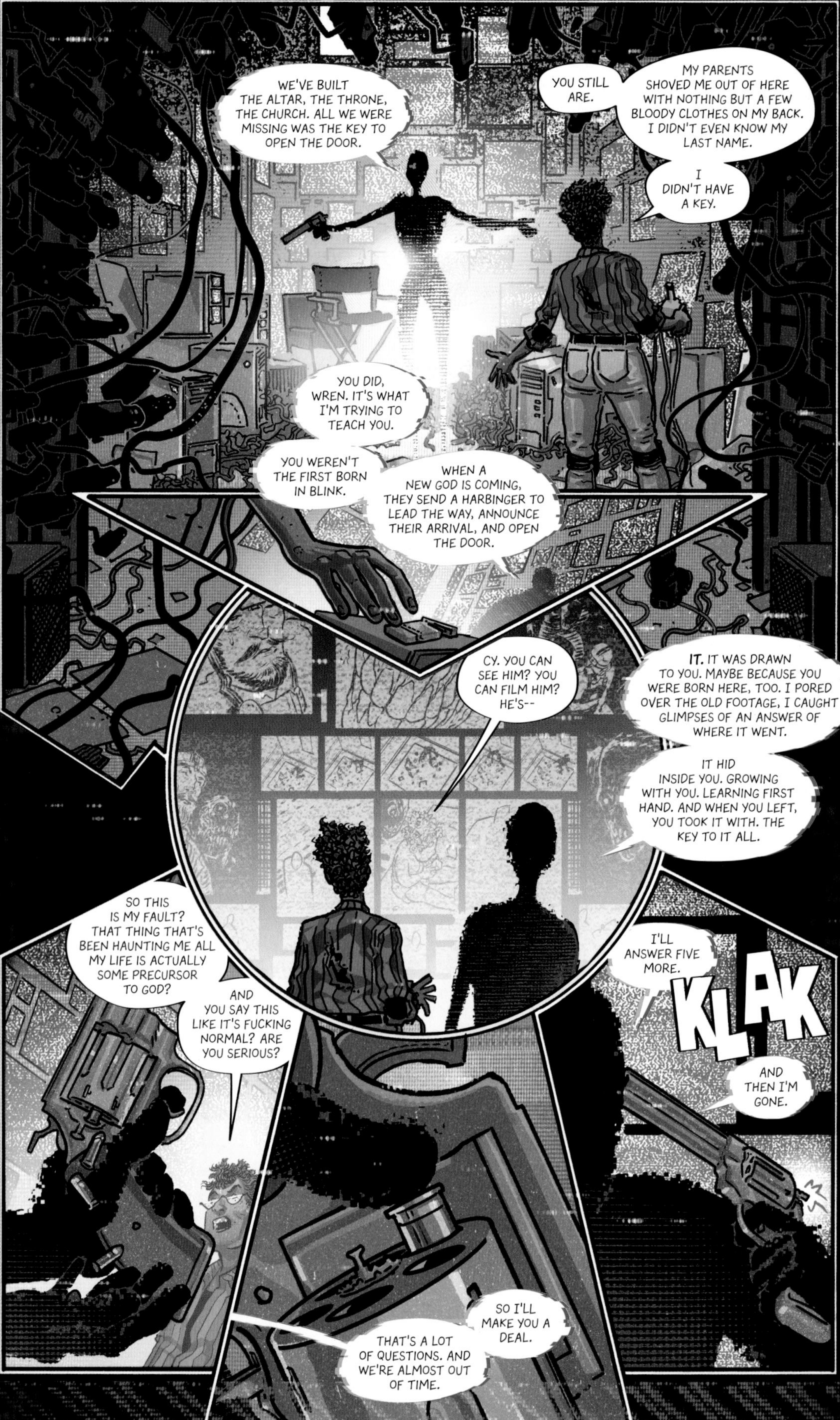
WE'VE BUILT THE ALTAR, THE THRONE, THE CHURCH. ALL WE WERE MISSING WAS THE KEY TO OPEN THE DOOR.
YOU STILL ARE.
MY PARENTS SHOVED ME OUT OF HERE WITH NOTHING BUT A FEW BLOODY CLOTHES ON MY BACK. I DIDN'T EVEN KNOW MY LAST NAME.
I DIDN'T HAVE A KEY.
YOU DID, WREN. IT'S WHAT I'M TRYING TO TEACH YOU.
YOU WEREN'T THE FIRST BORN IN BLINK.
WHEN A NEW GOD IS COMING, THEY SEND A HARBINGER TO LEAD THE WAY, ANNOUNCE THEIR ARRIVAL, AND OPEN THE DOOR.
CY. YOU CAN SEE HIM? YOU CAN FILM HIM? HE'S--
IT. IT WAS DRAWN TO YOU. MAYBE BECAUSE YOU WERE BORN HERE, TOO. I PORED OVER THE OLD FOOTAGE, I CAUGHT GLIMPSES OF AN ANSWER OF WHERE IT WENT.
IT HID INSIDE YOU. GROWING WITH YOU. LEARNING FIRST HAND. AND WHEN YOU LEFT, YOU TOOK IT WITH. THE KEY TO IT ALL.
SO THIS IS MY FAULT? THAT THING THAT'S BEEN HAUNTING ME ALL MY LIFE IS ACTUALLY SOME PRECURSOR TO GOD?
AND YOU SAY THIS LIKE IT'S FUCKING NORMAL? ARE YOU SERIOUS?
THAT'S A LOT OF QUESTIONS. AND WE'RE ALMOST OUT OF TIME.
SO I'LL MAKE YOU A DEAL.
I'LL ANSWER FIVE MORE.
KLAK
AND THEN I'M GONE.

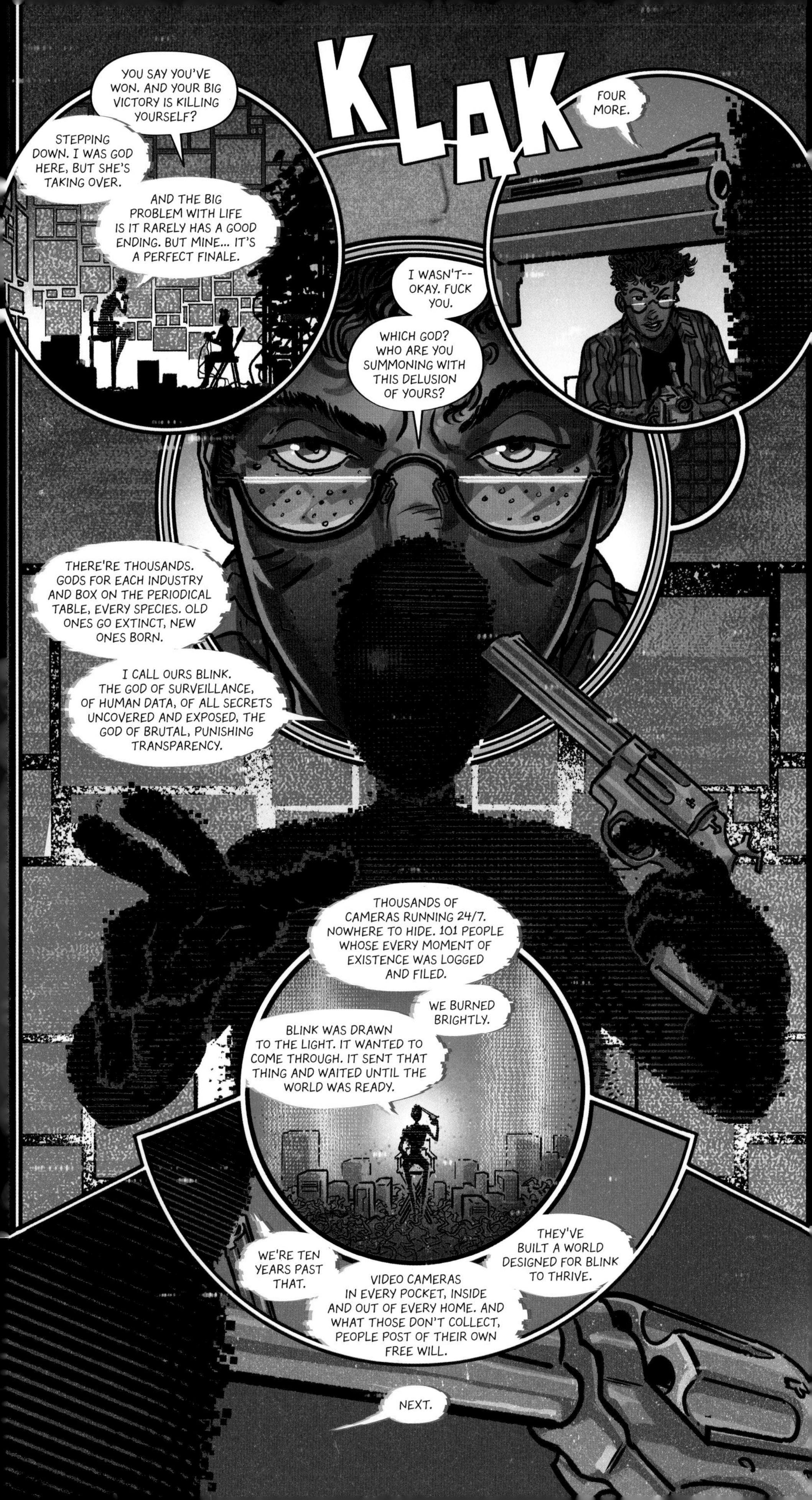
KLAK
YOU SAY YOU'VE WON. AND YOUR BIG VICTORY IS KILLING YOURSELF?
STEPPING DOWN. I WAS GOD HERE, BUT SHE'S TAKING OVER.
AND THE BIG PROBLEM WITH LIFE IS IT RARELY HAS A GOOD ENDING. BUT MINE... IT'S A PERFECT FINALE.
FOUR MORE.
I WASN'T-- OKAY. FUCK YOU.
WHICH GOD? WHO ARE YOU SUMMONING WITH THIS DELUSION OF YOURS?
THERE'RE THOUSANDS. GODS FOR EACH INDUSTRY AND BOX ON THE PERIODICAL TABLE, EVERY SPECIES. OLD ONES GO EXTINCT, NEW ONES BORN.
I CALL OURS BLINK. THE GOD OF SURVEILLANCE, OF HUMAN DATA, OF ALL SECRETS UNCOVERED AND EXPOSED, THE GOD OF BRUTAL, PUNISHING TRANSPARENCY.
THOUSANDS OF CAMERAS RUNNING 24/7. NOWHERE TO HIDE. 101 PEOPLE WHOSE EVERY MOMENT OF EXISTENCE WAS LOGGED AND FILED.
WE BURNED BRIGHTLY.
BLINK WAS DRAWN TO THE LIGHT. IT WANTED TO COME THROUGH. IT SENT THAT THING AND WAITED UNTIL THE WORLD WAS READY.
WE'RE TEN YEARS PAST THAT.
THEY'VE BUILT A WORLD DESIGNED FOR BLINK TO THRIVE.
VIDEO CAMERAS IN EVERY POCKET, INSIDE AND OUT OF EVERY HOME. AND WHAT THOSE DON'T COLLECT, PEOPLE POST OF THEIR OWN FREE WILL.
NEXT.

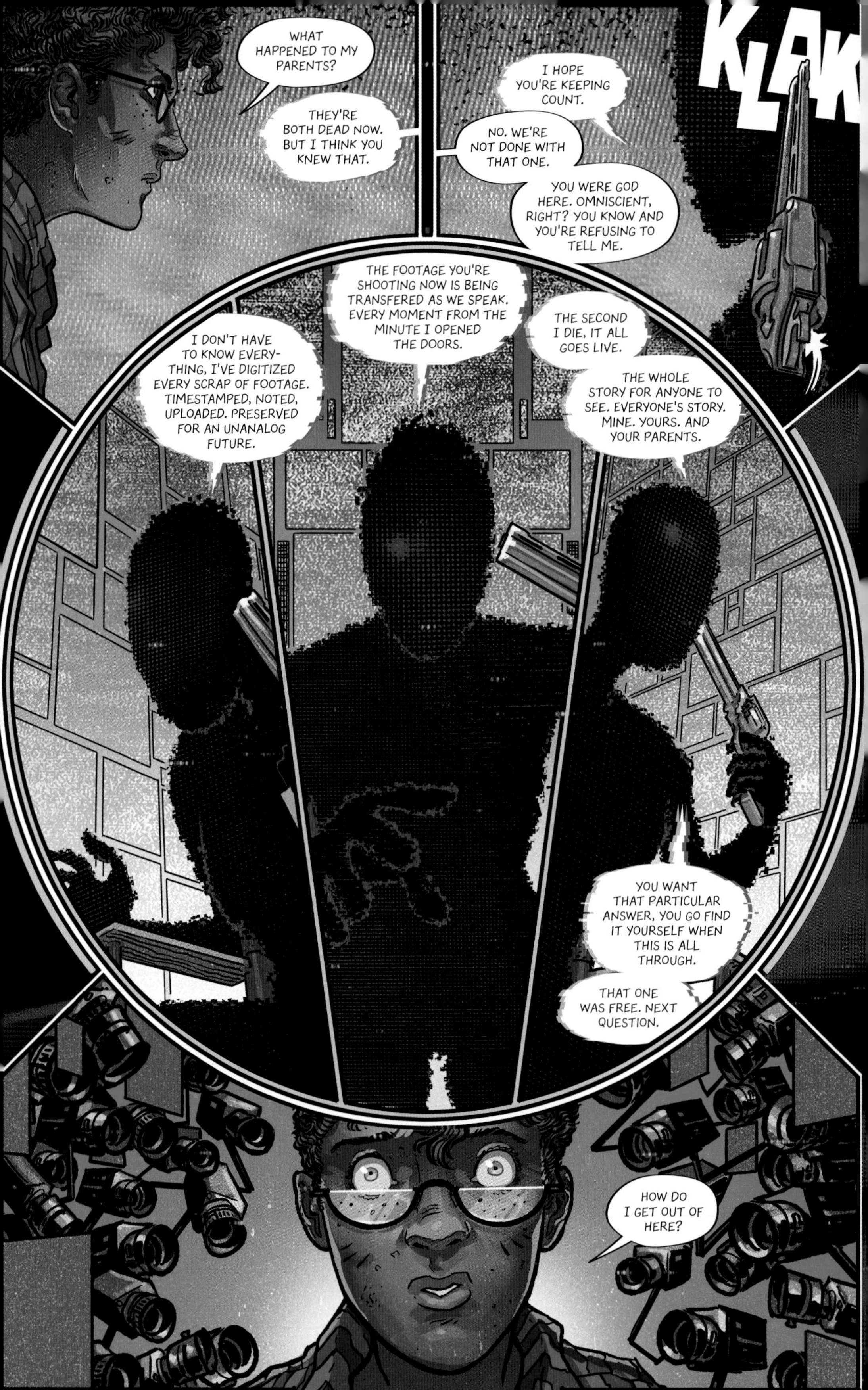
WHAT HAPPENED TO MY PARENTS?
THEY'RE BOTH DEAD NOW. BUT I THINK YOU KNEW THAT.
KLAK
I HOPE YOU'RE KEEPING COUNT.
NO. WE'RE NOT DONE WITH THAT ONE.
YOU WERE GOD HERE. OMNISCIENT, RIGHT? YOU KNOW AND YOU'RE REFUSING TO TELL ME.
I DON'T HAVE TO KNOW EVERY-THING, I'VE DIGITIZED EVERY SCRAP OF FOOTAGE. TIMESTAMPED, NOTED, UPLOADED. PRESERVED FOR AN UNANALOG FUTURE.
THE FOOTAGE YOU'RE SHOOTING NOW IS BEING TRANSFERED AS WE SPEAK. EVERY MOMENT FROM THE MINUTE I OPENED THE DOORS.
THE SECOND I DIE, IT ALL GOES LIVE.
THE WHOLE STORY FOR ANYONE TO SEE. EVERYONE'S STORY. MINE. YOURS. AND YOUR PARENTS.
YOU WANT THAT PARTICULAR ANSWER, YOU GO FIND IT YOURSELF WHEN THIS IS ALL THROUGH.
THAT ONE WAS FREE. NEXT QUESTION.
HOW DO I GET OUT OF HERE?

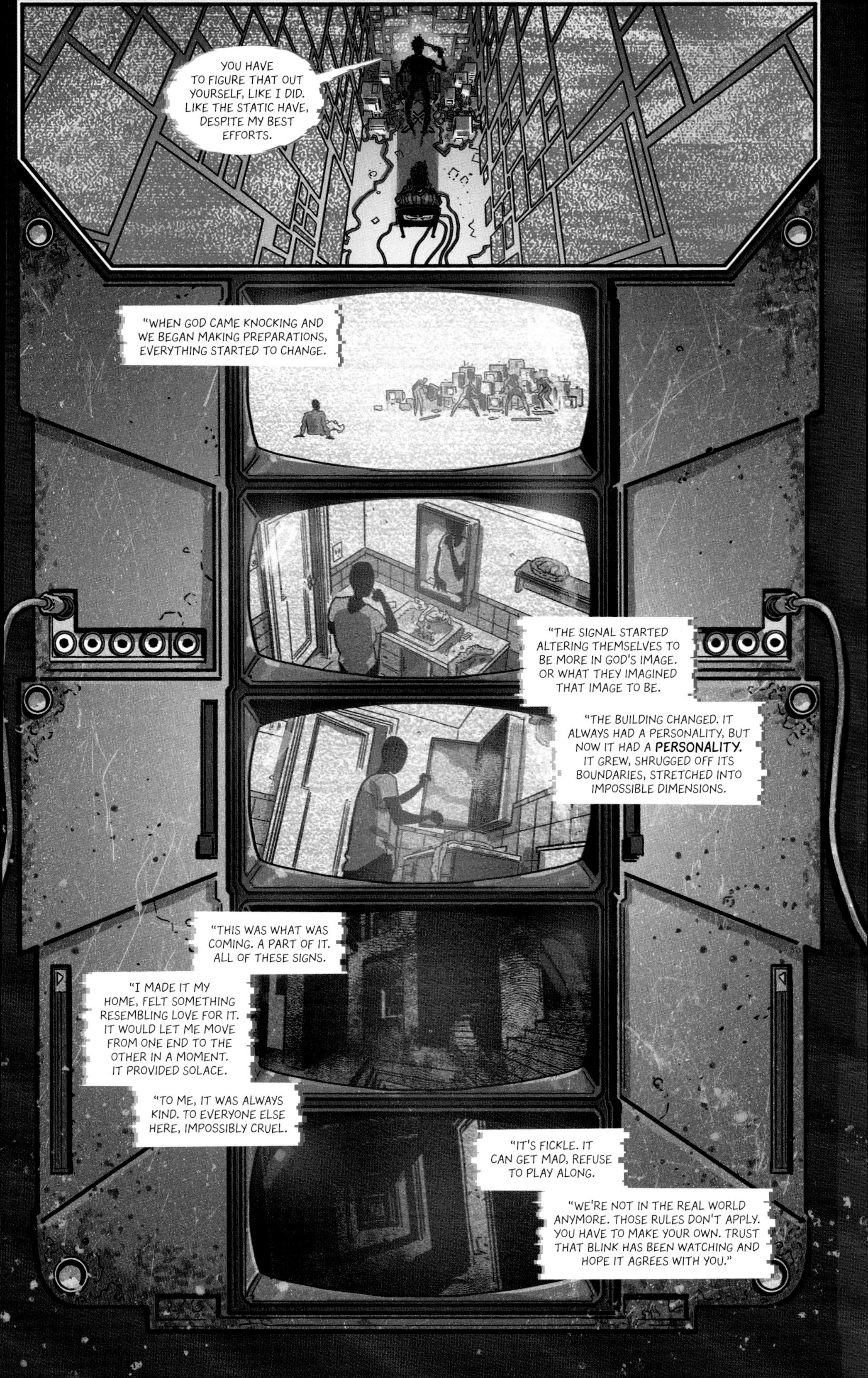
YOU HAVE TO FIGURE THAT OUT YOURSELF, LIKE I DID. LIKE THE STATIC HAVE, DESPITE MY BEST EFFORTS.
"WHEN GOD CAME KNOCKING AND WE BEGAN MAKING PREPARATIONS, EVERYTHING STARTED TO CHANGE.
"THE SIGNAL STARTED ALTERING THEMSELVES TO BE MORE IN GOD'S IMAGE. OR WHAT THEY IMAGINED THAT IMAGE TO BE.
"THE BUILDING CHANGED. IT ALWAYS HAD A PERSONALITY, BUT NOW IT HAD A **PERSONALITY.** IT GREW, SHRUGGED OFF ITS BOUNDARIES, STRETCHED INTO IMPOSSIBLE DIMENSIONS.
"THIS WAS WHAT WAS COMING. A PART OF IT. ALL OF THESE SIGNS.
"I MADE IT MY HOME, FELT SOMETHING RESEMBLING LOVE FOR IT. IT WOULD LET ME MOVE FROM ONE END TO THE OTHER IN A MOMENT. IT PROVIDED SOLACE.
"TO ME, IT WAS ALWAYS KIND. TO EVERYONE ELSE HERE, IMPOSSIBLY CRUEL.
"IT'S FICKLE. IT CAN GET MAD, REFUSE TO PLAY ALONG.
"WE'RE NOT IN THE REAL WORLD ANYMORE. THOSE RULES DON'T APPLY. YOU HAVE TO MAKE YOUR OWN. TRUST THAT BLINK HAS BEEN WATCHING AND HOPE IT AGREES WITH YOU."

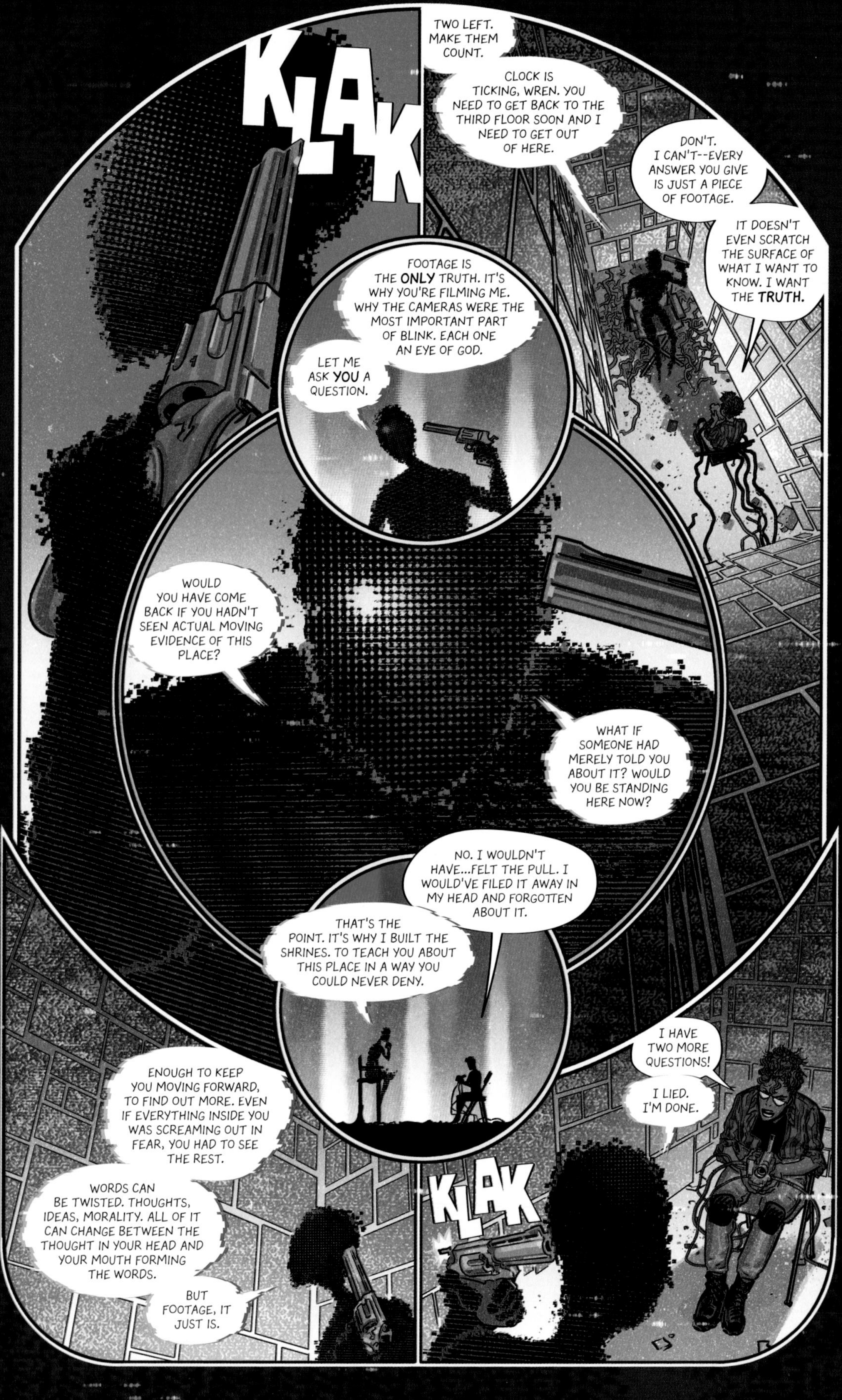
KLAK
TWO LEFT. MAKE THEM COUNT.
CLOCK IS TICKING, WREN. YOU NEED TO GET BACK TO THE THIRD FLOOR SOON AND I NEED TO GET OUT OF HERE.
DON'T. I CAN'T--EVERY ANSWER YOU GIVE IS JUST A PIECE OF FOOTAGE.
IT DOESN'T EVEN SCRATCH THE SURFACE OF WHAT I WANT TO KNOW. I WANT THE TRUTH.
FOOTAGE IS THE ONLY TRUTH. IT'S WHY YOU'RE FILMING ME. WHY THE CAMERAS WERE THE MOST IMPORTANT PART OF BLINK. EACH ONE AN EYE OF GOD.
LET ME ASK YOU A QUESTION.
WOULD YOU HAVE COME BACK IF YOU HADN'T SEEN ACTUAL MOVING EVIDENCE OF THIS PLACE?
WHAT IF SOMEONE HAD MERELY TOLD YOU ABOUT IT? WOULD YOU BE STANDING HERE NOW?
NO. I WOULDN'T HAVE...FELT THE PULL. I WOULD'VE FILED IT AWAY IN MY HEAD AND FORGOTTEN ABOUT IT.
THAT'S THE POINT. IT'S WHY I BUILT THE SHRINES. TO TEACH YOU ABOUT THIS PLACE IN A WAY YOU COULD NEVER DENY.
ENOUGH TO KEEP YOU MOVING FORWARD, TO FIND OUT MORE. EVEN IF EVERYTHING INSIDE YOU WAS SCREAMING OUT IN FEAR, YOU HAD TO SEE THE REST.
WORDS CAN BE TWISTED. THOUGHTS, IDEAS, MORALITY. ALL OF IT CAN CHANGE BETWEEN THE THOUGHT IN YOUR HEAD AND YOUR MOUTH FORMING THE WORDS.
BUT FOOTAGE, IT JUST IS.
I HAVE TWO MORE QUESTIONS!
I LIED. I'M DONE.
KLAK

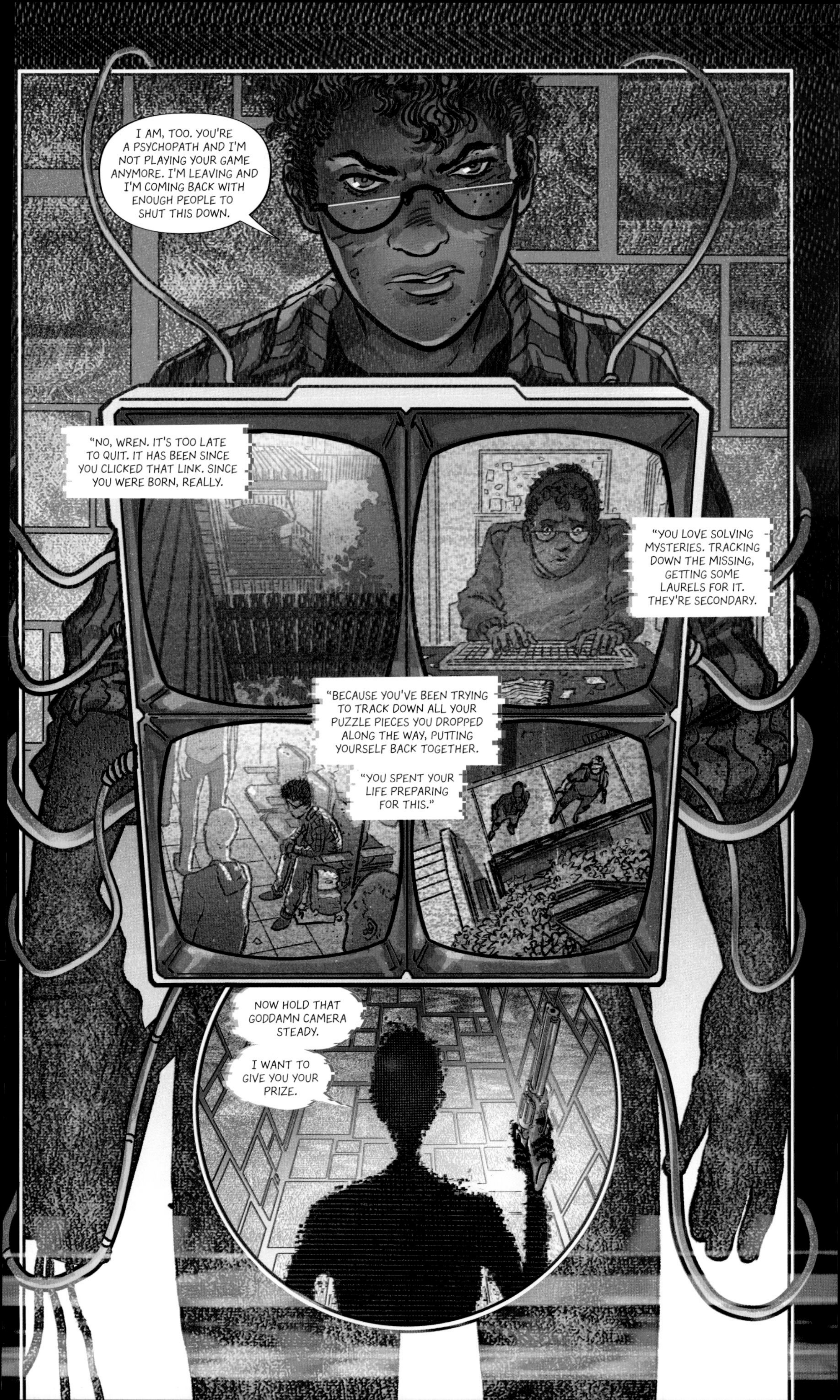
I AM, TOO. YOU'RE A PSYCHOPATH AND I'M NOT PLAYING YOUR GAME ANYMORE. I'M LEAVING AND I'M COMING BACK WITH ENOUGH PEOPLE TO SHUT THIS DOWN.
"NO, WREN. IT'S TOO LATE TO QUIT. IT HAS BEEN SINCE YOU CLICKED THAT LINK. SINCE YOU WERE BORN, REALLY.
"YOU LOVE SOLVING MYSTERIES. TRACKING DOWN THE MISSING, GETTING SOME LAURELS FOR IT. THEY'RE SECONDARY.
"BECAUSE YOU'VE BEEN TRYING TO TRACK DOWN ALL YOUR PUZZLE PIECES YOU DROPPED ALONG THE WAY, PUTTING YOURSELF BACK TOGETHER.
"YOU SPENT YOUR LIFE PREPARING FOR THIS."
NOW HOLD THAT GODDAMN CAMERA STEADY.
I WANT TO GIVE YOU YOUR PRIZE.

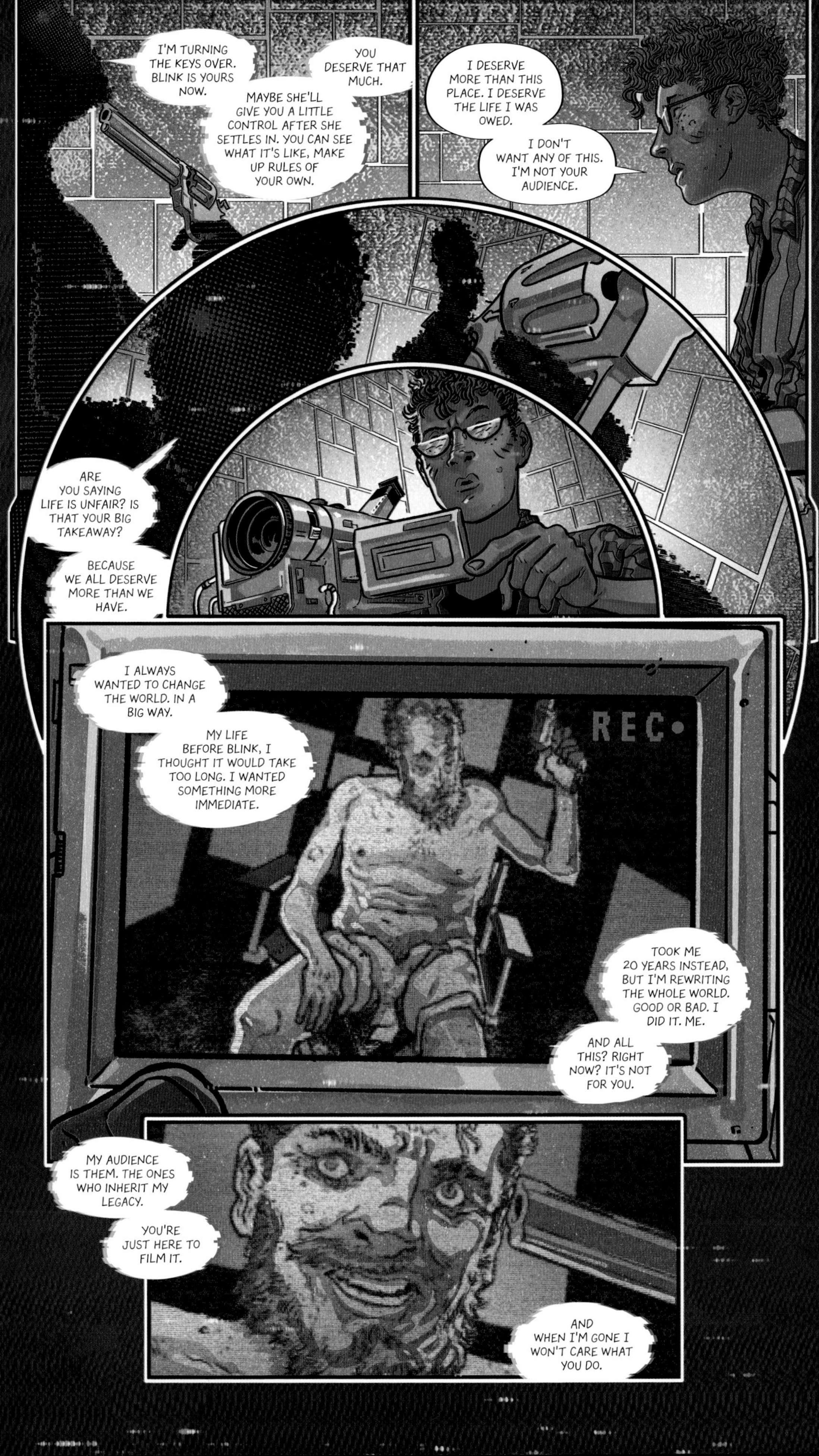
I'M TURNING THE KEYS OVER. BLINK IS YOURS NOW.
YOU DESERVE THAT MUCH.
MAYBE SHE'LL GIVE YOU A LITTLE CONTROL AFTER SHE SETTLES IN. YOU CAN SEE WHAT IT'S LIKE, MAKE UP RULES OF YOUR OWN.
I DESERVE MORE THAN THIS PLACE. I DESERVE THE LIFE I WAS OWED.
I DON'T WANT ANY OF THIS. I'M NOT YOUR AUDIENCE.
ARE YOU SAYING LIFE IS UNFAIR? IS THAT YOUR BIG TAKEAWAY?
BECAUSE WE ALL DESERVE MORE THAN WE HAVE.
I ALWAYS WANTED TO CHANGE THE WORLD. IN A BIG WAY.
MY LIFE BEFORE BLINK, I THOUGHT IT WOULD TAKE TOO LONG. I WANTED SOMETHING MORE IMMEDIATE.
REC
TOOK ME 20 YEARS INSTEAD, BUT I'M REWRITING THE WHOLE WORLD. GOOD OR BAD. I DID IT. ME.
AND ALL THIS? RIGHT NOW? IT'S NOT FOR YOU.
MY AUDIENCE IS THEM. THE ONES WHO INHERIT MY LEGACY.
YOU'RE JUST HERE TO FILM IT.
AND WHEN I'M GONE I WON'T CARE WHAT YOU DO.

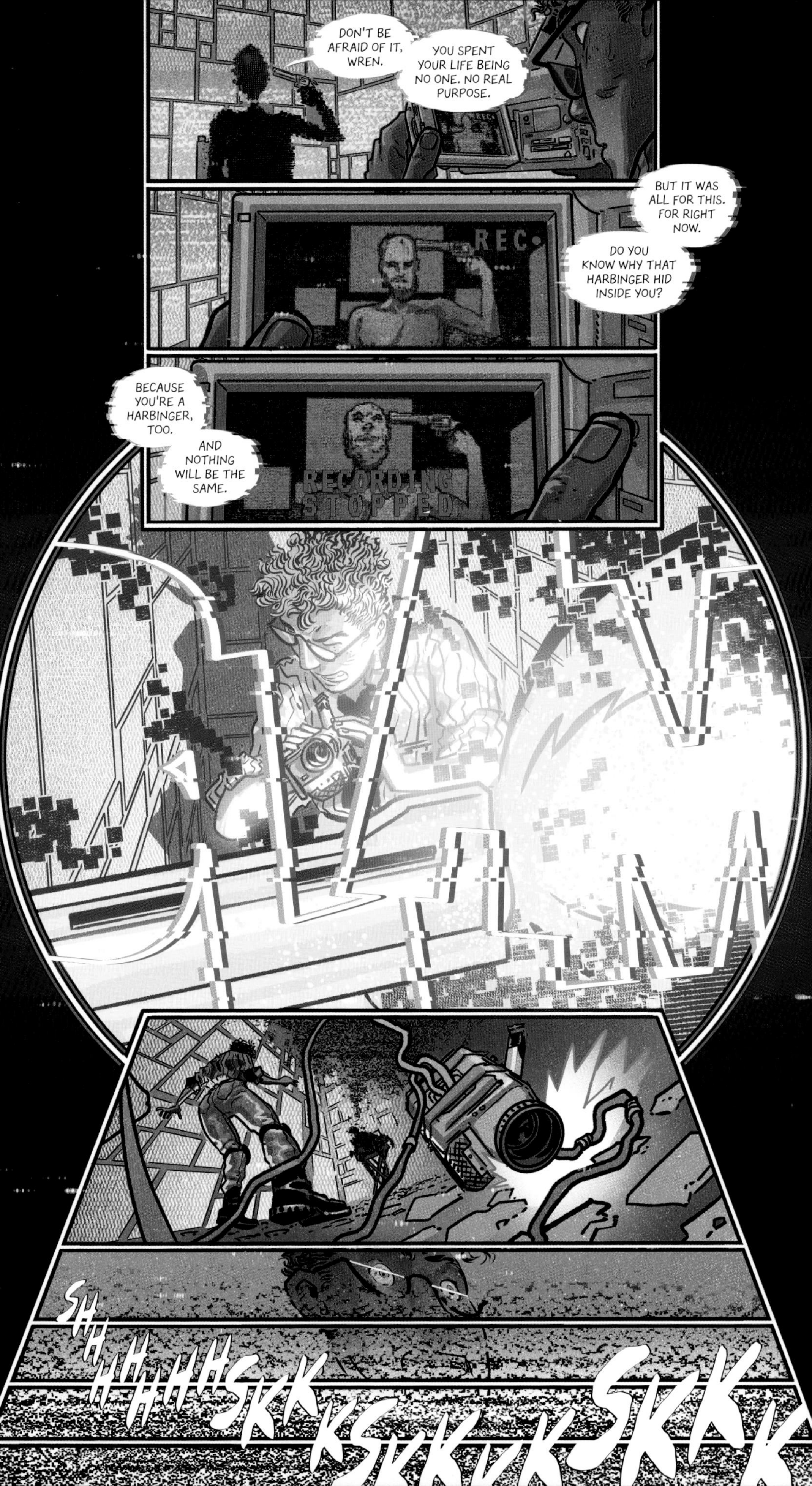

DON'T BE AFRAID OF IT, WREN.
YOU SPENT YOUR LIFE BEING NO ONE. NO REAL PURPOSE.
REC
BUT IT WAS ALL FOR THIS. FOR RIGHT NOW.
DO YOU KNOW WHY THAT HARBINGER HID INSIDE YOU?
BECAUSE YOU'RE A HARBINGER, TOO.
AND NOTHING WILL BE THE SAME.
RECORDING STOPPED
SHHHHHHHSKKKSKKKKKSKKK

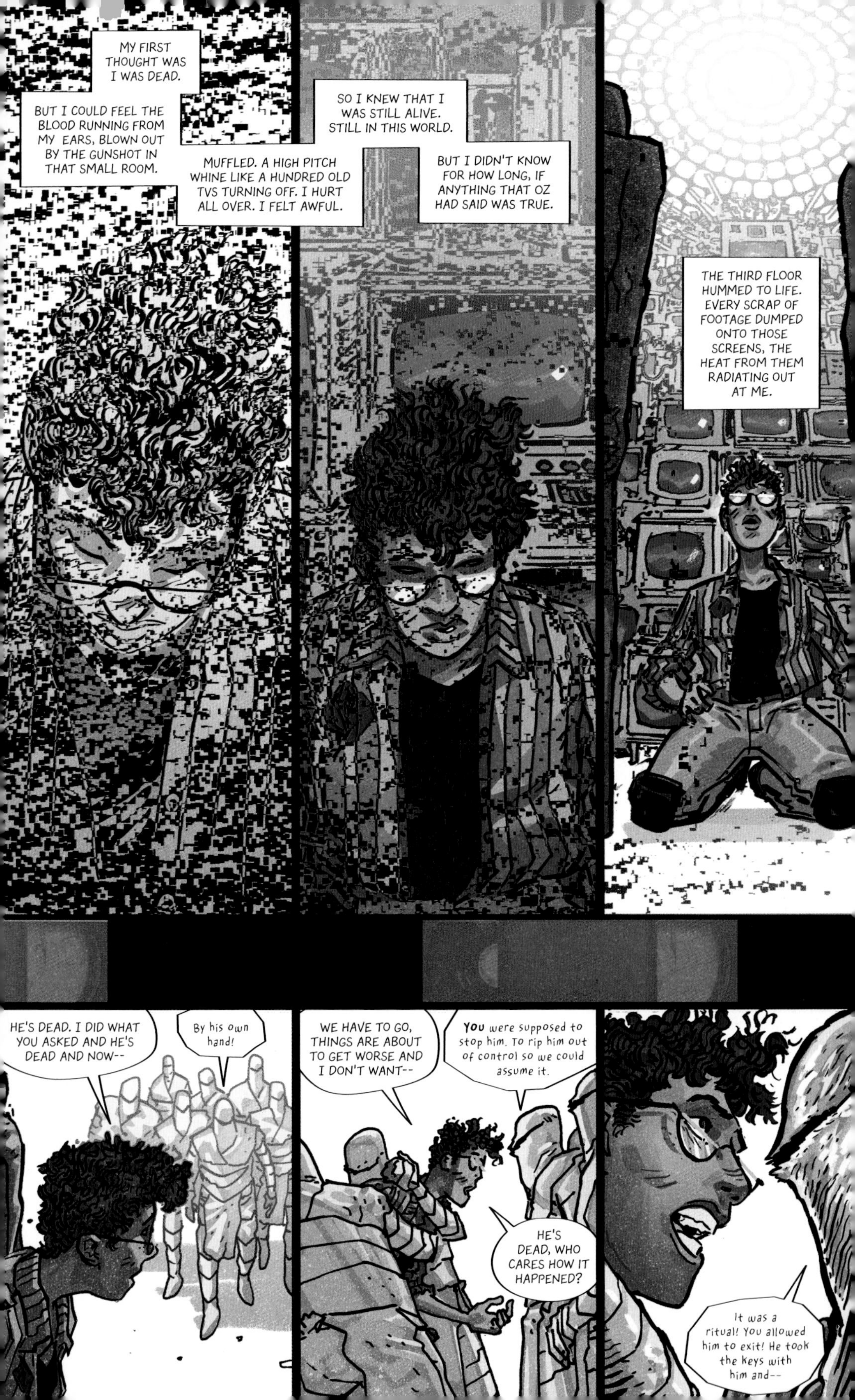
MY FIRST THOUGHT WAS I WAS DEAD.
BUT I COULD FEEL THE BLOOD RUNNING FROM MY EARS, BLOWN OUT BY THE GUNSHOT IN THAT SMALL ROOM.
MUFFLED. A HIGH PITCH WHINE LIKE A HUNDRED OLD TVS TURNING OFF. I HURT ALL OVER. I FELT AWFUL.
SO I KNEW THAT I WAS STILL ALIVE. STILL IN THIS WORLD.
BUT I DIDN'T KNOW FOR HOW LONG, IF ANYTHING THAT OZ HAD SAID WAS TRUE.
THE THIRD FLOOR HUMMED TO LIFE. EVERY SCRAP OF FOOTAGE DUMPED ONTO THOSE SCREENS, THE HEAT FROM THEM RADIATING OUT AT ME.
HE'S DEAD. I DID WHAT YOU ASKED AND HE'S DEAD AND NOW--
By his own hand!
WE HAVE TO GO, THINGS ARE ABOUT TO GET WORSE AND I DON'T WANT--
YOU were supposed to stop him. To rip him out of control so we could assume it.
HE'S DEAD, WHO CARES HOW IT HAPPENED?
It was a ritual! You allowed him to exit! He took the keys with him and--

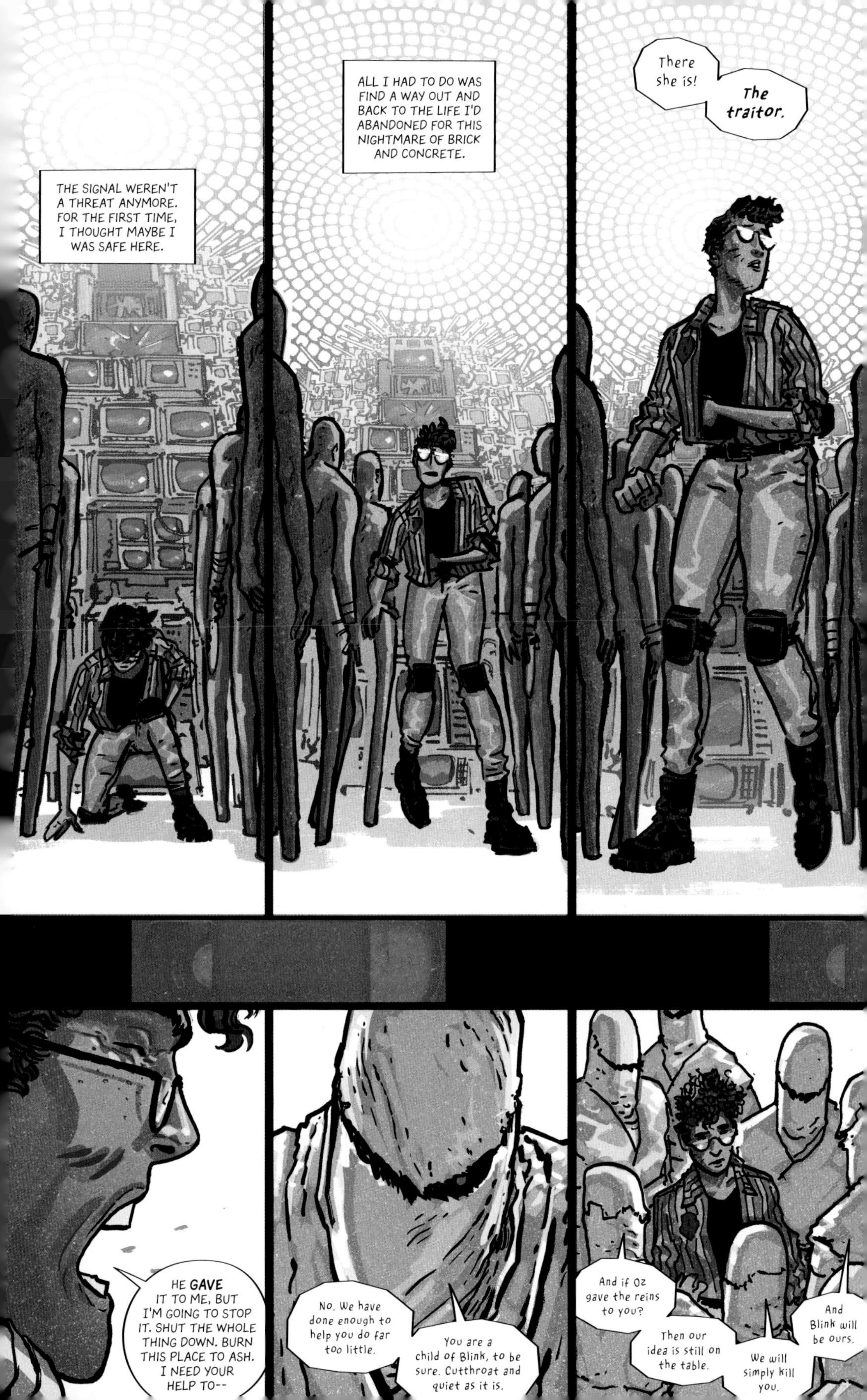
THE SIGNAL WEREN'T A THREAT ANYMORE. FOR THE FIRST TIME, I THOUGHT MAYBE I WAS SAFE HERE.
ALL I HAD TO DO WAS FIND A WAY OUT AND BACK TO THE LIFE I'D ABANDONED FOR THIS NIGHTMARE OF BRICK AND CONCRETE.
There she is!
The traitor.
HE GAVE IT TO ME, BUT I'M GOING TO STOP IT. SHUT THE WHOLE THING DOWN. BURN THIS PLACE TO ASH. I NEED YOUR HELP TO--
No. We have done enough to help you do far too little.
You are a child of Blink, to be sure. Cutthroat and quiet as it is.
And if Oz gave the reins to you?
Then our idea is still on the table.
We will simply kill you.
And Blink will be ours.

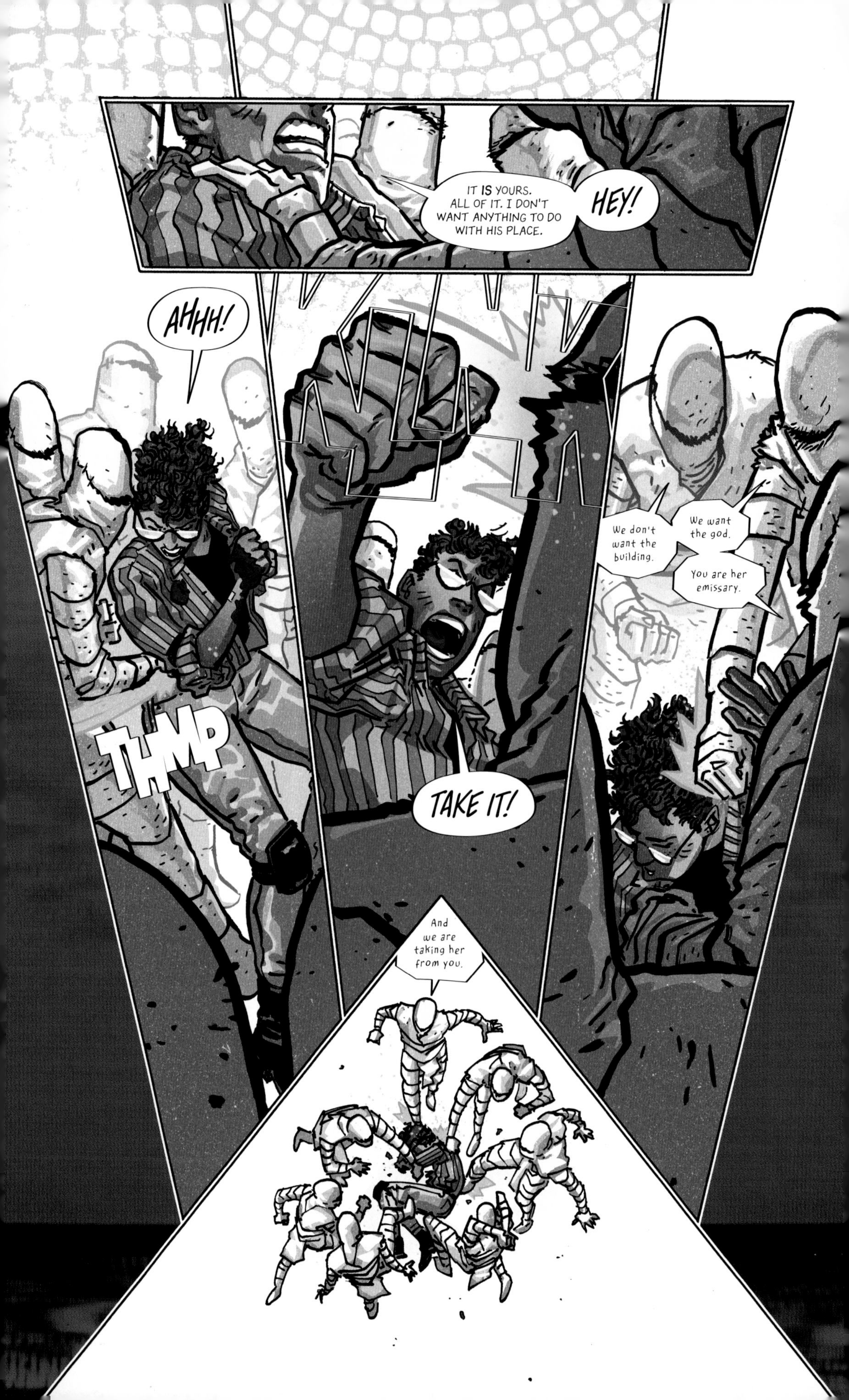
IT IS YOURS. ALL OF IT. I DON'T WANT ANYTHING TO DO WITH HIS PLACE.
HEY!
AHHH!
THMP
TAKE IT!
We don't want the building.
We want the god.
You are her emissary.
And we are taking her from you.

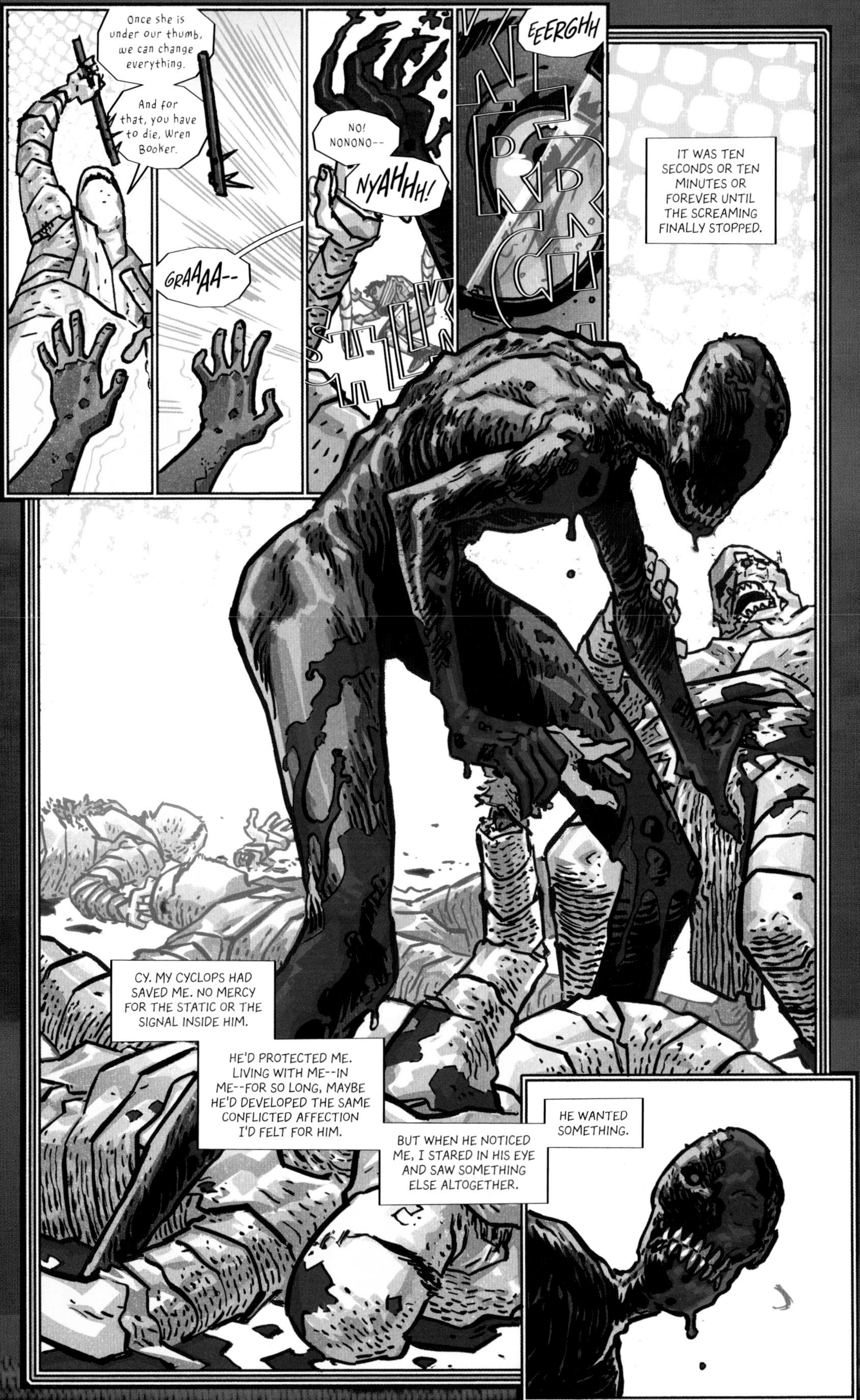
Once she is under our thumb, we can change everything.
And for that, you have to die, Wren Booker.
GRAAAA--
NO! NONONO--
NYAHHH!
EEERGHH
IT WAS TEN SECONDS OR TEN MINUTES OR FOREVER UNTIL THE SCREAMING FINALLY STOPPED.
CY. MY CYCLOPS HAD SAVED ME. NO MERCY FOR THE STATIC OR THE SIGNAL INSIDE HIM.
HE'D PROTECTED ME. LIVING WITH ME--IN ME--FOR SO LONG, MAYBE HE'D DEVELOPED THE SAME CONFLICTED AFFECTION I'D FELT FOR HIM.
BUT WHEN HE NOTICED ME, I STARED IN HIS EYE AND SAW SOMETHING ELSE ALTOGETHER.
HE WANTED SOMETHING.

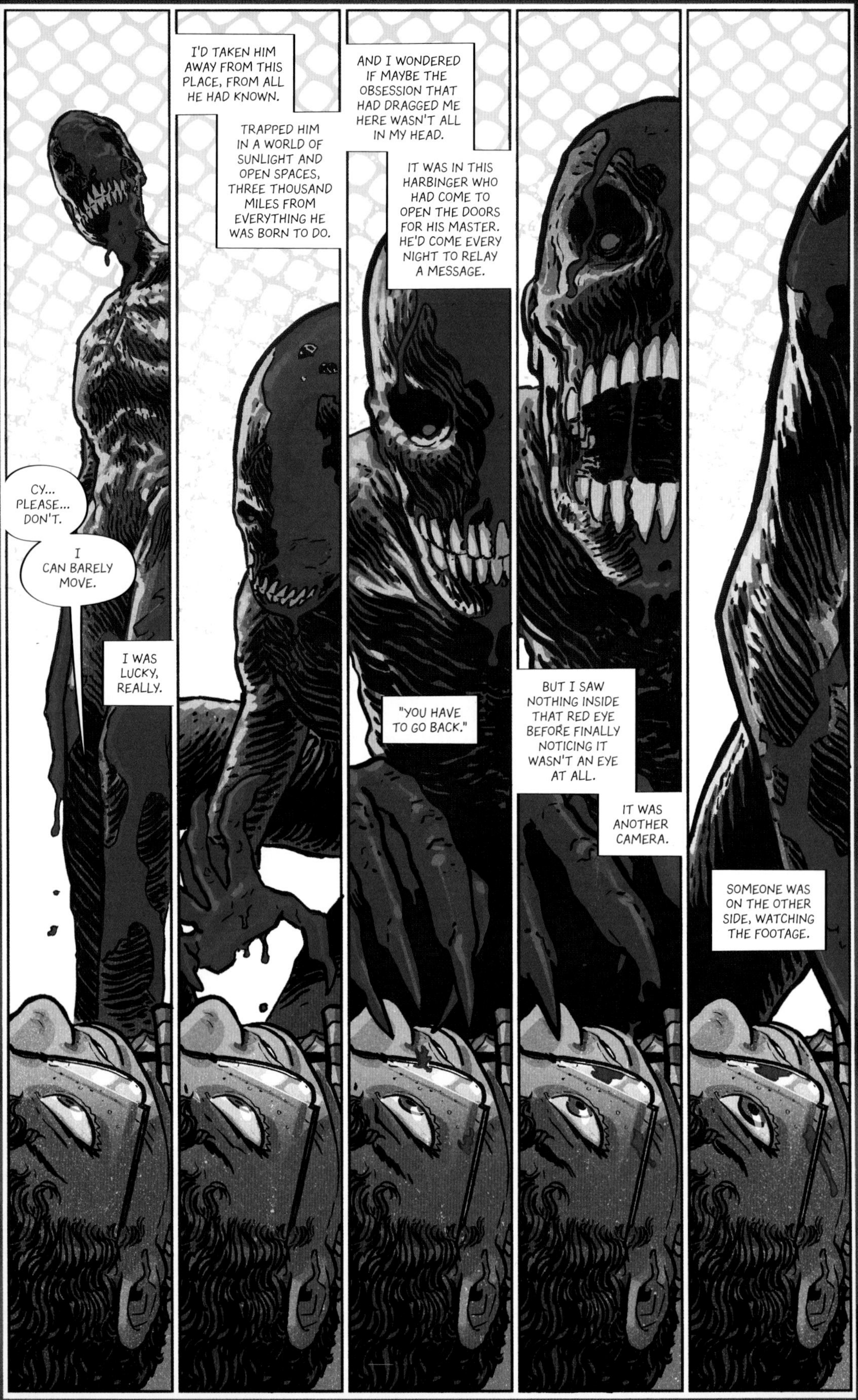
CY... PLEASE... DON'T.
I CAN BARELY MOVE.
I WAS LUCKY, REALLY.
I'D TAKEN HIM AWAY FROM THIS PLACE, FROM ALL HE HAD KNOWN.
TRAPPED HIM IN A WORLD OF SUNLIGHT AND OPEN SPACES, THREE THOUSAND MILES FROM EVERYTHING HE WAS BORN TO DO.
AND I WONDERED IF MAYBE THE OBSESSION THAT HAD DRAGGED ME HERE WASN'T ALL IN MY HEAD.
IT WAS IN THIS HARBINGER WHO HAD COME TO OPEN THE DOORS FOR HIS MASTER. HE'D COME EVERY NIGHT TO RELAY A MESSAGE.
"YOU HAVE TO GO BACK."
BUT I SAW NOTHING INSIDE THAT RED EYE BEFORE FINALLY NOTICING IT WASN'T AN EYE AT ALL.
IT WAS ANOTHER CAMERA.
SOMEONE WAS ON THE OTHER SIDE, WATCHING THE FOOTAGE.

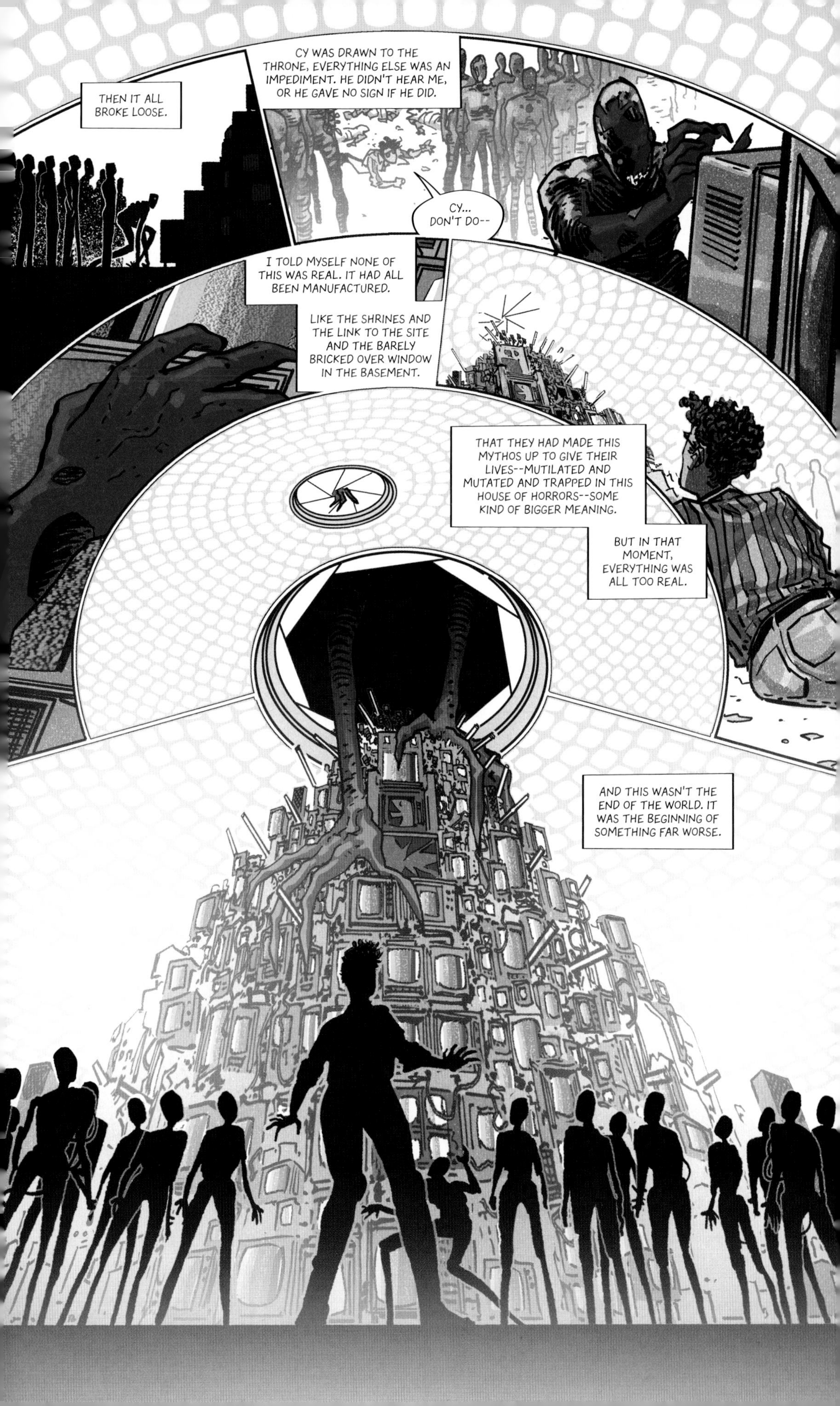
THEN IT ALL BROKE LOOSE.
CY WAS DRAWN TO THE THRONE, EVERYTHING ELSE WAS AN IMPEDIMENT. HE DIDN'T HEAR ME, OR HE GAVE NO SIGN IF HE DID.
CY... DON'T DO--
I TOLD MYSELF NONE OF THIS WAS REAL. IT HAD ALL BEEN MANUFACTURED.
LIKE THE SHRINES AND THE LINK TO THE SITE AND THE BARELY BRICKED OVER WINDOW IN THE BASEMENT.
THAT THEY HAD MADE THIS MYTHOS UP TO GIVE THEIR LIVES--MUTILATED AND MUTATED AND TRAPPED IN THIS HOUSE OF HORRORS--SOME KIND OF BIGGER MEANING.
BUT IN THAT MOMENT, EVERYTHING WAS ALL TOO REAL.
AND THIS WASN'T THE END OF THE WORLD. IT WAS THE BEGINNING OF SOMETHING FAR WORSE.

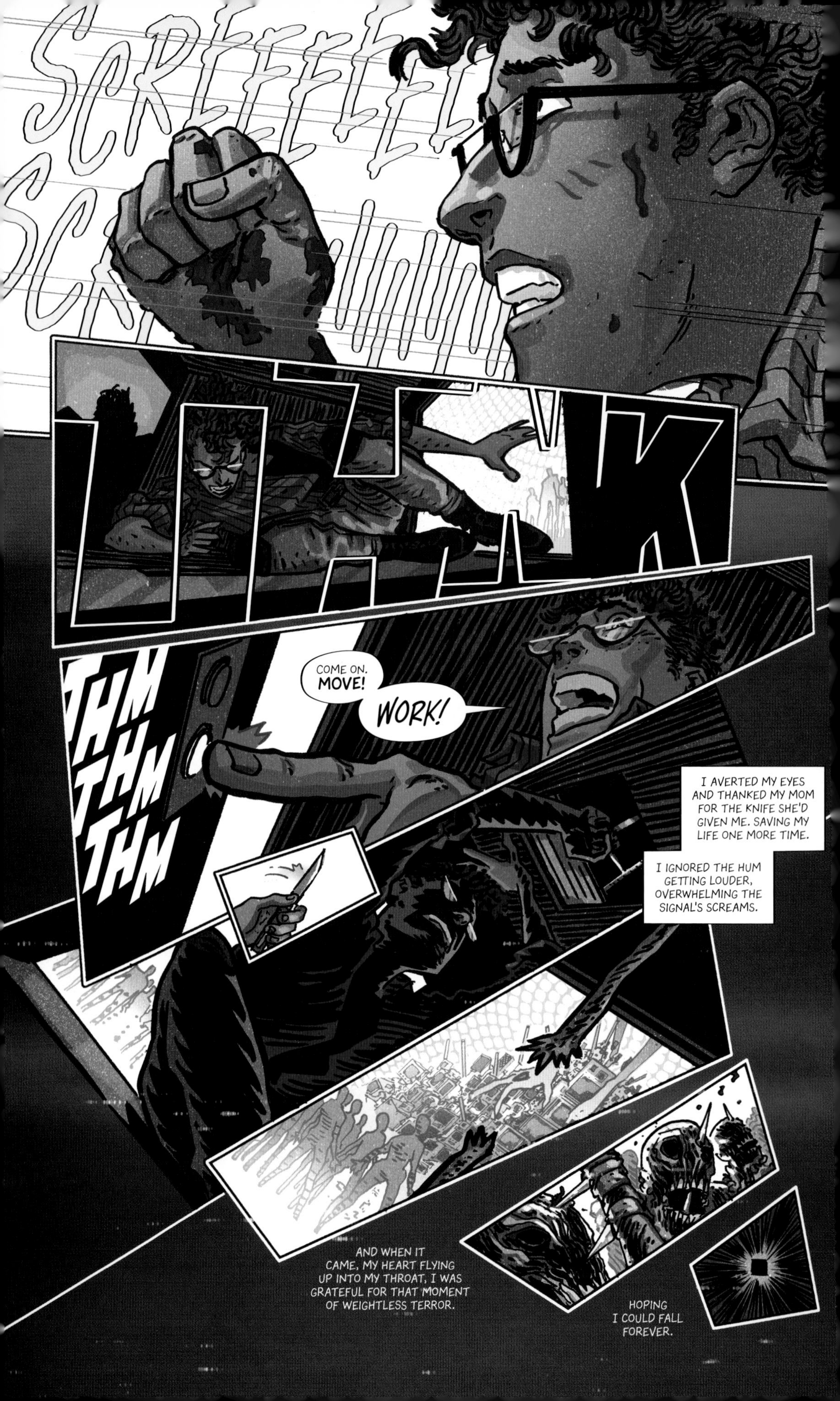
SCREEEEEE
COME ON. MOVE!
WORK!
THM THM THM THM
I AVERTED MY EYES AND THANKED MY MOM FOR THE KNIFE SHE'D GIVEN ME. SAVING MY LIFE ONE MORE TIME.
I IGNORED THE HUM GETTING LOUDER, OVERWHELMING THE SIGNAL'S SCREAMS.
AND WHEN IT CAME, MY HEART FLYING UP INTO MY THROAT, I WAS GRATEFUL FOR THAT MOMENT OF WEIGHTLESS TERROR.
HOPING I COULD FALL FOREVER.

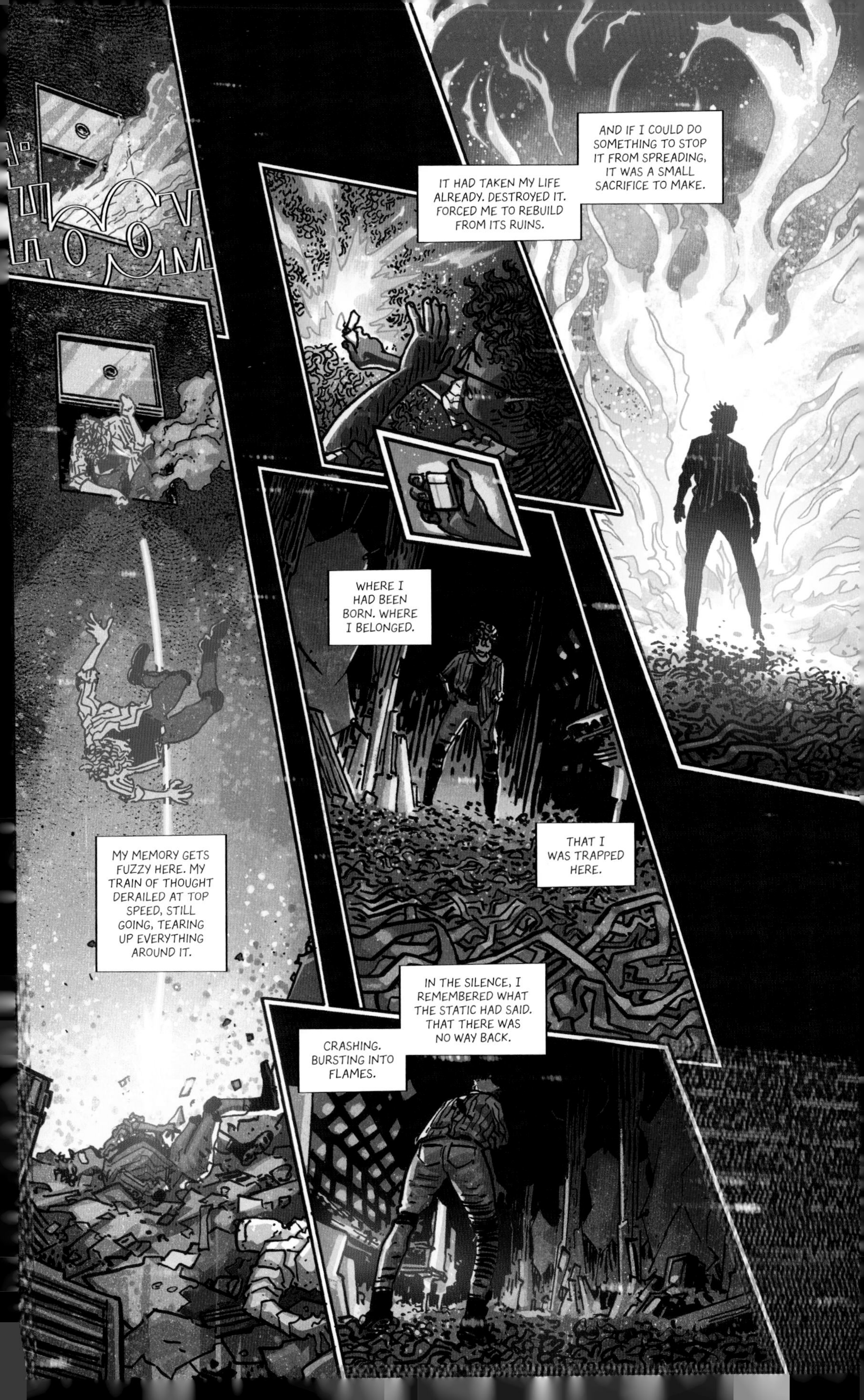
MY MEMORY GETS FUZZY HERE. MY TRAIN OF THOUGHT DERAILED AT TOP SPEED, STILL GOING, TEARING UP EVERYTHING AROUND IT.
CRASHING. BURSTING INTO FLAMES.
IN THE SILENCE, I REMEMBERED WHAT THE STATIC HAD SAID. THAT THERE WAS NO WAY BACK.
THAT I WAS TRAPPED HERE.
WHERE I HAD BEEN BORN. WHERE I BELONGED.
IT HAD TAKEN MY LIFE ALREADY. DESTROYED IT. FORCED ME TO REBUILD FROM ITS RUINS.
AND IF I COULD DO SOMETHING TO STOP IT FROM SPREADING, IT WAS A SMALL SACRIFICE TO MAKE.

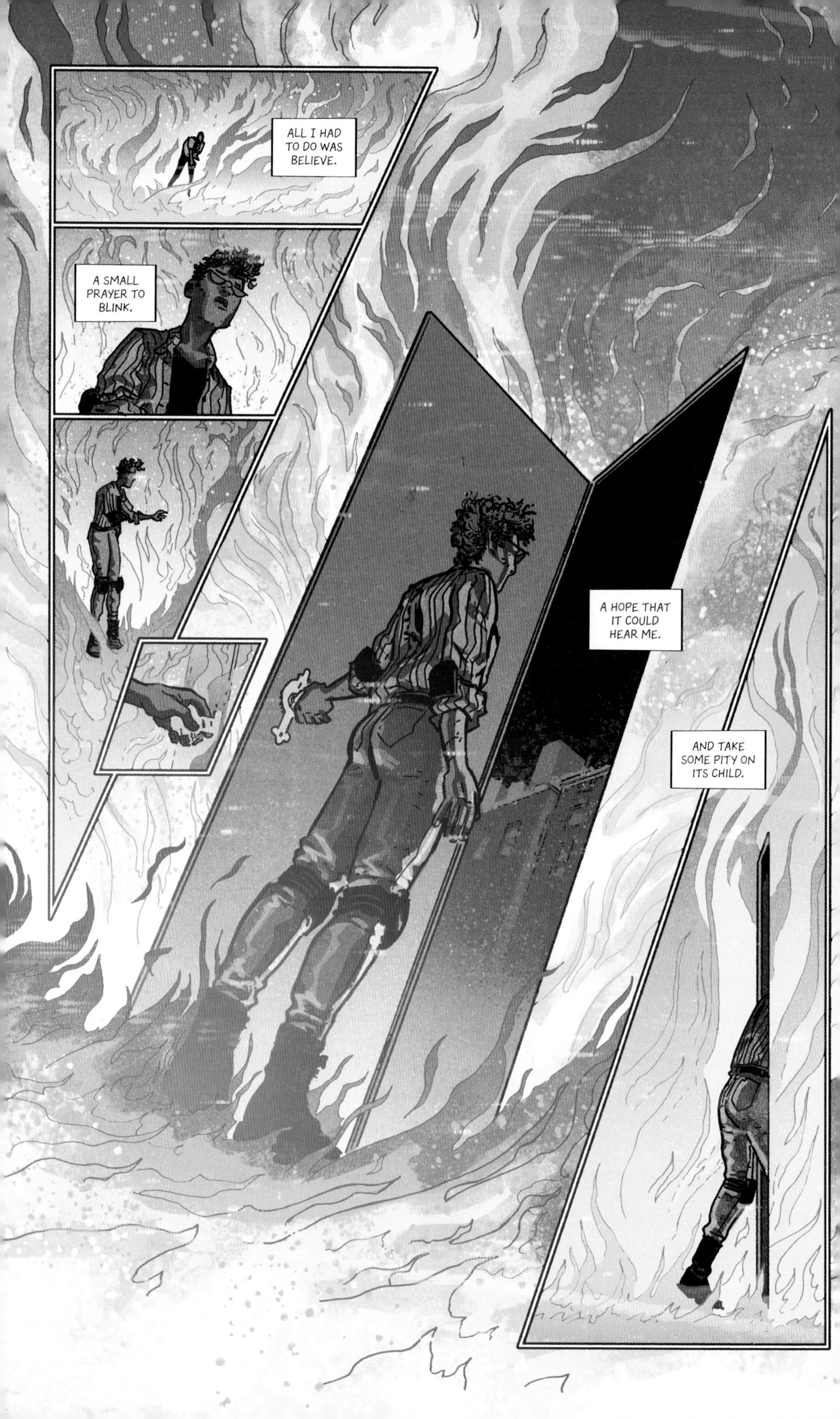
ALL I HAD TO DO WAS BELIEVE.
A SMALL PRAYER TO BLINK.
A HOPE THAT IT COULD HEAR ME.
AND TAKE SOME PITY ON ITS CHILD.

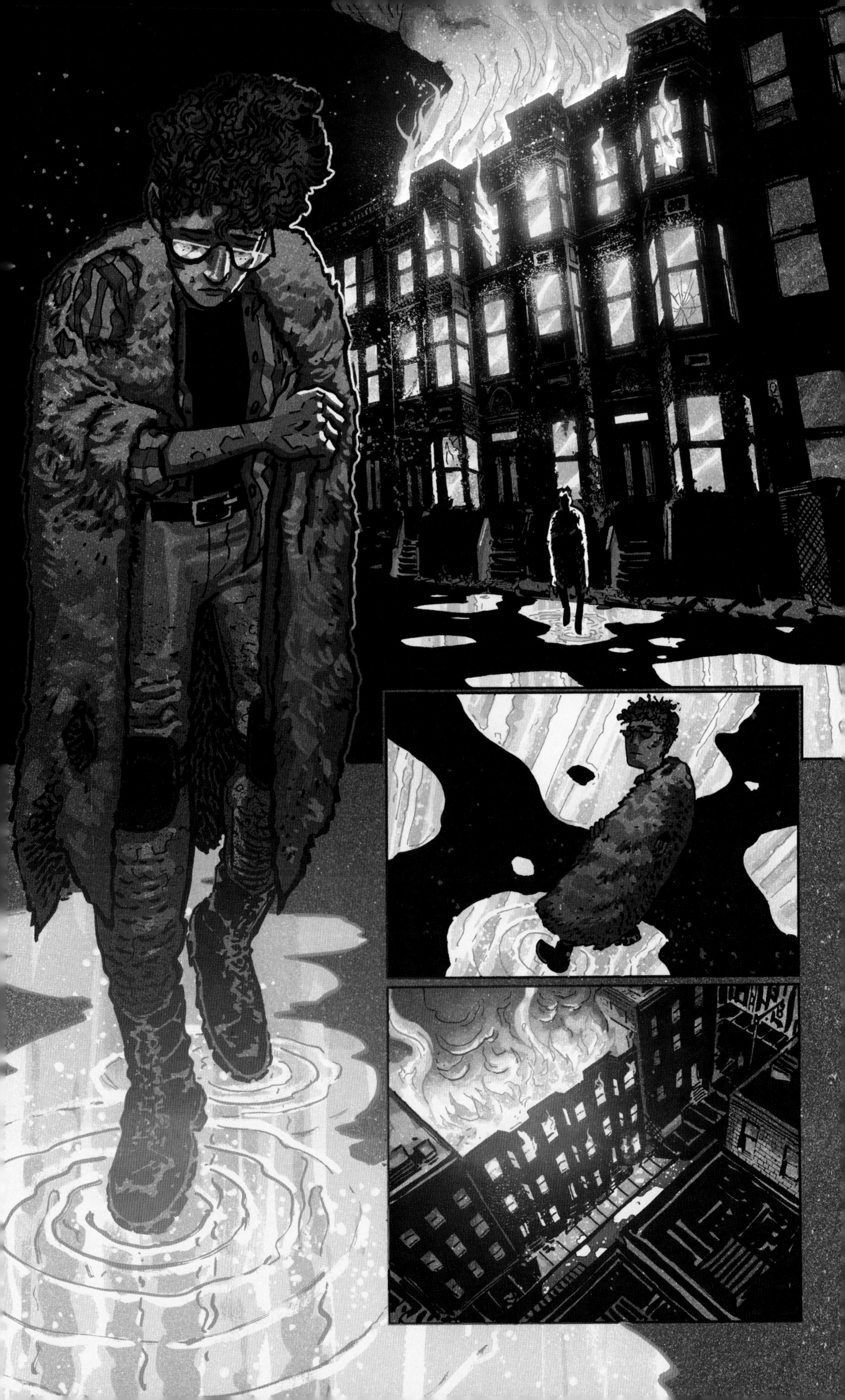

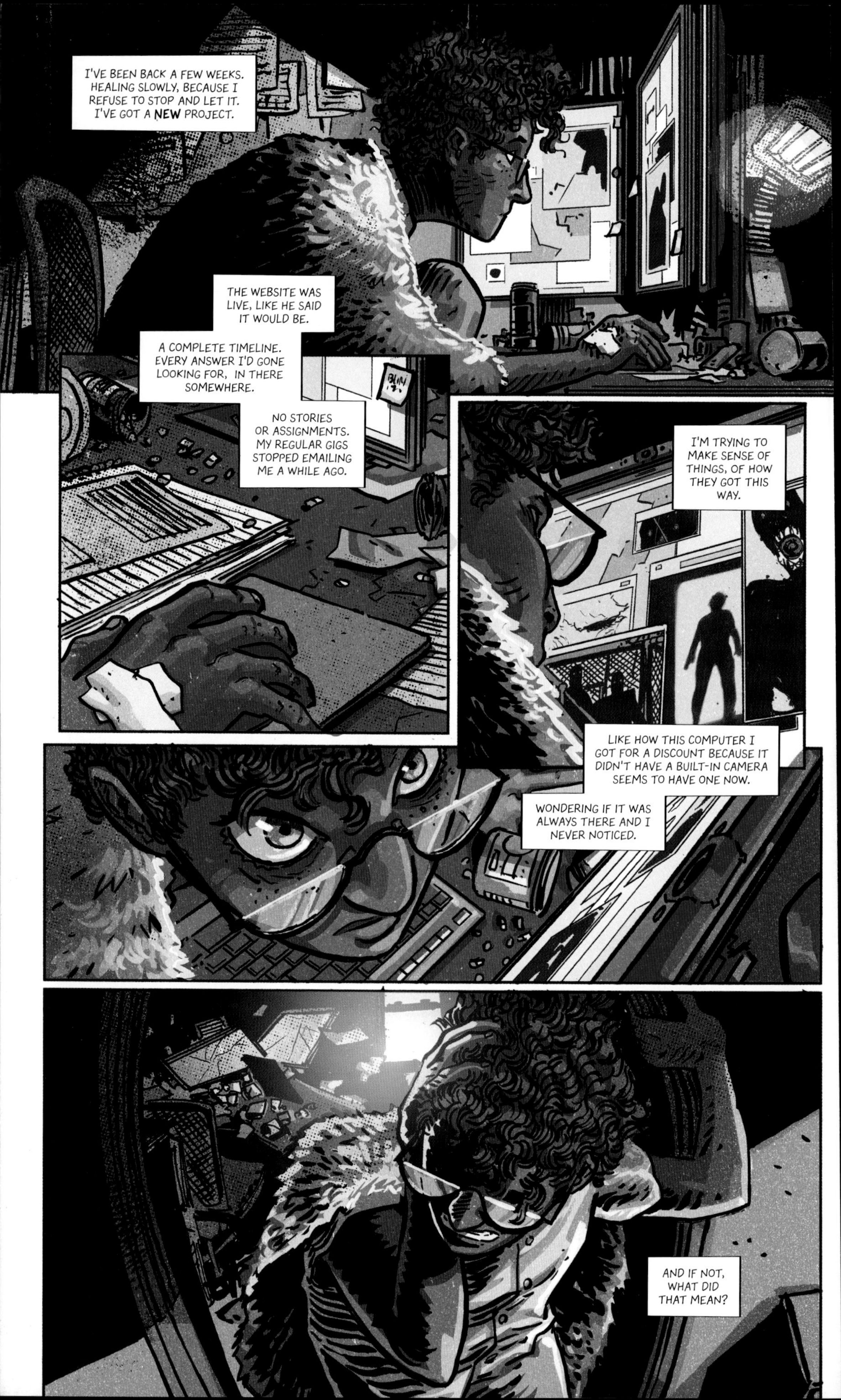

I'VE BEEN BACK A FEW WEEKS. HEALING SLOWLY, BECAUSE I REFUSE TO STOP AND LET IT. I'VE GOT A **NEW** PROJECT.
THE WEBSITE WAS LIVE, LIKE HE SAID IT WOULD BE.
A COMPLETE TIMELINE. EVERY ANSWER I'D GONE LOOKING FOR, IN THERE SOMEWHERE.
NO STORIES OR ASSIGNMENTS. MY REGULAR GIGS STOPPED EMAILING ME A WHILE AGO.
I'M TRYING TO MAKE SENSE OF THINGS, OF HOW THEY GOT THIS WAY.
LIKE HOW THIS COMPUTER I GOT FOR A DISCOUNT BECAUSE IT DIDN'T HAVE A BUILT-IN CAMERA SEEMS TO HAVE ONE NOW.
WONDERING IF IT WAS ALWAYS THERE AND I NEVER NOTICED.
AND IF NOT, WHAT DID THAT MEAN?

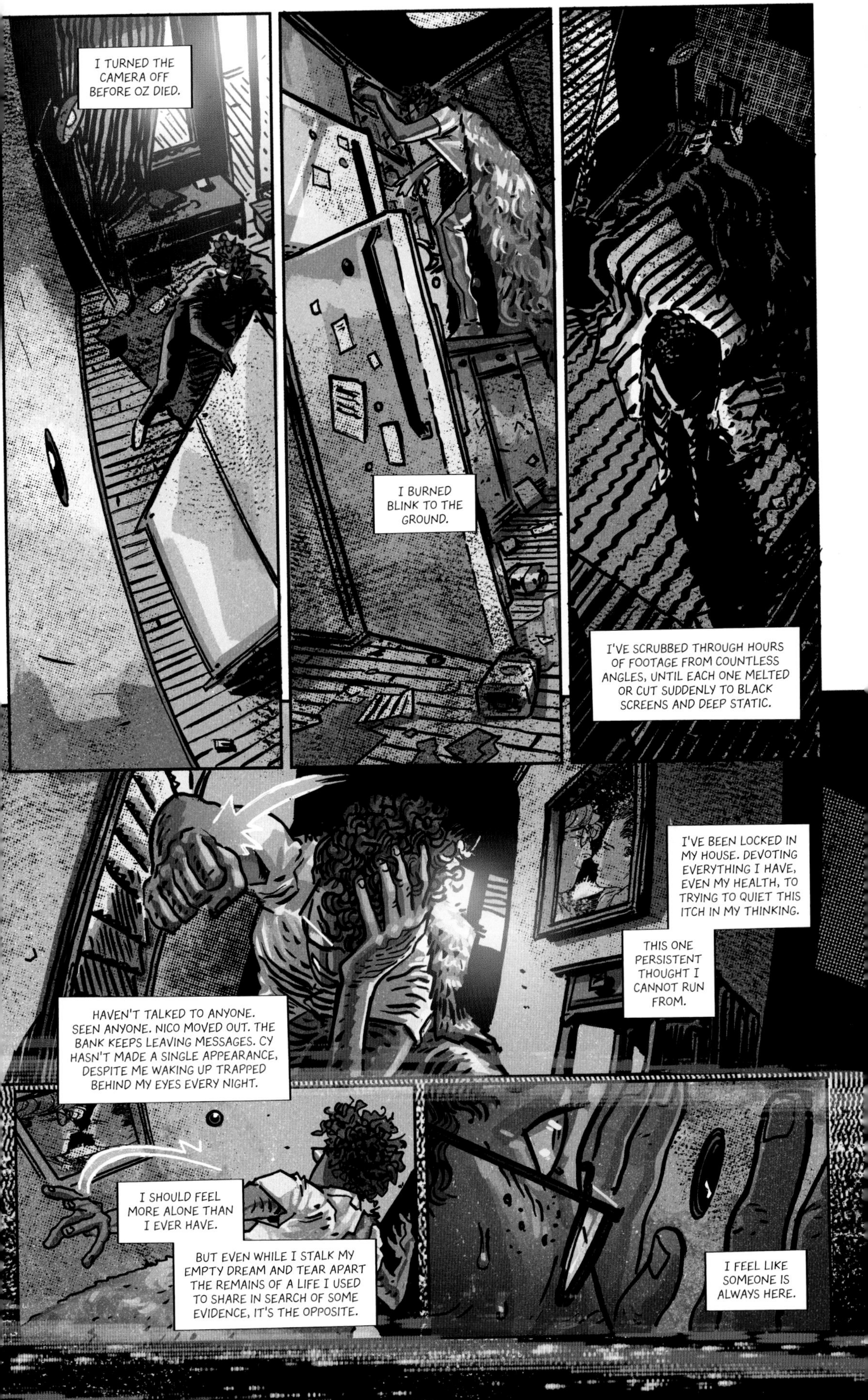
I TURNED THE CAMERA OFF BEFORE OZ DIED.
I BURNED BLINK TO THE GROUND.
I'VE SCRUBBED THROUGH HOURS OF FOOTAGE FROM COUNTLESS ANGLES, UNTIL EACH ONE MELTED OR CUT SUDDENLY TO BLACK SCREENS AND DEEP STATIC.
I'VE BEEN LOCKED IN MY HOUSE. DEVOTING EVERYTHING I HAVE, EVEN MY HEALTH, TO TRYING TO QUIET THIS ITCH IN MY THINKING.
THIS ONE PERSISTENT THOUGHT I CANNOT RUN FROM.
HAVEN'T TALKED TO ANYONE. SEEN ANYONE. NICO MOVED OUT. THE BANK KEEPS LEAVING MESSAGES. CY HASN'T MADE A SINGLE APPEARANCE, DESPITE ME WAKING UP TRAPPED BEHIND MY EYES EVERY NIGHT.
I SHOULD FEEL MORE ALONE THAN I EVER HAVE.
BUT EVEN WHILE I STALK MY EMPTY DREAM AND TEAR APART THE REMAINS OF A LIFE I USED TO SHARE IN SEARCH OF SOME EVIDENCE, IT'S THE OPPOSITE.
I FEEL LIKE SOMEONE IS ALWAYS HERE.

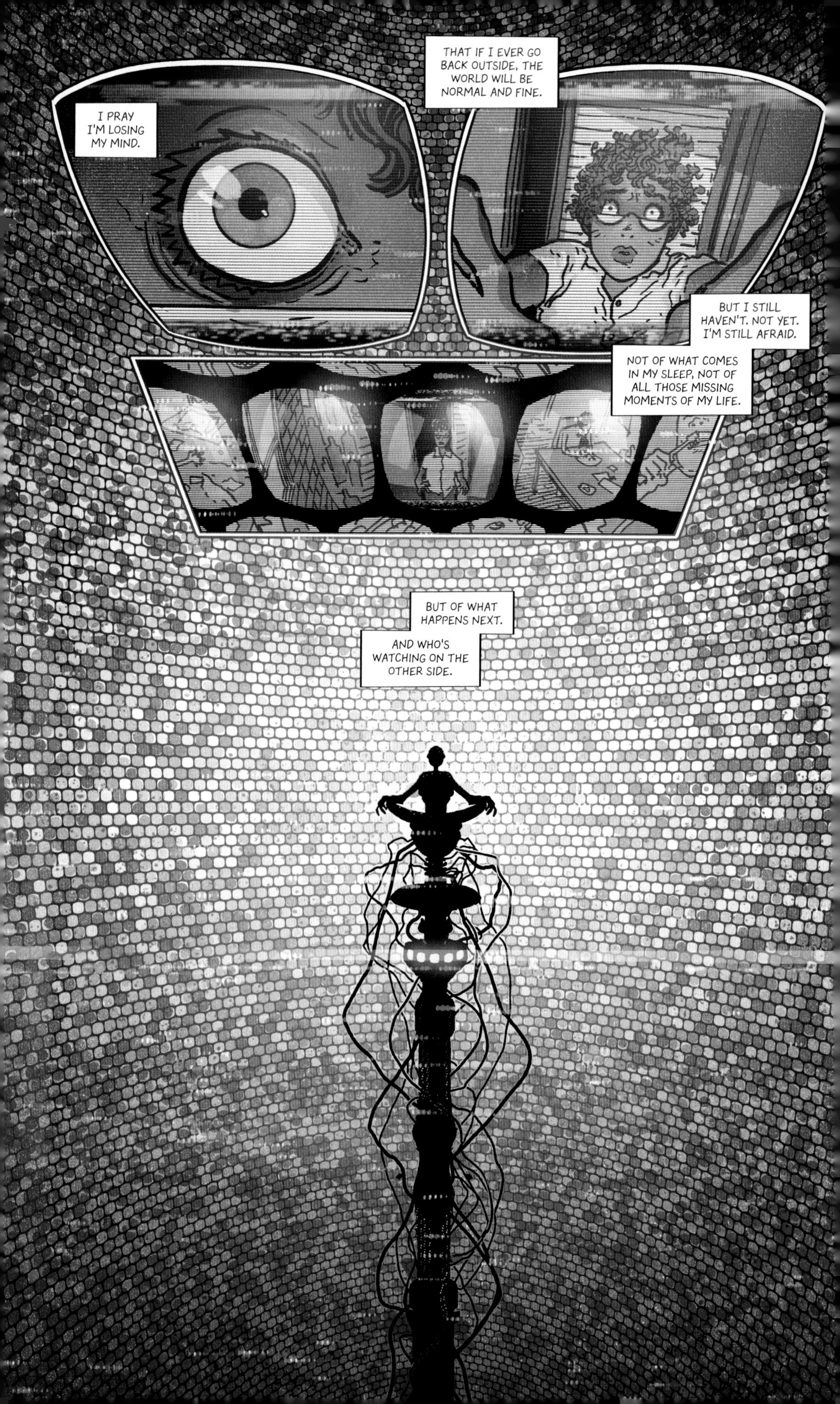
I PRAY I'M LOSING MY MIND.
THAT IF I EVER GO BACK OUTSIDE, THE WORLD WILL BE NORMAL AND FINE.
BUT I STILL HAVEN'T. NOT YET. I'M STILL AFRAID.
NOT OF WHAT COMES IN MY SLEEP, NOT OF ALL THOSE MISSING MOMENTS OF MY LIFE.
BUT OF WHAT HAPPENS NEXT.
AND WHO'S WATCHING ON THE OTHER SIDE.

BLINK

COVER GALLERY

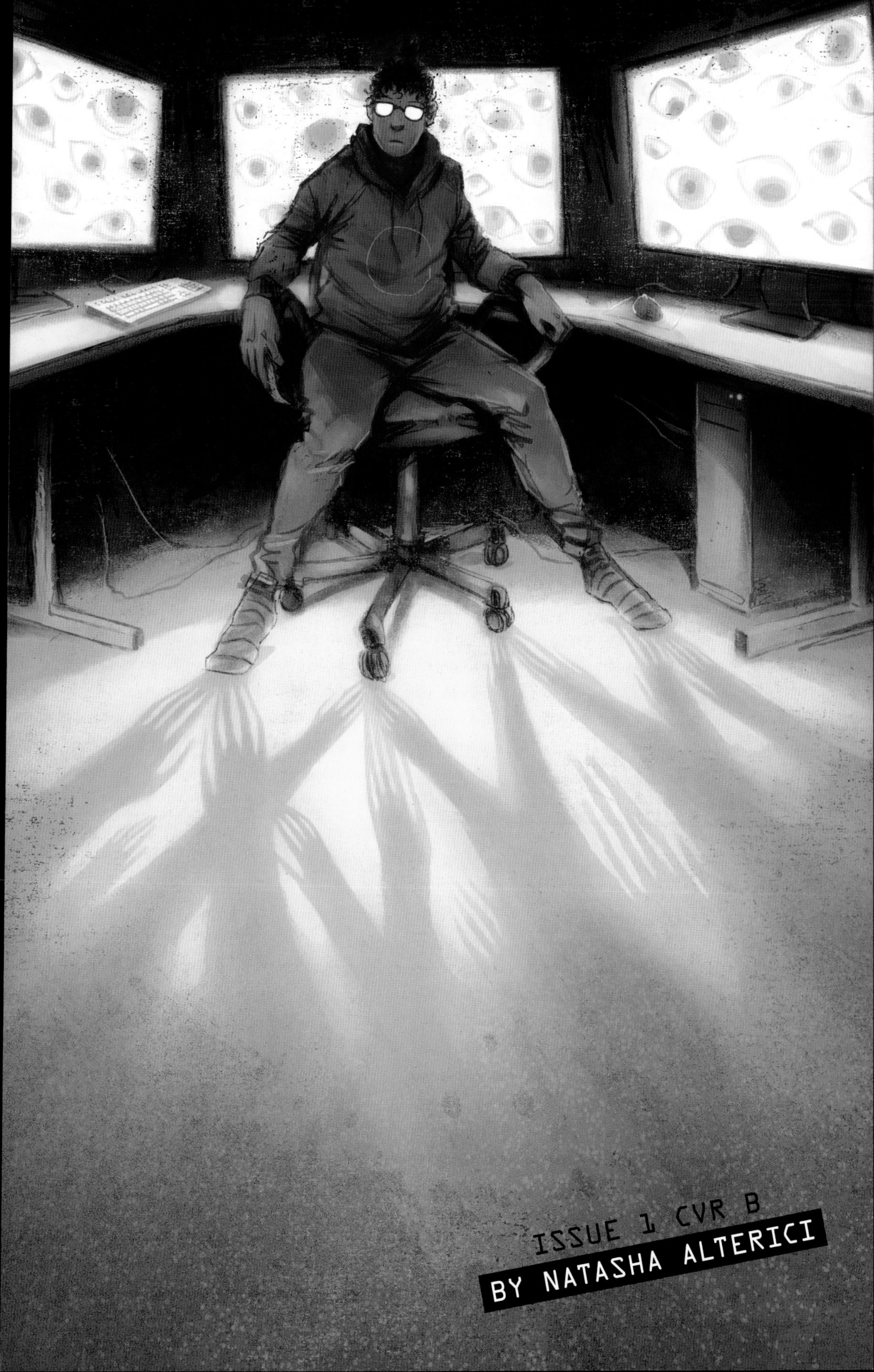
ISSUE 1 CVR B
BY NATASHA ALTERICI

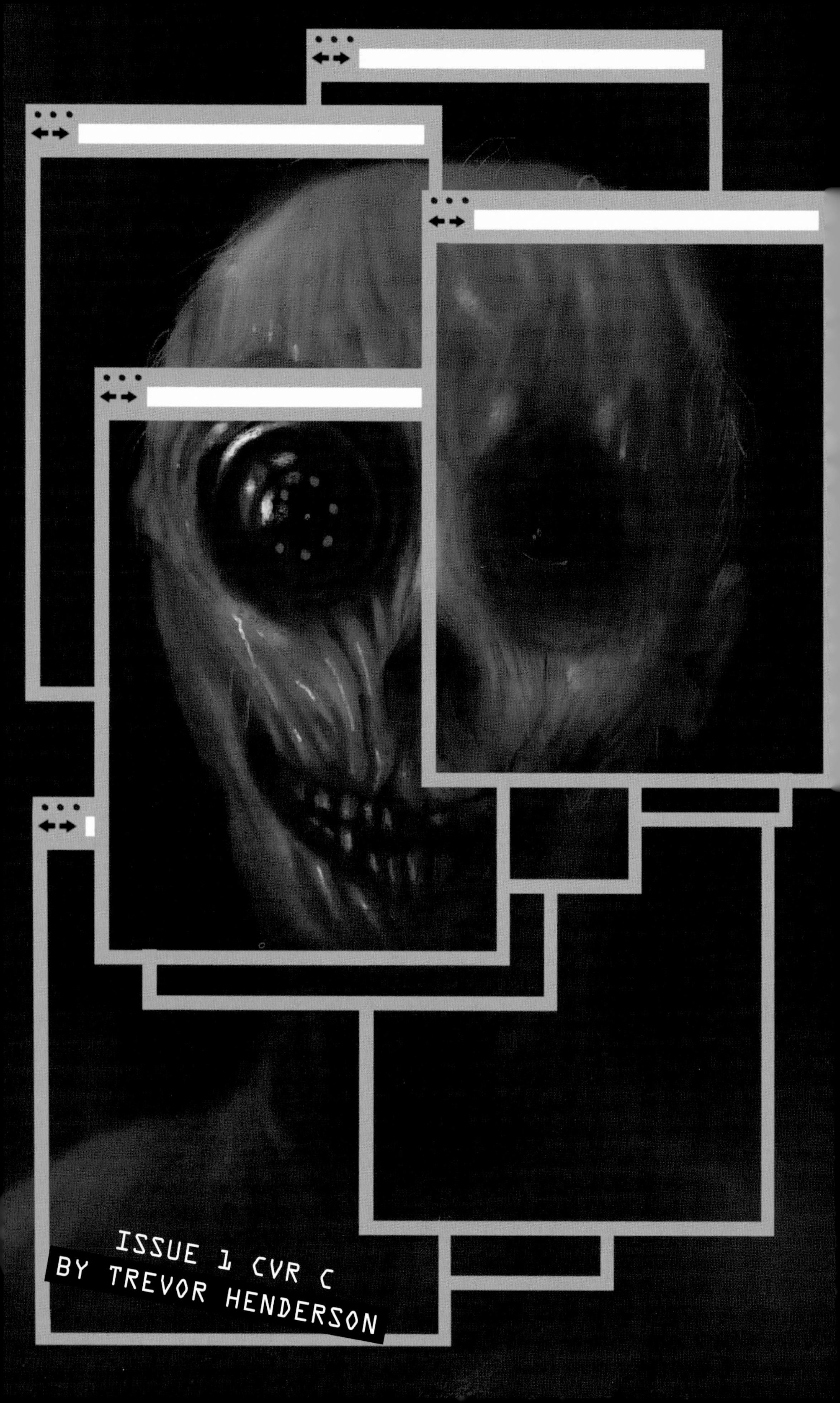
ISSUE 1 CVR C
BY TREVOR HENDERSON

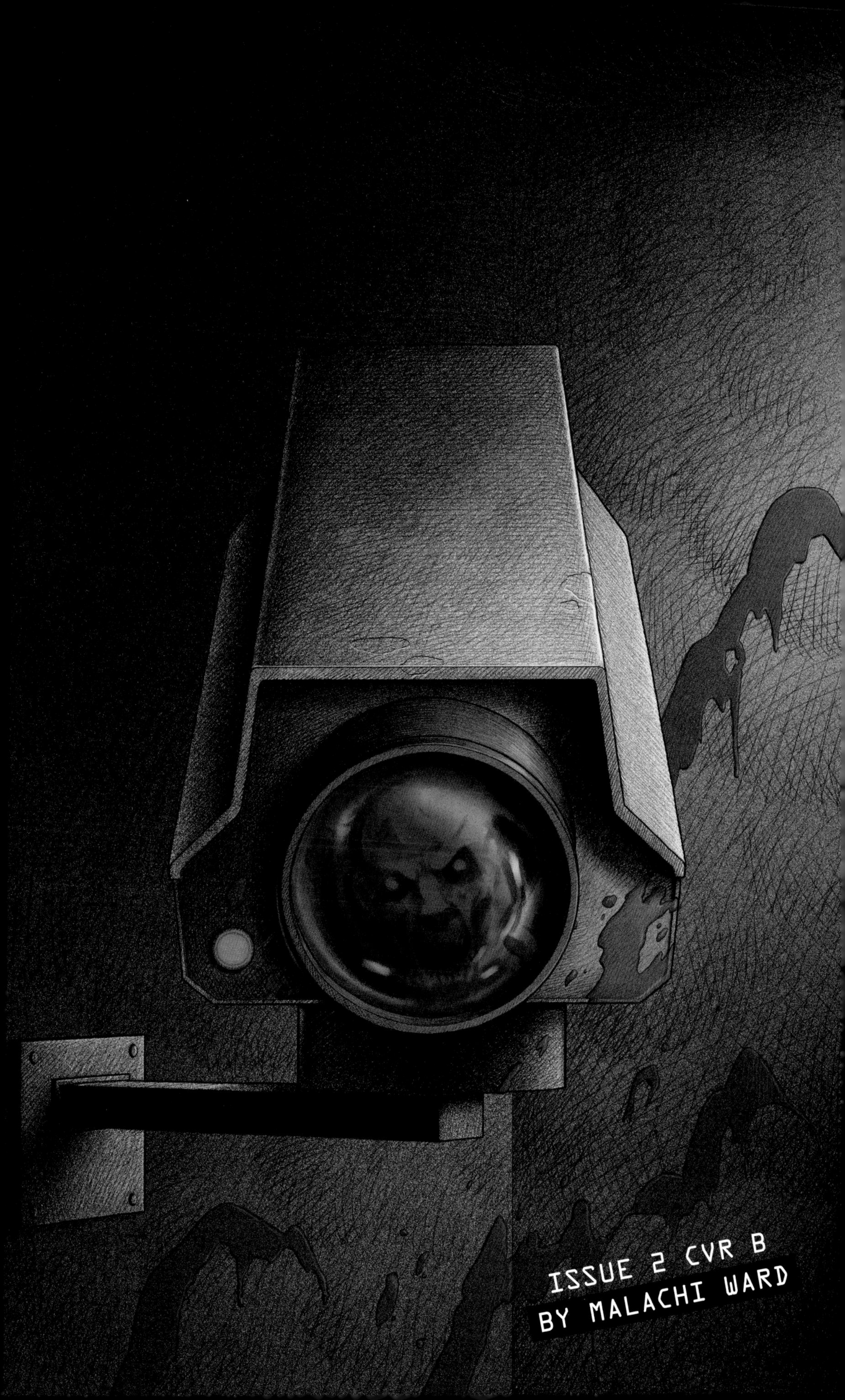
ISSUE 2 CVR B
BY MALACHI WARD

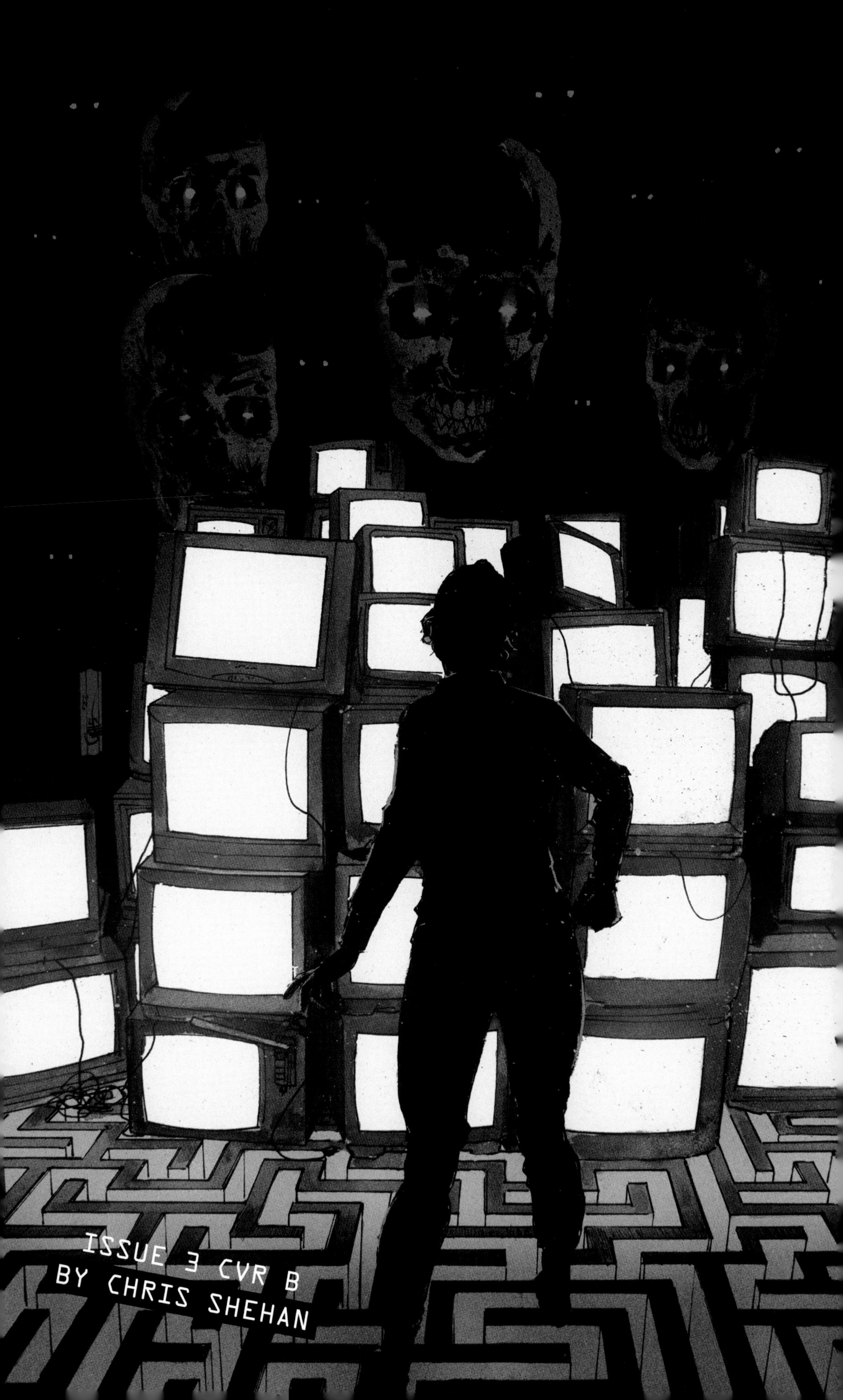
ISSUE 3 CVR B
BY CHRIS SHEHAN

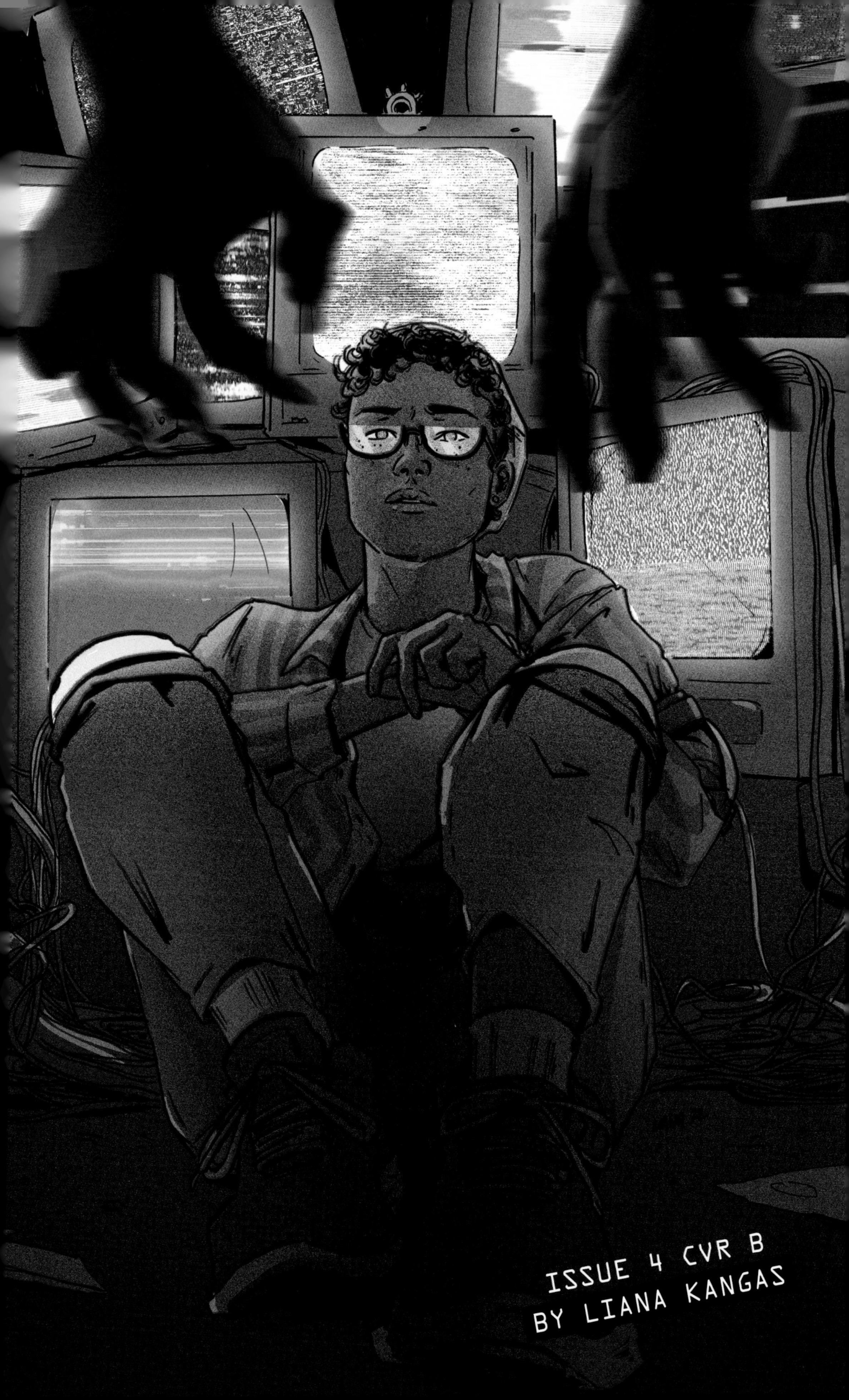
ISSUE 4 CVR B
BY LIANA KANGAS

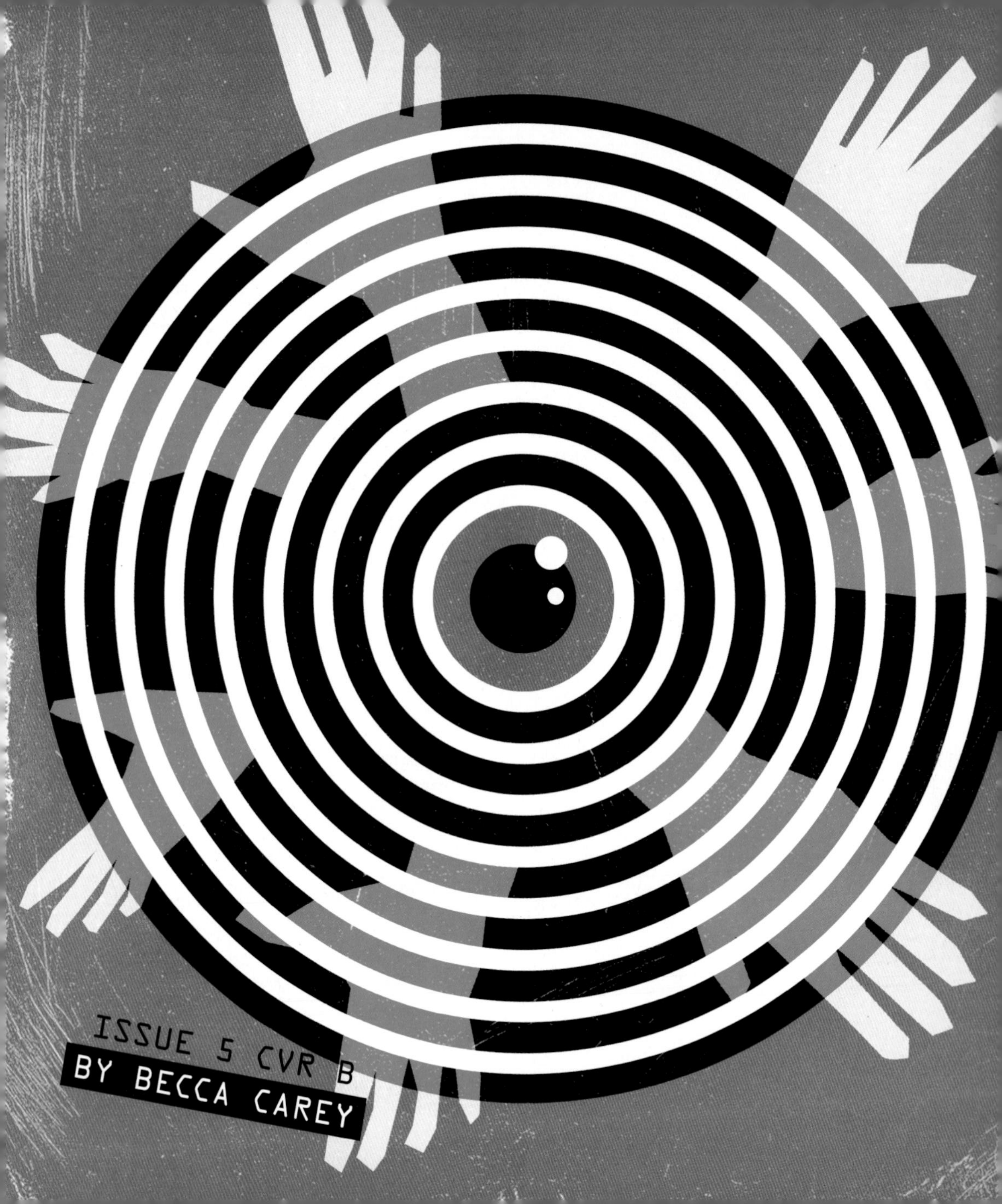
ISSUE 5 CVR B
BY BECCA CAREY

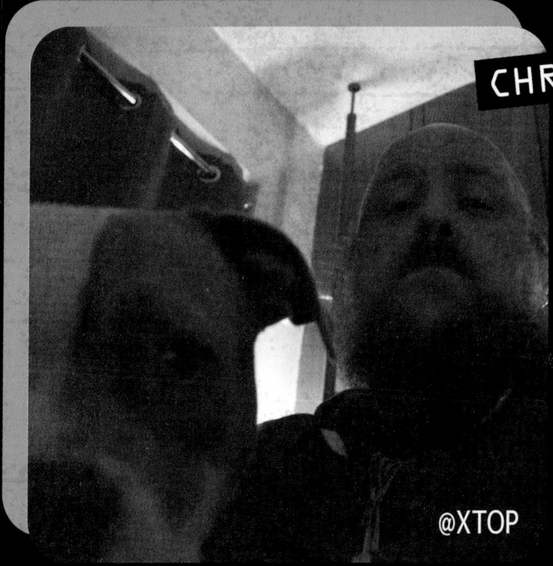
@XTOP

CHRISTOPHER SEBELA is a four-time Eisner-nominated writer, designer, and publisher. He's the co-creator of *Crowded, Dead Dudes, Test, Heartthrob,* and *Shanghai Red,* among others. He puts out his weirder work himself via a tiny publishing empire called Two Headed Press. Go see him at www.christophersebela.com

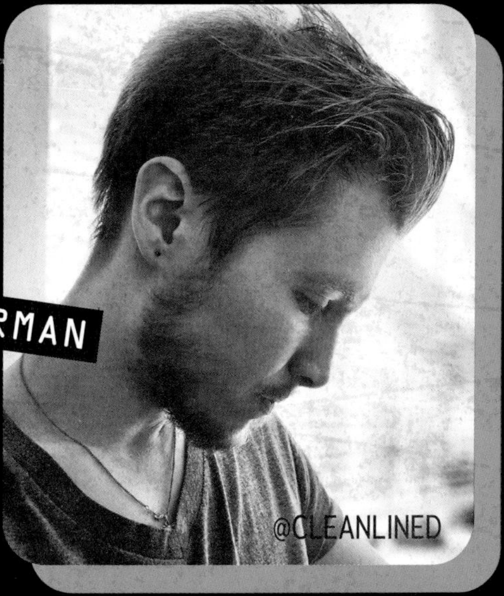
@CLEANLINED

HAYDEN SHERMAN is an award-winning comic artist whose work includes *Wasted Space, Thumbs, The Few,* and *Chicken Devil.* They're a lover of science-fiction and fantasy who has had the joy of illustrating for companies such as Oni, Marvel, Image, Dark Horse, Dynamite, AfterShock, Vault, and BOOM! Studios. They currently reside in Boston, Massachusetts, where they share an apartment with their significant other and an increasingly dumb cat.

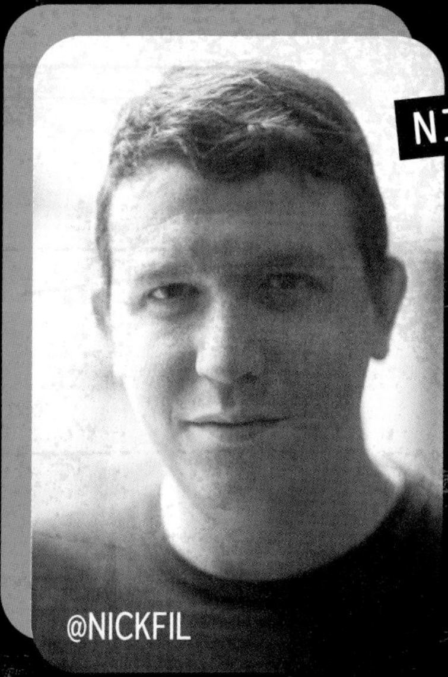
@NICKFIL

NICK FILARDI grew up in New London, Connecticut, listening to Small Town Hero and watching *Batman: The Animated Series.* After graduating from Savannah College of Art and Design in 2004, he colored for Zylonol Studios under Lee Loughridge in Savannah, Georgia, while maintaining the pretense of working an "office" job. He is currently living in Gainesville, Florida, with his three-legged dog, DeNiro. You can find his work in *Powers, The Victories,* and *Atomic Robo.*

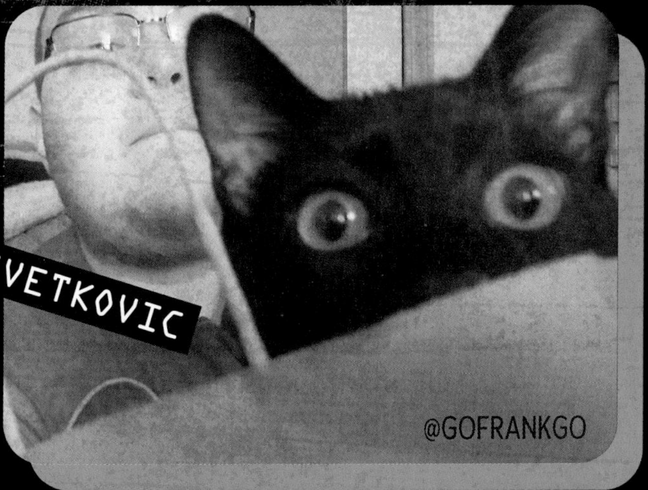
@GOFRANKGO

FRANK CVETKOVIC (He/Him) is a comic book letterer who hates when people assume that all he does is put words in bubbles. There's a little more to the job than that. For instance, sometimes he puts them in boxes. He currently lives in Cleveland, Ohio, where the rivers occasionally catch fire and the city sometimes shuts down due to deadly swarms of balloons.

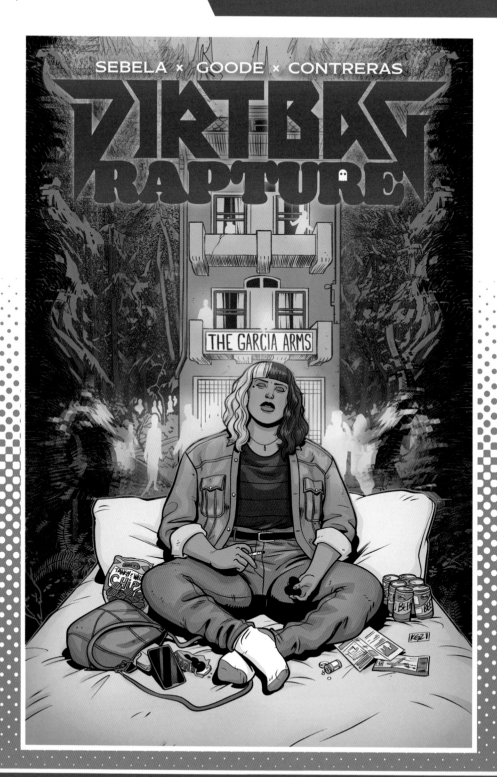

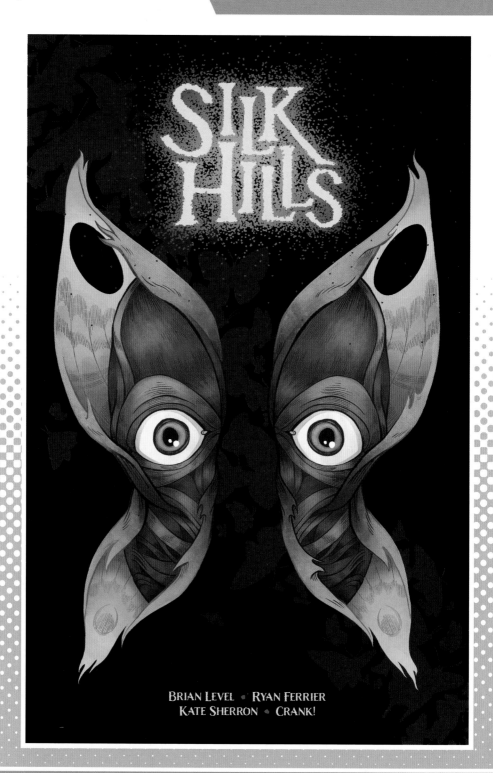

IN MEMORY OF
Vincent Kukua

On October 4, 2022, comics artist and Oni Press prepress technician Vincent Kukua passed away at age forty-five. Vincent was a beloved friend and member of the Oni staff, and his dedication to the craft of comics echoes through our books more than most people realize. When a professional handles the files and assembly of a comic, the result is the perfect meld of art and technical standards—a beautiful, readable, engaging book that doesn't distract from the creators' vision.

That behind-the-scenes talent is what Vincent brought to our books. His endless love and enthusiasm for the medium and deep well of camaraderie and support is what he brought to our staff as a friend, confidant, and coconspirator. If you had a crazy idea, Vincent was two steps ahead of you and ready to make it happen. If you needed a book recommendation, movie review, dinner idea, or a critical eye on anything, Vincent was the guy.

Friends, studio mates, and former colleagues have written beautiful memorials to Vincent, and we encourage you to seek those out and hear from the many people who love and celebrate him. Vincent's impact was great, and we feel this loss deeply. Making comics is the best way we can honor our friend's spirit and work. He'd be so excited to know you're reading this book.

With deep gratitude and love,

The Staff of Oni Press

Vincent was a prolific artist and member of Helioscope studio in Portland.
He drew the self portrait above, and you can check out more of his work on Instagram: @vkukua.